SPEEDSUIT POWERS

THE OPPOSITION

BOOK 2

Speedsuit Powers
The Opposition Book Two

By: Allen Paul Weaver III

This book is a work of fiction. Any references to historical events, real people, or real locales are used fictitiously. Other names, characters, places, and incidents are the product of the author's imagination, and any resemblance to actual events or locales or persons, living or dead, is entirely coincidental.

The poem, "What About Your Dreams" was written by Allen Paul Weaver III and is from the book, Transition: Breaking Through the Barriers. It was also used in Speedsuit Powers Book 1.

Conceptual designs for cover art and illustrations created by:
Allen Paul Weaver III / Radiant City Studios, LLC

Cover image designed by:
Shawn Alleyne, Allen Paul Weaver III

Cover Layout designed by:
Robert Giorgio & Jeff Tyler

Interior Design:
Robert Giorgio

Illustrations drawn by:
Allen Paul Weaver III

Artist 3D Renders created by:
Jeff Tyler

Speedsuit Powers Book 2
Copyright © 2014 by Allen Paul Weaver III

Published by: Radiant City Studios, LLC

Books may be ordered by contacting:
Allen Paul Weaver III at **www.allenpaulweaveriii.com**

ISBN: 978-0-9961045-3-1 (pbk)

Printed in the United States of America

This book is dedicated to the memory of
Rev. Dr. Shellie Sampson, Jr.

December 15, 1940 – January 20, 2014

For 16 years you treated me like a son and poured into my life in ways I am still discovering. You challenged me to become a person of significance. And you lived out your own significance: your multiple advanced degrees in science, theology and education; your desire for everyone to know God and their purpose. Your work in various communities in the United States and around the world… I pray your legacy of creative excellence will live on in everyone you touched.

To our youth who are struggling to survive
While trying to hold onto their dreams…
Keep pressing forward.

Contents:

Chapter One

To Whom Much is Given...

THE GOLDEN SUN RADIATES IN THE crystal blue sky. Seagulls surf the air as the sound of wind and waves can be heard mixed with laughter. A middle-aged father runs through the grains of sand with his two sons in tow – laughing hysterically while approaching the frothy waves. Their brown skin looking like roasted caramel in the daylight.

In this distant memory, a mother watches, as the sunlight illuminates her ebony skin. Her delight is apparent even through dark sunglasses and a flowery hat. She smiles with a wide grin while she lies on her lawn chair. Their eldest son runs back to be with her as a four-year-old Curtis jumps the waves with his father.

Malcolm and Curtis hold each other's hands tightly as they scale the oncoming waves. Omar laughs as Miranda snaps a candid shot of them from behind. Curtis looks up to his father as his father looks down at him. As father and son jump the next wave, Curtis looks away and feels a sudden drop as he finds himself under the blue water. Little fish swim by as bubbles flow from his little mouth.

Two hands firmly grasp Curtis by his sides and lift him from the ocean shores—which seems like the ocean depths to such a small boy. Water flows from his open mouth, nose and eyes as he lets out a gurgled series of coughs.

"Are you alright?" Malcolm chuckles with a concerned look on his face.

"Why did you let me go?" Curtis screams in fear.

Malcolm pulls his drenched son to his chest and holds him tightly as he rubs the back of his head.

"Curtis," he whispers softly, "I didn't let you go. You were the one who let go of my hand."

Curtis replies in the midst of his tears, "You - didn't – let me - go?"

Malcolm smiles broadly as he looks intensely into his son's eyes, "Curtis. I will never let you go. I will always be there for you...Always."

Malcolm's strong, smiling face slowly morphs into a lanky, weak and frowning gaze. The sunlight is overcome by florescent lighting as the sound of birds and the ocean breeze give way to high-pitched beeps and labored breathing. Now, a weakly held grasp is all that exists between father and son. And Miranda stands a distance away in a hospital room where Omar is nowhere to be found.

Malcolm's body is a shadowed shell of what it was less than ten years prior. Even so, as Curtis gazes into his father's gaunt eyes, he sees a vibrancy that wasn't present at the beach, even though now every other aspect of his form wreaks of death.

"Curtis…" Malcolm whispers in a hushed and labored tone, "I am so sorry I can't be here for you anymore."

Curtis doesn't speak, but merely rubs his fingers over his father's boney hand.

"Even though I can't be here with you," Malcolm continues, "God is with you."

"Dad," Curtis mutters, "don't—don't leave me."

Malcolm forces a smile. "There are many things I wished I could have said to you, Son. But don't forget the things I've taught you. Hold on to them."

Curtis jumps up in his bed with a start. His body covered in a cold sweat and his breathing heavy. He looks around the dark room and realizes that it was just a dream… or rather two memories played back at once. He rubs his hands through his hair and looks at the clock next to his bed.

"3:00 a.m." He sighs to himself. "I still have three hours."

Saturday. August 18, 2012. 9:00 a.m. A growing crowd gathers in anticipation of the morning's special event.

"Good morning America! I'm Caitlin Conners and we are live on Broadway and 66th Street—just across from Lincoln Center and several blocks from Central Park. Standing with me is a young man, whose name and exploits are known all over the world—Curtis Powers, also known as Jetstream! It's good to see you!"

"Thank you Ms. Conners," Curtis replies. "It's good to be here!"

"Now Curtis, we see you're wearing your Mach-1 Speedsuit. How did you feel running at the London Olympics just a few weeks ago?"

"It was literally a dream come true! Like… destiny. I really have no words to describe it."

"Yes. It sure seemed like destiny to have the world watch as you entered the stadium and ran with the Olympic competitors. That was your dream from when you were a child, correct?"

"Yes. When I was in elementary school my dad would always say that anything was possible, even with my deficits."

"And now you're ready for college!"

"I leave tomorrow," Curtis smiles.

"Your story is truly inspiring: how you lost your father to cancer and then encountered and overcame bullying in school. And of course there's your amazing invention! I understand an author has written about your life and there's already talk of the book becoming a film."

"Yes," Curtis adds, "But there's more to my story than just me."

"That's right," Caitlin adds, "there's also the team of family and friends—who we'll meet later—that provides support for your exhibition runs! And this brings us to why we are here today!"

"Yes," Curtis beams, "I've been asked by the mayor of New York City to do an exhibition run through Central Park as a way of highlighting the power of inspiration, motivation and education."

Caitlin smiles. "It's amazing that people are already making their way into the park to watch your exhibition run—which begins in three hours."

Several blocks away, a man drives a garbage truck on his usual route. His face suddenly grimaces as he clutches his chest with his right hand! The truck swerves as he slumps over the wheel. Everything blurs as his eyes glaze over with fluid and his body shoots up like a spring! His leg stiffens—wedging his foot between the gas pedal and the floorboard!

BOOM!!! A loud crash is heard near 67th and Broadway.

"Oh, my God! Did you hear that crash?" Caitlin asks as she, her cameraman and Curtis turn just in time to see a twenty-five ton garbage truck barrel through several stopped cars at red lights!

The massive vehicle hurtles directly towards them as Curtis grabs Caitlin and her cameraman and barely pulls them out of the way. Several nearby police officers jump into their cars, blast their sirens and accelerate down the road in pursuit. Caitlin struggles to gain her composure as Curtis puts on his helmet. With the press of a button he engages his Kinetic Redistribution Boots, fires up the Mach-1's Vortex Pack and takes off down the street in a burst of pressurized air!

Tons of mechanized metal careens down the street at 35 miles per hour, uncontrollably swerving from one side of the road to the other. Parked cars barely slow it down as it pummels a fire hydrant at 64th Street! A forty-foot spray shoots into the air as people try to take cover from this vehicular missile! Three police cars quickly close the distance, but the truck's massive body sideswipes the lead car! As it jumps a curb at 62nd street and crashes through a business storefront, the other officers slam on their brakes to avoid becoming the truck's next victims.

"How are we going to stop this thing?" one officer yells through the radio as they try to maintain a safe distance.

"Someone needs to get inside and hit the brakes!" The other officer squawks back.

"I'm not getting close to that thing," the first officer screams. "Did you see what happened to Menendez and Baker?" The words barely leave the officer's mouth as a blurred figure speeds past his car. As Curtis pulls away from the police cars and quickly approaches the truck, his mind jumps into high gear.

"If I don't do something, someone's gonna get killed out here! Hopefully, it won't be me." Curtis cranks the vortex pack into its highest gear! The thrust quickly propels him to the truck. "Only gonna get one chance at this!"

As he runs up to the driver's door the truck lurches in his direction, but Curtis moves with the truck and jumps up to the driver's door! He shuts down his Vortex Pack while screaming through the window to the driver.

"Hey! Are you awake?"

The driver groans as his slumped body barely moves. The vibration from this lurching vehicular beast causes Curtis to almost lose his grip! They just pass 60th Street as Curtis manages to get the door open. He pushes the driver over, grabs the steering wheel with one hand and turns the wheel hard to the right, barely missing the Columbus Circle architecture. As he enters the intersection, he pulls the wheel hard to the left and rounds the circle past the Time Warner building. The truck barrels through the Broadway and 58th Street intersection as Curtis dislodges the driver's foot from the gas pedal and slams hard on the brakes! The mammoth vehicle screeches to a halt, in a cloud of burnt rubber-induced smoke, stopping just shy of a sidewalk full of terrified people frozen with fear!

The crowd erupts into cheers as the police cars arrive!

"The driver needs a medic," Curtis yells as he moves out of the way so the officers can handle the situation.

"Thank you," the lead officer utters while shaking Curtis' hand. "You saved the day!"

Cheering crowds surround Curtis—showering him with handshakes and hugs while taking pictures and asking for his autograph. Caitlin and her cameraman pull up in their television van. The cameraman jumps out with his camera on his shoulder and begins filming as Caitlin runs through the crowd towards Curtis. She gets to his side with her microphone in hand.

"Curtis! You are a hero! You saved these people!"

"I don't know if I'm a hero," Curtis says somberly, "I just did what I could do to help. See you in a few hours Ms. Conners." Curtis waves to the crowd.

Mr. Grabowski arrives in his van. "Curtis! Get in." He opens the sliding side door, climbs in and closes it behind him. "Are you alright?" Jim asks as he drives off. "That was amazing!"

"It was," Curtis mumbles, "and I'm not."

Jim snaps his head back in Curtis' direction. "Are you injured?"

Curtis takes off his helmet and unzips his suit while shaking his head. Jim turns his attention back to the road and drives in silence. As the van stops at a red light, Jim looks at Curtis through his rearview mirror. They both sit in silence as Curtis looks down and notices the helmet shaking in his hands.

The light turns green as Mr. Grabowski slowly steps on the gas. "Your quick thinking saved the lives of many people today."

Curtis' breathing becomes labored as he weeps. Jim pulls the van over, puts it in 'park' and turns around in his chair.

"Look at me."

Curtis looks up at him with tears in his eyes, as he grabs his inhaler from the seat and shakes it. "Mr. G., I could have died." He takes a deep breath on his inhaler—Pshhhh. Jim sits quietly for a moment and allows Curtis to cry.

"Now that you're sitting still—it's hitting you. Yes, you could have died. But, look at what you did: you pushed through your fear and did what needed to be done. That's what it means to be 'courageous.'"

Curtis looks up at Mr. Grabowski and slowly wipes his eyes. "Yeah…"

"Just sit back and rest for a bit," Jim smiles as he turns back around and puts the van in 'drive.' "We'll go over to Central Park and wait at the starting point."

As Jim pulls out from the parking spot and drives along, he whistles to himself as he looks at the police and medical teams attending to the wrecked vehicles, damaged storefronts and injured individuals on the other side of the street. "Would you look at that…"

But Curtis is oblivious to everything as he thinks about his life in light of Mr. Grabowski's comments.

In an undisclosed location, a man sits in a dark room, bathed in blue and white light as he watches the events unfold on several television screens. His cell phone rings.

"Yes? I am watching it now. I agree. He is becoming quite the hero. Everything is going as planned. That's correct. It's time to initiate phase two."

Chapter Two

The Big Day

CURTIS SITS ON THE SIDE OF his bed with his journal. His desk lamp illuminates his visage from across the room. He looks at the clock on the side of his bed and shakes his head. With a deep breath, he picks up his pen and begins to write an entry in his journal.

Journal Entry 2,334. Volume 3. Sunday August 19, 2012. 1:27 a.m.
   "It's after midnight and I can't sleep. So, I figured I'd write. Everything's moving so fast. It's easy to get caught up in the blur. It's easy for me to lose myself. But I have to remember where I came from and how that makes me who I am today.

   "Back in 9th grade, when Treyshawn bullied me, I thought the safest place in the world was anywhere without conflict. The only way to avoid conflict, I thought, was to run away from it. What I didn't expect was what actually happened. Our worlds colliding actually set the stage for us to be set free!

   "That seems crazy... but when circumstances forced Treyshawn and me to stop running from our problems and face them head on, we saw beyond our differences and finally understood that we were the same. We were two boys trying to navigate a world without our fathers. It was here that we realized we were equals. And this newfound equality became the foundation to help us build lives we could be proud of.

   "What was meant to destroy me, actually became my greatest opportunity; and that opportunity changed my life and Treyshawn's and the lives of everyone around us. I was running into my destiny and figured everything would get easier. But today definitely was *not* easier! While I know more than I did back then, I see there's so much more to learn."

The room sits in darkness as shapes meld together into a continuous landscape of grey hues. Objects resemble monsters in the shadows as the stillness of the moment gives way to a slight muffled howl from the bed. The golden rays of dawn suddenly pierce through the window blinds and slowly rise until a broad swath of color streaks clear across the room. With each passing moment, the light intensifies until the room is fully lit.

Footsteps are barely heard approaching on the carpeted floor. A moment later, the door opens as Miranda stands—looking around her son's room—shaking her head.

"Nothing's changed," she chuckles to herself with a smile. Books, magazines and graphic novels lay open on the floor, along with several piles of dirty and, possibly, clean clothing. A pair of glasses and an asthma pump sits next to the alarm clock on the night stand.

"Just like when he started ninth grade." She looks at the foot of the bed and sees Curtis' feet dangling out from under the sheets, clearly off the edge. "Ok. Maybe some things have changed."

She notices a form standing in the corner. "And then there's that..." The Mach-1 Speedsuit stands in its holding cage at the ready—empty—waiting for its wearer. Next to it is a wall full of associated newspaper articles, magazine clippings and various photographs. Below these clippings is a table stacked with piles of fan mail from all over the world.

Miranda walks over to the suit and places her hand on its torso. "To think that this came out of my son's mind," she whispers. "And he's changed so many lives with it. I wonder what else he's dreaming about?"

She walks over to his desk and scans the many envelopes from people all over the world—people amazed at his Olympic run. She picks up several envelopes from the 'unread' pile and looks at the names: Emily Dickerson from Tuscaloosa, Alabama. Tommy Perez from Phoenix, Arizona. Stacy Blake from Casper, Wyoming. Matthew Hart from Harlem, New York. Justin Todd from Littleton, Colorado. She places them back on the pile where she found them. "We have to finish reading these…"

Next to the desk is a makeshift worktable with blueprints and two objects underneath a blanket. Curtis' journal sits next to the blanket, opened to its last entry:

Journal Entry 2, 335. Volume 3. Sunday August 19, 2012. 3:42 a.m.
"I'm not tired. So, I returned to my previous project. Ugh! This is so frustrating! I still can't get the electromagnetic repulsion system to work! The concept is sound… but I don't have access to the right materials to make this happen. My prototype is still too bulky and the magnetic field is nowhere near strong enough to support my body weight. If this works, it would give me way more versatility when running and jumping. I wish I had a billion dollar budget like Tony Stark or Bruce Wayne. For the time being, I'm stuck with the current design for my Kinetic Redistribution Boots. The spring-leveraging system will have to do."

Miranda picks up the blueprints, looking at them slowly, before taking a peak underneath the blanket.

"I see you," a tired voice moans through the rustling of sheets. Miranda jumps as she quickly drops the blanket and turns to see her son slowly pulling the covers back. As he sits up, she can't help but notice his lean, muscular physique through his tank top and boxers.

"I remember when you used to be a skinny string bean," she grins. "Now look at you."

"Wasn't that long ago," Curtis responds while rubbing his hands through his matted hair.

"You need a haircut," she laughs.

"Yeah," Curtis chuckles, "it's getting hard to put the helmet on."

"And by the way, I saw you yesterday on television. That was a good thing you did saving those people—absolutely crazy… but good." She stares into his eyes for a moment. "Were you… afraid?"

"Yes," Curtis diverts his gaze, "And I already had this conversation with Mr. Grabowski."

"Ok," Miranda says, her voice slightly elevated, "we don't have to talk about it if you don't want to. And since you want to change the subject," she crosses her arms, "just what precisely did you see me doing over here?"

Curtis smiles. "I saw you trying to peek. Take a look if you want."

Miranda pulls the blanket off, revealing an electromagnet apparatus and the workings of a mechanical arm. "What are these for?"

"They're still not finished." Curtis walks over to her. "The electromagnet is part of a reworked design for the inner workings of the KRB's. It doesn't work. I call the arm, 'Lift Assist.' When the wearer straps it on and powers it up, they'll be able to lift an extra thirty pounds or so."

"Wow," Miranda slowly shakes her head in awe. "Does it work?"

"Theoretically it should. But I haven't tested it, yet. It's still a bit heavier than I'd like."

Miranda hugs her son. As he hugs her back, a tear falls onto his arm.

He glances down at her. "Mom, why are you crying?"

She stands, smiling for a moment, taking it all in. Then she lets out a laugh while wiping her eyes. "I'm crying because my baby is growing up and leaving for college today!"

"You cried when Omar went to the navy," Curtis soothes before transitioning into a sarcastic tone, "but you survived."

"Curtis," his mother exclaims, before giving him her stern look while placing her hands on her hips. "Yes, I *did* cry when your brother left for the navy. And I will survive when *you* leave. Maybe I'll have some wild and crazy parties once I have the house all to myself!"

"Mom!" Curtis gasps.

Miranda laughs. "You wanted to be smart. I can play the game, too!"

"Point taken," Curtis holds his hands up in surrender.

"You may be growing up and going off to college, but you're *still* my baby."

Curtis smiles and kisses his mother on her forehead. "Don't you forget it, Mom."

"Your dad... he'd be so proud of you... of both of you."

"Yeah," Curtis turns and looks at a picture of himself and Omar wrestling with their dad at the old house. "I miss him."

"We all do, but he wouldn't want this to be a sad occasion. He would want a celebration! And what better way to start a celebration than with food. You know he always enjoyed a good breakfast."

"Like father—like son!" Curtis laughs.

"And since this is a big day for the Powers family, I'm making pancakes!"

"Yes!"

"Get dressed and come downstairs."

"Ok. Have you seen Omar?"

"He went to pick up the U-haul for the SUV. He should be back in an hour or so."

Miranda walks out of the room. Curtis sits on his bed, picks up his cell phone from the nightstand and sends a text message. He looks around his room for a moment.

"I'm actually doing this." He takes a deep breath and starts his morning routine.

Miranda stands in her kitchen, next to the electric grill, holding a large bowl, while stirring the pancake batter. The phone rings. She picks up the landline on the counter.

"Hello?" Miranda asks while continuing to stir the batter.

"Mrs. Powers?"

"This is she..."

"This is Attorney Noreen Phillips."

"Oh, good morning. How are you today?"

"I'm fine. Thank you for asking. How are you?"

"Well. Today's the day that my baby leaves for college!"

"So, it's finally arrived. I know you must be happy."

"I am," Miranda smiles. "But I know you didn't call to talk about Curtis."

"No, I didn't. I do have some initial news for you and I'm afraid... it's not good."

"Ok," Miranda sits her bowl down on a nearby stool, "tell me."

"After a thorough examination, I have been unable to unearth anything but the most basic life insurance documents. Everything I've found confirms what you were told: a computer glitch, coupled with non-payment and a fatal clerical error, caused your husband's life insurance policy to be canceled." She proceeds cautiously, "I do have to ask... why have you waited so long to pursue this?"

Miranda bites her lip and takes a deep breath. "Have you ever had two children to raise after your husband dies?"

"No," Attorney Phillips responds, "I have not."

"After the initial investigation confirmed there really was no money coming, I couldn't waste time pursuing the matter. My boys needed me and I had to make things work with what we had."

"I understand," Attorney Phillips says in a purposeful tone.

"Any other questions?" Miranda asks.

"Yes," Attorney Phillips hesitates, "Why start this up again?"

"I can't explain it, but something doesn't feel right about it. And for a while it's been sitting in the back of my mind. Now that I have more time, I wanted to take another look at it."

"I will do what I can," Attorney Phillips responds. "As I said, on the surface everything checks out, but for the length of time your husband was with the firm, I'd expect a longer trail of paperwork."

"Does that make you suspicious?" Miranda asks.

"It does," Attorney Phillips replies.

"So, what do we do now?"

"At this point? Nothing."

"Nothing?" Miranda huffs. "You just said you were suspicious!"

"Yes. That's true. But if something *isn't* right here, my inquiry might raise red flags for the very people who may be trying to hide something."

"So... I just sit and do nothing," Miranda says dejectedly.

"Until we have evidence revealing foul play—yes. I'm sorry. And I would advise you *not* to explore unofficial channels."

"Excuse me?"

"As an attorney, I must advise you *not* to attempt to contact any former coworkers of your deceased husband to see if they might have information that would be useful to you."

"Ah," Miranda says as she begins to understand. "Ok. Thank you for your time, Attorney Phillips."

"You're most welcome, Mrs. Powers. I will be in touch if anything comes up."

Miranda hangs up the phone in a huff. She takes a deep breath to calm herself down and then closes her eyes. "Ok, Lord... none of this takes you by surprise. So, now what?"

Ten minutes later, Curtis leaps down the stairs and walks into the kitchen, while buttoning his shirt. His mother is busy making the plates as he sits down. She places the pancakes on the table and, after a moment's grace, Curtis starts eating. The phone rings. Miranda answers.

"Hello? Well, hello to you too! How are you this morning? Good. Are you excited?" She looks at her son with a huge smile. "Yes, I can't wait to see you in a few hours. Hold on. I'll let you talk to him." She hands him the phone, with a grin. "You know, I always liked that girl."

"Mom, you say that every time." Curtis takes the phone.

"And every time it's true." Miranda turns to start eating.

"Did you say your grace?" Curtis whispers playfully before talking to Kelly. Miranda's eyes widen and then close tightly as she stops for a moment.

"Hey Kelly! Did you get my text?"

Kelly lies across her bed with her feet crossed in the air. She says somewhat sleepily, "Yeah. I just got it. Who stole the night? It seems like I just went to sleep ten minutes ago!"

"I know," Curtis chuckles. "But that's what happens when you go to bed late and get up early."

"We had a lot of packing to do," Kelly moans. "With my dad away, my mom wanted to make sure I had everything I need. I think I have too much."

"Too bad your brothers had to go back early for training camp."

"Yeah, coach's orders. That's why dad drove them down over the weekend."

"It's amazing that they're both at the same university. I feel sorry for whoever faces them on the court and on the field!"

"Yeah!" Kelly chuckles as she sits up on her bed.

"Ok. So, I'll see you later?"

"You trying to get rid of me already?"

"My pancakes are getting cold."

"You and your pancakes," she laughs. "Fine. Enjoy them. You spoke to Treyshawn yet? We're supposed to pick him up at 12:00 p.m."

"Was gonna call him after breakfast."

"Too bad Treyshawn has to fly by himself while the rest of us drive."

"Too bad his mom couldn't get off from work. He's still excited, though."

"Good. Tell him I said 'hey.' I'm gonna start getting ready. See you in a few hours."

Miranda sits in her bedroom with the door closed. She picks up her phone and presses a set of numbers she hasn't had to dial in several years. *It's amazing I still remember them*, she thinks to herself. After two rings, someone answers.

"Thank you for calling the Architect Firm of Pierce-Sterling and Whaley. How may I direct your call?"

"Yes, may I please speak to Margery Cunningham?"

"I'm sorry, she no longer works here."

"Really?"

"Yes. Just retired last year. Is there someone else I can direct you to?"

"No, thank you. Did she leave contact information? I'm a former associate of hers."

"I'm sorry, Ma'am, but she did not."

"Ok. Thank you very much."

"Have a nice day."

As Miranda hangs up the phone, she thinks to herself, *Now what? Margery was my one sure contact—someone I could trust.*

Chapter Three

Not Goodbye... See You Later

TREYSHAWN, KELLY AND HER MOTHER ARRIVE at Curtis' house. Jim is already inside talking with Miranda. Curtis and Omar are pulling bags and boxes outside, preparing to load up for the trip. Once pleasantries are exchanged and small talk ceases, everyone goes about the task of ensuring as quick a departure as possible. It will be a long flight to California for Treyshawn, and an even longer drive to Atlanta for Curtis and Kelly.

Treyshawn's cell phone rings. He puts a box down next to the car to answer it. As he answers the call, he can hear all kinds of chatter and sounds of dishes moving in the background.

"Hey, Ma!"

Shakira leans against a wall in the back of the diner where she works—in between the kitchen and storage room.

"Hey, Trey. I wanted to call you while I was on break."

"I'm glad you did," Treyshawn leans against the car.

"I really wish I was there with you."

"I do too, but I know you gotta work."

"It *does* feel good to be working now."

"Yeah," he smiles. "Besides, that's why we had that big going-away party last week. 'Cause everyone couldn't come today."

"That *was* a fun party," Shakira chuckles. "When I close my eyes, I still see you doin' the 'funky chicken,'"

"Ma! You can't tell anyone about that!"

Shakira laughs hard. "You ain't got to worry about me, Trey. But can the rest of the group keep the secret?"

Treyshawn turns with a spying eye, as he looks at everyone else moving boxes.

"So, seriously..." Shakira continues, "how you feelin'?"

"Good." Treyshawn turns back around. "I'm looking forward to the change," he catches himself, "although… I'm not looking forward to leaving you."

"Uh, huh. Good save," Shakira says sarcastically.

Treyshawn laughs. "And I'm definitely *not* looking forward to getting on a plane again."

Shakira is quiet for a moment as her stomach churns.

"Ma, you Ok?" Treyshawn asks.

Shakira smiles. "Perfect, baby. Just perfect. I am *so* proud of you, Trey. You saved me…"

Treyshawn pulls the phone away from his ear for a moment as he tries, to no avail, to contain his tears. He slowly brings the phone back to his ear. "I love you, Ma."

"I love you too, baby. I really do. You go get ready. Call me when you get to the airport."

"Ok. Talk to you then. And Ma?"

"Yeah?"

"I'm proud of you, too. Everything you been through and you *still* press forward…"

"We can choose. Remember?"

"Oh, I *definitely* remember," Treyshawn chuckles. "Talk to you soon."

Shakira closes her cell phone and leans against the wall. Tears stream down her face, as her manager glances at her while walking by. There are only a few minutes left on her break. She closes her eyes and thinks back to a few weeks before.

Welfare Office. Bronx.

"I know it's going to be hard," Shakira tries not to look at the dull colors on the wall, "but I want to get off welfare and make a way for me and my son."

The social worker stares at her unfazed. "How are you going to do that? You've never shown any type of initiative like this before."

"Things have changed," Shakira says, while wringing her hands nervously in her lap. "*I* have changed."

The social worker glares at her incredulously and then writes a couple of notes on her clipboard. Shakira forces a shaky smile.

"I know you deal with people like me—*like I was*—who abuse the system and make your life miserable in the process. Up until now, I never gave you anything but a hard time."

"That you did," interjects the social worker. The two women stare at each other for a moment and then break into a laugh.

"Believe me. I understand," Shakira empathizes as they both lighten up a bit.

"Ok," the social worker replies, "what are you doing to facilitate this change?"

"We'll... I started studying so I can get my GED. Thinking I can maybe get a job helping other single mothers see what options they truly have and how to take advantage of them."

The social worker raises her right eyebrow in surprise. She finds herself transitioning from a defensive, leaned-back position, to sitting on the edge of her chair. "That is a noble goal, but it will cost you money—money you don't have."

"I know. That's why I started singing again. Just had my first gig at a nightclub last week. And a friend of mine helped me get a waitressing job."

"Well, it seems you are on your way then. You need to be mindful of the requirements for you to continue to receive public assistance. To be realistic, I have to tell you that this will be an uphill battle. Old habits die hard, especially when new situations get difficult."

"True. But old habits *can* die. My son taught me that."

"And how is your son?"

"On a completely different path now. And leaving for college in a few weeks."

Shakira's watch beeps repeatedly—indicating it's time to get back to work. She opens her eyes, wipes away her tears and stands up straight. With a deep breath, she runs her fingers through her hair and gathers herself. "Thank you," she whispers before getting back to work.

The Powers House.

Miranda and Jim stand in the foyer.

"So, how does it feel to be retired?" she asks.

"It feels great, actually," Jim smiles broadly. "More time to sleep."

Miranda laughs.

"You think I'm kidding," Jim smirks.

"Well, thirty years of teaching is pretty long," Miranda responds. "You deserve an extended nap time."

"Actually, I may be busier now than when I was teaching," Jim laughs. "With your son's exhibition runs happening more frequently, 'Team Speedsuit' is always on call."

"Well, things should slow down a bit since Curtis, Kelly and Treyshawn are headed off to college. You know you don't have to travel to *every* venue. We can get someone else."

"If you are implying that I'm too old for this," Jim quips, "then thank you for your consideration. But being a part of this team helps keep me young!"

"Understood," Miranda smiles.

"Even so," Jim admits, "having a bit of a break is nice. I leave tomorrow to go visit my daughter's family in Cincinnati."

"The day has finally arrived," Miranda muses. "How long will you be there?"

"Three weeks."

"That's a long time."

"Not when you haven't seen your daughter in over ten years."

They both stand quietly for a moment, looking at each other before turning their attention to the rest of the group outside.

"So, how are you *really* doing, Miranda?" Jim asks softly. Miranda stares out the window for a moment, takes a deep breath and answers.

"How is a mother supposed to feel when her youngest son is going off to college for the first time? I just want to go and scoop him up—hold him tight and never let him go."

"They grow up so fast," Jim says retrospectively. "Next thing they're married with kids of their own and you're wondering where the time went."

"Don't rush the process!" Miranda laughs nervously.

"Sorry! Sorry." Jim raises his hands in surrender.

Miranda gazes at her son longingly. "I know Curtis will be Ok. It's just hard to let go. The world can be such a beautiful place. But there are areas that can eat you alive and spit out your bones if you're not careful. I just want to protect him."

"You have," Jim says confidently as Miranda looks at him with surprise. "You and Malcolm have done a great job with both of your boys. And even though he's not here, you both have instilled so much in them. When they need it—they'll be able to draw from *that* resource."

Miranda stares at Jim with tears in her eyes. "That was beautiful. Thank you."

"No need to thank me," Jim counters with a smile, "I only said what's true. Curtis and Omar will be just fine… no matter what they have to face in life."

"You *had* to mention Omar," Miranda interjects, "I was trying not to think about him having to leave in a few weeks. Tensions are increasing overseas."

"Omar has a good head on his shoulders." Jim puts his arm around Miranda.

"Well, I'm praying that God helps him use that mind of his… He'll most likely encounter trouble while back at sea."

They stand quiet for a moment, looking through the screen door, while listening to the sound of laughter from the group. Miranda walks over to the window and picks up a picture of her husband.

"Malcolm being gone has been unimaginably… difficult," Miranda says, "but you're right… his intentionality and impact before he died has been crucial in making the boys who they are today. In fact, he left something for both of them—which I'll give them before we all leave."

"That will be an amazing moment I'm sure." Jim smiles.

"I'm sure…" Miranda whispers. "But on another note, I did secure the lawyer you suggested."

"She's the best at what she does. Did she give you the discount?"

"Yes. When I told her you sent me, she said she'd handle all the legwork free of charge and only take a percentage if we win."

"It pays to keep in touch with former students," Jim smiles. "I don't abuse the relationship, but I do call in a few favors every now and then."

"Well, I appreciate it."

"Treyshawn is all set," Curtis tells Omar. "Can you believe he only has two duffle bags?"

"Sounds like he should join the military as I did," Omar chuckles.

"This is a new opportunity for him," Curtis continues, "but he's nervous about flying."

"I can't believe he'd never been on a plane before we all went to London," Omar adds.

"At least there's a barf bag in the seat," Curtis laughs.

"But what about you?" Omar asks, as he and Curtis hoist a large chest into the back of the SUV rental. "Are you excited?"

"For the most part," Curtis replies. "First time away from home, so I'm a little nervous."

"Technically, you've already been away from home. We did just get back from London a couple of weeks ago."

"You know what I mean."

Omar cracks a huge grin, as they continue putting boxes in the vehicle. "Yeah, I know."

"The Olympics was a great experience," Curtis says gratefully.

"It truly was," Omar adds. "Can't believe they invited us back for 2016!"

They both stand quietly, replaying memories of the exhibition run in their minds.

Omar looks at his brother. "Dad would have been proud."

"You got that right," Curtis smiles. "Real proud..."

"I remember when I left for the navy," Omar leans on the vehicle with his arms crossed.

"You were 'Mr. Cool,'" Curtis chuckles, "ready to go."

"What I *was*... was nervous."

"You were nervous?" Curtis stands in shock as they both recount that day.

"Ma made that big breakfast..."

"That was the best breakfast ever!" Curtis exclaims. "Eggs. Bacon. Pancakes. Sausage. Grits. Hash browns…"

"I could barely keep it down," Omar admits.

"Seriously?" Curtis shouts.

Omar belts out a laugh. "I wanted to vomit so bad!"

Curtis looks confused. "But you ate everything!"

"Yeah, I know!" Omar continues. "Ma went through all the trouble to make it, so I knew I had to eat it. And I wanted to eat it… But my stomach was tied in knots!"

"But, why were you nervous?"

"I was doing something new," Omar admits. "Taking a big step into the unknown… About to pledge my life and allegiance to my country, for four years."

"Four years," Curtis ponders. "Just like college."

"Except my classroom was an aircraft carrier," Omar grins.

"That's still so cool!" Curtis beams. "One day you have to get me a tour."

"Yeah," Omar agrees, "I wish you could see it up close like I get to do. At least you won't be alone like I was when I started at the navy. Lucky for you, Kelly will be nearby."

"Yeah," Curtis smiles from ear to ear, "I love that girl."

"I know you do, Bro. Make sure you treat her right."

"You don't have to worry."

"Yeah, but you might have to," Omar says seriously.

"What do you mean?" Curtis asks.

"I know you both care a lot about each other, but this will be a whole new ball game. She'll meet a whole bunch of guys who won't care that she has a boyfriend. Some of them will be working overtime to try and pull her from you."

"Are you serious?" Curtis asks in a state of unbelief.

"But don't let that intimidate you," Omar continues, "And don't go getting all insecure and try and hold her so tight that she doesn't have any freedom. Do that, and you'll push her right into another guy's arms."

"So what do I do?"

"Do you trust her?"

"Absolutely."

"Then just be you. Same thing you did to win her is what you do to keep her."

Kelly and her mother embrace.

"Your dad got to take your brothers and I get to take you. So, how *is* my baby?"

"I'm fine," Kelly looks down at the pavement.

Stacy's brow wrinkles as she sees her daughter's expression. "You don't *look* fine."

"It's just that," Kelly hesitates, "I'm not sure if I have what it takes..."

"What are you talking about honey? Sure you have what it takes!"

Kelly smiles a bit. "You're my mother. You're supposed to tell me that."

"Yes. And I'm also supposed to tell you the *truth*. You. Have. What. It. Takes."

"But girls will be there from all over the country. Even from other countries! What if I don't get along with people? What if we're all too different? I'll be so far from home."

"You are not that far away that we can't drive down to see you when we have to. We all go through the same feelings when we are about to go into something new. Just remind yourself about who you are, who you want to become, and what you've accomplished in your life so far: like dancing at Lincoln Center!"

Kelly smiles as her mom continues. "You are loving, kind, intelligent and strong-willed."

"Mom!" Kelly laughs.

"It's true!" her mom says. "Besides, your entire family is strong-willed!" She places her hands on Kelly's shoulders.

"Seriously. You have a family that loves you and friends that adore you. Not to mention, you also have Curtis. So you are definitely not alone. And if any or all of us fail you somehow, you always have God—who never fails."

"Thanks, Mom."

"Just be yourself. Pay attention in class. Have fun. And watch out for those boys!"

"Mom," Kelly laughs embarrassingly. "You know I'm with Curtis."

"And I know he knows how to treat you with respect. You always want to treasure that about him. But I also know there will be boys who will want to get close to you—even with Curtis around. And I know there will be girls who will want to get close to Curtis, especially if you are not around! So be mindful of that fact."

"Treyshawn sits on the curb as a car pulls up. Two familiar people get out.

"Mr. Andre? Mrs. Fuller? What are you two doing here?"

"We came to see you guys off," Mrs. Fuller replies.

"Especially you," Mr. Andre remarks. "People still call you 'lil' Trecherous'?"

They all laugh.

"I don't even call me that anymore."

"Now that's what I'm talking about," Mr. Andre gives Treyshawn a big hug.

Mrs. Fuller puts her hand on his shoulder, "Treyshawn, I want you to know how proud I am of you. We had a rocky start, but you've proven you have what it takes to succeed in life. Even more so, you've become significant because you have positively impacted the people around you. You keep pressing forward."

"Thank you, Mrs. Fuller. But you know I can't take all the credit."

"Oh, I know," she assures. "That is why I'm going to go say hello to Curtis right now."

They both laugh and hug.

"Any success I have is because of you all helping me," Treyshawn adds.

"And don't you ever forget that," she points at him with a smile. "But also, don't forget that even with all of our help, you are the one who did the work. Everyday, you *chose* to do the work." Mrs. Fuller smiles and walks away as Mr. Andre steps closer.

"We never really spoke about you turning your life around. But I was watching you."

"I remember what you said," Treyshawn replies, "about applying myself. You said I might be surprised at what I'm capable of."

"We'll, you surprised all of us." Mr. Andre stands confidently, sporting a huge smile.

"Thank you for standing up to me. I couldn't see the truth back then."

"But eventually you saw it," Mr. Andre interjects, "That is thanks enough."

"I was *always* comparing you to my father."

Mr. Andre chuckles. "If I had a dollar for every time you told me I wasn't your father...."

They both smile.

"Have you gone to see him?"

"Naw," Treyshawn looks away. "Last time I saw him, he told me never to come back."

"Since when do sons listen to their fathers?"

Treyshawn looks at Mr. Andre—like a light bulb just went off in his head. But then the pain of his reality overshadows him. "I don't know... Not really feeling that right now."

"A lot has changed for you since the last time you saw him," Mr. Andre adds. "Maybe a lot has changed for him, too."

"Maybe it hasn't," Treyshawn counters.

"You'll never know if you don't go see him."

"But what if he hasn't changed?" Treyshawn asks in an exasperated tone. "What if he still doesn't want to see me?"

"If he doesn't want to see you," Mr. Andre pauses while taking a deep breath, "then he's a fool and it's *his* loss. Either way, like Mrs. Fuller said, you keep pressing forward with *your* life. And you take *that* experience with your father and learn from it."

"Learn what?"

Mr. Andre looks at Treyshawn intently. "Learn how to be there for those who *need* you to be."

Miranda walks from the house and approaches her sons with something behind her back.

"Don't worry about the new school," Omar says to Curtis as their mother walks up, "you got this."

As Miranda stands in front of her sons, she presents a crumpled brown paper bag. "Your father wanted you both to have these." Omar and Curtis carefully open the bag and pull out two leather-bound journals.

"He wrote these himself," she says with tears rolling down her face. She continues as her sons slowly run their hands over the weathered leather covers. "That's everything he wanted to say to both of you. Everything he knew he wouldn't have time to share."

In a moment of silence, Omar and Curtis open their respective journals and see their father's handwriting on the first page: "To My Courageous Sons. From Your Father." They stare at that title for a moment before starting to slowly turn the pages.

"He saved that title for last," she utters, "after he had written everything else. I never did tell you about that day, when he wrote those words in the hospital room... before he died."

May 15, 2005.

A cacophony of hums and beeps from various monitors fill the sterile room as they keep track of Malcolm's vitals.

"God is good, baby," Malcolm's voice is hushed and labored. "I finally finished. Everything I could think of... and some things I didn't think of... all in these books for Curtis and Omar. Make sure you give these to them on the day Curtis leaves for college."

Malcolm's bony hands close both books. Miranda looks at her husband who lies before her, his body having wasted away to a mere shadow of the man he once was. But she can't focus on that... otherwise she'd miss the moment they were in.

"Why not give them the journals sooner?" Miranda asks.

"Because they'll have you for support until then. But when Curtis goes to college, and Omar is wherever he is, that will be an entirely new transition. You won't be with them and they'll need me to remind them about who they truly are. They'll also need to learn more about the man that I've become."

Miranda smiles slightly—acknowledging her husband's words—before turning away from him. She sits quietly gazing out the window, her mind suddenly lost in the sound of water droplets hitting the windowsill, as the rain streaks from the sky to the ground. Malcolm watches her for a few minutes—taking in her stunning beauty faded by wrinkled lines—before speaking.

"Going through this sickness with me has tired you," he interrupts her silence, "but your beauty hasn't diminished."

She snaps out of her gaze and turns back towards Malcolm. He sees the dried marks from the tears, which swam down her face minutes before. She closes her eyes and shakes her head.

"I... I can't do this."

Malcolm looks at her quietly as she starts to sob.

"How can I be happy about anything?" She asks in frustration. "How can I say, 'God is good' when the man I love is about to be taken from me? How is God *good* in this?"

Malcolm sits quietly for a moment and then musters all of his waning strength for one last Herculean feat: he slowly pulls the covers back from the edge of his bed and turns his body so he can place his feet on the cold floor. Miranda watches—through her tears—as he forges through unimaginable pain in order to stand up.

"Baby, what are you doing?" she says, alarmed, as she approaches to stop him."

"Don't. You. Move." Malcolm says with a whispered authority.

She halts and watches her husband intently. He tries to keep a straight face, but with each movement, his expression tells of his body's struggle as it silently screams at him! But through sheer willpower he forces himself up, reaches for the rack which holds his intravenous pain medication, and makes his way over to his wife. One. Agonizing. Step. At-a-time. Halfway to her, he loses his balance! Miranda moves like a bolt of lightning and catches him. She winces at the thought: *he weighs so little now*. But her thoughts burst like a bubble as her mind suddenly registers an insane request.

"What did you just say?" she asks.

Malcolm smiles slightly. "I said... dance with me."

She bursts into tears as she buries her face into his bony chest. It used to be firm and muscular… now it was so fragile. Miranda hears Malcolm's heart beating—as if it were outside his torso. Its irregular rhythm matched by the raspy sound from his lungs as they begin to slowly sway back and forth—humming to music only they can hear.

"*This* is why God is good," he whispers into her ear. "For *every* moment that we have had together." He lifts her head with his hand and gazes into her eyes. "We've been through this. We all have to die some kind of way. This is mine."

"I know," Miranda says softly. "Everything that could be done has been done."

"That's right," Malcolm smiles faintly as he inhales deeply. "Your hair smells *so* good."

Miranda can't help but laugh at such an unexpected comment.

"It doesn't make sense to be angry anymore, baby. You'll just miss the *beauty* of the moment that's right in front of you."

Miranda smiles softly as she pulls herself more closely to her husband. They continue to sway in the moment—their eyes closed—both seeing in a way they've never seen before.

The Present.

Miranda wipes tears from her eyes as she continues to speak. "Malcolm would have been so proud of both of you—how you've grown and matured—the way you seek to honor him with your lives."

As they begin to leaf through the pages, they notice something peculiar. They look back and forth at each other's journal before looking up at their mother.

"They're both the same," Curtis says.

Miranda smiles at their observation. "Your dad always liked to make an impression. That was intentional."

"Why?" Curtis asks.

"Yeah," Omar interjects, picking up Curtis' thought. "Why didn't dad just make a copy?"

"He didn't want *either* one of you to feel slighted because you got a copy and not the original. These are his words to you. Written by the same pen. Held in his hand. This is his love letter to you. Both equally his sons."

Tears stream down the boys' faces as they hold their father's words close to their chests. Miranda watches with a humbled pride, before being pulled into her sons' embrace.

"I know," she says, "we all miss him."

Curtis musters up the strength to speak. "Mom...You had these journals all this time?"

Again Omar finishes his brother's thought, but this time with a dejected tone. "You had these all this time and you're *just* giving them to us?"

"Yes," Miranda says solemnly.

Omar's eyes well up with tears as his voice rises. "After all these *years* without him. With everything we've been through and all the times we said 'we wished he was still here.' And *you* had these locked away?"

"I understand that you are upset Omar."

"Yes. I am," he says flatly.

"Omar," Curtis interjects. "We have dad's journals now. *That's* what matters."

Miranda turns towards Curtis. "It's Ok. Your brother asked a valid question." Then she turns back towards Omar. "You don't think I wanted to give these to you? With all of our struggles and sleepless nights, do you *really* believe that I didn't want to give these to you both? Your father made it *very* clear to me that unless there was some extreme emergency, I should wait until *this* day. This. Day! *This* is what *he* wanted and I was *not* going to deprive him of one of his last requests."

"Mom," Curtis says softly as he gives her a hug, "thank you." As they both hug, Omar's anger softens and slowly dissolves away.

"Ma..."

"There's no need baby," she says while reaching out for him, "There's no need."

The three of them embrace in a very long hug.

Treyshawn hears someone approaching and turns around to find a familiar face looking at him.

"I heard you was over here."

"Hakiim?" Treyshawn can't believe his eyes. They approach each other and embrace. "Man, it is good to see you," Treyshawn pounds Hakiim on his back.

As they hug, Treyshawn ignores the reeking smell of marijuana. They pull from each other and Hakiim takes a good look at his old friend as Treyshawn looks deep into the eyes of someone he used to know.

"Been a long time," Hakiim utters.

"Yeah, it has been a minute," Treyshawn responds.

"Look at you Trey," Hakiim smiles strong. "You doin' it."

"Doin' what?" Treyshawn asks.

"What you said you was gonna do. You fightin' for you... And now you 'bout to get up outta the hood. No basketball. No drugs. Just you."

"What about you?" Treyshawn inquires. "What you been up to?"

"You know... A little of this... a little of that."

"Your eyes are a bit glazed," Treyshawn adds.

"So, now you analyzin' me?" Hakiim counters.

"Just making an observation, bro. That's all," Treyshawn's eyes are sympathetic. "You know, it's not too late to go where I'm going."

"You sure 'bout that?" Hakiim objects. "We ain't talked in a couple of years."

"Don't mean you haven't been on my mind," Treyshawn counters. "Where's the rest of the guys?"

"You didn't hear? I'm the only one left."

"What you mean?" Treyshawn replies.

"Jay, Boz and Kuamane got locked up."

"What?" Treyshawn's face grimaces. "When did that happen?"

"Like six months ago. Surprised you didn't know. But you roll wit a different crew now."

Treyshawn ignores the side comment. "What about Remy?"

"Remy went down south for a drug run. Things went bad. He was killed two weeks ago."

Treyshawn looks at his old friend in horror. "What?"

Hakiim's steeled composure crumbles as he stumbles to the ground. "I don't know what I'mma do, Trey! I don't want to get locked up. And I don't want to die! But this is all I know!"

Treyshawn kneels down, takes his friend by the shoulders and helps up.

"Look at me, bro."

Hakiim looks at him intently.

Treyshawn continues without wavering, "If *I* can make it, *you* can make it."

"But I ain't like you!" Hakiim cries, "I don't have what you have!"

"What I *have*," Treyshawn counters, "is friends who care about me. Who pushed me. Who helped me. And now *you* got them too."

"I don't know," Hakiim states flatly as he slowly backs away.

Treyshawn grabs his friend's arm. "If you go back, you know where you're gonna end up. You ain't gotta go back to that life."

Hakiim looks at his friend. "Remy did say if you made it, we'd know it was possible."

"Yeah," Treyshawn whispers, "I just wish you guys would have come with me. Things would be real different for *all* of us."

Hakiim breathes deeply and then nods in his friend's direction. Treyshawn smiles brightly and walks Hakiim over to the group.

"Everybody? This is Hakiim. He wants to change his life and we gotta help him."

The group crowds around Hakiim to give him hugs and encouraging words. Treyshawn turns to Mr. Andre.

Mr. Andre smiles and puts his arm around Hakiim. "Have you ever met Mrs. Fuller? She's one of the best guidance counselors in the world."

After several minutes of intense and vibrant discussion, the group scatters as they begin their various journeys. Miranda, Omar and Curtis will lead the trip. Kelly and her mother will follow in their car. And Jim will take Treyshawn to JFK airport.

"Wait!" Miranda yells as everyone is about to pull off. "I forgot to check the mail!"

She gets out of the car, runs to the mailbox, grabs the waiting stack of mail and takes it inside the house to quickly sort. "Gonna be gone for a few days," she says to herself. "Don't want to miss something... important." Miranda's voice stops in a hush as she sees an envelope towards the bottom of the pile. Her name and address are in the center of the envelope. In the upper left are the initials, "M.C." and a P.O. box address.

I would know that handwriting anywhere, she thinks to herself as she holds the letter in her hands as if it were a sacred text. "On all the days for this to come." She snaps out of her trance, opens the letter carefully and begins reading—hearing the writer's words in a distinctly female, British accent.

Dear Miranda,

It has been a very long time since last we spoke. I remember your husband's funeral as if it were yesterday. I miss Malcolm very much and I know you do as well—only infinitely more.

For a long time, I wondered how you and your boys were doing. Imagine my surprise to turn on the news and see all of you setting a world record and attending the Olympics! Simply amazing is all I can say! Malcolm would be so proud! It is good to know that your family is thriving, even in the midst of so many setbacks.

We should meet for tea. It would be wonderful to catch up on recent developments and talk about the possibility of future endeavors. I will call you soon and provide a location.

By the way, we have a mutual friend who advised me not to contact you.

Sincerely,

M.C.

Miranda lets out a shout of jubilation that fills the entire house before covering her mouth! She then folds the letter, puts it back in the envelope and puts it in the inner lining of her purse. She quickly locks the door and makes her way out of the house and back to the waiting vehicles. Truly, a new journey is just beginning!

Chapter Four

College Bound

TREYSHAWN STARES OUT OF THE AIRPLANE window in awe. At 19 years old, this is only the third time he's had this experience—the first two times were the round trip flight to and from London for the Olympics. As he listens to the sound of the roaring engines, he chuckles, sits back, closes his eyes and thinks about his first flight.

July 20, 2012.

Jim, Omar, Miranda, Kelly, Curtis and Treyshawn find their seats and buckle in on the crowded British Airways plane.

"Are you sure this is safe?" Treyshawn asks nervously. Kelly and Curtis laugh hysterically.

"You should see your face right now," Curtis says.

"Yeah," Kelly chimes in. "For someone who's so tough, you're scared of flying on an airplane?"

"Hey," Treyshawn yells out. "It's my first time, alright. Cut me some slack!"

"It's Ok," Omar smiles. "We haven't even taken off yet."

"You're going to be alright," Miranda says assuredly. We are destined for too much greatness for something bad to happen to us now."

"Treyshawn," Curtis says as his laughter subsides, "you think we'd be on a plane if it wasn't relatively safe?"

"What you mean 'relatively?'" Treyshawn squawks back with a bewildered look.

"What he means," Mr. Grabowski interjects with a chuckle of his own, "is that nothing is 100% safe. But statistically, more people die from car crashes than from plane crashes."

"Can we *not* talk about dying, please?" Treyshawn retorts as his breathing gets heavier and he covers his mouth. "Aw man, I think I'm gonna hurl..."

The Present.

Treyshawn opens his eyes and laughs out loud. Several people turn and look at him.

"What you looking at?" he says, "A guy can't laugh when he wants to?"

The people turn back around in their seats.

Treyshawn thinks back to the moment after he said he was going to hurl and says to himself, "Man, the woman in front of me was not happy! How was I supposed to know there was a barf bag in the back of the seat?"

Kelly looks out of the car window at the passing trees. They look like stick figures dancing across the landscape—leaping across the horizon! She looks at the clock—five hours already and they were just getting to Washington D.C. Her mother quietly watches out of the corner of her eye. Kelly rummages through one of her bags and pulls out several key possessions: her first ballet shoes, her favorite three books, a photo of her family and a photo of her and Curtis. After taking a few minutes to look at each, Kelly smiles and puts the items back in her bag.

"A penny for your thoughts?" Stacy says while keeping her eyes on the road.

"Mom. Nobody says that anymore. Besides, with the cost of inflation my thoughts are worth way more than a penny!"

Stacy laughs, "Oh, really? Oh, how I miss the good old days!"

"What? Black and white television. Eight-track cassettes. Vinyl records. VCR's. Cell phones the size of bricks."

They both laugh.

"Somehow it was a simpler time then," Stacy adds. "You knew where people stood on things. But seriously, I know what you're doing."

"What am I doing?" Kelly asks—feigning ignorance.

"You're trying to redirect the conversation," Stacy says firmly.

Kelly grows silent.

"If you don't want to talk, that's fine. Just know that I'm here when you're ready. Besides, we have a long way to go before we get to our destination."

Kelly sits back in her chair and tries to get comfortable. A question lingers in the back of her mind and she's afraid to ask it out loud. So, she stuffs it down and replaces it with another one that is not so weighty.

"I wonder what Curtis is doing right now?"

Curtis sits in the back seat of the SUV staring at a copy of the photo Kelly was just looking at. He smiles as he rubs his finger over the image and looks into her paper-brown eyes. For a moment he gets lost in her gaze and thinks to himself, *Nice guys DO finish first.*

He puts the photo away and picks up his university's welcome pack. His smile lessens as he wrestles with several thoughts.

"Mom, I've got a problem."

Miranda and Omar look at each other.

"What is it baby?" she calls from the front seat.

Curtis hesitates before continuing. "I… won't be the only smart kid at school."

"You weren't the only smart kid in high school either," Omar says sarcastically.

Curtis shakes his head. "Omar, you *know* what I mean."

"What *do* you mean?" Miranda asks.

"*Every* student will be as smart as me—probably smarter. They'll be the valedictorians of their high schools. All 'A's'! Prodigies working on things I've never even imagined! I'll just be another smart kid which—on *that* level— makes me just another dumb kid."

"Hey!" Omar interjects. "No one there made the Mach-1 or the KRB's. *You* did that."

"And how could you believe what you just said?" Miranda reasons. "Every person has gifts and talents. And it's not for you to get caught up in what *others* can and can't do. You just have to make sure *you* work within your capability. Besides, like Omar said, *no one* else made the Speedsuit. *You did.*"

Curtis smiles and turns his gaze towards the scenery outside the car. "I guess you guys are right."

"There's no guessing to it," Omar says. "We *are* right. And remember what dad would always say, 'Do your best so that the miraculous can happen.' Don't start second-guessing yourself now. You've come too far. We all have."

Curtis takes out his dad's journal and rubs his hand across the cover. This simple act soothes his nervousness as he thinks about life.

His fame has brought more opportunities *and* more pressure. Because of his invention, the top colleges courted him and offered him unbelievable packages, if he'd agree to attend their educational institutions. Even private technology firms and the U.S. government's D.A.R.P.A. came knocking on his door. All he had to do was agree to work for them and his education—from Bachelors to Masters to Ph.D—would be funded. He had so many choices and so many opportunities for success, failure, and even deception. He wondered, *how does one weigh the pros and cons of a decision when all options provided promise everything beyond one's imagination? How do you decide where to go when everything is paid for and all you have to do is show up? How do you choose your course when every college and university rep puts on their best show in order to attract you—like the car dealer who points out the shiny paint, spinning rims and awesome stereo, but neglects to tell you that the car gets terrible gas mileage and has a poor-to-average safety rating?*

Curtis' mind draws back to his journal entries from earlier in the year.

May 21, 2012. Entry number 1,034.

"I can't tell the difference because every college is offering the best. God, where are you in this? Help me decide. Where do you want me to go?"

June 7, 2012. Entry number 1,035.

"It's funny how things work out. I've decided to go to Georgia Tech. And my decision was made after visiting all the colleges. I was an instant star at all of them. No one said anything negative. However, at Georgia Tech, while many were excited to see me, others could care less who I was. So, this place seemed more real... like I had a better chance of knowing where I really stood with people."

A cow slowly chews the cud as it lifts its head from the earth. Its ears flap every now and then to fan away the flies that are trying to make a meal of its head. The landscape is quiet, except for the mooing of the other cows in the green pasture. The cow cranes its head upward towards the deep blue sky, attracted by the sound of distant engines and the movement of a silver object reflecting the sun's rays. The cow tracks one object's movement across the sky—unsure of what it is—although it's seen these things before. But its interest wanes as it lowers its head back to the earth and grips more grass in its jaws.

30,000 feet in the air, the silver plane streaks through scattered clouds. Two and a half hours have passed as 256 passengers head to the same destination. Treyshawn still finds himself unable to peel his face from the window.

"Man," he says with a sense of awe, "big cities look like ant hills from up here. And the land looks flat with a bunch of squares on it." He peels his face from the window and glances at the guy next to him—a well-dressed white male, who returns his glance with a nervous smile.

Treyshawn thinks to himself, *Why is this guy so tense?* Treyshawn holds the guy's stare long enough for the silence to be broken.

"Ok, I've got to ask," the man says, "are you a rapper?"

"Are you serious?" Treyshawn responds incredulously. "You see a black guy wearing baggy clothes, fitted shirt and a ball cap and he's got to be a rapper?"

"I'm sorry," the man sputters while forcing a smile.

"Uh, huh," Treyshawn says. "Just because I don't dress in khakis and a dress shirt like you don't mean I'mma thug. That's what you really getting at, right? You afraid I'mma do something to you."

"No... No, I'm not."

"Man, quit lying," Treyshawn shoots back.

"Ok," the man concedes, "I was… a bit concerned." The man chuckles nervously as Treyshawn smiles and leans in his direction.

"A couple of years back," Treyshawn says, "you would have needed to be concerned. But not now." Treyshawn extends his hand. "My name's Treyshawn."

The man smiles as they both shake hands. "I'm Clarence."

"I'm on my way to Cali…" Treyshawn catches himself. "…*California* for college. I'm an artist."

"That's great!" Clarence says, "Congratulations. Your family must be proud."

"My mom is," Treyshawn says with pride, "I'm the first one to go to college."

"What about your dad?"

Treyshawn looks at him for a second. "You are one inquisitive white dude." They both laugh as all tensions melt away.

"I'm a lawyer. I get paid to be inquisitive."

"Uh, huh. Well, my dad's locked up. He doesn't even know where I'm going."

"Maybe you should tell him," Clarence says with a concerned look on his face.

"What is it with people telling me I should go see my father?" Treyshawn quips.

Clarence sits quietly for a moment. "I don't know you, but if different people have been telling you the same thing—without coming together and deciding to do so—then maybe that's a sign that you should go see him."

Treyshawn takes a deep breath and repeats his rehearsed lines like a broken record. "My dad wants nothing to do with me. Haven't seen him since I was a kid."

"People change."

"What kind of law you do?"

"Corporate. Making sure companies abide within the laws."

"And you probably help companies find ways around them laws too," Treyshawn interjects.

"If you're talking about loopholes," Clarence says, "there are legal ways to navigate some laws that work out for the best interest of the company."

"That's a very lawyer-like answer."

Clarence smiles a bit uneasily.

"What I was getting at is that you're a lawyer and you work with a lot of people—maybe even the same people over the years. Have *you* seen people change?"

Clarence sits quietly as he considers Treyshawn's question and contemplates his response. "People don't change unless there's a big enough reason for them to do so."

"By 'reason,'" Treyshawn asks, "you mean something happens that *forces* them to change what they do?"

"You know," Clarence says with a bit of surprise. "Your ability to read between the lines is impeccable."

"Thanks," Treyshawn smiles. "I'm from the 'hood. You gotta be able to do that."

"But back to your original point," Clarence continues, "maybe you're right and your father still doesn't want to see you. Maybe he hasn't changed. But maybe *you* changing will be a big enough reason for him to do the same."

Treyshawn sits back in his chair and thinks about Clarence's words. Clarence continues to stare at Treyshawn. "You know, the more I look at you, the more I think I've seen you before."

Treyshawn is happy to change the subject. "I've been on TV a few times."

"That's it!" Clarence exclaims. "I saw you on the news—on that segment about the teen who made the suit that enables him to run faster! Am I right?"

"Yep," Treyshawn says almost nonchalantly.

"What's his name?"

"Curtis Powers."

"Curtis Powers," he claps his hands together. "You are a part of his team!"

"No," Treyshawn interjects, "We're on the *same* team."

"Point taken," Clarence concedes. "So, how did you two meet?"

"You know," Treyshawn answers, "someone wrote a book about that. You should check it out."

"I'll do that!" Clarence smiles excitedly. "Wow. I'm sitting next to someone famous. I mean, in my line of work, I meet famous people all the time, but *this* is different."

"I'm not famous," Treyshawn says with a bit of introspection, "I'm just... lucky."

Just then, the flight attendant arrives with another round of complimentary beverages.

"I'll let you be," Clarence says. "Think I've talked your ear off already. And I'm sorry for the stereotyping."

"No problem," Treyshawn smiles. "I stereotyped you, too. You know, people may *look* different, but we all want the same things. Nice talking to you."

Clarence smiles and nods in agreement. Treyshawn turns back towards the window for a moment before becoming lost in his own thoughts. He sits back in his chair and begins to think back to how change happened in his own life. "Man, who would have thought..." he whispers to himself as his mind replays a series of memories in quick succession.

September. 2008.

"Check out this kid," Lil Treacherous says to Hakiim and the rest of their friends. "You see what he's wearin'? And look at his glasses..."

"Man, who you runnin' from? You're slower than my grandmother! And in case you wonderin', I'm one of the fastest cats in this school!

"Hey Smurtis! Been a few weeks. Where you been hiding?

"Did you...? Did you just do what I think you did?"

"Treyshawn, don't you ever hit Kelly again!"

Present day.

Treyshawn laughs to himself. "Who would have thought that bullying Curtis would change my whole life?

March. 2009.

3pm. The heavy steel doors opened as students exited the school building. Treyshawn stood in the parking lot as a crowd began to form around him.

"Talk to me," he said into his phone. "Where's this kid at?"

A reply came back from the speaker, "He's still in the physics lab."

"He can't hide in there forever. Don't lose him."

"You think he's gonna run?" the speaker squawked back.

"If he knows what's good for him," Treyshawn replied.

A few minutes later, Treyshawn's phone beeped. "He's on the move. Making his way to the main doors."

Treyshawn was actually surprised. "Huh, so he's really coming to face me?"

Several minutes later, the main doors, just off the side of the parking lot, burst open and Curtis leapt out!

"Finally! This dude's gonna catch it!" Treyshawn stood in momentary awe as Curtis leapt down an entire flight of stares and started running across the parking lot. *Did he just...?* Treyshawn ran to intercept—having no time to answer his own question—"How did he jump down the stairs like that?"

Curtis outmaneuvered Treyshawn by cutting between the parked cars. As he bolted across the school property, with his nemesis in hot pursuit, Treyshawn yelled to no one in particular, "Do I got rocks in my shoes?" He struggled to keep up with Curtis. "How is this kid faster than me now?" Treyshawn pushed his body to its limit, but Curtis stayed well out of reach! Treyshawn was so perplexed that he didn't even see the loose gravel spill that Curtis had just jumped over.

The next thing Treyshawn experienced was a sudden sense of weightlessness and the burning pain of asphalt scraping his face, arms, hands and back. The ground was unyielding to the impact of his legs and knees, as his body flipped, uncontrollably, several times before he came to a jarring halt. The world spun around him as he struggled to gain his bearings—unsure of where he was or what just happened. Pain sensors all over his body screamed at once — the internal sound being almost too much to bear. He struggled to get to his feet, unable to decipher the screams of other students and Curtis. The deep honk of a vehicle's horn didn't register with Treyshawn either, nor did his own name. As he looked up, all that met him were two white lights as a huge truck swiftly screeched towards him, in a cloud of rumbling smoke!

Treyshawn barely had time to yell, "No!" as something slammed into his side with enough force to push him out of the way of the hulking truck. Another impact racked his body with pain again. But, when his vision cleared, he saw Curtis on top of him.

"Treyshawn! Are you alright? Treyshawn! Can you hear me?"

This doesn't make sense, Treyshawn thought as he pushed Curtis off of him. His adrenalin spiked as he stood to his feet and looked around wildly at the scene, as the driver of the truck ran over in a panic.

"Are you two all right? I thought you were a goner! If it wasn't for that kid... Kid you're a hero!"

Treyshawn looked at Curtis in disbelief and thought to himself, *Did he just save me? Why would he do that?* He saw the crowd of students on the sidewalk. It angered him. He failed at his task—made a fool of himself in the process, and everybody saw it!

"Get your hands off of me!" he yelled at Curtis. "Don't think you're a hero. I didn't need saving."

Treyshawn stumbled away as quickly as he could in order to avoid the ambulance he heard in the distance. Hakiim and the rest of his friends caught up with him a couple of blocks away.

"Treyshawn! You alright?" they asked.

"Just leave me alone!" he barked as he walked away. Some time later, as he entered his house, his mother saw him from the living room. She quickly noticed his cuts, bruises and tattered clothing, but felt no sympathy.

"Treyshawn, you did somethin' stupid again, didn't you?"

Treyshawn didn't have strength to engage in their usual verbal fight. "Not now, Ma..."

"What you mean, 'not now'?" Shakira yelled back. "Doesn't matter. I don't want to hear it anyway! Since you up—go get me a soda!"

Treyshawn wanted to open the floodgates and tell his mother everything that had happened. But he knew it wouldn't do any good. So, he stuffed it all deep down inside and steeled himself. This was his lot in life: to suffer by himself. Nothing had changed—nor would it, ever. He needed a miracle... but there was nothing for him to believe in. He got his mother her soda: then, he went to his room and collapsed on his bed.

Present Day.

Treyshawn thinks about how his life had changed once he hit rock bottom. That was when he looked up and found Curtis standing there—willing to help. He smiles. Maybe Clarence was right. Maybe one person's change could be another person's miracle.

Chapter Five

Higher Education

THE SUV SLOWS TO A HALT outside the dormitories at Atlanta's Georgia Tech's campus. The area is busy as other students move in, with the help of their families and friends. Sitting next to a cart, in the midst of the activity, is a young man: Hispanic, slender-to-medium build, wearing a black 'Robotics will Rule the World' t-shirt, faded jeans, with holes in the knees, and sandals with no socks. His hair is a dusty brown, combed forward—partially covering his right eye—with a hint of styling gel to hold its inverted spiky appearance. He sits relatively motionless and relaxed until he sees his target. Like a bolt of lightning he makes his way through the crowd.

Curtis jumps out of the vehicle and proceeds to help Omar unload the boxes and bags from the trunk area. As he begins, he hears a voice boom from behind.

"You're Curtis Powers!"

"I am," Curtis says, as he turns towards the voice.

"I'm Gavin. Gavin Ortiz—from Chicago. You and I are roommates!"

"Really?" Curtis says, while shaking Gavin's hand. "So, you were just out here waiting for me?"

"I checked in this morning," Gavin smiles.

"Wait," Curtis interjects, "how did you know who I was?"

"Who hasn't seen a picture or video of the famous Curtis Powers? I can't say I'm your biggest fan, but I do know everything about you and your Speedsuit."

"That's amazing," Curtis jokes sarcastically, "Even *I* don't know *everything* about me!"

Gavin laughs. "You know what I mean. I've been following you since the world record. Your work is crazy! I've got some ideas for some robotic enhancements." Gavin invades Curtis' personal space like an overjoyed child. "Did you bring the Mach-1 with you? Is it in the truck?"

"No, it's not," Curtis laughs as he takes a step back. "But listen, you want to help us move my stuff inside? I'm sure we can talk tech later."

"Sure. No problem," Gavin says. "So, what should I call you? Curt? SP? Powers Man?"

"Let me think on that. But *Curtis* is fine for now." He throws his mother and brother a look. They do everything they can to keep from laughing. "Let me introduce you."

After they exchange pleasantries, the group begins to unpack the car. Ten minutes later, Omar loads the last box on the cart, as someone approaches them.

"You all must be the famous Powers Family!"

Curtis, Omar, Miranda and Gavin turn around and find an impeccably dressed black man standing in front of them. His smile displays warmth and his posture exudes confidence. They are all immediately taken aback—especially Miranda.

"Uh, yes," Miranda replies with a bit of hesitation. "That's us."

Gavin's expression is one of stunned awe while he fumbles out his words, "And I'm roommate... Curtis' Gavin—I mean—I'm Gavin, Curtis' roommate!" He leans over to Curtis and whispers while poking him in the side with his elbow, "Dude, do you know who this is?"

"No," Curtis whispers back. "Don't have a clue."

Before Gavin can respond, the distinguished gentleman speaks.

"Please allow me to introduce myself. My name is Chasm Montgomery: philanthropist, innovator, business mogul and alumni of this great institution." He extends his hand to Miranda. She smiles while returning the favor.

"It's a pleasure to meet you, Mr. Montgomery. I'm—"

"Miranda Powers," Chasm utters with a gleam in his eyes, before facing her sons and nodding in their direction. "And you are Omar, the strong, older brother to the famous Curtis Powers."

"Nice meeting you," Omar says, while he and Chasm exchange a sturdy handshake.

"Yes, nice to meet you," adds Curtis.

"The pleasure is mine," Chasm declares, with a slight bow of his head while turning from Curtis to address his mother. "I have been interested in Curtis ever since I first heard about him. The world record he set was marvelous. And his run in London was stunning. When I discovered he would be attending my alma mater, well, I knew you all needed a *proper* welcome."

"Thank you for your kind sentiments," Miranda replies—slightly blushing.

"Your welcome," Chasm smiles. "However, my remarks are more than just sentiments. With your permission, Ms. Powers, I would like to mentor your son as he seeks to navigate this next stage in life."

"I see you don't waste any time," Miranda chuckles.

"Time is precious," Chasm replies, "And I see no reason to not be upfront about my intentions. As someone who is very familiar with this institution, as well as private, public and government sectors of business, there is a lot I can offer Curtis. As you probably already know from the college application process, many people will try to capitalize on your son's intellect and ingenuity."

"Like *yourself*," Miranda states somewhat jokingly.

"Beautiful *and* quick-witted. I like that," Chasm says with a warm smile.

"Yeah, well as long as you look, but don't touch," Omar says, not-so-jokingly.

Miranda cuts her son a look. "Omar!"

Chasm reaches into his suit jacket pocket and pulls out his business card. "Any good son will make sure his mother is protected. That's what I do." He hands Miranda his card. "I would have drowned in college if not for my mentor. He helped make me the man I am today. I always like to pay that blessing forward to others I feel would best benefit from what I have to offer. Sure, there's money to be made; but not at the expense of a person's character. *That* is my agenda, Ms. Powers." Chasm reaches into a different pocket and pulls out another business card. "Do your due diligence and Google me if you'd like. You will see that I am, as they say, 'on the up and up.' May I give your son my card? I would like to take him to dinner once he's acclimated to his classes."

Miranda hesitates. "I suppose so."

"Ma," Curtis interjects, "People have been giving me their business cards since we set the world record."

"True," Miranda nods. "Mr. Montgomery. You may contact my son, but first give me your word that you will not try to sidetrack him from his studies."

"You have my word, Ms. Powers. All I want to do is make sure Curtis is in the best possible position for advancement during his college career and beyond. No strings attached."

Chasm hands Curtis his card. "This is to my personal line. Call when you are ready." He turns to everyone, "It has been a pleasure. Thank you for your time and enjoy your evening." As Chasm walks off, Curtis looks down at the card and then follows after Mr. Montgomery.

"Wait! There's no number," Curtis says confused. "Only your name and a red dot."

Chasm stops and faces him. "Take out your phone and place it next to the card."

Curtis does so and looks up in bewilderment at his new benefactor.

"Press your thumb on the dot in the bottom right hand corner."

As Curtis looks down and presses the dot, a portion of the business card flashes once as his cell phone automatically dials a restricted number. Chasm reaches into his jacket and pulls out his phone as it starts to ring. He turns the caller ID so Curtis can see his own name and number on the display.

"Whoa..." Curtis is almost speechless.

Chasm grins. "If you could see your face right now... This is new technology that I invented. Won't find it anywhere else."

"What about the card you gave my mom?"

"Standard business card I give to any interested party. But the card *you* hold I only give to people I have a vested interest in. Looking forward to being a help to you." Chasm walks off, leaving Curtis to his thoughts as he strolls back to his family and Gavin to continue the moving process.

"Dude," Gavin says. "I can't believe we just met Chasm Montgomery!"

"I *still* don't know who he is," Curtis chuckles.

"You may not, but I'm sure you know his work. The guy's got his hands in almost everything that's cool!"

Curtis looks down at the business card and mumbles, "You got that right."

As Curtis and Gavin make their way from the car to the dorm building, they are stopped by an upperclassman.

"Curtis Powers," The student says.

"Yeah."

"I'm Peter Broadman. Senior. Teacher's Assistant. I just wanted to introduce myself. You have classes with several professors that I work for. I wanted you to know that I'll be keeping my eye on you, so I hope you can keep up with the work load."

"I'll do my best." Curtis extends his hand. "Thanks for introducing yourself."

Peter looks at Curtis' hand and then back towards his face. "Don't expect everyone to fawn all over you because you're famous. Here... *every* student is smart, so you're nothing special."

"Man," Gavin says as Peter abruptly walks away, "it seems like that guy has it in for you—and it's not even the first day of class!"

"What gave it away?" Curtis jests. "Welcome to college."

Spelman College...

Kelly and her mother arrive at Spelman. It takes about an hour to move her belongings into the dorm room. As Stacy runs back to the car for a last check, Kelly surveys her room more closely. Her roommate, who is nowhere to be found, has taken all of the best spaces. Whoever this girl is, she sure has a full compliment: refrigerator, microwave, shoe racks, a vanity mirror and several closed chests filled with things unknown. Her thick, fluffy pillow adorns her fully made bed and she seems to have every cosmetic known and unknown to women.

Kelly opens the closet door—only a sliver of space remains for her clothes.

"I already don't like this girl," she says to herself.

Knock, knock, knock. Kelly opens the door to find her mother struggling with a handful of things. She walks in just in time for the objects to fall on the bed.

"That was close!" She looks around for a second, while catching her breath. "Alright, let's unpack!"

Kelly doesn't say anything as her mom begins to move around the room.

"Huh... Uh, huh..." Her mother turns in her direction. "Kelly, why does it seem like your roommate has sequestered more than her fair share of this room?"

"You just noticed that, huh?" Kelly answers sarcastically.

"Ah, college life," her mother responds while taking a deep breath. "An experiment in social consciousness. Your first day and I can already see we may have a conflict resolution situation on our hands."

"You think?" Kelly asks while crossing her arms.

"Don't worry baby. I'm sure this girl didn't fully realize what she was doing. Probably just caught up in the excitement of being on her own in a new environment."

Approaching laughter is heard from the hallway as a room key pierces the lock. The nob turns and the door opens, revealing three girls caught in a fever-pitch conversation drenched in southern drawl.

"Did you see the way he was lookin' at me?"

"An' he thought he was doing something—wearing a wife-beater over his scrawny chicken chest. That's supposed to be cute?"

They all laugh hysterically before seeing Kelly and her mother standing by the bathroom door. The three girls stop and stand quietly, looking Kelly up and down.

"You must be my new roommate," the middle girl declares with an ounce of disdain.

"Yeah. Hi. I'm Kelly." Kelly steps forward and reaches out to shake the girl's hand. The girl doesn't move.

"And I'm Kelly's mother—Mrs. Washington." Stacy's stern expression could move mountains.

The middle girl reaches out and shakes Kelly's hand. "I'm Clamille. These are my friends Shonda and Becka."

"Nice to meet you girls," Stacy interjects as they all shake Kelly's hand and then proceed to shake Stacy's hand as well. "It's nice to see that your parents have *taught* you the basic rules of socialization."

"Yes, Ma'am," the girls respond, while shooting cautious glances at each other.

"We came up together from Aiken, Georgia," Clamille adds. "Where are you from?"

"New York," Kelly replies. "The Bronx."

Kelly's mother can't help but notice Clamille seems to do *most* of the talking.

"We never met anyone from New York before—especially the Bronx."

"Well, I've never met anyone from Aiken, Georgia," Kelly replies.

"Is it as bad as everyone says?" Shonda asks.

"There are bad places everywhere," Kelly counters. "New York can be tough, but it's really not that different from any place else."

"You talk funny." Becka interjects.

"*I* talk funny?" Kelly looks dumbfounded. Her mother chuckles quietly as Kelly kicks back, "*You're* the ones with the accent!"

"What you mean me?" Clamille snaps. "Everybody from here talks like we do. You the one who don't belong here!"

"Now girls," Mrs. Washington interrupts. "Let's keep this conversation civil, alright?"

"Yes... Ma'am," the girls respond in unison.

"Now, I noticed that the majority of this room is filled with your things, Clamille."

"Yes, Ma'am."

"Somehow, you need to make room for my daughter's things. I'm sure the split in this room should be 50/50—not 80/20."

"Yes, Ma'am. I guess I got carried away trying to bring everything from home. It just helps me not to get homesick is all."

"Believe me, Clamille," Stacy smiles, "I understand the feeling, but I need you to work *with* my daughter—not against her. Now I have to get a few more things from the car. Shonda and Becka, would you mind coming to help me? This way Clamille and Kelly can get a moment to talk."

As soon as the door closes and Kelly and Clamille are alone, the conflict *really* begins.

"So, you had to get yo mamma to speak for you?" Clamille mocks. "You couldn't speak on your own?"

"What's your problem? We just met."

"But I know your type."

"How's that? You've *never* been to New York before."

"Don't have to," Clamille crosses her arms. "You think you better than me?"

"Oh, *now* you're talking crazy!" Kelly throws her hands up in frustration.

"Yeah, well let me tell you what's crazy," Clamille continues, "*you* thinking you're getting more space in here. My stuff isn't going anywhere."

Kelly leans back on the wall, crosses her arms and cracks a small smile. "You're good. You smile nice when it counts and then you act all *stank* behind people's backs."

"Who you calling stank?" Clamille yells.

"Better than some other words I could use. But let me tell you what's *really* crazy," Kelly pushes off the wall and walks right over to Clamille, "*you* thinking you can disrespect me. I like to be nice to people, but I don't let *anyone* walk over me. I *am* straight from the 'hood' and I'm not afraid of you! I'm not your enemy. But if you go down this road, you will wish you hadn't."

The door opens and Stacy walks in with several boxes that Shonda and Becka help carry. "So, how are you two doing? Are you getting to know each other?"

They both smile.

"Yes, Ma'am," Clamille says.

"We sure are," Kelly adds.

University of California, Berkeley

Blue sky and palm trees. Treyshawn has never seen anything like it, except on television.

"Man, this is gonna be nice," he says, smiling broadly as the taxicab approaches the school.

The taxicab lets Treyshawn, and his bags, off on the university's main street. Treyshawn steps onto the campus unsure of where he should go. He watches the flurry of activity that surrounds him as students and parents move about quickly. He attempts to stop several people to get directions.

"Excuse me…? Could you help…? I just need to know where…"

But no one stops as they all seem oblivious to him.

"Maybe I should have changed the way I dressed," Treyshawn says to himself.

Several white girls walk by and one of them looks at him with a smile. He looks back at her with a smile. "How you doin'?"

"Hey! Why you talking to my girl?" A voice booms just behind him.

Treyshawn turns around to find a tall, semi-muscular white guy approaching him. Before he can say anything, the guy is in his face, pointing his finger against Treyshawn's chest.

"You think you can just come here and take whatever you want?" The guy yells as the three girls look on quietly.

"Yo, you betta back up!" Treyshawn yells back.

"Or what?" The guy snarls.

"Or else I'll make you eat your finger." Treyshawn sneers.

Both boys stare each other down—neither one relenting.

"Johnny," the girl blurts out, "leave him alone."

"Yeah Johnny," Treyshawn adds, "leave me alone."

"You don't get to say my name!" Johnny pushes Treyshawn.

Treyshawn laughs to himself as he retains his composure. "I'mma let that one be free. And for the record, your girl looked at me first. So maybe you need to talk to *her* about your relationship! But touch me again... and you'll wish you hadn't."

"You think you scare me? Huh?" Johnny scoffs. "Where I'm from, we eat people like you for breakfast!"

"So, you're a cannibal?" Treyshawn responds. "Where I'm from folks like you are too afraid to come into my neighborhood."

"So, you're a thug-wannabe?" Johnny quips.

Treyshawn takes a deep breath and thinks to himself, *This is getting nowhere. I gotta think like Curtis.* He tries to relax.

"Look. Hold up." He raises his hands. "I didn't come *all the way* to California to get in fights. I could do *that* back home. I'm here for *school.* Let's try this again." Treyshawn extends his hand to Johnny. "I'm sorry for lookin' at *and* talkin' to your girl. My name's Treyshawn. Truce?"

Johnny looks at Treyshawn incredulously. Then he looks down at his extended hand and smacks it out of his way. "I don't care *who* you are. I don't care *where* you're from. And I *don't* like you. Every day I see you— you're gonna pay. So, you better stay outta my way!"

"What did I *ever* do to you?" Treyshawn asks.

Johnny and the girls walk away without a reply.

Treyshawn stands motionless as the group leaves. He slowly picks up his bags, looks around at the people and yells, "All these people around here and nobody stops to help a brother out!"

An hour later...

Treyshawn finally makes it to his dorm room and collapses on his new bed, in a vacant room. His roommate hasn't arrived yet. He tries to relax, but keeps replaying the altercation over and over in his mind.

"Man. New school. New kid. New drama. I will *definitely* have to avoid that guy. Good thing the school is a big place."

He takes a few relaxing breaths and thinks about this new situation. "I can't let one bad experience mess this up. My time here will be great. I've come too far from where I started."

As he thinks about his life, his mind drifts back to when he saw his father last—a few days ago. "Wish I didn't have to lie to Clarence on the plane, but I just couldn't deal with it."

Every piece of furniture was cold and uninviting. It wasn't designed to make a person want to stay long. Others talked in hushed tones while Treyshawn felt a growing lump rise in his throat.

"Maybe I should bounce," he mumbles to himself. "Don't know how I let them talk me into this anyway."

Before he could stand up, a loud buzzing drone was heard, as iron bars began to move. A moment later, a large man in chains and an orange jumpsuit was escorted into the room by two guards. He stood there, looking at Treyshawn. He didn't say a word. Treyshawn swallowed hard—forcing the lump to move from his neck to the pit of his stomach.

"You don't recognize me, do you?" Treyshawn asks.

The man stands silent, before speaking. "Should I?"

Treyshawn winces at the stinging words before replying. "The last time you saw me, I was four years old."

The man examined Treyshawn and when their eyes connected, a look of recognition faintly filled his face as he remembered the day he fought so hard to forget.

"I didn't want to see you then and I don't want to see you now." He turns to walk to the gate as Treyshawn's voice explodes.

"I didn't come here for *you!*" Everyone in the visitors center turns in his direction.

Treyshawn's father stops, but doesn't turn around.

"I came here for *me!*" Treyshawn yells. "Because my friends said I had to let my anger go!"

"Congratulations," his father bellows still with his back to his son. "Are you happy now?"

Treyshawn shakes his head in disbelief as he calms down. "Dad."

Treyshawn's father grimaces slightly, as if the title given to him by his son was a brick to the side of his head.

"You may not have changed… but I have."

Treyshawn's father says nothing.

"I graduated from high school. I'm leaving for college next week."

Treyshawn's frustration increases as his father remains silent. "You not wanting to be in my life almost destroyed me and mom. But you don't get to control us by your absence any more! If you don't want to change, then that's on you… But mom and me… We are free."

Treyshawn turns and walks to the exit. His father stands motionless in the visitor area.

"Get me outta here."

The two guards look at him, but say nothing as they escort Treyshawn, Sr.—stone face and all—back to his cell.

Present Day. Treyshawn's dorm room.

Treyshawn opens his eyes and gazes at the ceiling before looking around the entire room. It's so clean and quiet. He inhales deeply and thinks to himself; *well at least I am free.*

A key is heard turning the lock as the door opens and an Asian family happily enters the room. The parents' smiles quickly diminish as they see

Treyshawn.

"Hi," Treyshawn says as he rises from his bed. "You must be my roommate."

The young man shakes Treyshawn's hand. "I'm Hu."

His father frowns as he looks at a piece of paper and then steps outside to look at the number on the door. He speaks in his native language and Hu and his mother start picking up their things.

"What happened?" Treyshawn asks.

Hu forces a nervous smile. "My father says we have the wrong room."

A moment later, they are gone—leaving Treyshawn standing all by himself.

"More room for me," he says to himself, while trying to hide the sting of rejection.

He sits back on his bed for a moment before opening one of his bags. He pulls out a notebook—the very one he first used when he met Mrs. Fuller in her office. He chuckles as he opens the cover and sees the first two words: 'Sagacious' and 'Prolific.'

"Who would have thought," he says while sitting on his bed, "that admitting my ignorance would have been the key to me getting the help I needed." Treyshawn stands up and puts the notebook down, while pulling a picture frame from his bag. He also pulls out a small box of pushpins and proceeds to hang the picture frame on the wall. On the crinkled sheet of paper, inside the picture frame, is the poem that Mrs. Fuller first introduced him to: **What About Your Dreams?**

What about your dreams?
Don't you ever think about the future that's filled with possibilities?
Have you ever pictured in your mind, the coming day's light?
The day's light shines on your dreams:
The light of recognition –the light of realization
What about your dreams?
Do you choose not to dream to avoid the off-chance that it might
Not come true?
Are you afraid of broken promises? Is this what you do?

What about your dreams?
Is it stupid to dream of a future when you're trying to make it
Through today?
When you're just trying to overcome the struggles you must face?

With no dream for tomorrow can you really survive?
Something within you slowly dies…
With no joy in the morning will tonight draw you away?
What about your dreams?

Chapter Six

Stomp the Yard

CURTIS QUIETLY LIES ON HIS BED. He refused Gavin's invitation for dinner. Now he holds his father's journal in his hands. He opens up to the first entry.

To my magnificent boys... Omar and Curtis.

I thought long and hard about what my first entry should be to you. By the time you read this, I will have been dead for at least five years. I can't imagine how hard it's been for you to have to take this journey with your mother alone. I truly wish the circumstances were different—that I could have been alive to not only watch you grow and mature, but also help you develop into the strong young men I know you to be.

So let me start by saying, 'I love you!' I love you more than every sunrise and sunset, more than every scenic view, and ocean depth. I love you more than every building I've ever designed, more than the best restaurants I've ever dined in. I love you more than life itself... and I realized all of this when I began to write this journal. With only a couple of months left to live, you two were always on my mind. You were always in my thoughts. Curtis and Omar... you both were always in my midnight conversations with God and always in my midday conversations with your mother.

I hope you can remember what my voice sounded like, because the world will be a tough place and you will need to know - in the cold darkness of opposition - that you had a father who loved you and did the best he could to provide for you.

As much as destiny is something that you are waiting for, know that destiny is also waiting on you. As much as there are moments when opportunities beyond your imagination are presented to you, know even more so that those moments can only be fully taken advantage of when you do your best. If I've learned anything from life, from this cancer, from God, it's that - everything won't be handed to you, but you must make the most of everything that's in your possession. Only then, when you do your best, can the miraculous happen! And in your weakest moment, when you can't take another step, and the best you can do is barely cry out to God—then take heart and be encouraged. Because you are at your strongest when you are at your weakest. God's power is made perfect in our weakness.

Take care of your mother. Take care of each other. Enjoy the journey of life you are on. I hope that the words I share in this journal will move you towards greatness—in every sense of the word.

I love you. But God loves you more. I long for that future when we will all see each other again.

Your Father,
Malcolm Powers

Tears fall to the page as Curtis scrambles for some tissue from the bathroom. The ink blurs slightly as he dries the spots. He collapses onto his bed, clutches the journal, curls into a fetal position and cries uncontrollably. Old emotional scars tear open anew. And, amid a heaving chest and hyperventilating lungs, Curtis reluctantly admits to himself that the control he thought he had, was a myth. Reading his father's words has unleashed an emotional torrent! And even with all of his father's encouragement, he was barely holding things together.

A moment later... his cell phone rings. He lies motionless, determined not to answer it; but on the fifth ring, he swings his body around to look at the caller ID. He picks it up and swipes the green button on the screen, while taking a second to wipe the tears from his eyes and the snot from his nose, and to catch his breath.

"You Ok Curtis? Treyshawn asks concerned. "You don't sound too good."

"Hey," Curtis barely whispers. "Give me a second."

Treyshawn rises from his bed and listens intently through the phone as his friend takes several deep breaths and clears his throat.

"Ok," a slightly stronger voice responds, "I'm back."

"Bro, what happened?"

"Before we all left yesterday… my mom gave me and Omar journals that our dad had written for us before he died. I was just reading mine."

"You ain't gotta say no more," Treyshawn assures. "I get it."

They both sit on their beds in silence—holding the phones to their ears.

"I thought I had this under control," Curtis laments, "and then his words bring all my emotions back, like it was the day he died."

They sit in silence for another minute.

"I know you and your dad don't get along," Curtis adds.

Treyshawn laughs, "That's an understatement!"

The mood lightens for just a moment.

"I know," Curtis responds, "but at least your dad's still alive. There's still a chance you both might work things out."

"I won't hold my breath. But, about that," he says hesitantly, "I… lied to you guys."

"About what?" Curtis sits up on his bed.

"About my dad," Treyshawn continues. "I… went to see him last week."

"What happened?"

"Nothing's changed."

"I'm sorry."

"It's not your fault," Treyshawn sighs as he lies down on his bed. "Your dad may not be alive, but at least you got his journal. That's awesome."

"Yeah," Curtis says with a smile, as he looks at the journal cover. "It is."

"Listen, I know it's late there—me being three hours behind and all. I just wanted to check and see if you're good."

"Thanks," Curtis replies, "Things are good here. Been an amazing day already. Tell you about it later."

"Cool. Things are good here, but it's gonna take some gettin' used to."

"Well, if anyone can do this, it's you bro," Curtis says enthusiastically.

"Thanks," Treyshawn laughs and ends the call.

A Few Weeks Later...

Kelly walks across the quad on her way to her evening class: Introduction to English. Out of the corner of her eye she sees her roommate, Clamille, with her boyfriend standing next to a building stairwell. She tries to ignore her—since they still don't get along—but what she sees next draws her attention. She can't hear what's being said, but their body language speaks volumes!

Tyreese jerks Clamille's arm back with such force that she stumbles and almost falls to the ground. Her face contorts in pain as he grabs her cheeks with a vice-like grip. He points his finger in her face and barks at her, before seeing Kelly. Kelly recognizes the fear in Clamille's eyes, as Tyreese freezes and then yanks her around the corner. Kelly stands frozen in the moment— terrified by what she has just witnessed.

Later that night.

The door opens as sunglasses-wearing-Clamille tiptoes into the dark room. The light from the hallway illuminates the room enough for Clamille to see Kelly lying in her bed, presumably asleep under the covers. The door closes as Clamille quietly turns on her desk lamp, after repositioning it to shine in her direction. Kelly's voice speaks from the darkness.

"It's after midnight. Where were you?"

Clamille is startled before responding, "You're *not* my mother."

Kelly sits up in her bed and turns on the room light. Clamille turns away to hide her face.

"I'm serious, Clamille! Where have you been?"

"You think you saw something bad and now you want to act like you care?"

"You make it hard to care... but I do. Why don't you tell me what I saw."

"Nothing," Clamille says nonchalantly. "Tyreese gets physical sometimes. No biggie. He likes his women to be tough."

"He's not making you stronger, Clamille." Kelly walks over to see her face up close. They struggle as Kelly tries to remove the sunglasses from Clamille's face.

"Get off me!" Clamille yells as Kelly overpowers her.

Kelly gasps at the sight of Clamille's puffy, black eye. "He's abusing you!"

"What do you know?" Clamille pushes Kelly away from her and drops on her bed.

Kelly watches as her roommate begins to weep. "Clamille..." she utters calmly, "your man should *never* put his hand on you unless it's to help you up. Your man should be loving and kind and sweet. He should see the best in you and help you bring that out to the world. He should be your friend. And a real friend won't tear you down. That's the reason we call them *boy-friends*."

"What do you know?" Clamille yells! "Are you done with your lecture?"

"You're the one with the black eye!" Kelly huffs.

Clamille sits quietly for a moment. "You got all this wisdom... you got a man back home?"

"I have a boyfriend, but he's not back home. He attends Georgia Tech."

Clamille looks up at her roommate. "Does he put his hands on you?"

"If you mean, does he abuse me," Kelly responds, "no. Besides, if he ever tried, I'd kick his behind. Then my two older brothers would come and beat him to a pulp!"

"Two older brothers, huh?"

"Yep! And both are more than able to handle *any* issue."

Clamille looks out the window while thinking. "So, you and your boyfriend came from New York together?"

"Yeah."

"What's his name?"

"Curtis."

Clamille's eyes open wide as she stands up. "You're not talking about Curtis Powers," she says in a hush. "You *are* talking about him," she squawks excitedly. "I *thought* you looked familiar. I've seen you with him on TV! Girl, he is fine! *That's* your boyfriend?"

"Yeah," Kelly laughs. "How do you know about him?"

"I run Track," Clamille confides. "Saw his world record video like a hundred times! And I was glued to the television during the Olympics. Our coach was talking about trying to bring him to our high school, but we couldn't afford it. Could you introduce me?"

"I don't know," Kelly feigns hesitance, "are we cool now?"

Clamille looks Kelly up and down before responding with a smile. "I think we can be cool."

Kelly smiles back. "I'll introduce you if you seriously consider what I said about you and Tyreese."

Clamille's smile disappears. "I don't know," she says—flopping down on her bed. "I'll think about it."

Several Days Later...

Tyreese approaches Kelly as she walks across campus. He waves and flashes a big smile.

"Hey! It's Kelly, right?"

"Yeah," she hesitates, drawing her bag close to her.

Tyreese puts his arm around her. "How you doin?"

"What do you want?" Kelly asks defiantly, while pushing his arm off her shoulder.

"I was lookin' for Clamille. She hasn't been returnin' my calls."

"Haven't seen her since this morning," Kelly smirks.

"You wouldn't know *why* she's not returnin' my calls, would you?"

"Maybe she's busy with her classwork or something. I'm not a mind reader."

Tyreese laughs. "Mind reader... you funny girl. Tell me. What am I thinking right now?"

"I told you I'm not a mind reader!" Kelly tries to walk off.

Tyreese blocks her escape. "Yeah. You did say that. Make sure you remember you ain't a mind reader, cause some people's minds are full of a whole bunch of craziness."

Kelly looks Tyreese in his eyes. "Are you threatening me?"

"Naw girl," Tyreese grins from ear to ear. "I'm just sayin', you never know what a crazy person might do. Wouldn't want a cute girl like you gettin' caught up in the middle of something that ain't her business. Just tryin' to look out for you, is all."

"Uh, huh," Kelly responds while backing away. "Well, I can look out for myself."

"Hope so," Tyreese quips. "Tell Clamille to call me."

Tyreese walks away nonchalantly. Kelly keeps her eyes glued on him as she feels her knees starting to shake. She thinks to herself: *Dealing with Treyshawn and the other guys from my neighborhood was one thing—I grew up with them. But Tyreese... I don't know him at all. If he could hurt Clamille like that, then he's capable of anything!*

Bronx, New York

The house phone rings several times. Shakira runs from the kitchen to the living room and picks it up.

"Hello?"

"Ma?"

"Treyshawn!" she exclaims, "My baby finally called! So, Mr. College Man, how was your first few weeks?"

"It's alright..." Treyshawn paces around his room.

"Alright?" She responds surprised. "You fly all the way to the West Coast when you could've gone to school right here in New York and it's just... alright?"

"I know Ma... Maybe I should've just stayed home."

Shakira sits down on the couch. "No, baby. You needed a change of environment... a reset. You said you wanted to prove you could do this. Now really, how are things?"

"I'm seriously like the only guy from the 'hood out here," Treyshawn exclaims. "And all the other students are way ahead of me in class."

"Hey," Shakira interjects, "you are Treyshawn Jinkins—*my son*. And you don't give up."

"I'm not sayin' I'mma quit, Ma. I'm just sayin' things are hard. I have to take some remedial classes for things I should have known already."

"Baby, lots of students have to do that sometimes. But don't forget what you've done so far—what you've overcome. You found out about your learning disability. You got help and training. You turned your grades around and you graduated! So, you keep on doin' you and press forward, Ok? That's what I'm doin' too—pressing forward—one day at a time."

"Thanks, Ma," Treyshawn smiles. "Thanks for believin' in me."

"You believed in me, remember?"

"So, what's goin' on with you?" he asks while sitting down at his desk.

"Workin'. Job market's tough—especially with no resume!" Shakira laughs. "Right now the waitress position is all I got. And I wouldn't have that if Curtis' mom hadn't talked to her manager. I'm also tryin' to get my voice back together. And still tryin' to get off welfare. You know," Shakira huffs, "there's more paperwork to get *off* the system than to get on it!"

"But you're doin' it, Ma." Treyshawn looks at a recent picture of them both.

"Yeah, I'm doin' it. Me and Jesus! I ain't never prayed so hard in my life!"

"You goin' to church now?" Treyshawn asks curiously.

"Been there a couple of times with Miranda," Shakira leans back on the couch. "It's kinda nice. But, way different from when I was a kid."

"You used to go to church?" Treyshawn exclaims.

Shakira laughs. "Learn somethin' new every day, huh?"

"You never really told me about your life..." Treyshawn's voice trails off.

"Trey... I know I messed up a lot, but I'm gonna make it up to you. I promise."

"...I know, Ma."

"I never really talked about church *or* my life," Shakira pauses, "...I was ashamed of what I'd become. My mom warned me... but I didn't listen."

Treyshawn stands up. "You've never talked about grandma before."

"I know," Shakira whispers.

"Other kids would talk about *their* grandparents," Treyshawn continues, "but I thought I didn't have any. Never seen pictures. Never spoke to them on the phone. Don't even know where they live," Treyshawn pauses. "I... don't even know *where* you're from."

"South Carolina," Shakira replies softly. "I'm from South Carolina."

Treyshawn sits back down. "And that's where your parents live?"

"My dad died when I was three. I don't really remember him." Shakira pulls a dusty box out from under the couch and opens it. She holds a picture in her hands. "But my mother would show me photographs of him holding me—both of us smiling from ear to ear." She smiles as she rubs her fingers over the discolored photograph. "My mom said I was the apple of his eye."

Treyshawn asks hesitantly, "Is grandma still alive?"

"Yeah. She still lives in that old house where I grew up."

Treyshawn's frustration begins to rise. "All this time and you never once mentioned her!"

"I know," Shakira yells back before calming herself. "I told you... I was ashamed. She warned me... and she was right. She told me if I left with your father then nothing good would come to me."

"So, that includes me," Treyshawn says flatly.

"No," his mother reassures, "It doesn't include you.

They both sit quietly for a moment.

"What happened between you two?" Treyshawn asks.

"That's a conversation... for another time."

"When's the last time you spoke to grandma?"

"A few days before I gave birth to you."

"Are you kidding?" Treyshawn yells. "Do you know how long ago that was?"

"I know Trey... But she didn't want to be with me for your birth."

"What? How come?"

"I don't want to have this conversation yet." Shakira breathes heavily as she stands up and begins pacing. "Can we talk about this later?"

"It *is* later, Ma!" Treyshawn yells as he paces the floor of his dorm room.

"Trey," Shakira counters. "You didn't know for 19 years. What's another couple of months?"

"I can't believe you just said that, Ma! We talk about this now! I have a right to know!"

Shakira bites her lip. "I'm not sayin' you don't—"

"Now, Ma!" Treyshawn barely maintains his composure.

"Why is this so important to you?"

"Are you serious, Ma? I've spent my whole life not being wanted by you and my father. I spent my whole life thinking I was alone—that I had no family! And now you act like I'm crazy for wanting to know about my grandmother?"

"Trey," Shakira tries to hold back her tears. "Calm down, baby. I *will* tell you. I promise. Just... just give me a couple of days. This whole thing was... unexpected."

"Fine, Ma." Treyshawn wipes away tears from his eyes.

"Thank you, baby."

"Whatever. I gotta go."

"Trey. Wait!"

"What Ma? I got work to do."

"You didn't spend your *whole* life not being wanted." Shakira goes back to the box and pulls out a picture of Treyshawn as a baby. "There was a time—when you were small—when I *did* want you."

"You just did that to try and keep dad around."

"No!" Shakira counters. "I *kept* you because I wanted you. I just figured your dad would want you too."

"I gotta go."

"Ok. We'll talk soon. Ok?"

"Bye, Ma."

"I love you. Take care of yourself."

And with a click, Treyshawn is gone. Shakira holds the receiver to her ear for a few moments longer before hanging up. Her tears flow freely now as she bangs her hand on the sofa cushion.

The next day...

Treyshawn quickly enters the classroom.

"Nice of you to join us, Mr. Jinkins."

"Sorry Professor Slateman. I overslept. Won't happen again."

"I should hope not. It may be fashionable to be late in the inner city, but you need to be on time in *this* part of the world—especially for *my* class."

"Yes Sir," Treyshawn takes his seat towards the back of the class.

"And did you *complete* last night's homework assignment?" The professor asks with a knowing smile. "Since you're the *last* one here today, you can be the *first* to present."

Treyshawn exhales wildly while trying to keep his composure. "I didn't get a chance to complete it. I had a family emergency last night. Can we talk after class?"

"Why wait, Mr. Jinkins?" The professor arrogantly stands tall and crosses his arms. "You can talk to me now."

"In f-front… of… e-everybody?" Treyshawn stammers.

"You arrived *late* to my class in front of everybody."

"You know what?" Treyshawn says. "I worked really hard to get to this school."

"And why we let you into this school," the professor interjects, "is still a mystery to me."

The classroom full of students lets out a collective, "Oooohhhh."

Treyshawn gets out of his chair and walks right up to the professor. The professor backs up a few steps while trying to nervously maintain an air of superiority. The rest of the class also grows tense, unsure of what will happen next.

"You don't know me to be coming outta your mouth like that." Treyshawn's breathing is heavy.

"So, now what?" Professor Slateman says, with a shiver in his voice. "Are you going to assault me? Are you going to show us all how things are handled in the street?"

"Why you ridin' me like this?" Treyshawn closes the gap between him and his professor. "Why you disrespectin' me in front of the whole class?"

"This is Psychology 101, Mr. Jinkins. You show up to my class late and your assignment isn't done." Professor Slateman holds his ground while pressing his finger against Treyshawn's chest. "I want to see what-makes-you-tick."

One of the students in the front of the class laughs as he sits on the edge of his seat. He says to the students next to him, "Man I wish I had some popcorn for this." The other students laugh nervously as they look on.

"I *had* a rough night!" Treyshawn says, while slapping his professor's hand away.

"Take a number, Mr. Jinkins!" The professor yells. "We *all* have rough nights! But that does not excuse you from your responsibilities. And for the record, I am *'riding'* you just like I would any other student of mine who came to class both late *and* unprepared."

"That's bull!" Treyshawn counters. "You're doing this because you're the white privileged professor and I'm the black inner city student!"

"You're playing the race card," the professor smirks while shaking his head. "How typical. While race may play a factor in many areas of life, it does *not* play a factor here in my classroom."

"Yeah right!" Treyshawn yells. "You judged me the first day of class."

"Young man," Professor Slateman says sternly, "I judged *everyone* the first day of class. That's what a good professor does! I watched every student as they walked in. I studied them: how they dressed, how they walked, how they sat. Did they slouch or sit upright? Do students look me in the eyes? Do they take notes? Do they smile? Body language speaks louder than words. And these are just a *few* of the criteria I use during the first few minutes of class.

"*You* came in on the first day of class with your baggy jeans hanging half way down your butt. And your ball cap was turned sideways. *You* slumped into your seat towards the back of the class and kept your head down—only making eye contact with me occasionally. That tells me you don't want to be here. So please... use the door if you like."

Professor Slateman turns from Treyshawn and addresses the entire class. "*Any* student who doesn't want to be here is free to leave!"

Treyshawn begins to slowly back away towards his desk. He grabs his books and his bag and walks to the door. After opening it, he turns and faces the professor. "So, you think you got me figured out?"

"It appears that I do," Professor Slateman says flatly.

Treyshawn stands quietly for a moment before closing the door. He walks to the front of the class and looks at the student who wished he had popcorn. "You. Get outta my seat."

The student looks around at the others and then at the professor—who says nothing in his defense. He then grabs his books and heads to an empty seat a few rows back. Treyshawn sits down, takes out his notebook and pen and stares directly into his professor's eyes.

Professor Slateman cracks a slight smile and walks to his lectern. "Class. While we often make snap judgments daily based on exterior criteria—and our judgments may frequently be valid—your classmate here has just taught you a valuable lesson that lies at the core of Psychology. What matters even more than the validity of externally based judgments is the internal thought processes and the motivations for why we do what we do. And the content of our character is revealed as we respond to external as well as internal opposition. In essence—as the saying goes... you can't *always* judge a book by its cover."

The class collectively chuckles.

"If you are going to judge a book—and you should be taking notes when I talk—then you must read it! Engage with it. Then you can come to an *informed* conclusion. Sometimes the cover is agreeable and ostentatious, however, there is no substance to the story. Other times the exterior can look completely unassuming—uneventful even—but within its pages lies the stories of legends! In the end, perhaps our purpose is to discover a way to make the outside cover of the book equal to the quality of the story that's being told...

"Thank you, Mr. Jinkins, for this most wonderful lesson. One, I imagine, no student in this class will *ever* forget." Professor Slateman smiles. "Now, about your assignment... what's a syllabus but a plan that could be subject to change? I choose to make a change and give you all one more day to complete the five page paper. I'm sure Mr. Jinkins isn't the *only* one who would like more time."

The class lets out another collective laugh.

"The day after tomorrow, you will hand your papers in to me," Professor Slateman continues. "Those who don't have it will get a rather large zero for the assignment. Those of you who do hand it in will get whatever grade the quality of your work allows. You have been warned. Have a nice day."

Students look at each other—unsure if the class is truly over with forty minutes to spare. The professor motions with his hands towards the door and confirms their thoughts, "Yes, I am being very generous today."

The students begin to quickly pack up and leave in the midst of tremendous chatter. As they exit, the professor calls Treyshawn. "Mr. Jinkins. May I have a word with you?"

Treyshawn approaches the professors desk. The professor shifts his glasses onto his head and stands up. "First, let me say thank you for *not* hitting me." The professor wipes beads of sweat from his face with his handkerchief.

Treyshawn looks at him confused. "So, this was all a test?"

"Mmm..." the professor muses, "somewhat. I like to do unexpected things from time to time. It helps keep the class lively. Actually, it became a test for *both* of us. I wasn't quite sure how things would end up. But when you walked to the door and then took your seat, you confirmed what I had suspected from the first day you entered my classroom."

"What's that?"

"There's more to you than meets the eye. Although unsure of yourself—you are trying to find your way and make your mark. As a side note, it also helped that I had already reviewed your file from high school and saw how you had made a rather rapid turnaround in your grades. *And* your college essay was quite moving—well written and well executed. However, your appearance didn't match my preconceived notion about how you would look. So, naturally, I was intrigued to know more about you. This is why I've been—as you said—'riding' you for the past few weeks."

Treyshawn looks at his professor with a blank stare, before responding. "You know you're crazy, right?"

The professor gives a hearty belly laugh! "And you are straight forward, Mr. Jinkins! I like that!" He extends his hand, which Treyshawn slowly meets with his own.

"You can call me Treyshawn."

Professor Slateman looks amused. "I can call you anything I like Mr. Jinkins. However, I'd rather call my students by their last name. Helps them think more professionally. But thank you for the invitation. You showed us today that you can lead *and* follow. *That* ability will take you far. College is usually tough for freshmen—no matter where they're from. Just focus on developing your strengths and finding others to help you fill the gaps left by your weaknesses, and you will become increasingly successful and significant! Have a good day Mr. Jinkins and good luck on your paper. I look forward to reading it."

The Mirage Diner

"Listen Shakira," the scheduling manager says, while looking down at his clipboard, "I understand what you're saying."

"Do you?"

"Yes, I do."

"I need more money, Mr. Howard. I can work more shifts."

"With the economy the way it is, *everyone* here is looking for more shifts."

"You know I'm a hard worker," Shakira counters. "And the customers—"

"And the customers *really* like you. Yes, I know." Mr. Howard takes a deep breath. "I'll see what I can do."

"Thank you." Shakira walks off to begin her shift, muttering, "Easier to make more money on welfare..." But then she catches herself. "No. I gotta stop thinking that way. Something's gotta change. And it starts with me." Shakira approaches one of her tables.

"Welcome to the Mirage Diner. What can I get for you today?"

The two elderly patrons look up from beneath their rather large hats. "Hey Shakira! How are you today?"

Shakira breaks into a wide grin. "Well, if it's not my favorite couple! Didn't recognize you with your new hats and sunglasses."

"Yes, well it's warm and sunny outside," the gentleman says, "and you know us old folks have to be mindful of the sun."

Shakira's phone vibrates in her pocket.

"I'm sorry, that's my phone."

"Well, take a look at it then," the elderly woman says with a smile. "It could be important."

Shakira pulls her phone out of her pocket and looks at it. "It's my son."

"The new college freshman?" the elderly man says. "Answer it!"

"I'll be right back," Shakira says as she smiles and walks off.

"We'll be right here!" the elderly woman says.

Shakira walks to a quiet spot while answering her phone. "Hello?"

"Ma!" Treyshawn yells.

"Baby, what's the matter?" Shakira yells back. "Are you Ok?"

"Everything's good, Ma!" Treyshawn says excitedly as he walks across campus. "I just had this *awesome* experience in psychology class!"

"That's great baby!" Shakira smiles. "Listen. I'm at work..."

"Nah, that's no problem, Ma!" Treyshawn says excitedly. "We can talk later."

"Baby... thanks for calling me. You sound like you're on cloud nine. Wish I could be there, too."

"You can Ma," Treyshawn says confidently. "We're in this together, right?"

Shakira smiles. "That's right baby. We're in this together."

"And Ma, whenever you're ready to talk about grandma, you just let me know. No, pressure."

Shakira's eyes swell with tears. "Ok, baby. Thank you."

"Love you, Ma."

"I love you too, baby."

Treyshawn ends the call and continues marching across campus, as if he's the king of the world. A new flame has been lit within him.

Shakira leans against the wall while holding her phone tightly in her hands. She raises it to her forehead and squeezes her eyes shut as she smiles. She puts her phone in her pocket, wipes her moist eyes with her skirt, takes a deep breath and makes her way back to her customers. Her customers and coworkers notice her renewed vigor as she moves with greater enthusiasm and determination. When her favorite elderly couple prepares to exit, they leave something for her.

"You are the best waitress we've had in a very long time," the elderly woman says.

"We know that you're trying to make a change in your life," the husband adds, "as well as make a difference in your son's life."

"So please accept our gift." The wife grabs Shakira's hands and discretely transfers a wad of bills into her grasp. "Don't make a big commotion when you see the tip." The wife releases her hands, making sure Shakira's hands remain closed. She and her husband get up from the table, and then head for the front door.

As they are about to go out the exit, they turn back and wave. "We'll see you soon!"

Shakira waves and then looks down at her hand. She slowly opens it and finds twenty one hundred dollar bills, neatly folded. She gasps and looks up just in time to catch a glimpse of the elderly couple walking outside the diner and then disappear out of her sight.

Several days later...

Curtis' face is glued to the 49th floor window of The Commerce Club. On this beautiful sunny day, he can see Atlanta's downtown and suburban landscape for miles.

He and Chasm Montgomery have finally been able to schedule their first mentoring lunch. Classical music plays softly in the room. Interacting sounds of silverware, china and light conversation pepper the symphony. A rich tapestry of aromas fill the air—each complimenting the other. Chasm's platter sits empty, with only a citrus residue of his Alaskan salmon and stir-fried vegetables visible. Curtis' platter of Shrimp Parmesan is two-thirds finished.

"Thanks again for lunch, Mr. Montgomery. I can't believe you ordered food that wasn't even on the menu!"

"Curtis, you have thanked me several times already," he laughs. "And please, call me Chasm. In reference to the menu," he smiles slightly, "I've learned you can get almost anything, if you know how to ask."

"I'll have to remember that. You know, your business card is amazing!"

"You like it?" Chasm crosses his legs and sits back in his chair.

"Like it!" Curtis exclaims. "That's an understatement! I looked at it with a microscope in the science lab and I couldn't even tell how it works!"

"That was the objective: to miniaturize several technologies down to the Nano-scale."

"Wow. So, if I lost the card—"

"*Don't* lose that card," Chasm counters with a sly smile.

"I won't. But if I did or if someone else tried to use it?"

"It uses biometric haptic technology," Chasm responds rather nonchalantly. "Once the card is activated on its first use, it will only work for *that* user until it is reset. And it is traceable, so it can *never* be lost once it's activated."

"Wow! How did you even think to come up with something like that?"

Chasm smiles slightly. "What you give your time and focus to is what you will ultimately come to understand. This is what most people don't realize. They go through their lives jumping from one thing to another—ready to give up as soon as things get difficult." Chasm leans in slightly. "But the adventure is *in* the difficulty. It is the fruit of a challenge that has been met which yields the greatest results. Start with the end result—in this case creating a business card unlike any other. Define the parameters and then reverse engineer the solution."

"You make it sound so easy," Curtis huffs."

Chasm laughs. "Oh, it was far from easy!"

Curtis listens intently while trying not to cram too much of his lunch down his throat. The shrimp tasted so good! But this restaurant was such a high-end establishment that he needed a certain level of poise and restraint—otherwise he would look uncouth. And Curtis noticed as soon as they entered the main entrance that the entire restaurant staff treated Mr. Montgomery like a king. By extension... that made Curtis a sort of 'prince,' and he didn't want his lack of restraint to reflect poorly on his new benefactor.

"But you understand the power of focus, don't you Curtis?"

"Huh?" Curtis looks up from his plate. "Sorry. Yes, I do understand it. Especially now..."

Chasm laughs. "It *is* difficult when the food tastes so good, isn't it?"

Curtis freezes, with his mouth full of shrimp. "How did you know?"

Chasm breaks out into a hearty laugh that echoes throughout the entire restaurant. "I can see the look on your face," he says while gaining his composure. "It's the same look I had when my mentor began bringing me here years ago. The food is so exceptional it makes you want to lick the plate!"

"Yes, it does," Curtis agrees. "So, did you meet your mentor when you were in college like me?"

"Actually, it was Dr. Winters who found me a few months before I began my advanced studies. I was going through a rough period in my life... and there he was." Chasm leans in again and whispers. "But let me tell you what he told me when I wanted to lick my plate."

Curtis' chewing comes to a halt as he leans towards the center of the table with great expectation. "What did he say?"

A smile slowly forms on Chasm's face. "Go ahead."

Curtis looks dumbfounded, as if to say 'are you serious?'

Chasm laughs again as he sits back and relaxes into his chair. "That's what he said. And I quote: 'Go ahead, Son. You only live once.'"

Curtis looks down at his now finished plate and grasps it with both hands. As he slowly lifts it from the table, feeling its sturdy weight in his grasp, he stops. *Wait*, he thinks to himself. *What if this is some kind of test?* Curtis looks back up at Mr. Montgomery.

"So," he says, "when Dr. Winters said 'go ahead,' what did you do?"

Chasm smiles. "Good... You want to know the rest of the story."

Curtis nods his head.

Chasm makes sure his tie is aligned as he sits up in his chair. "I didn't lick the plate."

Curtis slowly sits his plate back down on the table.

"Oh, but I wish I had!" Chasm smiles as he brings his own plate to his mouth and loudly slurps up the remaining sauce. Curtis looks around at the other people in the restaurant who look in Chasm's direction. Some do so with disdain, most see the humor in it. Some look completely nonchalant and then turn back to their own plates.

Chasm sets his plate back on the dinner table. "People will always be looking at you, Curtis. No matter what you do, you will *never* satisfy everyone. So focus on satisfying only those who matter to you. If you do, you will live a much freer life that's not bound by undue, suppressive expectations." Chasm nods in Curtis' direction. Curtis smiles, picks up his plate and licks the Parmesan remnants—giving the plate a seemingly spotless appearance. Chasm smiles approvingly.

"My mentor was testing me. He was from a different generation where the right answer was 'to refrain.' Even though I followed his lead, it didn't make sense to me. If we paid for the food and it tasted good, why couldn't we finish it to the last drop? So, I adopted the same test, but *my* 'right' answer was to lick the plate. Let me ask you... who was right? Me or Dr. Winters?"

Curtis' heart skips several beats as his palms began to sweat. He clears his throat and begins to speak. "Well," Curtis hesitates as he thinks about the entire conversation. "I'm sure both of you think you are right."

Chasm's right eyebrow rises. "Go on..."

"Well," Curtis continues as his line of thought solidifies, "you mentioned you two are from different generations. So one generation always thinks they're right while the other is wrong—or at least misinformed."

Chasm chuckles lightly.

"But, there's something to learn from each generation," Curtis continues. "Maybe his lesson was... when you're not in control you have to live by someone else's rules. And maybe your lesson is... when you are in control, you can make your own rules."

Chasm sits quietly—studying the young man sitting before him. Curtis' anxiety builds as he tries his best to calmly meet his benefactor's gaze.

"I want you to come by my facilities next week for a tour." Chasm motions for their waiter.

"A tour?" Curtis exclaims. "That would be awesome! Wait. What did you think of my answer?"

"Did I not just invite you to tour my facilities?" Chasm's waiter arrives at his table.

"Shall I charge this to your account Sir."

Chasm nods. "Yes. Thank you Sergei."

Curtis sits back and smiles, as the waiter walks away.

"Curtis. Very few people have sat in that chair and seen the lesson on their own. That is something to be noted. Now the key to the lesson is this: you must understand the times when you have control and the times when you don't."

Later that night...

The phone rings at the Powers' home. Miranda picks it up.

"Hello?"

"Hi Mom!"

"Curtis! How's my baby doing?"

"Great! I finally had lunch with Chasm today."

"With who?"

"Chasm. Chasm Montgomery."

"Oh, you just had dinner with Mr. Montgomery," she corrects.

"Yeah, Chasm," Curtis says in a matter-of-fact tone.

"Baby, why are you calling Mr. Montgomery by his first name?"

"That's what he told me to call him."

"It's fine that he wants to be relatable, but a teenager calling an adult by their first name is a sign of disrespect."

"Mom, I am eighteen."

"And 'teen' is *still* behind your number."

"Mom," Curtis counters, "I'm practically an adult!"

"Not the same as *being* an adult," Miranda says in her motherly tone.

"I can go fight for my country, like Omar," Curtis quips.

"True, but you aren't of legal age to rent a car or even drink alcohol—not that you should be drinking alcohol!"

"I know, Mom, but maybe you're just being old fashioned. What works for your generation doesn't work the same way for my generation."

"Curtis," Miranda speaks sternly, "what kind of nonsense is that? And since when have you ever given me *any* backtalk?"

"Mom, I'm just saying—"

"No," Miranda interrupts. "*I* am saying that this is not up for debate. Until you are an adult, working in a professional business environment, you address women and men who are older than you by their last name. It is a sign of respect. Am I understood?"

Curtis breathes heavily, "Yeah... I understand you."

After a moment's pause, Miranda speaks.

"Baby, I know you're getting older and you've achieved more in the last year than most people do their entire lives—but don't forget who you are—even while you flex your wings and try to fly in life."

"Thanks Mom," Curtis smiles. "Actually, with my Speedsuit, your metaphor isn't accurate."

"Good night, Son!"

"Night, Mom."

"And I love you, Son. Don't you forget that."

"I know, Mom. Have a good night."

Chapter Seven
Tour Guide

SEVEN DAYS LATER CURTIS GRINS FROM ear to ear as he rubs his hands over the plush white leather seats. His attention is averted as the high-end luxury automobile arrives at The Montgomery Group facility headquarters. Eight buildings sit on a sprawling twelve-acre gated campus. Walls, trees and security watchtowers clearly define the campus perimeter. Chasm Montgomery's driver goes through three security checkpoints before gaining direct access to the main building. Along the way, Curtis looks out the window at the pathways that intersect between fountains, trees and other foliage.

As the automobile approaches the seventeen-story main building, Curtis immediately notices its unique architecture, which consists of a wide base with several overhanging structures that rise at sweeping inclines towards a convergent roof.

"It kind of looks like an 'A'," he mumbles to himself before noticing a solitary young woman, wearing a lab coat, standing near the curb. The vehicle stops right in front of her, as the driver engages the brake, exits the vehicle and opens the rear car door.

"This is where you disembark, young sir," the driver says with a smile and a slight tilt of his head.

Curtis exits the car and finds himself standing in front of the professionally dressed young woman. Her hair is pulled back in a simple fashion. Her silver-rimmed glasses are moderately styled. Yet, he notices an excitement in her expression that is not diminished by her reserved look. He nervously adjusts his glasses in an attempt to divert his attention away from her sheer beauty. However, even with her white technician lab coat on, he can see hints of her hourglass shape accentuated by her violet colored blouse, textured navy blue skirt and dark grey high-heel shoes.

"Welcome," she says in a chipper tone while displaying piercing brown eyes, glossy white teeth and luscious dark red lips. "You must be Curtis."

She has one of the most beautiful smiles I've ever seen, Curtis thinks to himself before responding to her welcome. "Y-Yes," he stutters, "I'm Curtis Powers."

She responds with a slightly flirtatious, but professional tone, "Of course you are. It's a pleasure to meet you." She extends her hand.

"And you are…?" Curtis inquires, while shaking her hand.

"My name is Erica Cosway. I am Chasm's executive assistant of projects."

"Nice to meet you," Curtis smiles while seemingly caught in her gaze. *And her eyes…* he thinks to himself. "Chasm—Mr. Montgomery—never mentioned you."

"I guess he wanted to surprise you." Erica motions for Curtis to follow her towards the main entrance.

"Well, he sure did," Curtis responds under his breath.

"I hope you are ready for this." Erica looks over her shoulder at him. "Chasm has asked me to show you as much as you'd like to see. We'll start with our main headquarters. We affectionately call it the 'A' building."

They enter the metallic and glass building, walk past several security guards, and with a swipe of her identification card, enter an elevator. Curtis clears his throat. "So, how long have you worked with Mr. Montgomery?"

"Since I started college," she smiles while pressing the top button on the number pad. "I'm a second year graduate student now."

"Wow. So what's your major?"

"I have dual engineering degrees from undergrad. My current degree focuses on Biomimetics. What about you?"

"Too soon to tell."

"Well, with everything you've already accomplished, it looks like the sky's the limit. It seems like we are both prodigies."

"I suppose. So what do you do here?" Curtis asks as he tries to focus on the aesthetics of the elevator.

"Whatever Chasm needs me to do." Erica gazes into Curtis' eyes.

He laughs a bit awkwardly. "Figured that… since you said you are one of his assistants," Curtis counters sarcastically.

"You're handsome and quick-witted," she quips. "I like that."

"So does my girlfriend," Curtis laughs nervously.

Erica looks at him with a raised eyebrow as the elevator doors open.

"That's good to know." She walks out and down the hall with Curtis in tow. "But back to your question, Chasm hired me because I like a good challenge and can get things done. Of course it helps that I'm at the top of my class in math and the sciences."

"Wow," Curtis says—both at Erica's comments and at the view of the skylight-lined employee cafeteria they just entered. A host of well-placed seating fills the area, accented by several giant flat-screen televisions. A chef station is prominently positioned in the center of the room to catch the attention of all who enter.

"It's said that the quickest way to a man's heart is through his belly," Erica smiles. "Here, you can order whatever you want and the chefs will make it for you."

"*Whatever* you want," Curtis repeats in disbelief.

"If they have the ingredients, they will make it," Erica says confidently. "You can even text in your order so it's ready by the time you take your lunch break. Chasm feels that happy employees are loyal, hardworking and creative employees." She points to a full-service juice-bar to the right of the chef station and to the ice cream and yogurt bar to the left.

"Since there's always someone working at these facilities, and often times employees may have to pull long hours working on time-sensitive projects, the cafeteria is open twenty four hours. When we're done with the tour, we can come back here to get something to eat."

For the next two hours, Erica gives Curtis a cursory tour of the Campus, which consists of: research and development labs, testing facilities, a ballistic range, a test-driving course, a vehicle hangar, a water treatment plant, solar and wind energy conversion fields, fitness gym, dormitory, helipad, sanitation facilities, security stations, fire safety and landscape control units.

"This place is like something out of a dream," Curtis utters to Erica, as they sit in the cafeteria and drink exotic fruit-smoothies. Erica smiles as she lets her hair down and exhales deeply. She looks at Curtis over the rim of her glasses and sips her smoothie. Curtis looks away nervously, trying not to notice her flowing, black, shoulder-length hair.

"I hope you don't mind me letting my hair down. Having it up all the time makes me feel stuffy."

"It's your hair," Curtis responds with a slightly awkward smile.

"Thank you," she smiles. "It's not everyday I get to meet another prodigy who's close to my age. And your comment about this being a dream is exactly how I felt when I started interning here. This has been the best job I've ever had... so far."

Curtis looks around the cafeteria. "It would be great to work here."

"Why do you think you're here?" Erica asks.

"What do you mean?"

"Chasm wants you to intern here," she smiles.

"He said that?"

"Yes. That's why he asked me to give you the tour. He'll probably mention it to you the next time you see him."

"Which happens to be now," a voice bellows from behind them.

Curtis and Erica turn to find Chasm standing there, dressed in an impeccable charcoal grey pinstripe business suit. "So, what do you say, Curtis? Do you want to intern here?"

Curtis' eyes almost jump out of his head. "Sure! I'd be crazy not to!"

"Excellent. Finish up here and then Erica will bring you down to my office in about fifteen minutes to discuss the details."

Chasm Montgomery's Office...

Curtis and Erica sit in Chasm's office suite, which takes up half of the floor. It's very sparse in decoration—having more of a Japanese sensibility to it. The images and items that do populate the room, all make a statement of power, creativity, fluidity and innovation. Curtis steals glances of the space, while trying to keep focused. He notices that Erica hardly pays attention to the environment at all—as she sits next to Chasm taking notes.

"Curtis," Erica smiles, "you were saying?"

"Sorry. Got caught up in my thoughts. I always have so many ideas in my head," Curtis continues, "I can barely keep up. Biomimetics, aerodynamics, urban mobility... When an idea hits, I write it in my journal and then when I have time to flesh it out a bit, I create a file. The way I figure, it doesn't matter how crazy the idea seems... if I like it, I want to try it. Even if it doesn't work, you never know what other opportunities might open up from trying it."

"That's what I like about you," Chasm responds. "You are inquisitive and willing to take risks, to try new things—like building your Mach-1 Speedsuit."

"The funny thing is," Curtis reflects, "I never set out to create the Mach-1. I was just trying to keep from getting pummeled by a school bully. That's how I came up with the idea for my Kinetic Redistribution Boots. Once those were successful, I got other ideas for different components, which lead to the Speedsuit."

"What amazes me," Chasm adds, "is that you and your friends were able to create the boots and Speedsuit on a shoestring budget—using off-the-counter parts from a hardware store. Did you even spend a few thousand dollars on everything?"

"Hmmm," Curtis recollects, "about twenty five hundred dollars."

"That's why I want you to be one of my key interns. Imagine what you could do with your ideas if you had access to my resources. The sky would no longer be your limit."

Erica looks at Curtis with a slight smile.

"This is all so amazing. But, why are you doing this?"

"You mean, why you and not someone else?" Chasm asks.

"Yes," Curtis says hesitantly.

"You were a big fish in a small pond. Your accomplishments made you a household name, but now you find yourself in an ocean... a school where everyone's as smart—if not smarter than you. You find yourself second guessing things and then an opportunity of a lifetime is presented to you. Your question is one that Erica and I have asked. It ties into whether we think we're good enough or privileged enough... After all, we are African Americans and we find ourselves in a world that often values the lives of others who don't... share the same hue. Honestly, I'd be worried if you weren't second-guessing yourself." Chasm smiles slightly. "The way I see it, you need this grand opportunity and I need your creative ability. Learning is a two-way street. Together, we can help each other grow."

"So..." Curtis says slowly, "What would I be doing?"

"For starters, you have been assigned a workspace at the school. It's not big, but it will allow you to continue working on your own ideas for the Speedsuit and anything else you can imagine. This internship will be done in phases. For the first year, your freshman year, you will be an unpaid intern.

You will tour and observe each of my divisions. Take in all the information you can. Ask questions. Learn. Grow. We will also give you opportunities to weigh in on some of our design processes.

For your sophomore to senior years, you will be a paid intern. I will assign you to assist with several projects and you will have your own designated workspace—here. Once you graduate, you can work for me—if you wish. If you desire to further your education... it will be paid for by my academic foundation all the way to your Ph.D."

Curtis can't believe what he's hearing. "Are you serious?"

Chasm looks at him confidently. "Completely."

"Thank you," Curtis shakes his hand. "Thank you Mr. Montgomery."

"Please... call me Chasm."

Chapter Eight

Anonymity

THE TAXICAB PULLS TO A STOP as the passenger door opens. Out steps Miranda, into a new land, surrounded by rustic buildings etched with a history that spans hundreds of years.

She whispers at the sight. "Toto, we're not in Kansas anymore." Before her is an opulent restaurant, sitting right on the bank of a beautiful river. She retrieves her bag from the back seat, thanks the driver and proceeds to walk judiciously towards the entrance.

The attendant at the door bids her to enter, "Welcome to Niagara-on-the-Lake." Once inside, a greeter escorts her through various levels of the eatery to the Bacchus Lounge. The room is full of well-dressed individuals, seated in plush leather chairs around decadent wood tables. The multiplicity of their conversations somehow meld into an acoustic banter that is both inviting and intelligible. The stained-glass windows that line the lounge denote beauty and conceal a secret just beyond their borders.

The greeter opens the door to the outside dining area and leads Miranda to a stunning view of the Niagara River. To her left sits a beautiful patio overlooking the waterway. At the far side of the patio, a woman dressed in white, smiling warmly, rises from her chair and waves with the elegance of a queen.

Miranda's pace quickens as she makes her way through the maze of guest-filled tables, until she stands directly before her host. For several minutes, they hug and quietly weep, before sitting. Miranda gazes at the woman through teary eyes, as the warm breeze blows through their hair.

"Marge, thank you for inviting me and paying my way."

"You are most welcome, Miranda. It's the least I can do to see an old friend."

"I have never seen you this relaxed."

"Well," Marge chuckles, "this is what Canada does to people. How was your train ride?"

"Longer than I expected," Miranda laughs. "When you said in your letter that we should meet for tea, I figured you had retired and stayed somewhat close to the city."

"My dear, I knew once I retired it would be best for me to get as far away from New York City as possible. The things I was privy to… being 'just out of reach' seemed the logical thing to do."

"And what were you privy to?" Miranda asks as the waiter approaches the table.

Marge smiles and orders for the both of them. "Two teas, please. English. Earl Grey. With lemon and cream on the side."

As the waiter leaves with their order, Marge leans in towards Miranda, "I so love a good spot of tea."

Over the next thirty minutes—in between sips of tea—they catch up on their family life, and recount fond memories of Malcolm. After the pleasantries, the conversation changes.

"Now let us discuss why we are here," Marge declares with a quiet confidence.

"My husband's life insurance policy wasn't canceled by accident," Miranda states flatly.

"No," Marge confirms. "It was not an accident."

"What do you know?" Miranda presses. "How do we fight this?"

"Your husband did so much for me while we were at the firm. His kindness. His trust. I owe him a great deal. Even so, if I can be honest with you, I was afraid. Aspects of the firm reach far and wide. There were certain things that were done in the past to propel it to international prominence. In my opinion, many of these things were unethical."

"Are you saying that my Malcolm was involved in illegal activity?"

"Not at all, Miranda. Many of the questionable practices were done well before your husband was even hired. But these practices served to build the foundation for the company. As far as I could tell, Malcolm had no involvement at all. However, I think as he worked his way up to Partner, and had been in that position for a while, he was beginning to see some things."

"And you think they killed him for it?"

"Now, I have no proof of that. I doubt John or any of the other founding members would do such a thing, but I did see how they tried to win your husband over. No surprise, Malcolm couldn't be bought, so, they did an even better job of covering things up. Then when your husband was diagnosed with cancer, I believe a plan was put in place to make sure that his life insurance policy would be canceled."

"They did all of that out of spite—as some kind of retribution because he wouldn't do what they wanted?"

"I'm not sure what the exact reason was, but I am sure that the documents I have show the cancelation of the life insurance policy was deliberate."

"Did John do this to us?"

"What I've seen is inconclusive. It could have been John or any of the three other partners."

"Well, you have to give me copies of what you have! I'll look everything over myself."

"All in due time, Miranda. All in due time."

"Haven't we waited long enough?"

"My fear kept me quiet. But when our friend contacted me for her investigation—when I realized you were looking into things—I knew the time to act was at hand."

"So, let's act!" Miranda urges.

"That," Marge states calmly, "is what we are doing."

"I'm sorry," Miranda huffs. "I don't see your logic."

"I understand your frustration," Marge concedes, "but you have to trust me. We have to be very methodical about everything. There's a reason I retired, moved to Ontario and have been silent for these past few years. I had joined the firm shortly after its inception. I was one of those tasked with keeping company files: public, private and secret. There were entire sections of files that we had to manipulate and destroy over the years. As a sort of life insurance policy for me, I kept copies of key files. I can't draw any attention to myself. Just meeting you today is a risk. If our attorney friend has been digging around, there is a chance that someone associated with the firm has been made aware of her 'excavating' process. Hopefully, the digging didn't go deep enough to set off any red flags."

Miranda gazes at the lake. "I hope you're right."

Marge smiles slightly. "The next time we convene, I have someone I want you to meet. His name is Emmanuel Hart. He was one of the chief accountants when your husband worked at the firm. Nobody follows a money trail better than him."

"Thank you, Marge. I do appreciate your help. So, what can I leave here with today?"

"You leave here with a better sense of the big picture. You leave here knowing you have the upper hand, because you know something they don't. You leave here with another ally who desires to see that you and your boys receive what is due you. And the allegiance I gave to your husband, I now pledge to you."

Chapter Nine

Pushed Too Far

JUSTIN TODD SITS QUIETLY IN A corner of the Colorado high school cafeteria, trying to eat his lunch in peace. Today he has a pen and notebook in his hands. As usual, he sits alone. On the surface, there is nothing spectacular about him. He rarely makes deliberate eye contact with anyone. And he does his best, through the use of nondescript clothing, to make his 5 foot 6 inch lanky frame invisible to the naked eye. He even went so far as to dye his blond hair a dark, sandy brown in order to avoid attention. *Attention is the enemy...* he often thinks to himself. But actually, his bullies are; and *attention* is their opportunity to use him as the butt of their jokes—literally.

But that is not his focus today as he tries to hide his smile while writing a letter. October 12, 2012 sits on the top line. Three words sit below the date. *"Dear Curtis Powers..."* Justin has watched every video newscast and has read every blog post he could find about Curtis. *"This is my second letter to you. It's amazing the things you've done..."* Justin could have sent an email to Curtis' website, *"I figured you probably get thousands of emails a month, so I decided to write you by hand, thinking maybe my letter will stand out."*

Justin's hand can barely keep up with the stream of thoughts in his mind. *"I don't know if you had a chance to read my first letter, but I know everything about you and how you had problems with being bullied. I'm going through that right now and it's really, really bad. Please help me. I read the book that was written about you and I know how you and Treyshawn became friends—how you got him to stop bullying you. But I don't know if that will work where I am. I can't figure out how to get Jock and his crew to leave me alone. His name isn't really 'Jock.' That's just what people call him. But, I don't know why he keeps at me! I have never done anything to him!!!"*

A hand reaches into Justin's private space and strips his notebook from his grasp!

"Hey! Give it back!" Justin leaps up from the bench. Standing in front of him is the bane of his existence: Chad Roaming—AKA—Jock. Chad laughs hysterically while holding the notebook high in the air. The inequality in size is all too apparent as Chad's 6 foot 3, 225 pounds of molded muscle towers over Justin's 5 foot 6, 115 pounds of lankiness.

"What have we got here?" Chad asks sarcastically, as he pushes Justin back onto the bench. Justin lands with a thud and almost falls over as the other kids laugh. Chad continues with the spectacle: "This looks like a letter," Chad shouts loudly. "Is it a love letter? Let's take a look!"

A crowd gathers as Chad begins to read the letter. "Dear... Curtis... Powers..." Chad points at Justin with wild eyes. "Isn't this that Speedsuit guy? You think he's got time for you?" Chad reads bits and pieces of the letter in his sarcastic tone. "Please help me... I'm being bullied... And I don't know how to make them stop!" Justin sits quietly through Chad's mockery and the other students' laughter. His gaze pierces the floor—like always—as he stuffs his frustration down.

Chad laughs hysterically before looking incredibly serious. He turns and points at Justin. "That's just it! You *can't* make us stop! You don't have it *in* you! If you *had* the guts to stand up here in my face—right now—then *maybe* I'd think about backing off of you a bit."

You can hear a pin drop in the cafeteria as the students and even some of the adult monitors wait to see what will happen. A very menacing looking Chad towers over Justin.

"So, you got the guts to get in my face?"

But Justin doesn't move. He just sits on the bench, with red eyes and a quivering lip, while trying to fight back his tears.

"I thought so!" Chad yells. "So you gonna cry now?" Chad slaps Justin across the top of his head. "Huh? You gonna cry now?" Chad strikes Justin again—harder. Justin takes the hit—again saying nothing. "See, I gave you a chance to change things, but you couldn't do it!"

Just then, the assistant principal—Mr. Miller—walks into the cafeteria and speaks to the nearest adult. "I'm surprised it's so quiet in here. What's going on?" The monitor motions across the room.

Chad gives an evil grin as he backs up, raises the notebook in the air and grasps it with both hands. Justin stares in horror as the sound of ripping paper and cardboard fills the air.

"No!" Justin's shout pierces the silence as Chad rips the notebook in two and then tears the letter into small pieces! Justin jumps to his feet and rushes Chad—only to get knocked down by Chad's knuckle sandwich!

"Chad," yells an approaching Mr. Miller! "Leave him alone and get in my office, now!"

Chad drops the mangled notebook to the ground, shrugs to his friends and walks off to the main office.

Mr. Miller tells one of the hall monitors, "Take Justin to the nurse and have her look at his face." Then he turns to the rest of the students, "Alright everyone! Show's over! Time to get to your classes! Now!"

As Justin is escorted out of the cafeteria, his eyes catch Amanda's. If Justin is non-spectacular, Amanda Ramone is just plain ordinary. She is 5 foot 2 inches tall, with a head full of red hair that she often wears in two ponytails. She dresses as though she came straight off the farm, standing slightly hunched at the shoulders from all the heavy book bags she's carried over the years. Some of the mean girls take special delight in making her feel less than human. Fortunately for her, today's focus was on Justin. But tomorrow might not yield the same results.

She and Justin are two sides of the same coin—both endured years of torture at the hands of people like Chad and his cohorts. They've never really talked much, but they do understand their plight. Mere days after the new school year began, an anonymous student survey circulated through the school via the Internet. The survey rated students in a number of different categories. At the top of the list were Chad and his girlfriend for "most likely to succeed." Justin and Amanda were at the bottom of the list for: "most likely to be bullied for the rest of their lives."

Justin and Amanda quietly hoped things would change. At several points, they even got their parents and school administrators involved in an effort to get the bullying to stop; but down through the years, everything remained the same. Now, as they make eye contact, she smiles at him. He cracks a faint smile back at her and then disappears around the corner—into the hallway with the hall monitor.

SLAM!! Mr. Miller's wooden office door closes with significant force—

sealing the two occupants inside. Chad sits nonchalantly in one of the chairs. Mr. Miller paces behind his desk as Chad opens his mouth.

"Mr. Miller. Before you say anything, I want you to know that I'm practically doing that kid a favor."

"That kid's name is Justin. And just how are you doing him a favor?"

"I'm toughening him up!" Chad scoffs. "You see how small he is. He needs to grow a spine."

Mr. Miller stands motionless—stupefied—shaking his head. "Oh, I have heard it *all* now. So, I should be thanking you; is what you're telling me?"

Chad arrogantly smiles. "That is correct."

"We'll, Chad... *Thank you.* Thank you for continuing to show me who you really are. I keep trying to give you the benefit of the doubt, but thank you for opening my eyes to the truth."

"You're welcome," Chad answers smugly.

Mr. Miller sits down hard in his chair and leans forward very intently over his desk. With his index finger pointing right at his egotistical student, he continues. "You know what your problem is, Chad?"

"No, but I'm sure you're going to tell me," Chad replies.

Mr. Miller shakes his head in a huff. "You think you're untouchable!"

"I *am* untouchable—on the field and in life. I'm a force of nature and can't be stopped! That's why our team is undefeated."

"See? That's *my* problem. You are *supposed* to be a leader, but all you focus on is winning at all cost."

"What else is there?" Chad asks loudly.

"What else is there?" Mr. Miller shakes his head in disbelief. "There's losing. That's what else!"

"I don't lose. That's what *other* people do."

"Just because you're the captain of the football team doesn't mean you can push others around *off* the field. You're supposed to be inspiring everyone, not intimidating them!"

Chad's smile disappears. "I don't think I like your tone, Mr. Miller."

"My tone? You don't like *my* tone? I don't like *your* tone!"

"Don't forget my father paid for *all* of this school's renovations and the new educational wing. My family practically owns you and everyone here."

Mr. Miller sits quietly for a moment. "I'd call your parents, if it would do any good."

"You know what they say," Chad replies, "the apple doesn't fall far from the tree."

"And that's the tragedy for you, Chad. You have wealth, physical dexterity and intelligence. Everything the rest of us want. Yet none of those things have helped you develop any sense of morals, compassion, or heart. You know, there's *another* saying, 'the bigger they are... the harder they fall.'"

Chad sits up in his chair. "Are you threatening me, Mr. Miller?"

Mr. Miller smiles slightly and sits back in his chair. "Not at all, son."

"I'm *not* your son," Chad says forcefully.

"Oh, I am *so* glad about that!" Mr. Miller chuckles. "Believe me... I am just saying that you may think everyone else is beneath you—like ants. But if you step on an anthill hard enough, they will come out ready to fight. For your own good... grow up. Stop being a bully and leave Justin alone."

Several weeks later...

It's late in the afternoon on a warm, breezy fall day. Justin leaves his house and walks through a path from his backyard into the woods. As Justin ventures deeper into the woods, he accidentally encounters Amanda in a secluded part of the woods near his house. She's standing on a large boulder with a noose, strapped to the branch of a tree, around her neck. The instant she sees him—she jumps.

With a snap, the rope goes taut as she dangles by her neck. Time seems to slow as he watches Amanda thrash around—her feet just inches from the ground. The grimace on her face is evident as the weight of her body causes the noose to grip her neck like a vice. Asphyxiation begins to set in as her eyes meet Justin's. From twenty feet away, Justin sees—very clearly—the fear in her eyes and recognizes it as his own.

As her hands fumble with the tightening noose, he jumps into action! Justin runs to Amanda's side, grabs her legs, and tries to support her weight. She fights for a few small gasps of air and looks around wildly with reddened eyes. Her fingers claw their way in between the rope and her neck. Justin struggles—his muscles straining to lift her up—holding her as high as he can as Amanda moves back and forth.

She finally loosens the rope from around her neck, in a wave of deep coughing. Both of them fall hard to the ground. Justin scrambles to sit up as Amanda smothers him in a tight hug.

"Thank... you," she cries. "Thank you."

"It's Ok." Justin whispers as he holds her close.

"I thought I wanted to die," she coughs, "until the rope tightened around my neck!"

"It's Ok," Justin assures her. "You're safe now."

Amanda sobs on Justin's shoulder, as his face grows red with emotions swelling beyond his control. Minutes pass, as they sit under the dimming light of the setting sun. Justin eventually pulls back and looks at Amanda's face in the shimmering light. A thought enters his mind as he stares at the bruises on her neck.

"Why should they win?" he mutters, as Amanda looks at him with searching eyes. "Why. Should. They. Win?" Justin asks again, as he grabs her by the shoulders.

"What are you saying?" Amanda asks as she wipes away her tears.

Justin's gaze doesn't break. "I almost died two days ago."

"You... you tried to kill yourself, too?"

"Yeah." Justin looks away.

"What... What did you do?"

"Doesn't matter," he says abruptly. "*What matters* is if we kill ourselves then the bullies win. Then *everybody* will remember us as two bullied kids who couldn't handle the pressure. We'll *always* be the kids who never fought back—who never stood up for ourselves!" He looks back at her intently and speaks with great disdain. "We deserve to win—not them!"

"What... what do you want to do?"

"We kill them. We kill them all. Then people will take us seriously."

Late November. 2012.

Mr. Grabowski and Curtis sit at separate computer screens in separate locations, connected by the Internet and their cell phones. Notes are everywhere as they look over the Speedsuit event calendar for the rest of the year.

"Ok. I had to deliberately keep most of the calendar clear, due to your school schedule," Mr. Grabowski says. "Don't want to use all of your downtime gallivanting all over the country."

"Thanks, Mr. G. I could use some breaks. These classes are no joke!"

"That hard, huh?" Jim replies.

"It's like the professors are *trying* to kick our butts!" Curtis exclaims. "We sit in a two-to-three hour class and the professor gives us three to six hours worth of homework! And each professor acts like we don't have other classes!"

Jim chuckles. "Welcome to college."

"Chasm has been helping me adjust," Curtis says matter-of-factly.

"Chasm? You mean that alumnus you met, Mr. Montgomery?"

"Yeah."

"So, you are on a first name basis now? What does your mother think about that?"

"She's not too happy about it," Curtis complains as he imitates his mother: "*Calling an adult by their first name is a sign of disrespect.*"

"I can see where she's coming from."

"Can we talk about something else, please?" Curtis huffs.

"Sure," Jim assures, as he rummages through his papers. "Let's go back to the schedule."

"You're still using pen and paper?" Curtis asks.

"Some tricks an old dog can't learn," Jim quips. "There's something visceral about pen and paper. Besides, what do you do when your iPad runs out of power and you can't plug it in?

They both say in unison: "Get pen and paper!"

After a moment of laughter, they focus on the schedule. "Ok, the next event we have is scheduled for three weeks from now at a high school in Colorado."

"Standard run?" Curtis asks.

Jim looks over his notes. "Yes. A run around the indoor track. Motivational speech. And a meet and greet. I'm glad we made the suit-up and monitoring process simpler. Hopefully, we can pull this off with just you and me. Treyshawn's staying out in California for an art exhibit. Kelly has a dance recital in Atlanta. Omar's still out at sea. And your mom is working."

"Yeah, I spoke to them," Curtis adds, "But Gavin is free!"

"Your roommate? You've only known him a few months."

"We get along great! He's down-to-earth. And he's a robotics major. I'm sure he'll be useful. Besides, he's really itching to see the Speedsuit up close!"

"Ok," Jim says a bit warily. "If you trust him... then the three musketeers it is!"

Curtis pulls up the school's website on his computer. "So, what do we know about the school?"

Jim ruffles through his papers until he finds the specific details. "Ah, here we go. The student population is just over 1500: primarily White with a mix of Black, Latino, Asian, Indian, and Native Americans. It's in an upper middle class area, but students are bused in from all over the county. The school has strong sports, science, literacy and creative arts programs. It also boasts a no-nonsense anti-bullying campaign. But there have been a few incidents over the last two years due to socio-economic issues. The principal feels that our visit will help motivate students to see their differences in a positive light and help each other strive towards excellence in their studies and in life."

"That's a pretty tall order..." Curtis whistles. "Ok. When do we leave?"

"It's a long drive to Colorado." Jim takes his glasses off and rubs his temples. "We should leave early enough to arrive at least a day or two before the event."

Curtis leans back in his chair and puts his hands behind his head while looking up at the ceiling. "Man. Too bad we couldn't just put all of the equipment on a plane and fly there."

"Do you *remember* how hard it was to get everything over to London?" Jim asks exasperatedly.

"Yeah," Curtis moans, "I'm trying to forget."

"They lost half of our luggage, and it took them a day to find it and get everything to us! If we hadn't arrived several days in advance, the expedition run for the Olympics wouldn't have happened!"

Curtis says nothing as he lets Mr. Grabowski vent. Jim continues in an even louder voice. "We pay all this money just for the tickets, and then extra for our luggage, just so we get a 50/50 chance of our bags making it on the flight with us?"

Curtis closes his eyes and tries hard not to laugh.

"And *don't* get me started about the quality of the food portions! A good meal used to be *included* in the price of the ticket! Now we have to pay extra for that, too!"

"Mr. G..." Curtis speaks softly.

"I remember when you used to get *real* service..."

"Mr. G..." Curtis speaks a little bit louder.

"Now they take *everything* away and then charge you—and say it's a benefit!"

"Mr. G! You're doing it again," Curtis laughs.

Jim abruptly stops his tirade. This isn't the first time this subject has come up. Probably won't be the last either. "I'm sorry, Curtis. Got a little carried away. It's just that the Olympic exhibition run almost didn't happen because of delayed luggage."

"It definitely *was* a tense moment," Curtis interjects. "But everything worked out! I just wish flying was an option. We could do so many more events that way."

"I know what you mean," Jim responds. "But airlines are too unpredictable... unless you only have carryon. We'll just have to wait for you to buy a private jet. Then we can travel in true Tony Stark fashion!"

Curtis chuckles. "I've never even been on a private jet, let alone thought about owning one. But who knows. Anything is possible."

"That's right," Jim responds in a chipper tone! "In the meantime... I *do* have a surprise."

Curtis sits up in his chair. "What's the surprise?"

Jim smiles towards the web camera. "It wouldn't be a surprise if I told you right away."

He sits quietly, savoring the moment before he speaks.

"Spit it out already," Curtis laughs. "You're killing me here!"

"Let me just say that our legs won't be cramped while driving cross country."

Curtis' eyes open widely. "We got it?"

"We got it," Jim confirms.

"We got the RV!" Curtis shouts.

"We got the RV!" Jim repeats. "Our very first major sponsor sent over the paperwork this morning."

"When can we see it?"

"You won't see it until the day we leave. *I*, on the other hand, will see it tomorrow."

"No fair! You have to send me some pictures!"

"I'll think about it," Jim laughs."

"Hey," Curtis responds with an equally robust laugh, "That's not funny!"

"Why, sure it is," Jim, counters sarcastically.

They both laugh for a moment before getting back to the task at hand.

"Ok. That's enough funny business," Jim declares. "We still have to flesh out the plan for this event."

Colorado…

"So, what's the plan?" Amanda asks as she and Justin huddle together at a table in the school cafeteria. Their hushed words are drowned out by the noisy conversations of a couple hundred students.

"First, we'll analyze our targets. We'll know their every move, in and out. Second, we stock up on guns and bulletproof vests. We'll also need to find a place to practice shooting. There are some abandoned areas behind my house—way back in the woods. Those should work. Third, we study the school layout, security shifts and restricted areas. We find the best spot and the best time of day to pull this off—when Chad and his friends are all together. This'll send a real message to everyone: if you push people too far, they will push back!"

As Justin and Amanda talk, they are unaware that others are staring at them.

"Look at them," Chad addresses the rest of the group sitting at his table. "What do you think they're talking about?"

"Who cares," his girlfriend says while pulling his face back in her direction. "They're nobodies."

Chad swats her hands away. "So, now you're sticking up for them, Claire?"

"Did you hear what I just said? They. Are. Nobodies! Sometimes, for someone so smart—you can be so dumb." The rest of the table laughs.

Chad smiles slyly. "If I'm so dumb, why you still with me?"

Claire smiles back, "Dumb don't mean stupid. Besides, you have other attributes I like." She rubs her hands over his shirt, feeling his chiseled chest through the expensive fabric. "I'm just saying they're not even worth our time," Claire continues. "You're always messing with them. Just give it a break."

"Says the 'head of the mean girls' that love to cause 'redhead-pigtail-girl' over there so much trouble."

Claire smiles. "It *has* been fun. Just sometimes… it gets old."

"We just need to find a way to make it fun again." Chad motions to two of his boys and the three of them get up from the table.

"I don't know Justin," Amanda cautions. "Do you think we can pull it off?"

"Sure," Justin answers confidently.

Amanda sits hesitantly. "Once we do this, there's no going back."

Justin sits quietly for a moment as Amanda holds his hand. "There's gotta be another way to get back at them."

"I wish there was. But we've tried the rules. And where did that get us? We're ostracized and they get a slap on the wrist! No. Rules are only as good as the people who enforce them. And I am not crying over this anymore! Aren't you tired of crying, too?"

Amanda notices motion out of the corner of her eye. "Someone's coming." They turn around to find Chad and his two friends approaching.

"What are you two talking about over here?" Chad asks.

Justin wastes no time standing up to face them. The volume level of the room lowers as the surrounding students take notice of the confrontation. Chad and his two friends surround Justin, but they are slightly surprised when Justin doesn't cower in fear, but looks them all in the eyes.

"What we're talking about," Justin replies with a seething confidence, "is *none* of your business… yet."

"What's that supposed to mean?" Chad shoves Justin into the wall. "Are you threatening me? Do you know what I could do to you?"

"That's enough," a security guard yells, as several adults quickly advance.

"Back away Chad," Mr. Miller commands, while approaching the boys. He stands between them. "What's the problem here?"

Chad smiles as he raises his hands in feigned ignorance. "There's no problem."

"Uh huh," the assistant principle says. "It looked like you shoved him."

"Justin didn't see me coming when he got up from the table. His 'buck-115' frame couldn't handle my '225'."

"It's Ok Mr. Miller," Justin interjects in a joking manner. "Sometimes my eyesight isn't so good."

He grabs his backpack from the table and motions to Amanda. She gets up and they both head towards the exit as Justin says over his shoulder, "I'll be seeing you real soon Chad! Real soon..."

Chapter Ten

Sacrifice

STEAM CATAPULTS HISS AS THE SOUND of jets thunder through the hangar. Vibrations cause grates to tremble as multiple helicopters sit on deck preparing for takeoff. Their rotors chop the air—straining to lift several mechanized tons into the atmosphere.

The U.S.S. Hightower has been on high alert for the last three hours. Fighter jets have been scrambled to provide air support for troops engaged in combat just beyond the shoreline. Explosions blast in the distance as mechanics move about the hangar bay.

Omar works at a feverish pace. Sweat pours from his forehead as he takes his goggles off and tries to keep his eyes clear of dirt, moisture and oil while hauling heavy machinery.

"O," yells a crewmate named Quade. "Where are we?"

"Don't know!" Omar yells back while unhooking a pressure hose. " C/O hasn't said, but we're somewhere in the Middle East."

"Tell me something I don't know," Quade laughs nervously. "I heard the fight is thick on the ground!"

"Wouldn't know, Quade. Too busy trying to repair this engine so we can get this plane back in the air. Besides, how'd you hear anything if you've been in here all day?"

"You know, I hear things." Quade laughs while checking the control panel for the engine's electrical systems.

"Yeah, you do," Omar laughs. "Those *voices* in your head."

Just as they laugh, three gaskets eject from the engine casing, as oil and hydraulic fluid spray everywhere—covering most of their uniforms.

"I *hate* hydraulic fluid!" Quade roars.

"Part of the job," Omar shouts as he wipes oil from his face. "Shoulda put my goggles back on! They really shot this plane up good."

BOOM! An explosion blasts just off the starboard bow—causing the ship to rock from the concussive force!

Quade panics. "That sounded close! I thought they couldn't reach us from this distance!"

"Apparently they can," Omar replies calmly. He looks at Quade with steady eyes. "Q. Calm down. Focus on the task at hand. I'm sure Captain has everything under control."

BOOM! BOOM!! BOOM!!! The aircraft carrier rocks back and forth as fire erupts from the side of the ship! Thick, black smoke rolls into the hanger bay. Sirens blare as a voice squawks over the intercom.

"This is the Captain! We've taken three direct hits. All hands not directly involved in securing the damaged areas head to extraction points!"

BOOM! Another explosion rocks the damaged carrier as Omar and Quade tumble to the floor. "This is the Captain! All hands abandon ship! I repeat! All hands abandon ship! The U.S.S. Intruder is approaching to assist with pickup!"

Omar and Quade drop their tools and make a run for the nearest exit.

"It's blocked," Quade yells as he looks at the fallen debris and mangled metal! "I don't want to die, O! I don't want to die!"

"You're not going to die!" Omar shouts. "Stay close and follow me to the other exit!"

Omar runs in the other direction, but notices Quade is not with him. He turns to find Quade still at the previous exit, trying to clear away the obstructions.

"Quade," Omar bellows! "Leave it and get your butt over here, now!"

"But this is the quickest way to the emergency exits," Quade yells back. Several other mechanics approach and begin helping Quade remove the debris. Omar quickly assesses the situation. The corridor is rapidly filling with smoke.

"Omar!" Quade yells, "Stop standing there and start helping us!" Omar looks across the hanger at another door where other sailors are exiting without a problem. He looks back at Quade and the other mechanics. They have managed to clear some of the debris.

"Guys! Leave it! We need to get to the other exit!"

"That's clear across the garage!" Quade grunts. "We'll never make it! We almost got this bulkhead moved! The four sailors lift with all their might and move the steel beam just enough for them to exit. Omar runs back over to them.

"I am giving you a direct order Quade! There's too much smoke! We need to use the other exit!"

"You may outrank me," Quade says, "But you don't know what you're talking about!"

The wreckage falls away from the doorway as more dark smoke fills the area. "See," Quade says with a smile. "Let's go!"

The group pushes past Omar and enters the corridor. A blast erupts from the other end as flames and water shoot towards them! The three mechanics barely retreat in time while Quade catches the brunt of the engulfing blast. The concussive force throws him some thirty feet out of the corridor as he slams onto the unforgiving deck with a crunch! Omar helps the three other mechanics to their feet and then runs to Quade's position. Quade lies motionless with second-degree burns on his face and hands.

"Quade! Quade!! Can you hear me?"

BOOM!!! Another blast sends the ship rocking, knocking Omar and the other mechanics to the floor. The force of the blast also causes several large pieces of machinery to break free of their restraints and cascade across the deck.

"Get to the other exit!" Omar yells, as he picks Quade up and throws him over his shoulders. Omar runs with his crew, toward the hangar doors, on the far side of the garage while dodging pockets of flames. As they exit, Omar notices a nearby munitions pad sitting directly in the path of an oncoming trail of fire. He looks in the other direction and sees many of his fellow crewmen trying to board the lifeboats. He yells to the nearest sailors and they run over to help.

"Take him!" Omar points to the pad and the oncoming flames. "I gotta move that munitions pad or none of us will make it off the ship!" The crewmen nod, grab Quade and run for their lives. Omar rushes back into the hangar bay garage and jumps on the nearest forklift. He fires up the engine and begins to pick up the munitions pad and move it from the path of the flames.

I gotta buy everyone some time! He jumps off the forklift, grabs a nearby extinguisher and tries to put out the flames closest to his position. A few moments later, the extinguisher is empty. Omar throws it down and runs for the exit.

BOOM!!! The ship rocks again—this time throwing Omar completely off his feet and into a nearby guardrail. His back slams into the railing—hard.

"Ahh!" Omar cries as he falls to the ground at an awkward angle. His body lies partially between the open doorway and the wall. As the ship rocks again, a heavy metal crate tumbles towards him and smashes into his legs. Omar hollers out in excruciating pain, just before losing consciousness. The last thing he sees, before being swallowed up by darkness, are flames.

Chapter Eleven

Firstborn

CURTIS AND GAVIN SIT IN THEIR dorm room eating Chinese food and laughing while trying to do their homework. Their light-hearted conversation takes on a serious tone as the subject of their fathers is brought up.

"I know you know about my dad," Curtis says. "But what's your dad like?"

"I just met my dad earlier this summer," Gavin says with a forkful of shrimp and broccoli in his mouth.

"For the *first* time," Curtis says in shock—almost choking on a mouthful of vegetable lo mien.

"I know. Crazy, right?" Gavin says with a slight smile while shaking his head. "I almost can't believe it myself." He swallows and takes a bite of his eggroll.

"Are you gonna tell me what happened?" Curtis asks. "You can't say something like that and not tell what happened." Gavin smiles and doesn't move—holding Curtis' growing anticipation for a moment longer before beginning to recount the story.

August 2012...

The 747 airliner lands at Atlanta International Airport. Gavin doesn't move while everyone else disembarks from the plane. Then he gets up from his seat, grabs his suitcase and book-bag and walks to the front of the aircraft. As he thanks the flight attendants, he gazes into the cockpit in awe of all of the controls.

"This is my first plane ride."

"Really?" the pilot asks. "How old are you?"

"Seventeen."

"Well, make sure this won't be your last flight," the pilot smiles.

"Oh, I will definitely be flying again!"

As he walks through the corridor towards the terminal, he can feel the nervousness swelling inside of him. *I've wanted this my entire life*, he thinks to himself, *and now that it's here, I don't know what to do with it.* He enters the terminal and sees a man standing about thirty feet away—looking at him nervously. Their eyes lock as Gavin slowly approaches.

"Gavin?" the man asks.

"Dad?" Gavin responds.

"You look bigger than in your pictures... more mature."

"You too," Gavin responds, thinking to himself, *You too? That's the best I could do?*

They stand a few feet apart—unsure whether to hug or shake each other's hand. The tension lessons as Gavin's dad slowly extends his hand. As Gavin shakes his dad's hand for the first time, he asks, "So it's just you picking me up?"

"Yes," his dad responds. "Do you have more bags?"

"I checked a couple."

"Alright then. Let's go get them from baggage claim."

As they make their way through the parking lot, Gavin's dad asks, "You sure you don't want help with your bags?"

"Nah, I got them."

His dad pulls out the keys to his vehicle and deactivates the alarm. CHURP! CHURP! Gavin stops. His mouth gapes and his eyes open wide. Sitting in front of him is a silver 2012 Mercedes-Benz GL-Class SUV—with all the trimmings.

"This is *your* ride?" he asks in astonishment.

"Yep," his dad smiles as he opens the trunk.

"You rent it?"

"Nope. It's paid for—clean and clear."

"I mostly see drug dealers drive these back home."

"Well, I am definitely *not* a drug dealer."

As they leave the airport, Gavin begins to notice the stark contrast between his new life and the one he left behind. "We don't even own a car back home..."

"Yeah," his dad adds, "I know what it's like to live without a car and have to rely on public transportation."

"What do you know?" Gavin interjects. "You were only in Chicago for college and then you split."

They drive in silence, with Gavin's face glued to the window and his dad's hands glued to the steering wheel. *I knew this wasn't going to be easy,* Gavin's dad thinks to himself, *but knowing something and walking it out in real life are definitely two different things.*

Soon, their vehicle slowly passes Georgia Tech Institute of Technology. Gavin smiles excitedly as he takes in the view. His father smiles, "A couple of weeks from now you'll be a student there."

"I know," Gavin says with a sense of awe. "It's crazy that I'm even here."

"I'm glad your mother agreed to let you come early and stay with me," Gavin's dad adds. His son says nothing.

"This way we can get to know each other better."

"Better?" Gavin counters, "we don't know each other at all!"

"You're right. But regardless of our past and my mistakes, we can get to know each other now. And you can get to know Atlanta, too."

"Look," Gavin retorts, "just because I agreed to stay with you don't mean this is easy."

"You think this is *easy* for me?" his father asks—his pitch slightly elevated.

"I'm not the one who left!" Gavin shouts. "You left me and you left my mom! So, if this situation is hard on you—good. It should be!"

They drive a few more miles in a tension-filled quietness, as the cityscape transitions to the residential areas. Gavin notices the change in topography as office buildings and apartments give way to houses, which grow larger by the block. Soon, every house looks like a mansion.

"Where are we?"

"Buckhead," Gavin's father replies. "It's one of the wealthiest residential neighborhoods in Atlanta. They turn off the main road onto a side street. After a few minutes driving, they turn off the side street and pull to a stop at a gated entrance. Gavin notices a security camera aimed at the vehicle. At the touch of a button, the large gates open swiftly—ushering them onto a long, private, gravel driveway. Gavin watches in the side view mirror as the gates close as quickly as they opened. The SUV makes its way up the winding path, which reveals a massive structure sitting at the top of the hill.

"You live here!" Gavin blurts out.

"Yes," his dad chuckles. "Now you do, too." A moment later they arrive at the front of the mansion. Gavin stumbles out of the vehicle and surveys the expansive manicured lawn, uniquely shaped shrubbery, and tree-lined walls. His dad exits and walks to his son.

"We're sitting on eight acres of land, which includes a lake. So, what do you think?"

"What do I think?" Gavin's awe slowly gives way to anger as his face transforms like a contortionist. He turns and faces his father. "What kind of man lives like this—surrounded by... opulence... while his baby's mama and son live in poverty? We live on welfare! And you livin' on an estate with a lake? We can barely afford a one bedroom apartment with leaking faucets and rats the size of cats!"

"Gavin. Listen—"

"No. *You* listen! You have all this peace and quiet, while me and Ma have to listen to gunshots almost everyday! You get to breathe fresh air, while our living room smells like marijuana from the neighbors next door! You can leave your front door wide-open! We can barely get ours closed with six locks! What kind of man are you to leave us in that?"

Gavin's father looks away for a moment as he tries to fight back his tears. He turns back towards his firstborn. "Son..."

"Oh, now I'm your son?" Gavin yells.

"You've *always* been my son, Gavin."

"Yeah? Well you got a crappy way of showing it!"

"I *gave* you my name. You *are* my firstborn. And I'm proud of you."

"Proud of me?" Gavin's hands clinches into fists. "Are you serious? You barely even know me!"

"Listen," Gavin's dad holds his hands up calmly, "you've overcome extreme conditions to get to this point."

"With no help from you!"

His dad stops and looks at his son with an air of realization. "You don't know, do you?"

"Know what?"

He takes a deep breath and looks away for a second. "She *never* told you..."

"Told me what?"

"Your mother never told you about the private schools you went to— who got you in and who paid your tuition all those years."

"She said I was chosen by a wealthy... benefactor," Gavin's words slow as he begins to realize the truth. "Mom said that someone... had seen my struggle and potential... and wanted to pay for all of my schooling... to give me a chance…"

"...at a better life." Gavin's father finishes his son's sentence with a comforting smile.

Gavin stands motionless. "The wealthy benefactor... the scholarships... that was you?"

Gavin's father nods his head.

"But why? Why would you pay my tuition, but not be around?"

"Honestly, sometimes your mother can be stubborn," Gavin Sr. says jokingly.

Gavin's eyebrows pinch together as he tackles his father to the ground. "You don't get to talk about my mother like that!"

Gavin's dad grabs his son's wrists and forces his arms into the air. "Gavin! You need to calm down."

"Don't tell me what I need!" Gavin pulls away and scrambles to his feet. "So, my mother was good enough to sleep with, but not good enough to marry? I guess she *wasn't* stubborn enough!" Gavin swings wildly at his father.

"That's *not* what I meant," Gavin Sr. yells as he parries his son's strikes. "I *meant* that your mother doesn't like to receive help from others!"

Gavin looks at his father as he slowly lowers his hands.

"You know I'm right about that, Son."

"Sometimes… she *can* be like that."

"She can," Gavin Sr. agrees, "but she did ask me to help with one thing."

"What's that?"

"You."

Gavin looks away.

"Your mother and I *couldn't* be together. So, she was determined to raise you herself. But when she saw how bad the schools were around your neighborhood, she asked for my help. She wanted you to have a good education... something she never had. I gladly did what I could."

Gavin sits on the grass. "How come she didn't tell me?"

His father sits near him and looks at the trees, which surround the property. "I'm sure she had her reasons. I guess there's a lot she hasn't told you."

Gavin slowly looks at his father. "All I know is you broke her heart."

"I did," he replies softly, "but it wasn't by choice."

University of Chicago. September 3, 1991.

Gavin's dorm room door bursts open as Jackson, Joe and Carlyle rush in. "Dude," Jackson yells, "Joey found this new coffee shop. Let's go!"

Gavin pours over his books at his desk. "I can't, Jackson. I have to finish this assignment. Professor Clementine is brutal!"

"Come on," Carlyle counters, "you haven't slept since yesterday! It's break time!"

"Yeah," Joe adds, "this spot is supposed to have the best coffee and scones in the city!"

Gavin's friends dismiss his response as they wrestle him out of his chair, dragging him—kicking, screaming and laughing—to the coffee shop. Once there, they all clump in a booth. Gavin slowly begins to drift off to sleep until he glimpses movement out of the corner of his eye. As his eyes train on the source of the approaching motion, his fatigue immediately vanishes.

He quickly sits up and focuses on their waitress—the most beautiful woman he's ever seen. It was her eyes that caught him—shaped like almonds. He notices the curvature of her lips and the dimples that appeared when she smiled. And her voice—to him—was like a soothing, gentle breeze as she spoke in broken English.

"Welcome. I am Elena. What I get for you today?"

The four young men sat speechless at the beauty of her caramel skin, her pear-shaped figure and her braided black hair, which reached all the way down her back. But Joe, Jackson and Carlyle saw how Gavin looked at her, so Jackson spoke up.

"We'll take two lattes and our friend, Gavin, will have five Espressos."

Elena responded in broken English. 'With the bags under his eyes, you friend looks like he need ten Espressos.' Gavin had never laughed so hard. All he could think was, *her voice is the sweetest sound I have ever heard.*

Ten days later… The café door opens with a ring of the bell. The place is half empty. Gavin walks in with a smile and sits in his usual spot.

"Hi Elena," Gavin Sr. says with a wave, as she approaches.

"You back again?" She smiles. "That makes ten days in a row."

The Present.

Gavin looks at his father's intense euphoric expression as he sits—lost in his memories.

He smiled as he spoke. "Everyday I came by—trying to win her affection. It took three months before she finally agreed to go out with me. That first date was… wonderful. From that first date, our relationship grew into love."

"If you guys loved each other," Gavin inquired, " why did you break up?"

Gavin Sr. turned to his son as his smile disappeared. "My parents."

University of Chicago. March 12, 1992.

Gavin and Elena walk out of the dormitory and up the front sidewalk past the parking lot as a familiar looking sedan parks nearby. "Oh, no," Gavin says under his breath as he sees the car's occupants. The car horn beeps twice, indicating that Gavin has been seen. As they approach the car, the doors open and his parents step out.

Gavin's mother and father are impeccably dressed: he in glossy black shoes, grey slacks with a light blue shirt and navy blue sports jacket; she in a flowered dress, gleaming high heels, a black hat, and matching purse.

"Mom! Dad! I didn't know you were coming by," Gavin says nervously.

"We wanted to surprise you," his dad responds with a smile.

"And who is this?" his mother inquires with a strained politeness.

Gavin forces a smile. "Mom… Dad. This is Elena… my girlfriend."

Gavin's parents glance at each other swiftly.

"Elena… these are my parents: Jonathan and Margaret Pierce."

"How do you do?" Elena asks with a warm smile, while extending her right hand.

Jonathan and Margaret do not move—making no attempt to hide their displeasure.

The Present.

"They wouldn't even shake her hand?" Gavin Jr. asks, as he and his father sit in silence—staring off into the distance. "You don't have to tell me anymore. I'm starting to see why you had to leave."

"I have to tell you," his father counters. "As much as it hurts me, you need to know everything." Gavin slowly turns his gaze back towards his son. "When they discovered your mother had only been in the country for two years—and wasn't even a university student—things got worse."

Pierce Estate. April 23, 1992.

Gavin's parents tower over him as he sits in his father's study.

"Dad. I love her."

"Son, she's a waitress!" Jonathan sternly retorts. "Are you out of your mind?"

Gavin counters with an air of conviction his parents have rarely experienced. "I've never seen clearer, Dad." But his conviction does nothing to deter them.

"Gavin," Margaret interjects in a scoffing tone. "*That girl* isn't even a United States citizen! She's probably here illegally!"

"Mom," Gavin responds barely hiding his frustration. "Elena *is* here legally. And she's not a *'girl'*; she's a woman."

"What she *is*," Margaret scowls, "is a girl who's trying to *attach* herself to you so she can get *our* money!"

"That's crazy, Mom!" Gavin immediately stands up. "I haven't even told her about our finances or who our family is!"

"You haven't?" Margaret asks with a bit of surprise. "Why not?"

Jonathan responds. "Because he wants to be sure that she loves him for him..."

"And she does," Gavin exclaims. Jonathan and Margaret look at each other knowingly as their expressions soften.

"Son, this... relationship of yours will never work."

"Why not, Dad? Because she's from another country?"

"I'll admit it doesn't help that she's Mexican."

"She's from Costa Rica."

"What's the difference?" Margaret huffs.

"Are you serious?" Gavin yells. "You have six degrees between the two of you and you've traveled the world! You both should know the difference! And both of you should be ashamed of yourselves."

"Now you're trying to lecture us?" Jonathan asks. "Do I need to run down the laundry list of your past indiscretions?"

"Don't try and change the focus, Dad! This conversation has nothing to do with my past mistakes. But it has *everything* to do with your narrow perspective!"

"Son," Margaret interjects. "She's not even a university student! If you're going to fall in love with someone outside of your race, at least find someone who can help propel your career forward! Someone with some goals and aspirations!"

"That's just it," Gavin says with a mix of defiance and passion. "You don't even know her! You won't even take-the-time to get to know her! If you did, you'd know that she has goals and dreams... wonderful dreams of opening up her own business once she gets her citizenship."

"Let me guess," Margaret replies sarcastically. "She wants to open a

Spanish food shop."

"Not *just* a food shop mother," Gavin declares passionately, with a glimmer in his eyes. "She wants to create an exclusive Costa Rican dining experience."

"That's a *nice* sounding dream," Jonathan states. "But you do realize the obstacles a person has to overcome to open such an upscale establishment? It will be even harder for her. She's not in college. Her English is less than adequate. And she's working for minimum wage!"

"What could she possibly give you," Margaret quips.

"Love mother! She gives me love! She looks into my eyes and sees who I am! Not me the 'rich guy'. Not me the 'smart guy'. Not me the 'overachiever.' Just me, Gavin Preston Pierce."

"Love will not pay the bills young man," Margaret remarks sternly.

"So, I guess you didn't marry dad for love, huh mother," Gavin answers sarcastically.

"We married," Jonathan interjects, "for expedience."

"And eventually," Margaret says, "we *grew* to love each other."

"That might have worked for you. But, what's wrong with us being in love and *then* getting everything else together? Besides, there's enough money in my trust fund that we would have no financial problems at all!"

"You *can't* touch your trust fund until you are 21," Margaret counters.

"And let's see how much love can buy," Jonathan adds, "if your mother and I stop paying your tuition and cut off your discretionary spending fund."

"Are you threatening me?" Gavin approaches his father.

"Son," Margaret steps in between them. "What your father is saying is what I also believe." She grabs his face and looks deeply into his eyes with as much empathy as she can muster. "We raised you for something better— something significant. We just want you to do better. That's all."

"You mean you want me to be with someone *you* think is better. Why can't you guys just give her a chance," Gavin asks, while wiping tears from his eyes.

"Look at you." Jonathan shakes his head. "Ready to burst into tears over a woman. She's *already* made you weak. This proves she's not right for you. We've worked too hard to create the life you are now living. And if you want to keep living it, then I strongly suggest you end this foolishness."

Gavin slowly backs away from his parents. "You keep acting like what you're saying is for my own good. But you're both bigots."

"Gavin!" Margaret yells.

"Let him speak," Jonathan says in a cool and calculating voice, which momentarily surprises his son.

"You both talk about diversity in business and the need for teams to be made up of people with a variety of skills and experiences. But when *your son* falls in love with a woman who doesn't look or talk or live like you..." He hangs his head, sighs and continues. "I'm ashamed to call you my parents."

"Well," Margaret interjects, "we are ashamed of you!"

"Gavin," Jonathan replies sternly. "I will only say this once. I have no problems with you calling us bigots. You are free to say what's on your mind. Besides, in my years of business I have been called worse. But if you continue these shenanigans with this girl, you will do so without us and without our resources. You will be completely and utterly on your own. Now you decide… is she worth it?"

The Present.

Gavin sits on the ground with his dad next to him—both of them dealing with a range of emotions: from sorrow, to anger, to disbelief.

"I'm sorry, but your parents are crazy!"

Gavin Sr. laughs while he looks at his son. "I told you that breaking your mother's heart was not my choice. I just… I just wasn't strong enough to stand up to my parents."

"So, you broke up with her?"

"Not exactly..."

Gavin looks wildly at his father and breaks into a laugh. "You kept things on the down-low!"

Gavin Sr. laughs again. "I wouldn't use that terminology—but yes—we secretly kept seeing each other. And I got a college friend of mine to be my fake girlfriend for when my parents were in town or when I had to go home to see them."

"Oh, I done heard it all now! That's wild!"

"Yeah, well, about a year later, they hired a private investigator because they suspected something wasn't right. The PI came back with photos of my fake girlfriend out with another guy and me at the coffee shop with your mother. I made up a story about my fake girlfriend and I breaking up and told them that your mother and I were just friends."

"I take it back. You're parents aren't crazy. They're wicked."

"It gets worse. They couldn't prove I was lying, so they transferred me to a closer school."

"So that's how it happened... That's how you and mom broke up."

"Yes. Until your mother called me eight months later saying that she was pregnant with you."

Gavin's eyes grow wide. "What did you do?"

Gavin's father takes a deep breath. "She didn't want me to *do* anything because she knew what the consequences would be. She just wanted me to know that we were having a son, and that one day she hoped you and I would be able to meet."

"Did you ever tell your parents?"

"Not to this day."

"Mom painted you like a villain. Said you left us."

"She had to paint that picture to keep you from trying to find me. Can you imagine my parent's surprise if you showed up on their doorstep or if a letter came in the mail?"

"*That* would be crazy!"

"Yeah. It would be. But your mother and I wanted you to have my first name. And I told her to contact me if she ever needed anything. When she needed to return to work after you were born, she called me. She didn't have funds for childcare and she had no family. So, I secretly siphoned money from my savings account to cover your childcare. And I've been paying for your schooling ever since."

Gavin Sr. and Gavin Jr. sit quietly on the lawn and stare off into the distance.

"Dad..."

"Oh, so now I'm your Dad, huh?"

They both laugh.

"Seriously... I'm sorry about all the drama with me trying to beat you up."

"Hey," Gavin Sr. assures, "you didn't know. If I were in your shoes I would have done the same thing."

"So…" Gavin Jr. says in a hesitant tone, "when are you going to tell your parents about me?"

Gavin's father sits quietly for a moment. "My parents died in a plane crash last year." Gavin looks at his father in astonishment. "That's why I was surprised she never told you about me paying your tuition. My parents gave almost everything they possessed to me: money, properties, estates." Gavin Sr. looks down and picks up a blade of grass—twisting it between his fingers. "Even with what they did—how they hurt me and your mother—they were still my parents. They did a lot of good for a lot of people. I'm just sorry they couldn't conquer their own biases and truly see my heart. I called your mother a few days after they were buried."

Chicago. August 12, 2011.

Rain falls from the dark sky as thunder rolls behind several bolts of lightning. Elena sits in the living room reading a book. The phone rings.

"Hello?" she says in almost perfect English.

"Elena."

Her heart skips a beat. "…Gavin?"

Gavin can barely speak. "How… how are you? How's our son?"

"We… we're fine," Elena whispers. "He tries to hide it, but everyday he misses you."

"Without ever having met me…"

"But he has," Elena says, "…through me. I showed him a picture of us. He liked it."

"My parents…" Gavin mutters.

"Please. I don't want to talk about your parents."

"They're dead…"

Elena inhales so abruptly that she barely remembers to exhale.

"Their plane crashed."

"I'm… Oh, Gavin. I'm so sorry to hear that."

Gavin chuckles slightly as he wipes his bloodshot eyes. "No, you're not."

Elena doesn't even smile as she speaks with absolute compassion. "You are who you are because of them—even if the three of you couldn't agree on us. If you are in pain, then I am too."

Gavin sits speechless. "Why... why didn't you ever marry?" he whispers.

"You already know the answer." Elena wipes away her swelling tears. "Why didn't you fight harder for me?"

Their words hang heavily in the air. "I... I wasn't strong enough."

"So, we both made our decisions. Tell me, how... how are your wife and kids?"

Gavin doesn't want to answer her. "They are fine."

Elena diverts the conversation. "Our son will graduate soon. He is almost top of his class and is planning on applying to Georgia Tech University."

"That's great!" Gavin exclaims. "Do you think... he'd be willing to come stay here with me before he starts?"

"That would be a great idea. A boy needs his father, especially when his father lives a significant life."

"Thank you, Elena."

"You're welcome. We'll talk soon."

The Present.

"Now it all makes sense," Gavin says to his father. "I thought my mom was loco when she said she wanted me to stay with you."

Elena's apartment. July 2012

Gavin covers his ears with his hands at the sound of his mother's words.

"What you mean you want me to go stay with him?"

"Gavy," Elena pleads, "he's your father."

"And I don't know him! He up and left you! He's never been around at all! Besides the picture, you've never told me a thing about him! I don't want to stay with him!"

"Gavy. He was respecting my wishes."

"What you mean, Mama? You… you told him to stay away?"

Elena quietly nods.

"But, why would you do that? With everything we've been through—I've gone through—why would you keep him from me?"

"That is for him to tell you. But I will say, your father is a good man, Gavy. And I want you to spend time with him. Whatever you ask… he will tell you."

The Present.

"I got it!" Gavin jumps up. "You can divorce your wife and marry my mom! Then we can all be together!"

"Gavin," his father stands to his feet. "Your mother and I—that was a long time ago."

"But you still love her!" Gavin exclaims.

"We will *always* have a special place in our hearts for each other. But I do love my wife and children."

"But my mom was first. *I* was first!"

Gavin Sr. takes his son by the shoulders and looks deep into his eyes. "The most important bond your mother and I have… is *you*. And while we may not be married, *she* is your mother and I *am* your father. That will *never* change. And now that I am free to do so, I will 'do right' by your mother."

"What do you mean?"

"My wife and I already discussed everything and are in agreement. It's time to get you guys into a better neighborhood and help your mother get her dream off the ground."

A father and son embrace for the first time. Minutes pass without either of them pulling away. Tears stream down their faces as a boy's dream has finally come true and a father's burden has finally been lifted.

Chapter Twelve

Payback

IT'S NOVEMBER 5TH. THE TIME FOR payback has finally come. The first three gunshots reverberate like firecrackers through the lower-level halls of the school's sports wing. Eugene Cartman, the football coach, hollers as he falls to the ground—gripping his thighs. Justin and Amanda stand above him with their guns drawn.

"You always spoke to us like we were nothing!" Justin yells angrily, while putting away his pistol and pointing his shotgun at the coach's head. "And when I told you what Chad was doing to me, you smirked and just walked away!"

"Don't kill me," Coach Cartman begs—throwing one of his bloodied hands up in terror.

"If we wanted you dead—you'd be dead," Justin says. "We want you to suffer for every time you refused to help us!"

"But you *can* help us," Amanda adds while lowering her gun to her side.

"How?" The coach asks confused.

"When they ask *why* we did this," Amanda answers, "tell them the *truth*."

They turn and walk down the hallway, heading for the main block of the high school. "Feel free to call the police if you like," Justin shouts over his shoulder. The football coach slowly crawls into his office—leaving a trail of smeared blood in his wake. He fumbles to pull the phone off the desk by its chord. As if adding insult to injury—the phone falls—landing on his head with a hard thud. Once the pain subsides, he dials 911.

Justin and Amanda rush the halls—shooting at any and all reminders of their oppression: sports trophies, banners, photos and plaques. Students scream and run away as teachers gather as many of them as they can into their classrooms. A security guard confronts the shooters as they come around a corner.

"Hey! What are you two doing?" the guard asks while holding out his nightstick.

"You've always been nice to me, Mr. Rogers," Justin asserts. "I don't want to shoot you."

The security guard slowly approaches Justin and Amanda with his hands slightly raised. "Justin, you don't have to do this."

"Yes I do!" Justin yells as he cocks his gun. "And if you don't back up, I will shoot you!" The security guard stops in his tracks and slowly backs away.

"Get as many people out as you can," Justin shouts as he and Amanda walk past Mr. Rogers. "Only four people have to die today!" As the shooters return to their mission, the guard begins to evacuate students to the nearest exits.

Just outside the gymnasium, next to the indoor track field, Mr. Grabowski, Curtis and Gavin finish up the startup protocols for the Mach-1 Speedsuit. The gymnasium double doors burst open as students, teachers and security guards run for their lives. A janitor and a security guard carry Coach Cartman outside.

Mr. Grabowski stops the group. "What's happening?"

"Two students have guns and are shooting! I called the police..."

Growing symphonies of sirens are heard in the distance.

"Who are these students?" Mr. Grabowski asks.

"Do you know anything about them?" Curtis adds.

The football coach hesitates. "They're... students who've been bullied repeatedly." He breaks down in tears and sobs. "They asked for help... but nobody did anything to help them... Now we're paying the price for our own negligence."

Curtis unhooks his suit from the diagnostic equipment and grabs his helmet from the nearby rack.

"Curtis, what are you doing?" Gavin asks.

"I'm going in," Curtis states with a steely resolve in his voice.

"Are you crazy?" Gavin yells. "There are two students in there with guns!"

"But they're not after *me*," Curtis says while putting his helmet on. "Maybe I can talk them down before someone gets killed."

"I know I can't talk you out of this," Jim says. "So be careful!"

"You got it Mr. G." Curtis presses his belt buckle, which activates the power supply for the Speedsuit. He runs towards the double doors to the school and disappears inside.

"What are we going to do Mr. G?" Gavin asks.

"What do we do?" Jim repeats, as his mind kicks into high gear. "We come up with a plan."

Police and media helicopters swirl overhead—jockeying for the best view of the unfolding events on the ground. Law enforcement officers set a perimeter around the school's campus. A growing number of citizens gather just beyond the blockades. SWAT teams and K-9 units prepare for deployment.

The police chief speaks: "Listen up! Coach Cartman says there are two fully armed students inside—a boy and a girl. He thinks they're on their way to the main quad to settle a score with several bullies. I want teams Two through Seven at every major exit to get students and teachers out! I want team One at the quad. Find the shooters and take them out if necessary. We've got birds in the air but no eyes inside, so use extreme caution!"

"Chief!" yells a quickly approaching officer. "I've got that physics teacher from Team Speedsuit!"

"Tell him we're a little busy here."

"He says he can help."

The chief stops for a moment and then motions for them to advance beyond the barricade. Mr. Grabowski approaches with a bunch of cables and a wireless receiver box in his hands. Gavin's right behind him, carrying a sizable video monitor.

"Jim," the chief says, "I'm sorry we had to cancel the afternoon school event. My guys were looking forward to it. But, as you can see, we have a big problem on our hands. So, please tell Clark—"

"Curtis," Jim interjects.

"Right. Curtis. Please tell him that we're sorry."

"But that's why I'm here!" Jim exclaims. "Curtis is inside!"

"What?" the police chief replies. "What is he doing *inside*?"

"He's going to try and talk the shooters down!"

"Unacceptable!" the chief shouts. "What your boy has done is stupid!"

"Maybe you're right," Jim replies. "But what he's *done* is given you eyes and ears inside."

Screams are heard from almost every room as the sound of rapid gunshots fills the air. Wounded students and teachers lay in the wake of Justin and Amanda, as they walk expeditiously through the hallways making their way towards the quad—the main hangout area where all of the hallways meet. Chad, his girlfriend Claire and their group of friends huddle in a corner, unsure of what to do. The gunshots echo through all the hallways, making it difficult to tell where they are coming from.

"The gunshots are getting closer!" Claire screams. "What are we going to do?"

"I don't know!" Chad shouts back.

"You need to do something, Chad! Do something right now!"

"Shut up! Alright?" Chad yells. "Just shut up and let me think!"

Their terror turns into horror as two double doors towards the end of the hallway open. Justin and Amanda enter the quad with their guns trained on their targets.

"Justin?" Chad yells in shock and disbelief. "What are you doing?"

Justin gives a quick pull of his gun's trigger. A bullet bursts from the rifle's nozzle, at the speed of sound and almost instantaneously finds its target in Chad's right leg—shattering his femur bone. Claire and the others scream as Chad falls to the ground. Their friends make a run for the nearest exit, but a hail of bullets from Amanda's semi-automatic rifle cuts off their path. They cower together as Amanda walks up and slams the butt of her rifle into the side of Claire's left knee—snapping it! A screaming Claire falls to the ground in excruciating pain.

"You're not so tough now," Justin says as he approaches a crumpled Chad.

Chad raises his hand and mumbles. "Justin—"

"Shut up!"

"Please," Claire cries. "Please don't do this..."

"Funny," Amanda quips. "That's what I used to say to you. And did *you* ever listen?"

Suddenly, two school police officers barrel around the corner with their pistols drawn.

"Freeze! Drop your weapons!"

Justin snaps around, ready to open fire, but the officers shoot first. The students duck for cover as the bullets find their mark in Justin's chest and Amanda's back! Both fall to the ground as the officers empty their clips. Smoke emanates from the holes in Justin's bulletproof vest as the officers slowly make their approach. But as they begin to reload, Justin jumps to his feet!

For a moment, everything seems to move in slow motion as Justin grits his teeth in seething anger and brings his assault rifle to bear on them. A split second before he pulls the trigger, a roar echoes through the side hallway as a blurred body hurtles through the air and tackles the two officers—forcing them out of the way as a hail of bullets burn through the air and hit the wall behind where they stood! The three crash hard into a side enclave!

"Wha—" Justin says in a huff, unsure of what happened. He quickly turns and calls to Amanda as he helps her to her feet.

"Ow... That hurt," she mutters.

"Doesn't matter," Justin interrupts, "Did you see what just happened?"

"No," Amanda stutters.

Justin sees movement out of the corner of his eye and turns towards his prisoners who are trying to escape. "Don't even think about it!" he yells, with an intense ferocity that even startles Amanda. "Get back together!"

"Are you guys Ok?" Curtis asks as he stands up.

"I think my arm is broken," one officer replies.

"Sorry about that."

"If you hadn't shown up, my arm would be the least of my problems."

Thanks," the other officer adds. "That was close."

"Well you guys sit tight." Curtis turns towards the main hallway.

"Wait!" shrieks the first officer. "What are you doing?"

Curtis takes a few deep breaths. "I'm going to talk to this kid."

"Is your suit bullet proof?" the first officer asks.

"Nope."

"Then you're crazy!" snaps the second officer.

"Maybe... but I may have a chance at this." Curtis turns and slowly sticks his head out into the main hallway to assess the situation. He quickly pulls his head back as several bullets whizz past where his head was just a second ago.

"Don't shoot!" Curtis yells. "I am coming out and I am unarmed!"

His words are met by silence.

"Did you hear me?" Curtis shouts.

"Yeah, I heard you," Justin barks back. "But, why should I let you come out? You'll just shoot me again!"

"I'm not a cop and I didn't shoot you! My name is Curtis. Curtis Powers."

"Curtis Powers..." Justin mumbles as his eyes open widely. *Could it really be him?* He thinks to himself. *Could he really be here?* He looks at a nearby wall and sees a poster with a picture of Jetstream prominently displayed on it. He notices the caption: "Curtis Powers will be at our School." He sees the date—today's date.

"Is it OK for me to come out now?" Curtis asks.

Justin feels like there's a frog in his throat. "How do I know you're really Curtis?"

"If you don't shoot, you can see for yourself," Curtis says with a bit of sarcasm.

"What about those cops you saved?"

Curtis looks at them and they nod back at him. "They are going to stay put."

"And what about the cops outside?" Justin asks. "If you're who you say you are... then I don't want any other cops coming in here!"

Curtis suddenly hears Mr. Grabowski's voice in his earpiece. "Curtis, I'm with the police outside. We can see and hear everything through your communications array."

"Tell the cops to hold up a minute," Curtis whispers back.

Jim looks at the police chief, who hesitates for a moment before picking up his radio. "Team One: Hold your position."

Team One moves through the hallways swiftly and quietly with their guns drawn. The team leader stops as the order comes in over their communications channel.

"We're two minutes from the target area," the team leader says.

"I repeat. Team One: hold your position. We have eyes and ears on targets and may be able to talk them down."

"Copy. Holding position," the team leader says, while looking at the rest of his men. He turns his communications link off. "You two check these rooms for students. The three of us will move slowly towards the quad... just in case things go south."

"What about those cops?" Justin hollers again.

Jim's voice comes through the earpiece. "The police have stopped, Curtis... for now."

"They've stopped," Curtis yells back.

"How do I know you're telling the truth?" Justin replies.

"I've got a link to them through my suit. They stopped so you and I can talk for a bit."

"Ok." Justin runs his hand through his hair nervously. "Come out slowly and keep your hands where I can see 'em!" Justin, Amanda and their hostages watch eagerly as Curtis slowly steps out from the side hallway with his hands raised high. They all gasp as a hush falls over them. Justin watches in astonishment, with a growing smile. For a moment, all of the stress and tension leaves his face as he's caught in a child-like wonder.

"You... you're here..." Justin quickly wipes the sweat from his brow. "You're actually... here."

"Yeah," Curtis smiles slightly as he walks slowly towards the group. "I'm here."

Justin looks around in a daze. "I didn't expect... I didn't... expect *you*...

to be here."

"You didn't know I was coming?" Curtis inquires calmly.

Justin shakes his head. "Haven't been to school for the past three weeks... Been too busy planning for today. Didn't even notice the flyers on the walls... until now."

"So," Curtis' smile increases, "you wanna talk about this?"

"I wrote a letter to you... two actually."

"That's cool. When did you send them?"

"I sent the first one over the summer. Figured you get a ton of mail, so I wrote another one a couple of months ago." Justin's child-like wonder is overtaken by a wave of anger. "But I didn't get a chance to send the second one." He turns and points his gun at Chad. "This moron took it from me and shredded it in front of everyone!"

"Listen," Curtis tries to get the attention away from the hostage. "You wanted to talk to me... Here I am. No one has to die today."

Justin's anger gives way to rage as he looks at Curtis and then back at Chad. "Yes, someone does!"

"Hey." Curtis takes another step. "Look at me."

"Stop right there!" Justin yells, while bringing his rifle to bear on Curtis once more. "Don't take another step!"

Outside, several news reporters are live on air—regurgitating the same information over and over again: "Shots fired. Several people injured. Many students rescued. Hostages."

"I'm Laura Ling, reporting at Mid West High School. Back to you in the studio."

"And... cut," says Javier—the camera man.

"Javie," Laura says in a huff, "we have the same info everyone else has! And that's practically nothing!"

"What do you want me to do?" Javier asks.

"I don't know," Laura looks around. "We need a break..." As the words exit her mouth, she notices the group of police huddled around a table near their command center.

"Javie," she motions in an almost whisper. "What are they doing?" As they both approach the blockade, Laura suddenly pulls her cameraman to the side. "Javie." She looks squarely in his eyes. "I bet my career they're watching a camera feed! I want that picture!"

"Shouldn't be too much of a problem." Javier smiles as he runs over to his truck and grabs some equipment. He then finds an elevated spot with a direct line of sight to the police monitor. He breaks out a secondary high definition camera with an extended zoom lens, plugs an amplifier box into the audio jack and attaches a parabolic microphone to the amplifier. Once powered up, he zooms in tight on the police monitor, capturing a decent picture and solid audio coming from the monitor's speaker system.

"Excellent!" Laura exclaims as she and Javier quickly reposition themselves using the main camera. A moment later, she is back on the air.

"This is Laura Lin, bringing you exclusive footage of the Mid West High School shooting and hostage situation—only seen here on Channel 4. We have been able to access a live feed broadcasting from inside the school to law enforcement officers! We go to that footage right now."

All across the state of Colorado and around the nation, hundreds of thousands of people focus on their televisions and mobile screens. Each wonders the same thing: *How will this situation be resolved?*

Chad, Claire and their friends sit on the floor as a makeshift barrier—separating Justin and Amanda from Curtis.

"Do you mind if I put my hands down?" Curtis smirks. "My arms are getting tired."

"Sure," Justin says quietly.

"What's your name?"

"I'm Justin... This is Amanda."

"It's nice to meet you Justin and Amanda. Although I wish it were under different circumstances."

"That would have been cool," Justin smiles slightly before the reality of the situation sets in again, "but this is what we've got."

"What do you want to do now?" Curtis probes.

"You really *are* Curtis Powers," Justin looks dumbfounded. "I can't believe you're standing in front of me."

New York City…

Miranda and Shakira turn around quickly as they hear Justin's voice on the diner's big screen television. They both freeze, with their hands full of plates, as they watch the news feed. Everything they see is from Curtis' perspective. And right now, he is staring down the barrel of a loaded gun.

"Curtis…" Miranda whispers as her plates fall from her hands and shatter into a hundred pieces.

California…

Treyshawn sits in a dorm lobby swarming with fellow students. The sound of the television news is overwhelmed by the noise of the students as Treyshawn reads the caption, "Curtis Powers tries to negotiate a school hostage situation."

"Everybody shut up!" Treyshawn yells. Immediately a hush falls over the students as every eye is on Treyshawn. He points to the screen. "That's my friend Curtis right there! Somebody turn up the volume!"

Atlanta…

Kelly leaves her class and begins her trek across campus to meet one of her professors as her phone rings.

"Hello?"

"Kelly, it's Miranda. Are you watching television?"

"No. What's wrong?"

"Turn on the news. Curtis is in trouble!"

Miranda hangs up abruptly as Kelly checks out her local news station's website on her phone. She gasps at the sight, as she covers her mouth with her hand.

Erica bursts into Chasm's office with her tablet in hand.

"Turn on the news!"

"I'm already watching," Chasm says, as he points to the flat screen television hanging on the wall.

The world at large…

Across the country and around the world, viewers sit breathless. Routine interactions have halted in many places as social media blazes with activity! Millions of people focus on something they never get a chance to see—this one, intimate moment.

Inside the school…

Justin and Amanda stand in silence—looking at each other and at their enemies. Chad, Claire and their friends all look at the two they had bullied for so long. S.W.A.T. Team One quietly arrives at the quad and takes their positions. Several officers silently signal—indicating they have eyes on the targets. The team leader pulls back and talks into his microphone.

Outside the school…

"Sir, we have a shot," rings out over the police radio. Unknown to the officers, those words have also been broadcasted around the world.

"*Do not* take that shot!" the chief declares.

"But sir, we can end this right now," blares back over the radio and out to the world.

"I'm giving you an order. *Do not* take that shot. Things have changed. Everyone's about to walk out alive!"

"Sir, you don't know that," the team leader's voice responds over the radio.

"If you or any of your men shoot these kids, I will have your badges!" the chief yells back. "No one's dying today!"

"If we don't take this shot," the radio blares, "and this Justin kid kills someone, then that'll be on *your* head."

"Shut up and hold your position," the chief barks. "*Do not* take that shot! Do you copy?"

A moment passes before the voice squawks back, "Copy. Holding position."

"Come on Powers," the chief whispers, as he looks intently at the television monitor. "Please God, let him do this."

"How did you get Treyshawn to be your friend?" Justin asks quietly as sweat drips down his forehead.

Curtis looks surprised.

"Yeah, I know all about your story. That's why I tried to write you. How did you get Treyshawn to stop bullying you?" Justin asks desperately. "I've tried..." he looks at Amanda, "*we've* tried to get these two to leave us alone for years... but they never stopped. So, how did you do it?"

Curtis takes a breath as he looks from Justin and Amanda to their hostages and back at them again. "I... I treated Treyshawn the way I wanted to be treated."

"That doesn't work!" Amanda yells. "The more we tried to be nice to them, the more they laughed and humiliated us!"

"And the more we *tried* to play by the rules," Justin interjects, "the more we told our parents and our teachers and the principal and our friends, the more retaliation we got!"

"When their parents were forced to meet with our parents and the principal, you know what they said?" asks Amanda.

Curtis shakes his head. "What did they say?"

"Grow a backbone," Amanda utters flatly.

"Yeah," Justin interjects with an angry laugh. "Chad's dad actually told my parents that they should be thanking him because he was helping me grow a 'thick skin!'" Justin turns and kicks Chad in his back. Chad yells out in pain as Justin shouts in his ear, "Is my skin thick enough now?"

"I'm sorry," Chad cries.

"Oh, no," Justin shouts as he towers over Chad. "That's not good enough! I want you to suffer for everything you did to us!" Justin stands up straight and grips his gun as he aims it at Chad's back. "And then I want you to die!"

"Justin wait!" Curtis shouts from across the barrier. "No one has to die today!"

Justin looks at Curtis—his eyes swirling with pain and anger, "You keep saying that. But someone has to die! It's the only way to make all of this stop."

"No it's not," Curtis counters. "You and Amanda can walk away from this. We *all* can."

"No!" Justin yells. "If we don't do this, then these gooseballs get away with years of making our lives a living hell!"

"And if you kill them," Curtis counters, "then you become *monsters* and they win. Think about how the media will spin this! Students and teachers and parents are scared for their lives. People have been shot. Cops are ready to rush in here and take you out! You'll be labeled mentally disturbed."

"I don't care what people call us!" Justin shouts. "Do they think someone can be pushed to their breaking point and there wouldn't be consequences? We'll kill Chad and Claire and their friends and then ourselves! Then all the pain will be over. There's nothing to live for anyway."

"There's *everything* to live for!" Curtis responds.

"There's… *nothing*," Justin yells. "If we do what you say and let everyone go, then we go to jail for the rest of our lives! Or maybe the cops shoot us anyway. But if we follow our plan, at least the pain ends. Do you think we'd be here if we weren't ready to die?"

"But if you die, then you don't get to tell the world your story! Others will tell *their* version… and they won't get the facts straight."

"Look," Justin mutters, "Everything worked out for you before things got too crazy. It's not the same for us."

Outside the school, the police chief looks at Jim and shakes his head. He grabs his radio. "Team One. Get ready to move on my command."

"Chief," Jim says, "you can't do this."

"I don't want to, but your boy's losing ground in there. Justin's about to snap and we've got to act. I'll give Curtis another couple of minutes and then I'm ordering my men to move in."

Inside the school, Claire whispers to Chad, "We're not going to make it."

Chad grunts a response while shaking his head—trying to remain conscious.

"Claire," Chad whispers as he looks at her, "I'm sorry…"

"For what?" Claire asks while wiping away her running mascara.

"You told me… to back off a bit," Chad continues, "and I didn't listen. Now we're here in this mess… about to die."

Curtis hears Jim's voice through his earpiece. "Curtis, you've got another couple of minutes. If they don't back down, S.W.A.T. is coming in."

"Justin… Amanda…" Curtis says in an exasperated tone, "*No one* has to die today."

"I keep telling you," Justin interjects, "someone is dying today."

Curtis looks at the terrified hostages and then at Justin and Amanda. He can feel their desperation and lack of hope—and it's overwhelming. *If I don't do something, then these kids are gonna die.* In that moment, he makes a critical decision and takes off his helmet. "If someone has to die… then let it be me."

Justin, Amanda, Chad, Claire and their friends look at Curtis in shock.

"What?" Justin mumbles, as his mind tries to process what he just heard.

"That's stupid," Amanda blurts out. "You didn't do anything wrong!"

"You're willing to die… just to save them?" Justin probes. "So you're on *their* side?"

"I'm not on *anyone's* side," Curtis says firmly. "I'm doing this for *everyone.*"

Justin shakes his head. "You're not making any sense! Why are you doing this?"

"I travel the country with this suit—telling kids like you that their lives matter… that their lives mean something. I tell them that with help from others they can overcome *any* obstacle. I tell them that if they do their best…"

Justin finishes Curtis' sentence. "…then the miraculous can happen."

Curtis and Justin stare at each other in silence.

"That's what your dad always told you," Justin half whispers. "I remember you saying that in an interview after you set the world record."

Curtis shakes his head, almost in a state of disbelief. "The fact that you knew that quote and this situation still happened..."

"My best wasn't good enough." Justin's upper lip starts to quiver. "Miracles don't happen for me." Justin drops his assault rifle and pulls a pistol from his waist belt and raises it to the side of his head."

Curtis throws his hands up. "Justin wait!"

"Why should I?"

"Because you just helped me realize that my words won't always be enough! It's my actions that matter most!" Curtis takes a step towards Justin. "So, take *my* life! Not yours."

"You haven't done anything wrong!" Justin cries. "But what I've done... I deserve to die!"

"No!" Curtis takes another step forward. "You *deserve* to live!" Justin pauses at the statement. "With everything that's happened to you... you deserve to live. I want you to live!" Curtis extends his hands towards Justin and Amanda. "Both of you. Just put the guns down. Please... Just give me the guns."

"I just want the pain to stop." Tears roll down Justin's face. "I just want people to know that bullying hurts; that when they don't stop… it changes people." Justin continues as he looks at Amanda, who can barely hold back her tears. "It makes us into something else... forces us to do things... to find a way to make others take our pain seriously."

Amanda takes Justin's hand in her own. "I don't want to die anymore."

Justin holds her hand for a moment before letting it go. He turns back to Curtis and slowly walks over to him, while lifting his hands. As he surrenders his gun, he crumbles into Curtis' arms. Amanda drops her gun as well and collapses to the floor. Their captives cry sighs of relief as the tension lifts.

The police, surrounding the command post monitor, erupt into a rousing cheer! Pockets of people in the community applaud as well, as the word spreads: *The situation is over. Everyone is alive.* All over the country and the world, cheers are heard, tears are shed and hugs are exchanged! Social media explodes with comments that cover the gamut of the emotional spectrum!

The double doors at the main entrance of the school open as two police officers exit with Justin and Amanda in restraints. Several officers exit behind them with the wounded group of students. Curtis exits last with the two school guards he had initially saved. The awaiting community cheers as paramedics and officers swoop in to assist in a number of ways. Media reporters jockey for position in order to get the best footage and any possible verbal statements. "Boos" are heard from some, as Justin and Amanda are escorted to a waiting police vehicle.

In the midst of all of the commotion, a man bursts through the police barrier, with a loaded gun, and runs towards Justin and Amanda. Before anyone realizes what's happening, the man aims and fires several shots! The crowd reacts in horror as the nearest police officers wrestle the man to the ground, while Justin and Amanda fall next to the police vehicle. As the officers take the gun from the man and put him in handcuffs, he looks through the fray at Justin and Amanda's felled bodies and hollers repeatedly, "That was for my son!" When they pull him to his feet, the police chief recognizes the man: Chad's father.

"Dad! What are you doing?" Chad shouts from the back of a nearby ambulance.

His dad turns towards him. "I did this for you, Son!"

"But they let me go! Now you killed them!"

"Serves them right!" his dad laughs. "They got what they deserved!"

Just then, their attention is drawn back to the police vehicle. Chad's dad watches in disbelief as several officers help Justin and Amanda to their feet. Again, their bulletproof vests had saved their lives. Chad's dad shouts repeatedly, "No!" as he's thrown into the back of a police car. After a quick-but-thorough examination by paramedics, Justin and Amanda are placed in the back of the waiting police van. Curtis approaches as the officers prepare to close the doors.

"So, what now?" Justin asks, as he sits with his hands handcuffed behind his back.

"You both take responsibility for your actions and face the toughest situation you've ever had to deal with," Curtis replies.

"But at least we're *alive* to tell our side of the story," Justin says in a sarcastic tone.

"Right," Curtis smiles. "At least you are alive. And you won't be going through this alone." Justin and Amanda smile as the police van doors are shut. The officer slaps the back of the vehicle twice as the van's sirens blare and it pulls away.

Thirty minutes later, after a complete search of the school and every student and faculty member are accounted for, a press conference takes place in the parking lot. After the police chief gives his initial comments about the order of events, he allows Curtis to make a statement. Curtis stands at the podium, still wearing his Mach-1 Speedsuit. He squints for a moment under the glare of the video lights and the continuous strobes from the many cameras. He stands there almost motionless, trying to bring his words together.

"No one expected today to happen like it did, but our lack of expectation doesn't get us off the hook. We must take responsibility for what happened today. I came to do an exhibition run and talk to students about overcoming obstacles and reaching their potential. Instead, I found myself staring down the barrel of a loaded gun. If we as students, parents, teachers and community members don't take bullying seriously, more situations like this may happen… and the outcome may be drastically and tragically different."

"Justin asked how my own bullying situation turned around because he knew that Treyshawn—the guy who used to bully me—is now my friend. The fact that he asked, showed me that he didn't want to be where he was— holding that gun—doing what he was doing. He and Amanda felt that they didn't have any other options. So, let today be the beginning of a new journey for us all! Either we *all* win or we all lose. There is no 'us' verses 'them!' There is only 'us!'"

Chapter Thirteen

Regaining Consciousness

DARKNESS GIVES WAY TO AN UNCOMFORTABLE stimuli of sound, smell and pressure. Omar slowly opens his bloodshot eyes—his vision met by blurred white and blue images. A dull ringing swells in his ears and then gives way to a rapid succession of high frequency beeps. His mouth feels like gravel as he tries to swallow. His tongue feels like sandpaper as it clings to the roof of his mouth. His nostrils are obstructed by something he can't discern.

His arms move with sluggish starts and unresponsive stutters. After a moment of intense concentration, he manages to raise his left arm; bringing his hand shakily to his face. Pain receptors fire up to his mind as he struggles to make sense of a white blob, which is his hand wrapped in bandages. Omar blinks repeatedly, trying to focus. Slowly, formless hues and shapes become distinct. His eyebrows wrinkle as he painfully breathes out a single word.

"…Water…"

An attentive nurse approaches with a smile. "You're finally awake." She pours water into a cup and brings it to his mouth. Omar struggles to raise his right hand to take the cup. As his hand comes into his line of sight, he notices the bandages. Unable to take the cup, he lowers his arm to the bed as the nurse slowly pours the cool liquid into his mouth. A few drops dribble down his chin as he attempts to gulp it quickly. The nurse pulls back a bit.

"Not too fast, sailor. This is your first drink in several days."

Omar purses his lips and smacks them together several times as moisture begins to return to his mouth. "…My… skin," Omar says rather dryly. "…It… itches."

The nurse rubs his arms slightly, but he moans in pain.

"Sorry. You're still badly bruised and your skin is pretty raw under those bandages."

"Where... where am I?" he mumbles.

"You're in the naval hospital." Omar winces in pain as he grabs the sides of the bed and struggles to push his body into an upright position.

"Slow down," the nurse cautions, "your hands have first and second degree burns!"

"How did I...get here?"

"You were brought here—"

"Is this a dream?"

"No."

"Am I dead?" he asks with more force.

"No. You're not—"

"Dad?" Omar yells out. "Dad! Where are you?"

"Your dad isn't here," the nurse replies in a stern, but caring voice. "Again, you are in the hospital!" Omar pulls the long tube out of his nose—gagging in the process—and moves to get out of the bed.

"Slow down!" The nurse tries to restrain him. "You can't get out of bed!"

"My journal! I had... a journal..."

"Yes. We have it! It was strapped to your back, underneath your shirt." The nurse pushes Omar back onto the bed, picks the journal up from the table next to him and hands it over. He takes it in his arms, hugs it tightly and relaxes back into the bed.

"I'm... not dead... I'm not... dead." Tears flow from his eyes as he cries out for his father. "Dad..."

As she sees him calming down, the nurse turns away to look at the monitor. Suddenly, Omar struggles to get up again, but then realizes a lack of sensation.

"My legs... I can't feel my legs. Why can't I feel my legs?"

"That's what I was trying to tell you before."

Just then, Omar sees Quade lying unconscious in the bed next to him. Most of his body covered in bandages.

"Quade!" Omar yells as he tries to reach for him. "Quade! Is he alive?" Omar's breathing increases uncontrollably as another nurse comes over.

The nurse reaches for a syringe. "He's hyperventilating. We need to sedate him!" The nurse injects him, and moments later his breathing begins to stabilize as he reclines into his bed once again. As his eyes close, his surroundings drown into obscurity.

Darkness gives way to light as Omar regains consciousness. A doctor stands at the front of his bed.

"The nurse said you were about to wake."

Omar looks at the doctor and then down at his restraints.

"Even in your condition you're pretty strong." She smiles. "How do you feel?"

Omar looks around the room and then back at the doctor. "Better... You can take these restraints off now."

"After we discuss a few things and ascertain whether you're a danger to yourself." The doctor looks down at the checklist on her clipboard. "Tell me... What's your name?"

"Powers... Omar Powers."

"Good. Where are you?"

"In... a hospital."

"Good. What's the last thing you remember before waking up here?"

"I was... trying to put out a fire... on my ship. We were under attack... I was trying... to buy my guys more time... to abandon ship."

"Good. So you're memory is still intact."

"What about... my legs?" Omar looks the doctor in her eyes. "Why... can't I feel them?"

"Your legs are still there," the doctor grins confidently. "They are badly bruised, but still intact. They should heal over time." The doctor's smile lessens. "According to several of your shipmates, you took a pretty big blow to your back—which affected your spine."

Omar's mind floods with a thousand questions as he replays the incident. His eyes scan back and forth as he sorts the mental chaos and comes to a singular focus. "So, now I'm paralyzed?"

"Partially," the doctor says softly. "The damage is bad, but not severe. Actually, if your hefty journal hadn't been strapped to your back, the damage could have been much worse. I'm not sure how long it will take, but you should make a full recovery or at least very close to one."

"And Quade?"

"He's not your concern."

"I saved his life! He is my concern."

The doctor sighs. "He's heavily sedated. Third degree burns over twenty percent of his body. His uniform did help to prevent further damage, but it didn't help shield him from the concussive force of the blasts. He's already had several skin graft surgeries. I can't tell you any more than that."

"So what now?" Omar asks.

"For you? Physical therapy. Then you go home for a while until it is deemed that you are fit to return to active duty."

"Home..." Omar whispers softly. "Did anyone call my mother?"

"Not to my knowledge. We needed to determine your condition first. Now that you are conscious, you may call home whenever you wish."

Chapter Fourteen

Aftermath

CURTIS WISHED LEAVING COLORADO COULD HAVE been uneventful. He, Gavin and Mr. Grabowski walking through the airport terminal with a police escort brought much unwanted attention. Cell phone cameras flashed all around him as crowds took notice of their presence. His image was on every television screen, at every gate, as analysts and experts weighed in on the school shooting and hostage situation. These experts dissected every moment and extrapolated apparent meaning from each action and lack of action of the police, teachers, students, parents and even Curtis himself.

But Curtis was too dazed to pay the broadcasts any real attention. The unexpected had happened, and while Curtis was found to be prepared—the situation had left him shaken. And with no time alone to examine his feelings, the best he could do was "stuff them down" for later.

The nearest police officer leans in and comments as they walk. "Don't worry about the news broadcasts."

"I'm too tired to worry," Curtis chuckles.

"Well, at least you'll be able to get some good sleep in first class."

Once the rest of the passengers were aboard, the police detail escorted Curtis, Mr. Grabowski and Gavin to their seats. Then the police chief addressed the passengers and announced his gratitude for Curtis' heroism. They cheered for what seemed like several minutes as Curtis stood and waved before taking his seat again. After the police officers disembarked and the plane's main door was closed, Curtis sank into the plush first class seat and was almost immediately engulfed by sleep. But when his eyes closed, the faces of Justin and Amanda flashed through his mind—causing him to wake up after a few moments.

Twenty minutes later, the plane is cruising at thirty thousand feet. Curtis, Gavin and Mr. Grabowski are exhausted. Just a couple of days ago they were literally at the center of attention. Now, after acting to save numerous students and administrators, debriefing with law enforcement and being interviewed by a number of media outlets, they are finally heading home.

Mr. Grabowski looks at Curtis. "I thought you'd be asleep by now."

"Me too." Curtis huffs. "But I'm too tired to sleep."

"That doesn't even make sense," Jim laughs.

"Yeah, well... that's my reality," Curtis groans in a sarcastic tone.

"Well, I'm tired, too," Jim says, "but the thought of going home has me a bit energized. You know, it was nice that they paid to fly us back instead of us having to drive."

"Yeah," Curtis agrees. "Good thing there was a drop off station nearby for the RV. Don't know how driving back across country would have been after everything that just happened."

"We would have made it," Jim responds confidently. "But it *is* nice to fly first class."

"I just hope the Mach-1 and the rest of our equipment makes it back in one piece."

"Ugh," Jim grunts. "Please don't remind me about London. Getting the Speedsuit there was a nightmare!"

"At least we don't have to go through Customs," Curtis shakes his head.

"Thank God," Jim agrees. He and Curtis chuckle as they look over at Gavin who has his seat fully extended into an almost horizontal position. Drool pools around the corners of his mouth as he snores loudly.

"You know Mr. G," Curtis muses as he looks at Gavin, "*that* would be so much more difficult in economy."

"Yes," Jim chuckles. "He'd probably be lying on both of us!" They laugh for a moment before Curtis' expression reveals the seriousness of his thoughts.

"How could something like this happen?" Curtis looks down at his hands.

Mr. Grabowski's smile disappears as he stares out the window. "I don't know..."

"I mean," Curtis speaks in frustration, "how does it get *so bad* that someone has to use a gun to try and solve their problems? And how do adults see what's going on and do nothing to make things better?"

Jim sits quietly for a moment. "Those are two questions that parents, school administrators and community leaders have wrestled with for a long time."

"Well, they're not wrestling enough," Curtis replies. "It's like people don't care!"

"I think people are afraid… more than anything," Jim replies. "The situation seems so large that people aren't sure *what* they should do. Bullying is a complex problem. *You* know this better than most. Kids have issues. Parents have issues. Schools… well they have bureaucracy."

"That *doesn't* mean there aren't solutions," Curtis snaps before catching himself. "I'm sorry, Mr. G. That wasn't meant for you."

"I know, Curtis," Jim grins. "So… what kind of solutions are you considering?"

"I don't know…"

Chapter Fifteen

Phone Home...

A NURSE WALKS THROUGH THE HOSPITAL'S burn unit, passing several rows of active treatment patients. She turns a corner, enters room 603 and assesses the occupant.

"Omar," the nurse says as she updates his vitals sheet. "It's been several days and you still haven't called home."

"I'm not ready yet," Omar replies while holding his father's journal. "I still don't know what's going to happen with me, so I don't want to worry her."

"What if she's already worried about you? What if she's seen the news and knows about the attack on your ship?"

Omar sits quietly in his bed.

"Ok," the nurse raises her hands, slightly shaking her head, "I can take a hint."

"Thanks." The nurse walks away as Omar opens the journal and flips to a new entry: *Why We Quit.*

Omar,

You are my firstborn and there were many times when I felt inadequate for the task of raising you. I wasn't sure if I had what it took to be a good father... to ensure your success and safety and development in life. Sounds insane, right? I could design skyscrapers that kissed the sky and sprawling homes that stretched across acres of land. But how do I take care of a small boy who looks up at me with eyes beaming with wonder? There were no classes to teach me that.

I understand why grown men quit... why they give up on life, but most importantly, why they give up at raising their sons. If I had a dollar for every time I felt unsure of myself—like I couldn't measure up to the challenge that was before me—I would be a millionaire. We often give up for fear that we will fail. And it is only by the grace of God that we don't retreat, but stay in the fight until the end.

A mother's maternal desire to take care of her child is built-in (even if some deliberately choose to ignore it). But fathers don't have such wiring. Becoming a good father takes a great effort! Raising you was on-the-job training!

I never told you... don't even know if I told your mother either... but they say 'confession is good for the soul.' So, here it is: I dropped you on your head when you were almost two. It was a complete accident! Your mother was out and I was watching you at home. You liked your playpen, so we let you stay there a lot. On this particular day, I picked you up and the phone rang. I turned with you in my arms and as I turned to the right, you fell backwards to the left. It happened so quickly, and before I could react, you had already hit the floor!

You cried so much! And I held you so tight, consoling you and checking you out. You stopped crying after a few minutes. You wanted to go to sleep in my arms, but I had to keep you awake for at least an hour to make sure you were truly Ok. You didn't like having to stay awake! By the time your mother came home, you were fine. But for the next two weeks, I would stay by your bedside every night, praying to God that you wouldn't experience any after effects from that fall. Your mother thought my sitting by your bed was so cute... but if she knew the real reason... well, you know your mother. I might have left this world much sooner!

But to be serious... that one experience traumatized me. Even these years later it still affects me. I tell you this because I know my illness has put you through your own trauma. The last time we talked, I told you that you were stronger than you realized. You told me that you were not strong and couldn't handle the pressure. But a man's character isn't measured by how he handles himself when things go great for him. No. The truest test of a man's character is how well he handles himself when everything falls apart. Even the Bible says in Proverbs, that the person who faints in the day of adversity has small strength.

Omar, you know this in the gym. You continue to bring your body under subjection so that it can operate at its peak efficiency. But you know physical strength isn't measured by how good you look with your shirt off, but by how much weight you can move and by how many repetitions you can endure. This is easier said than done, but you only have to translate what you know in the gym to comprehend the rest of the real world.

I don't know where you will be when you read these words. I don't know what you will be going through—whether you will be experiencing a time of joy or a season of pain. But what I do know is that in whatever state you are… you don't have to give up on life. I mentioned the word 'quit' earlier in this entry, but let me say that there is a difference between 'quitting' and 'giving up.' To 'quit' is to examine the situation, acknowledge the challenges and your capabilities to meet them, and then decide to stop the journey because you desire to do something else. 'Giving up' is something else entirely. 'Giving up' means you allow your sense of inadequacy to determine your actions—despite the facts or potential opportunities.

Know this, Son: you turned out to be and will continue to be a strong and honorable man who is capable of more than you can imagine. I will always love you.

Your Father,
Malcolm Powers

In the Bronx... Miranda sits in front of her computer screen, inputting her household bills into a budget management program. Her frustration is apparent as the sum still shows that she has more "outgo" than she does income. Her phone rings. She looks at the clock—2:00 a.m.—and thinks to herself, *Who's calling this time of night?* She looks at the caller ID, but it registers "Private" on the screen. She hesitates, but slowly picks up the receiver.

"Hello?"

"Ma..."

Miranda practically melts into her chair as she hears the voice of her firstborn son.

"Omar!" she shouts. "Baby, you have been on my mind so much these past few weeks. For some reason, I have been praying like nobody's business! Please tell me you're Ok."

"I'm Ok Ma. Now I am." Omar tries to hold back his tears.

"Where are you?" Miranda asks. "Why haven't you called?"

"Ma, I don't want you to panic."

"Panic? Panic about what?"

"I'm in a naval hospital."

"A hospital!" Miranda yells while jumping up from her seat. "What happened?"

"Our ship was attacked. We took heavy fire."

"But you're Ok, right?" Miranda asks as her eyes well up with tears.

"I was injured while trying to save my shipmates."

"What *kind* of injury do you have?" Miranda looks over at a picture on the fireplace mantel: a picture of Omar wearing his United States Navy uniform.

"I'm temporarily paralyzed from the waist down."

Miranda stands in silence before slowly walking over to her son's picture. Tears begin to stream down her face as she holds the picture frame in her hand.

Omar hears his mother's quiet cries through the phone receiver. "Ma… are you alright?"

Miranda makes her way back to her desk and slumps into her chair. "Omar… I *can't* do this… First Malcolm. Then Curtis puts his life in jeopardy to save some kids he doesn't even know. Now you… I can't do this…"

"This is why I waited so long to call you. I didn't want you to worry. Ma, you've always been so strong—much stronger than me. I can't do this if you can't pull yourself together."

Miranda hears her son's voice and continues to stare at his picture. She then looks at the family picture of the four of them—taken years earlier when they didn't have a care in the world.

"Ma?" Omar interrupts her silence. "Ma, do you hear me? I *need* you."

Miranda slowly grabs a tissue and wipes her eyes and nose. She takes a deep breath and corrects her posture. She whispers, "Lord Jesus help me," and then clears her throat. "Alright… I'm here."

"We just take things one day at a time," Omar smiles softly.

"That's right baby," Miranda concedes, "one day at a time. So tell me about your temporary condition."

"The doctor says I should make a full or at least almost full recovery. While the damage to my spine was extensive, it wasn't severe."

"Ok. That's good to hear. So what are you doing now? What's the next step?"

"I just started physical therapy. Oh, and I do have some burns, but those are minimal."

"Ok." Miranda thinks through possibilities. "So, are you coming home at all?"

"Yeah," Omar smiles. "I should be home next week, a few days before Thanksgiving."

"Thank God," Miranda smiles with a sigh of relief. "I'll have your favorite meal ready."

"Thanks," Omar smiles widely. "I can already taste your good home cooking."

Miranda laughs. "You know, it seems that you and your brother love to visit hospitals," she says sarcastically as the mood lightens.

"It seems that way," Omar laughs.

"Well, is there anything I can do for you?"

"One of the best things you did was give me Dad's journal," Omar replies. "Reading his words has really been helpful. I can't even begin to explain it."

"He hoped his words would be timely for you and your brother."

"Well," Omar smiles, "His hope was right. Wait a minute, Ma. What did you mean Curtis put his life in jeopardy to save some kids he didn't know?"

Chapter Sixteen

It's Good To Be Back!

THE SUDDEN JOLT OF TIRES HITTING the runway wakes Curtis with a start. He looks around rather wildly as he tries to get his bearings. Mr. Grabowski and Gavin laugh as they look at him with amused expressions.

"Who's the one drooling now?" Gavin asks.

"Didn't realize how tired I was." Curtis yawns and stretches his weary limbs. The three of them turn on their cellphones as the plane taxis to the gate.

"My mother texted me ten times since we've been in the air!" Curtis laughs.

"My parents too," Gavin adds.

"My daughter called," Jim interjects. "I'll call her when I get to the hotel."

"You know you could have just gotten a straight flight back to New York," Curtis says.

"And have to deal with your mother?" Jim laughs nervously. "I don't think so! Your mother was already worried out of her mind. Me making sure you made it back to campus actually helped to put her at ease."

Minutes later, the three men descend the escalator to baggage claim as impatient news reporters take notice.

"There he is!" one of them shouts—a sudden commotion of activity roars to life as lights and chatter overtake the area.

"Aw man," Curtis huffs. "Not again..."

"Smile for the camera," Jim says. As soon as the words hit Curtis' ears, he sees a very good reason to smile. He immediately exits off of the escalator and walks past the reporters without saying a word. He rushes the last few meters and embraces Kelly who has been eagerly waiting.

"Curtis!" Kelly exclaims while hugging him tightly.

"Hey Kelly," Curtis says warmly, as he drops his bag and embraces her. They both hold each other for what seems like an eternity—oblivious to the prying "eyes" of the lights and cameras as they share a strong kiss.

"I wasn't sure if I was going to see you again." Kelly wipes away her tears.

"I know. I'm sorry."

"Don't you *ever* do something like that again!"

"Can't promise you that," he smiles softly.

"I know." Kelly buries her face into his shoulder.

"Wait." Curtis pulls away from her so he can see her face. "How did you get here?"

"That would my doing," a voice declares from a nearby corner. Chasm Montgomery reveals himself, causing the media to be whipped into an unexpected frenzy.

"Chasm!" Curtis exclaims, while giving him a firm handshake. Chasm laughs and pulls Curtis into an embrace. "Curtis! No need to be so official in front of the cameras. With everything you've been through, I wanted to be here on your return."

"Wait. You and Kelly never met. How did you know to pick her up?"

"You've mentioned her enough," Chasm smiles. "It was easy to have Erica track her down and make the necessary arrangements."

"So, you've met his assistant, Erica." Curtis tries to hide his nervousness.

"*Did I?*" Kelly responds. "She's top notch!"

"I do my best to pick the finest students," Chasm interjects.

"Speaking of students," Mr. Grabowski adds as he walks over, "Curtis was my best in high school."

"Mr. Grabowski, it's nice to finally meet you!" Chasm extends his hand. "I'm Chasm Montgomery."

"It's a pleasure to finally meet you, too." Jim smiles as he shakes Chasm's hand. "Curtis talks of you often."

"As he does of you," Chasm affirms with an air of diplomacy.

"Thank you for everything you're doing to help him."

"I am merely paying forward what others have done for me."

Gavin's eyes almost bulge out of their sockets as he nudges Curtis.

"Chasm, you remember my roommate, Gavin?"

"It's great to see you again sir! I'm a big fan!"

"So I hear," Chasm laughs. "It's good to see you again as well."

As media personnel begin to press with their questions, Chasm steps forward.

"Ladies and gentlemen of the Press. I know you've been assigned to gather as much information as you can. However, given recent events and the number of interviews young Mr. Powers has already done, I'm sure you understand our need to move expeditiously. So, we will not provide any further comments at this time. Thank you for your understanding."

As Chasm motions for the group to move towards the exits, several of his private security guards step out of the crowd and clear a path. Once outside, they find Chasm's assistant, Erica, standing in front of three black sedans. Curtis notices her long flowing hair and lack of glasses.

"Curtis!" Erica beams as she steps forward and hugs him tightly. "I wasn't sure I'd see you again." Kelly raises her eyebrow at Erica's remark as Curtis returns her hug—quite hesitantly—with a loose embrace.

"It's good to see you," he nervously mumbles. "Where are your glasses?"

"I've got contacts. Which do you like better? Glasses or no glasses?"

Curtis can see Kelly's expression out of the corner of his eye—and it's not a good one.

Moments later, the sedans drive away with their occupants and precious cargo. In the first sedan, Chasm and Erica talk business. In the second sedan, Mr. Grabowski and Gavin talk physics. In the third sedan, Curtis and Kelly sit quietly. Curtis is lost in his thoughts as he gazes out the tinted windows. His cell phone rings.

"Hello? Hey mom. Yeah, we're back. On our way to campus now. I miss you, too. Yes, I'll call you later. Bye." Curtis hangs up his phone as Kelly gazes at him.

"My mom says 'hi.'"

Kelly smiles. "You know that Erica seems like a *real* hottie—in a nerdy kind of way."

"Really?" Curtis feigns ignorance. "I hadn't noticed."

Kelly sits up and looks at Curtis. "You *haven't* noticed?" she asks flatly.

Curtis throws his hands up in surrender and cracks a smile. "Ok, maybe I *have* noticed."

"Maybe?"

"Ok, I give up! I've noticed," Curtis confesses. "She's cute."

"She's *hot*," Kelly counters.

"Ok! She's hot—*really* hot," Curtis concedes. "There! It's out in the open. We have now named the elephant in the room!"

Kelly sits quietly and smiles. "I have no problem with you noticing beauty, Curtis."

Curtis looks at her confused.

"After all," she continues, "you did notice *me*, right?"

Curtis smiles from ear to ear. "Absolutely. And for the record, I don't deliberately think about her."

"So, you think about her?"

"That's *not* what I meant!" Curtis exclaims.

"I know," Kelly laughs. "But I do know, from the way she hugged you, that she *deliberately* thinks about you."

"You think so?"

"Well," Kelly muses, "you *are* smart, handsome, extremely gifted and a gentleman. What woman wouldn't be attracted to those qualities? But you make sure you let her know that you are taken."

"I already made that clear to her."

"Well, make sure it's *crystal* clear," Kelly counters. "And for the record, she's not the elephant in the room." Kelly rubs his hand softly. "Something else is on your mind."

Curtis pulls his hand away and turns back towards the tinted windows in silence.

Kelly slowly takes his hand again and moves closer to him. "You can tell me... What's wrong?"

"Maybe... everything."

"What do you mean?"

"I haven't... I haven't slept much. When I close my eyes, I keep seeing a loaded gun pointed at my head. You know Justin and Amanda are only a few years younger than we are. Bullied for years... facing an impossible situation."

"But everyone's alive because of you. Because *you* were there."

"But what happens now?" Curtis looks into Kelly's eyes intently. "Do I just... go back to taking classes while kids in schools across the country are bullied? I thought Treyshawn was intense. But what Justin and Amanda went through..." Curtis' voice trails off as he looks away.

"You found the solution to your bullying situation," Kelly consoles, "and now *everyone* is better off because of it."

"That's what I'm saying!" Curtis huffs. "Maybe I'm *supposed* to help find a solution. And maybe that solution... won't be found while I'm *sitting* in a classroom."

"Curtis, are you saying you're going to quit school?"

"I don't know what I'm saying," Curtis replies solemnly. "While I'm in class, kids' lives are being destroyed. I just feel like I should *do* more. But I don't know what *more* is."

"Well, here's what I do know," Kelly declares confidently as Curtis looks at her. "Your Speedsuit may have gotten you into that situation with Justin and Amanda, but it was your heart and mind that got you out. So, before you do anything drastic, you need to think things through."

On Campus...

Curtis and Kelly embrace next to their sedan as the drivers unload the luggage.

"I'll talk to you later?" Kelly asks.

"You bet," Curtis assures. "Thanks for meeting me at the airport. I really needed that."

She kisses him. "You would have done the same for me." With a smile, she turns and gets back into the sedan. "See you all later!" she yells.

"Bye Kelly!" they respond. As Kelly is driven away, Curtis, Gavin and Mr. Grabowski make their way from the sedans to the dormitory. A crowd of students begins to gather.

"I think I forgot something in the car." Mr. Grabowski turns around. "Be right back."

Many students congratulate Curtis, while others inquire about the details of the incident. Within the crowd is upperclassman Peter Broadman, the teacher's assistant for several of Curtis' professors.

"Well if it isn't the famous Curtis Powers," Peter blasts sarcastically, as he approaches.

"Not now," Curtis says as he passes him.

Peter blocks the path. The crowd grows quiet.

Peter eagerly breaks the silence. "Your stupid track suit on steroids wasn't enough, huh? So, you had to go and be a glory hog too?"

"Are you serious?" Gavin yells angrily. "People almost died!"

"That's right," Peter concurs sarcastically. "But the *great* Curtis Powers saved the day."

"You don't even like me," Curtis responds. "Why are you wasting your breath talking?"

"Because I want you to know that everyone isn't going to fall all over you and bow at your feet just because you expect them to do so," Peter retorts.

"I don't expect them to do anything," Curtis counters. "But let me tell you what I think. You don't even know me, but you're mad at me because of your own feelings of inadequacy."

"You don't know what you're talking about," Peter snaps.

"Yeah? Before I came to this school, *you* were the big man on campus."

"That's right I was!" Peter shouts back.

"But I'm not trying to take your place. I don't want to be you. I'm just me. So don't blame me for things not working out the way you wanted them to in your own life."

"How dare you..."

"How dare me?" Curtis retorts. "I've never done a bad thing to you, but you're the one who keeps verbally attacking me every chance you get! You may be an upperclassman, but I'm not going to let you push me around."

"You're talking big with this crowd around." Peter invades Curtis' personal space. "I could make your life very difficult around here."

"You could," Curtis responds without flinching, "but I'm not your enemy."

"Besides," a voice booms from just beyond the crowd, "you don't want to be an enemy of Curtis Powers, Peter." The crowd parts to reveal Chasm, Erica and Jim standing nearby. Peter's expression changes from an arrogance-fueled anger to a cowardly fright. "Chasm!"

Chasm slowly walks towards the center of the confrontation, making sure everyone hears him. "If you were an enemy of Curtis... since he is under *my* tutelage... then you would be my enemy."

"Chasm, I'm... I'm sorry," Peter averts his eyes to the ground.

"It would seem that you have allowed your former position with me to go to your head," Chasm says firmly. "From this point forward, Peter, you will address me as Mr. Montgomery. And if you wish to remain a student at this school or be a student at any other, you best rein in that temper and do *more* than be sorry."

"Yes, Mr. Montgomery," Peter quickly replies.

"Now, be a good fellow student and carry Curtis and Gavin's bags to their room. Going forward, if I even suspect a hint of animosity on your part, your life here will become very difficult."

"Understood, Sir." Peter backs away from Chasm, slowly grabs the luggage and proceeds to follow Curtis and Gavin to their room amidst the snickers and cheers from the students.

Later that night...

Curtis stares down the barrel of a loaded gun. The muzzle fires! Curtis wakes in a cold sweat, yelling as he looks around wildly. A moment passes as his heaving chest relaxes. Gavin's loud snoring fills the room.

Curtis wipes the sweat from his brow and crawls from his bed to his desk. As he turns on his desk lamp and pulls his father's journal from one of the desk drawers, his eyes focus on Gavin's limp frame and gaping mouth. *He sleeps like a log!* He thinks to himself while shaking his head. As he returns his focus to the journal, he leafs through the pages until coming across a title that catches his attention: *Our Greatest Opportunity.*

Curtis,

Sometimes in life... necessity is laid upon us. It's not something that we seek after and pursue, but it pursues us. It may be something we don't want. It may be something we have never expected. But often times, what was meant to destroy us could lead to our greatest opportunity. And the greatest men and women who have ever lived—both famous and unknown—are not those who were the most talented or who had the most wealth. The greatest people who live are those who are confronted by a desperate need, and, though they might want to ignore it or run from it, they refuse to turn their eyes away. They sit at the table of necessity, with all the utensils at their disposal, and eat what is served.

Popular wisdom would say that you discover your passion and then pursue it. But life doesn't always work that way. Sometimes you have to pursue a need that you have been confronted with… and that need becomes your passion. Your talents alone are merely indicators of possibilities. Your creativity and intelligence will help open doors of opportunity. But your greatest power comes from your ability to serve those around you who are in need. It is your character (good or bad) that will make the greatest impact on the world.

I don't know what you are doing at this point in your life. I don't know what struggles you may be facing. I wish I could be there with you to help guide you. But what I do know is that God has given you the ability to make a difference in the lives of others. And that difference can be multiplied when you do what you can do, while working with other like-minded individuals.

There is an African proverb: "If you want to go fast, go alone. But if you want to go far, go together."

God has no problem with you being great, Curtis. His problem is when we think that our greatness makes us better than others. So, BE GREAT, SON! Welcome necessity! And do what only you can do so you can inspire others to the greatness that is waiting for them to discover in their own lives.

I will always love you,

Malcolm
Your Father.

Curtis leans over the journal while thinking, *This can't be coincidence.* He rereads the letter, again. As he finishes, his cell phone rings.

"Hello?"

"Curtis. This is Chasm. I just wanted to see how you were doing. You've been through a lot these past few days."

"Yeah. Thanks, Mr. Montgomery."

"Are you having problems sleeping?"

"How did you know?"

"My boy, you stared down the barrel of an assault rifle. And it's *late*, but your voice shows no sign of grogginess. I simply put two and two together."

"I'm exhausted, but I haven't slept more than 20 minutes at a time since the shootings."

"Your mind is still experiencing the trauma," Chasm responds knowingly.

"I can't seem to shake the emotions of that moment."

"And how *did* you feel?"

"I was terrified! When I stepped out from around that corner and stood in front of Justin and Amanda, it was like I was facing death."

"But you kept engaging," Chasm probes.

"I had to."

"No," Chasm counters. "You could have run away. And with your Speedsuit, no one would have caught you."

"My parents didn't raise me like that. They didn't train me to run away when I knew there was something I could do to help."

"So, you kept moving forward," Chasm concedes. "What else were you thinking?"

"Besides dying?" Curtis asks sarcastically. "I figured I had the best possibility of talking them down because of my past bullying experience."

"And it appears you were right," Chasm agrees. "They are *all* alive because of you."

"I never prayed so hard in my life!" Curtis laughs.

"I'm not a proponent of prayer," Chasm states flatly. "Making a difference has more to do with a person's analysis, strategy and execution in the midst of a situation, than with receiving guidance or intervention from some supposed deity in the sky."

"I can see why many people feel that way..." Curtis says.

"I'm sorry for inadvertently diverting this conversation from finding a remedy to your sleeplessness," Chasm admits. "Your comment about prayer… took me by surprise."

"Well, I think there's room for intellect *and* prayer," Curtis replies. "Especially when we encounter situations that are beyond our control."

"Since it's late," Chasm says a bit curtly, "let's just agree to disagree."

"That works for me," Curtis responds nonchalantly.

"If you *want* to go to sleep," Chasm adds, "don't open your eyes when those images appear. Keep your eyes closed and face what you see. You've already lived through the situation, so you know how everything ends."

"You know," Curtis smiles, "I didn't think about that."

"I know," Chasm responds. "Sleep well."

With that, the call ends. Curtis lays his phone on top of his father's journal and lies down on his bed again. He takes a deep breath and slowly exhales through his mouth.

"Lord, thank you for that remedy," he whispers. "Help me to sleep well." Curtis turns off his desk light and slowly closes his eyes. The images begin to appear in his mind's eye as feelings of inadequacy rise up within him. He forces his eyes to remain closed. And as he faces his fears, he says to himself, "I already know how the story ends..." Minutes later, Curtis is sound asleep.

Chapter Seventeen

Homecoming

THE SUN SLOWLY SETS IN A golden-orange hue as the smell of roasted lamb, mashed potatoes, cornbread, collard greens and sweet potato pie fill the air. Thanksgiving has arrived again, and a black sedan, with government plates, arrives in front of Miranda Powers' residence. The driver exits the vehicle, opens the trunk and retrieves a wheelchair. He opens the chair and rolls it to the back passenger door. Omar opens the door and swivels his body as he prepares to get into the chair. The driver motions to help him.

"It's OK. I got it," Omar responds. In a couple of fluid motions, Omar moves from the car to the chair. The driver grabs Omar's blue duffle bag and straps it over the back of his chair. They both salute each other and exchange a handshake. Omar grasps the sides of the wheels, turns his chair towards the front of the house and rolls from the street to the sidewalk.

Suddenly, the front door bursts opens as Miranda bolts out of the house towards her son.

"Omar!" She swings the yard gate open and all-but-jumps into his chair! Omar lets out a hearty belly laugh as he embraces his mother with his strong, chiseled arms.

"I missed you, Son!"

"I missed you too, Ma!"

"Let's get you inside. Your homecoming meal is ready!"

"Thanks," Omar smiles widely. "I smelled it as soon as the car door opened!"

As Omar and Miranda approach the front door, they see a box next to the doorstep.

"Is that yours?" Omar asks.

"No," Miranda responds, "That wasn't there earlier." She looks at the address label. "It's from Chasm Montgomery. And it's for me?" She and Omar look at each other as she struggles to pick it up. "It's... heavy."

Once inside, they stare at the box as it sits on the table in the living room.

"What do you think is in there," Miranda asks.

"Open it up and see," Omar responds.

Miranda takes a pair of scissors and cuts the box open. She pulls back the lid and gasps.

"What is it, Ma?"

She peels back several layers of colorful, high quality wrapping paper, which reveals a well-adorned Thanksgiving gift basket. On top of the basket is a card, which reads:

Miranda,

As we celebrate this time of Thanksgiving, I wanted you to know that I am very thankful for you allowing me to be a mentor to your son. Please enjoy this gift basket. I am looking forward to seeing you again, soon.

With Warm Regards,

Chasm Montgomery

"Who talks like that?" Omar asks sarcastically. "'With warm regards.'"

"Apparently, Chasm Montgomery does," Miranda chuckles. "It is a nice gift. That was very thoughtful of him. I will have to call to say thank you."

"I'm sure that's what he wants."

"What do you mean?"

"A handsome man with wealth. A single, attractive woman."

"Omar, please. I'm sure it's not like that."

"Maybe not, but you never know."

"Well, why don't you take your deductive reasoning with you and go get ready for dinner. I made your favorite meal."

"Alright! I am starving."

Miranda watches Omar roll towards the bathroom and then looks back at the card and the gift basket, with a slight smile.

"'With warm regards…'"

After dinner...

"Ma, this was the best meal I've had in a long time," Omar wipes his mouth as his mother takes his plate to the kitchen.

"Thank you! I know meals from the military can't compare to your mother's cooking."

"You got *that* right," Omar laughs.

Miranda walks back over and looks at her son's face. "It's *good* to have you home."

"It's good to *be* home," Omar beams. "And I can't wait to see everyone in a few days."

"Now that you're in the wheelchair," Miranda says softly, "Jim and I were wondering if we should have Thanksgiving dinner over at his house again, since he has more room."

"Our house *is* kinda small, Ma. The extra space will be good."

"So, it's settled then," Miranda says between lively hand claps. "We'll celebrate Thanksgiving at Jim's! It'll be great to have all of our families together."

"So, how are *you* doing Ma?" Omar asks solemnly.

"I'm doing alright." Miranda hesitates slightly as she sits on the couch.

"And the bills?" Omar probes.

Miranda runs her hand through her hair. "Thanks for sending what you can every month. And the money from Curtis' Speedsuit events definitely helps."

"But we still have a lot of debt left," Omar states knowingly.

"We're managing," Miranda replies softly, "even though my business degree seems useless in helping me get more revenue."

"I still don't understand how dad's life insurance policy could have been canceled like that," Omar huffs. "If we had *that*, we wouldn't be in this mess."

"True," Miranda tries to maintain an even keel in her response. "But, like you said, we just try and take things one day at a time."

Later that night...

Omar tosses and turns on the couch. While partially awake, he hears the sound of footsteps and hushed talking. He forces himself awake and remains motionless in an effort to hear and identify the sounds. *Are we being robbed?* He thinks to himself. A moment later the voice becomes clear. *It's Ma!* He looks at the clock. "Who is she on the phone with at 2:30 a.m.?" he mumbles to himself before trying to go back to sleep.

In the morning...

Omar awakes to the smell of homemade waffles, turkey sausage, eggs and hash browns. He rolls his wheelchair into the kitchen and finds his mother making his plate.

"Rise and shine, sleepy head," she utters cheerfully.

"Wow, Ma. I didn't expect this."

"I wanted to surprise you!"

"You're in a good mood." He moves over to the kitchen table.

Miranda smiles as she places the plate and syrup in front of him on the table.

"My eldest son is home," she smiles. "That's a good reason to be grateful. Now let me get my plate and we can eat together."

As they eat, Omar comments. "Ma, I woke up this morning at 2:30 a.m. and you were talking to someone on the phone."

"Are you sure?" She feigns ignorance. "Maybe you were dreaming."

"No, I wasn't."

"No, you weren't," she smiles. "I *was* on the phone."

"You're not going to tell me with who?"

"I didn't know I *had* to tell you."

"Ok," Omar says as he places a forkful of food in his mouth. Miranda takes advantage of the silence and places a forkful of food in her mouth as well.

"Are you and Mr. Grabowski seeing each other?" Omar blurts out.

Miranda almost chokes on her food. "Omar!" She tries to gain her composure. "The relationship Jim and I have is one of mutual friendship. Nothing more, OK?"

"Look, I don't have a problem if you and Mr. Grabowski *are* seeing each other."

"We are *not* seeing each other, Omar!"

"It doesn't matter if he's almost twenty years your senior."

"Omar! I am *not* in a relationship with Jim Grabowski!"

"I mean, Curtis would probably be happy. I would be happy, too."

"Omar," Miranda interjects forcefully. "Read my lips. I am not in a romantic relationship with Jim Grabowski."

"Ma," Omar responds, "It's OK. I think dad would approve. And we just want you to be happy."

"I *am* happy!" Miranda huffs. "And once again, Jim and I are *not* in a relationship."

"Ok," Omar says, a bit nonchalantly. "No need to get bent out of shape." He eats another forkful of food. "Are you going to tell him about the gift basket from Mr. Montgomery?"

Miranda looks at her son while shaking her head. "I can't believe you."

"Forget it, Ma. You don't have to answer that. But answer this. Have you ever *thought* about being in a relationship with Mr. Grabowski?"

"That, young man, is none of your business."

"So you *have* thought about it," Omar exclaims while pointing at his mother.

Miranda laughs as she rests her head in her hands and takes a deep breath. "Of course the thought has crossed my mind. Jim is kind, caring, smart and funny. And he gets along very well with you and Curtis. What widowed mother wouldn't think about the possibility? But again, Jim and I are just friends. Ok?"

"Ok. I won't mention it again."

"Good," Miranda says sharply.

They both finish their glasses of milk in silence while pretending not to watch each other.

"So, who were you talking to on the phone?" Omar probes.

"Omar," Miranda yells before calming herself. "All I can say is that I was talking with a former colleague who is helping me with a project. Alright?

That is *all* I can tell you. This subject is now closed to further discussion." Miranda gets up from the table and takes her dishes to the sink. She then comes and grabs Omar's dishes.

"Wait, Ma! I wasn't done—"

"Oh, yes you are!"

"But I was going to eat another couple of waffles!"

"Oh, no you aren't!"

Omar laughs at the situation. "Ok, Ma. You win."

"I know I win. That's what mothers do." Miranda clears the table and begins putting the extra food away. Omar watches her for a moment before asking one final question.

"Do you think Mr. Grabowski has thought about you, too?"

Later that day...

Jim and Miranda stand anxiously in the baggage area at LaGuardia Airport. Miranda slightly paces back and forth. "I can't wait to see my baby,"

"The plane just landed a few minutes ago," Jim replies with a smile. Minutes later, Curtis and Kelly descend on the escalator and arrive in the baggage area.

"There's my baby!" Miranda breaks into a run and throws herself into his arms.

"Mom!" Curtis laughs as he drops his carryon bags in order to catch his mother.

"My baby is finally home!" Miranda gives her son hugs and kisses. Kelly laughs at the sight, as Jim makes his way over to the group.

"It's great to see you, Mom!" Curtis gives her a big bear hug.

"It's good to see you again, Kelly," Jim says enthusiastically.

"You too, Mr. Grabowski," Kelly replies as she gives him a hug.

They both turn to Curtis and Miranda. "You'd think they hadn't seen each other in twenty years," Jim remarks while pointing at them with his thumb.

"Yeah," Kelly laughs.

Miranda pulls away from Curtis and faces them. "Sorry Kelly." She gives her a long hug. "It's just that this is the first time I'm seeing my baby since the school shooting."

Kelly returns her hug. "I know Ms. Powers. *That* was a tough situation." Miranda pulls back from Kelly while grasping her shoulders with her hands, "It's *really* good to see you. And I'm glad you were there to meet Curtis when he came back from the Midwest."

"Curtis," Jim extends his hand, "it's good to see you." Their handshake turns into a hug.

"I feel like we just saw each other a few weeks ago," Curtis jokes.

"We did," Jim laughs. After a few moments of small talk, the group gathers their luggage and exits the terminal.

"Thanks for giving me a lift home," Kelly says to Miranda and Jim as they all walk to the car.

"Not a problem, Kelly," Jim smiles.

"With both of your parents at work, it's the least we can do," Miranda adds. "After all, you're a part of the family."

"So, how's Omar?" Curtis asks excitedly. His mother's eyes meet his with a solemn expression.

"Curtis," Miranda takes a deep breath. "Your brother… on his aircraft carrier… he was injured."

"What!" Curtis shouts, unable to hide his alarm. "What kind of injury? Why didn't you tell me?"

Miranda looks at her son and forces a smile. "We didn't want to worry you, so we figured we'd wait until you came home."

"Why would you do that?" Curtis replies emphatically.

Miranda takes a step back, crosses her arms, cocks her head to one side and says, "Who was the *last* person to find out that you were being bullied by Treyshawn?"

Curtis stands in silence.

"*Uh, huh*," Miranda shakes her head. "It was *me*. Everybody else knew… but me!"

Jim and Kelly look away into the distance while slowly moving back.

"You didn't want to worry *me*. We didn't want to worry *you*."

Curtis lowers his head. "Sorry Mom."

Miranda looks at her son—her attitude melting away in mere seconds as she steps towards him, cupping his chin with her hands. "That's OK, baby." She smiles deeply without breaking her gaze. "Let's go home and see your brother."

Powers' Residence...

Curtis opens the door and runs in—followed by his mother and Kelly.

"Omar!" Curtis runs into the living room and stops by the couch. "Mom... why is there an empty wheelchair here?"

The toilet flushes. A moment later, the bathroom door opens and Curtis and Kelly watch in unexpected horror as Omar crawls from the bathroom to the couch. He turns and looks at them.

"Hey Guys."

"Omar!" Curtis shouts as Kelly bursts into tears. Miranda tries to hold back her own tears as Curtis runs over to his brother and starts to help him get onto the couch.

"Hold on, Curtis." Omar balances himself on one arm and holds out the other to stop him. "I can do this on my own."

"But I'm here!" Curtis interjects. "Let me help you!"

In a few swift moves, Omar turns over and climbs onto the couch. As he repositions his legs, he looks at his brother. "I appreciate what you're trying to do, little bro. I would have done the same thing if you were in this chair, but I've been having to go to the bathroom like this for the past month."

Curtis straightens his stance and collects himself, before forcing a slight smile. "Well, it's a good thing your upper body is so strong." He gives Omar a long hug.

"Don't worry." Omar chuckles. "The doctors say my injury is temporary. I should be walking again at some point... Already starting to get some feeling back in my legs."

Omar turns and looks at Kelly. "So, how's my brother treating you?" he smiles.

Kelly forces a smile and gives Omar a hug. "Besides giving me a scare with the school shooting a few weeks ago... not bad."

Omar looks at his brother and then back at Kelly. "You know, I didn't hear about that until I got back to the States. Last thing I wanted to do while in the hospital was watch television." Omar extends his hand to Curtis who reaches out and grasps it. "That was a good thing you did, little bro. I know you were probably scared out your mind, but you demonstrated courage. And courage is about doing what's right... *especially* when you are afraid."

"Thanks for the encouragement," Curtis smiles. "So... tell me what happened to you."

For the next hour, Omar recounts the events, which led to his injury and the steps he has already taken on the road to recovery.

Two hours later, Kelly arrives home to the smell of chicken roasting in the oven.

"Mom? Dad?" No response. She walks up the stairs to a dark living room and looks around. "Where *is* everybody?"

"Surprise!!!" The lights flick on as Kelly's mother, father and brothers jump from behind the couches. Kelly jumps back with a start and screams hysterically! They all laugh at her reaction.

"You guys!" She laughs. "That's not funny! You almost gave me a heart attack!"

"Mom knows C.P.R." Kevin says, as he walks over and gives his little sister a big bear hug. "We missed you, Kelly."

Kelvin is next in line as he hugs his sister. "Glad to finally see you, Sis!"

Her father gives her a long hug and a kiss on her forehead, "My baby girl is home!"

Lastly, her mother stands silently with her hand over her mouth, slightly shaking her head. "Three months away and you already look so grown up!"

"Mom..." Kelly smiles as she walks over and embraces her.

"So," her father says once the hug is over, "how's college life?"

Kelly hesitates, "It's... great."

"Hold up," Kelvin says. "Yeah," Kevin adds, "you hesitated."

Kelly glances down before forcing a smile.

"Kelly," her mother and father say at the same time. "Is this about your roommate, Clamille?" her mother asks. "I thought that was getting better."

Kelly breathes deeply before throwing her hands up in a huff, "We *are* getting along better. And college is great... except for Clamille's boyfriend—Tyreese."

"Did he do something to you?" her father asks protectively.

"No… But he was abusing her."

"Oh, no," her mother responds.

"I finally confronted her about it and she agreed to get some help," Kelly sits on the couch. "Then Tyreese noticed the change in her behavior and confronted me."

"Did he hit you?" Kevin asks heatedly.

"Oh, man," Kelvin adds, "now we gotta make a trip to your school."

"He didn't hit me," Kelly says, "but he did make it clear that something could happen to me if I didn't mind my business."

"Ok, we're *definitely* going down to your school," Kevin and Kelvin say in unison.

"Now boys," their father interrupts, while raising his hands to calm them down, "let's not do something rash."

"Dad," Kevin replies, "if we do nothing and something happens to Kelly, we won't be there to protect her."

"I'm not saying we don't do anything," their father interjects, "I'm just saying we should think through the ways in which we *can* act. Let's look at all of the options and then determine a course of action."

"Does anyone else know about this?" their mom asks.

"No. I didn't even tell Curtis yet," Kelly responds. "I didn't want him to worry."

"Well he's the closest one of us you got down there," Kelvin counters. "So you need to tell him."

"Before you do that," their father adds, "we need a plan."

The next day...

Treyshawn unlocks the front door and runs into the house.

"Ma! I'm home!" He drops his bags and runs through the small single-family dwelling.

"Ma?" he says while looking around. Silence greets him. As he sniffs, he notices a faint smell of food in the air. Treyshawn walks into the kitchen and finds a solitary piece of paper folded in the center of the table. He picks it up. It reads:

Treyshawn. I am SO glad you are home! Sorry I missed you! The diner called with a shift that opened up. We need the money, so I couldn't turn it down. I made you some dinner. (Actually, I brought you a meal from work… You know I can't cook!) It's in the oven. I don't get off till after 2am. See you in the morning.

Love,
Mom

Treyshawn holds the paper in his hand for a moment and then places it on the table. He opens the oven and pulls out the foil covered plate, grabs a fork and knife and sits down at the table. He smiles as he unwraps the plate and sees a juicy hamburger and fries with a few ketchup packets on the side. He looks at everything and thinks about the very first time his mother ever cooked a meal for him. The first time she ever told him she was sorry. He smiles at the memory triggered by the similar sight before him and begins to eat. A hamburger and fries never tasted so good.

Chapter Eighteen
Past Life

IT'S 3:30 A.M. A TIRED SHAKIRA STANDS in the doorway of her son's room. Light from the hallway streams past Shakira's frame and illuminates her view. She stands with a weary smile as she looks at her son who lies across his bed in a deep sleep. A moment passes before she slowly closes his door and prepares to go to sleep.

Morning time...

Sunlight streaks through the window as Shakira wakes up to the smell of eggs, waffles, bacon and coffee. As she makes her way from her bedroom to the kitchen, she's astonished to see her son at the stove.

"Trey," she mumbles.

Treyshawn turns, looks at his mother and chuckles. "Morning, Ma. I like what you've done with your hair." Shakira turns to a nearby mirror and sees her unkempt hair.

"Yeah, well... It's not everyday that I wake up to the smell of breakfast. And good morning to you, too."

"Sit down, Ma. Food is ready."

"Since when do you cook," Shakira almost shrieks while taking her seat at the table.

"I am a man of *many* talents," Treyshawn smiles back.

"Apparently," she responds.

Treyshawn makes his mother's plate and places it in front of her. He also pours her a cup of coffee and puts it on the table. He then quickly makes his plate and joins her. Shakira smiles while taking hold of her son's hand.

"Thank you, baby."

"You're welcome, Ma."

From her first bite, Shakira immediately notices the quality of the food. "Wow, Treyshawn!" She exclaims, her eyes bulging. "This is *really* good."

"Thanks," he smiles.

She chews another forkful and continues her line of thought. "Tastes almost like the breakfast... from the diner... *down* the street." She looks around the kitchen as Treyshawn tries to maintain his composure.

"This *is* from the diner isn't it?" Shakira asks as she spies the diner bag partially sticking out of the trashcan.

"You got me!" Treyshawn replies while holding up his hands in surrender.

"But you *told* me you knew how to cook!"

Treyshawn laughs. "You said you didn't *know* I knew how to cook. I simply said 'I'm a man of many talents.' But I would have told you... eventually."

Shakira laughs. "Well, you sure know how to heat up some food in a pan."

"Thank you." Treyshawn nods in her direction with the attitude of a diplomat.

"Speaking of talents," his mother continues, "How's college?"

"First couple of months was tough." Treyshawn gulps down a glass of milk and wipes the excess from his mouth with the back of his hand. "But things are better now."

"It's *a lot* different out in California." Shakira says matter-of-factly.

"Who you tellin?" Treyshawn agrees. "But I'm adjustin'. Wait. You've been to Cali?"

"Long time ago." Shakira takes another bite of her food. "I am so proud of you, Trey... you are the first in the family to go to college."

"Ma, you told me that already."

"I know. But you're doing what none of my immediate family has been able to do." Shakira contemplates her own words as she remembers a conversation from her past. "Actually," she says softly, "*I* was supposed to be the first to break that cycle and go to college."

"Well, now you can be the second." Treyshawn declares with a twinkle in his eyes.

"To go to college?" Shakira blurts out.

"Sure," Treyshawn laughs. "Why not?"

Shakira explodes into a fit of uncontrollable laughter. "Imagine me... in college..."

Treyshawn smiles in his chair while his mother laughs. She looks at him. "You're serious!"

"You should do it, Ma," he smiles.

Shakira looks at her son in bewilderment. "Trey, I'm too old to be startin' college."

Treyshawn smirks. "There's a grandmother in some of my classes, doin' college for the first time. She's in her sixties. So, if it's not too late for her, it's not too late for you."

Shakira quietly looks at her son with a mixture of resistance and admiration.

"So, you're *Mr. Motivation* now?" she quips, sarcastically.

"Nah, I'm just me, Ma."

"Yes, you are." She smiles as she slowly leans across the table. "You keep being you, Ok? You keep fighting to make your life better. You hear me?"

"I hear you." Treyshawn smiles.

"Good. Cause when you work to make your life better, you force *everyone* around you to make decisions about their own lives."

"So, you goin' to apply to college?" Treyshawn asks excitedly.

"Slow your roll, Ok?" Shakira chuckles nervously. "One thing at a time."

"So, you'll think about it?"

"That's better," Shakira mumbles through a deep breath. "I'll *think* about it."

"Ok, cool." Treyshawn smiles.

"But there is something I want to do." Shakira leans back in her chair.

"What's that?" Treyshawn asks—his tone laced with curiosity.

"I wanna answer your question from before... and tell you about my past."

1990. South Carolina.

"'Kira! You are making a *big* mistake," Shakira's mother shouts as she rushes down the hall towards the front door. "If you walk out that door don't you *ever* come back!"

170

Shakira stops in the opened doorway with the screen knob in her hand. Her mind is reeling as her mother's southern drawl weighs almost as heavily as the words themselves. She turns sharply and faces her mother—her flowing tears evident.

"I told you when I graduated from high school I'd be gone, Ma!"

"Shakira Antwanet Rollins," her mother yells in a tone just as fierce, but layered with a fraught disappointment, "this is *not* God's plan for you."

"How do you know, Mama?" Shakira shouts back. "I love him!"

Her mother's head snaps back dismissively. "He's a grown man you just met a few months ago! Show'd you some attention at the State talent show—flashed his card, some money and a big title. Says he's gonna make you a star... Baby all he gonna do is use you!"

"No, Mama!" Shakira cries. "He loves me for me!"

In the silent moment between words, Lucinda Rollins' expression softens as she gazes into the eyes of her only daughter and sees the evidence of her hurt and pain.

"Baby... he only wants to use you to make him some money."

"No," Shakira turns away.

Lucinda grabs her daughter's arm softly and turns her back around. "He wants that beautiful voice of yours—that gift from God—even your father recognized it before he died."

"Don't you bring daddy into this!" Shakira interrupts. "Why do you *always* try to use him against me?" She whimpers.

"Baby, your daddy and I were married for 14 years." Lucinda's eyes fill with tears as she thinks about her deceased husband. "I *loved* that man... and he loved you. But you don't *remember* him like I do. So, I simply tell you what I believe he would say." Lucinda raises her hands to her daughter's face and plants them sweetly on her cheeks.

"He wanted the best for you—only the best—even till his last breath. And what you are fittin' to do is *not* the best."

"This is *my* life to live, Mama!" Shakira brushes her mother's hands away. "And daddy died at a gas station mini-mart while tryin' to get gas and some cigarettes!"

Lucinda's expression shifts from disappointment and compassion to anger as she quickly raises her right hand and brings it swiftly to bear on her daughter's face. SLAP! Her next words are spoken through quivering lips. "Your father died at a gas station mini-mart while tryin' to protect us!"

Shakira rubs her stinging cheek and struggles to hold back the resulting tears. "What you mean, Mama?"

Lucinda steps back a few paces. "I never told you the *whole* story 'Kira. It was too painful."

1975. 15 years earlier.

Ding. Ding. Ding. Ding. Ding. White numbers on black backgrounds rise in their display housing as the repetitive sound of the dispenser chimes in rhythm.

"Gas prices keep going up, Lucinda. At this rate we'll hit $0.60 cents soon. Cost me a whole $10.00 to fill up the tank!"

A tired, coughing Elton Rollins replaces the gas nozzle and closes the gas tank on his 1974 Oldsmobile Cutlass Supreme. He then wipes the pooling sweat from his forehead.

"Been here all my life and still don't like this heat," he mumbles to himself. "'Cinda," he calls to the car, "I'm gonna get me some cigarettes."

"You know I don't like you smoking anywhere near our babygirl!" Lucinda calls back from the car.

"You remind me *every* time." Elton rolls his eyes. "You know my job is rigorous. Cigarettes help with the stress is all."

"Jesus can ease your stress," she counters. "And without all those bad side effects."

Elton looks at his wife and smiles. "You right, baby." He walks over, kisses her and looks at Shakira asleep in the back seat. "I'm gonna stop soon. I promise."

"Hm, mm," she smirks. "Christmas is coming, too."

They both laugh.

"Let me go pay for this gasoline." Elton makes his way to the station. As he enters, he sees a man leaning against the far side of the building— nervously looking around.

"Call the cops will ya?" Elton says to Joseph—the attendant, "there's a guy out back—"

"Nobody move! Gimme the money! Now!"

Elton and Joseph turn towards the direction of the voice, as the front door bursts open and a man enters with a gun!

"Sure thing, buddy," Joseph concedes. "Ain't no reason to get violent."

"Don't try to smooth-talk me!" the man yells. "There's *always* a reason to get violent!" He throws a bag at the attendant. "The money. Now!"

Elton keeps his arms up, as he focuses on his family outside and then back to the gunman.

"What you looking at?" the gunman yells as he rushes over to Elton and puts the gun in his face. "You studyin' me?"

"No, brother," Elton replies calmly.

"I'm *not* your brother!"

"Ok, friend."

"I'm not your friend, either!"

"Ok. No problem. Just be cool."

The gunman studies Elton's eyes. "Gimme your wallet." Elton hands his wallet over to the gunman. "It's cool man… Only money."

"And gimme your car keys."

"Listen," Elton's tone moves from cool to serious. "You can have my car, but let my family get out of it first."

The gunman smiles a sly grin. "You mean that lovely wife of yours sittin' in the front seat? And that baby girl sleeping in the back? How old is she? About three? Maybe four?"

Elton clenches his fists while trying to keep calm. "Just let them go and the car is yours."

"Maybe, I'll take your car *and* your family. Ain't got one of my own no more."

Elton snaps as he lunges at the gunman! "You ain't touchin my family!" He knocks the gun from the man's hand. It slides across the floor as they both exchange punches and kicks. Joseph pulls his shotgun out from underneath the counter and takes aim, but can't get a clear shot with Elton in the way. Both men leap for the gun on the floor.

Lucinda hears the commotion from the car and looks towards the station just in time to see the muzzle flash and hear the 'pop' of the gun discharging a single round.

BLAM!

Lucinda's body shudders at the sight and sound as her heart swells up with her worst fear. Inside the gas station, the struggle ceases. A second later the door flies open as the gunman runs out. Joseph quickly fires one round, which shatters the gunman's shoulder! The gunman cries out in pain, dropping his gun as he falls to the ground. He staggers back to his feet and disappears into the night. Joseph calls the police, as Elton stands to his feet and stumbles out of the station.

"Elton! Wait!" Joseph yells. "You've been shot!"

Lucinda watches as Elton exits the station and wobbles across the lot. Her body freezes as she hardly catches her breath. Only her eyes move—trained on her husband's steps—until he stops, looks at her with a painful smile and collapses into a motionless heap on the gas-stained cement. At that very moment, her body convulses as a gut-wrenching cry erupts from the pit of her stomach, rises up through her diaphragm and escapes her mouth at the speed of sound.

Shakira cries uncontrollably—scared awake by her mother's scream. Lucinda fumbles to open the car door and rushes to her husband's side. As she cradles his body, Joseph exits the station and runs over to them. "Help is comin'!"

Lucinda looks up at Joseph with desperate eyes and then down at Elton. She presses her hand hard over his bleeding wound.

"You don't get to leave me!" She glares through her tears into her husband's eyes.

"Shhhh," Elton whispers, "you and Shakira... are Ok... so everything's... Ok..."

"Elton," Lucinda whispers, "please, don't leave me. I don't know what to do without you."

Elton's pained smile turns into a solid frown. "Sorry... 'Cinda. You'll have to... figure things out on your own." Elton coughs a few times with increasing intensity. As his coughing quiets, he can hear his daughter's cries carry through the night air. "Bring her... to me."

Joseph runs over and gets Shakira from the car.

"She shouldn't see you like this!" Lucinda whimpers.

"It's Ok..." Elton replies. "This is the last time... I will see her."

Joseph brings Shakira to her mother, who holds her up in front of her father.

"Daddy!" Shakira cries, as she reaches out to him. He looks at his daughter with a smile, reaches up and takes her hands in his.

"Daddy... has to go away... babygirl. But, I... will always love you..." Elton turns back towards his wife. "At least... I can quit smoking now."

Lucinda crumbles over her husband as he whispers into her ear. "Take care of our daughter..." Tears stream down his cheeks.

"Elton?" Lucinda looks at her husband's face. His expression relaxes as he exhales his last. "Elton!!" Lucinda shakes him. "Elton!!!" With that... he's gone.

1995.

Shakira stands in the doorway. "I... I... remember."

"At some point," her mother whispers, "you blocked it out."

"Why would you let me block it out, Mama?" Shakira's voice scratches.

"I looked at it as a blessing."

"A blessing? I couldn't remember his face or what he said to me!"

"And you wouldn't remember the most painful moment of our lives!" Lucinda interjects. "Yes. I saw *that* as a blessing! Only I had to be burdened with the pain and suffering."

"But I was *still* in pain, Mama!" Shakira shouts. "Pain that daddy was dead! Pain that he died over some gas and a stupid pack of cigarettes!"

Shakira's grandmother steps into the hallway from the living room, and approaches the front door. Mama Rollins speaks with a soft authority that only a grandmother can possess.

"Kira, we're *all* in pain, baby." Mama Rollins places her hands on the shoulders of her daughter and granddaughter as she continues. "And if you walk out that door... you will continue to be in pain for the rest of your life. And your pain won't end until you come back home."

Shakira stands motionless, pensive, contemplating her past, present and future.

"You were *his* babygirl... Shakira," Mama Rollins says with a warm and full smile.

Shakira looks softly at her grandmother and then turns her gaze to her mother. Her mother stands quietly with steely eyes. In a moment's time, Shakira's softness gives way to her anger towards her mother.

"Mama Rollins, I can't stay a little girl forever." Shakira opens the front screen once more.

"Shakira," Lucinda says firmly, "if you walk out that door... and get caught up with that man... then don't expect *any* help from me."

"...Goodbye, Mama." Shakira walks out—letting the screen slam shut behind her. She marches defiantly to Treyshawn Sr.'s black Mercedes at the edge of the Rollin's property and never looks back.

Bronx. The Present.

Shakira sits quietly as Treyshawn looks at her from across the table.

"Wait. That's it?" Treyshawn asks.

"For now," Shakira replies.

"But what happened after you left?" Treyshawn says hurriedly, "When you got in the car? After you drove off? What was life like?"

"That's... another story for another time," Shakira says as she prepares to get up.

"Another time?" Treyshawn asks incredulously.

"Trey, I have to get ready for work."

"Ma' you sure know how to leave a brotha hanging."

"Hey!" she laughs.

"I'm just sayin'."

Shakira pauses for a moment as she looks away. "I never looked back," she states with a quiet agony. "I don't even know what their expressions were as I walked up the driveway and got into your father's car."

Treyshawn sits quietly with his head down.

"Now you see why I never told you."

Treyshawn slowly looks up at his mother. "You need to call her."

"What?"

"I want to meet my grandmother and my great grandmother. You need to call them."

"Trey, I haven't spoken to my mother since you were born. And even then she didn't want to have anything to do with me or you!"

"I get it. You're scared. But you gotta do this, Ma. Tomorrow's Thanksgiving. We all need this."

"Trey..." Shakira hesitates, "I wouldn't even know where to start..."

"You start," Treyshawn states firmly, "with a phone call..."

Chapter Nineteen

Blast from the Past

SEVERAL HOURS LATER, TREYSHAWN PREPARES TO go outside as he finishes up a phone conversation with Curtis. "Yo, I can't wait to see you and Kelly tomorrow! Everybody back together again! That's going to be funlarious! What? I know it's not a word. You said that last time. But you watch... The more I say it—the more it'll catch on! One day, everybody's gonna be saying it!" Treyshawn laughs. "Ok, bro. See you guys tomorrow."

Treyshawn puts his cell phone into his pocket, grabs his keys and heads out the door. Within minutes, he's lost in his thoughts as he walks down a familiar street. He watches people engaged in at-risk behavior and thinks, *wow, not much has changed.* This stretch of concrete jungle casts long shadows in the reddish-gold sunlight. *It's like the neighborhood is stuck in a time loop*, he thinks to himself, *destined to forever repeat the past with every generation.*

"We really are products of our environments," he says out loud as he considers how Curtis' help to change his environment forever affected his life. "How can I help others see that the world is bigger than this?" Treyshawn is so deep in thought that he doesn't realize someone is approaching him.

"What's up, Trey?" Treyshawn glances up and then jumps back into a defensive position. Melvin stands several feet in front of him. "Smelvin! What you want?"

"Whoa, whoa, whoa," Melvin throws up his hands. "I'm not here to fight. You wasn't lookin' for me—I wasn't lookin' for you—but here we are standin' in front of each other."

Treyshawn relaxes... slightly.

"Besides," Melvin smirks, "you couldn't beat me before, so what makes you think you can beat me now? Been a long time Trey."

"Apparently not long enough," Treshawn counters.

Melvin laughs. "Still mister funny man. Heard you in college now. Good for you."

"You keeping tabs on me?" Treyshawn clenches his fists.

"You *and* your mother." Melvins states flatly without smiling.

"Are you serious?" Treyshawn responds with a mixture of disbelief and anger.

Melvin laughs again. "Boy, I'm just kiddin', alright? I ain't been keepin' tabs on you or your mother. You know word gets around! Seriously, I only heard about it the other day!"

"You know you supposed to leave us alone!"

"Look, I just asked how you were doin'. That's all. The last time I saw you and your moms I said, 'I didn't want to go to jail.' And I still don't. Just tell Shakira I said, 'hey.'" Melvin starts to walk away, but Treyshawn blasts him.

"How do you expect me to act after everything you did to my moms? After everything you did to me? Now you expect me to be happy to see you? I ain't tellin my moms nothin'."

Melvin stops for a moment and faces Treyshawn. "You talkin' about almost three years ago, Trey. A lot can change—"

"And a lot can stay the same!" Treyshawn interjects. "You were with my moms for five years and nothin' changed! Not till she stood up to you!"

Melvin and Treyshawn exchange stares, as neither one looks away from the other. Treyshawn does notice that Melvin seems different. He can see it in his eyes, but he'll never admit it. What Melvin perceives in Treyshawn's eyes—behind the anger—is pain. It's a look he's seen before and had always exploited. But like he said, things are different now.

"Have you seen your father?"

"Don't you *ever* talk about my father, Treyshawn yells as he pushes Melvin. But Melvin, who could easily pummel Treyshawn, doesn't resist or retaliate.

"I'm not talkin' *about* him," Melvin retorts. "I'm *askin'* if you've seen him."

Treyshawn grabs Melvin by his shirt. Melvin smirks as he looks from Treyshawn's hands to his face. "Who's being the aggressive one now?"

Treyshawn yells with all of his might as he punches Melvin in the face. Melvin stumbles back a bit before regaining his composure as Treyshawn grabs his shirt again.

"You got stronger," Melvin says while wiping a spat of blood from his mouth. "Guess I deserved that. You wanna hit me again?" Treyshawn looks warily at Melvin, unsure of what to do. He slowly releases his grip on Melvin's shirt.

"I'm not tryin' to make you feel bad, boy." Melvin steps back.

"I'm not a boy! I'mma man!" Treyshawn shouts as he steps forward.

"True. But if you gotta tell someone you're not a boy, then chances are you're still one."

Treyshawn sucks his teeth. "What's that supposed to mean?"

"It *means* that you, me, your dad—*every* man—if we haven't dealt with our 'daddy issues' then we are *still* boys."

Treyshawn looks silently at Melvin. "Why you telling me all this?"

"You and your mother standing up to me was the best thing that happened to me in a long time. I couldn't see it then, but it was."

"So, now you're a *good* guy?" Treyshawn scoffs.

"In my life, I've been *far* from good," Melvin says with a bit of remorse. "I'm just tryin' to repay the favor."

They both stand in silence.

"I went a while back," Treyshawn admits. "It was a disaster. I'm never going again."

"Your dad and I shared the same cell block." Melvin reveals. "We looked out for each other. Not that we liked it—but we did what we had to so we could survive."

"What's that got to do with me?" Treyshawn asks.

"If you shut up and listen, then you'll see," Melvin responds.

Treyshawn bites his lip and suppresses his impulse to punch Melvin again.

"One day," Melvin continues, "we were talkin' about our fathers. Really, *I* was talkin' and he was listenin'. My 'old dude' was always there for my mom, my sisters and me. He never left us and wouldn't raise a hand to us unless he absolutely had to. It was all about love and discipline with him. He was a good man: tried his best and gave his all… But the pull of the streets was too strong for me. I loved it: the danger, the rush, the conquests. Eventually, that's what I chose, even though he always fought to pull me back."

"Where's your dad now?" Treyshawn asks.

"Dead," Melvin responds sadly. "Died a long time ago." For the first time, Treyshawn looks at Melvin with an ounce of pity.

Melvin continues. "But back to what I need to tell you. When I finished tellin' your pops my story, he just sat there in silence. I'll never forget it. I asked him if he was going to say somethin'. And he just sat there. A couple of minutes later, he spoke."

Treyshawn waits with an unexplained eagerness. Melvin can see it in his eyes and deliberately holds the moment for a bit longer.

"What did he say?" Treyshawn blurts out.

"Your dad said... 'My old man beat me... constantly.'"

"That's it?" Treyshawn asks.

"That's what I thought," Melvin chuckles. "I had gone into this whole speech about my father and all your pops could say about his 'old dude' was one sentence. But I slowly realized his one sentence said more than I ever did."

They both look at each other.

"When you go to see him again—"

"I told you, I ain't going back!"

"I know what you said," Melvin concedes. "But when you do... Don't just look at him all rough and tough. That's just the shell he put up to protect himself. Even in his silence he's speakin' volumes." Melvin starts backing away. "Well, I did my good deed for the day. Now we're even. Next time I see you, I'mma punch you in your jaw!" Melvin laughs. "Just kiddin' Trey."

"You're funny," Treyshawn sarcastically replies.

"I know, right?" Melvin shouts. "Tell your moms I said, 'hey'. Keep your head up, Trey!" With those last words, Melvin turns and walks off.

Treyshawn stands motionless. The sun has set far in the distance. Now, in the darkness, he remembers that night when he was a scared, young boy trying to act like a man. The night when he ran through the streets, blinded by tears, crying out to the sky and wondering why he couldn't get his father out of his mind... wondering if he was destined to become just like him?

Now, he was living proof that change was possible. But there was still this nagging question he couldn't shake. And no matter how hard he worked to tell himself it didn't matter, it was still there in the recesses of his mind. In that moment, he knew his life wouldn't be fully lived until he had a genuine answer to his question—even if he didn't like what he heard. Treyshawn takes a deep breath before verbalizing his thoughts.

"Melvin's right... I have to go back. I have to find out why he doesn't want me."

Chapter Twenty

Mama?

SHAKIRA SITS ON A CHAIR IN her bedroom—her knees shaking. She's been staring at her phone for twenty minutes. Finally, she picks it up, begins dialing and is amazed that she so easily remembers a phone number she hasn't called in over 18 years. It's as if it had been waiting all this time to be used. She puts the receiver to her ear and listens as the phone begins to ring. Beads of sweat pool between her wrinkled eyebrows, as she bites her lip. Her heart beats in her ears as she unintentionally holds her breath. Six times the phone rings.

In South Carolina, Lucinda finishes up in the bathroom and rushes to get to the phone while drying her hands. She doesn't recognize the number on her caller ID, but picks up the phone anyway.

"Rollins residence," she announces in her southern drawl.

Shakira's eyes widen at the sound of her mother's voice.

"Hello?" Lucinda beckons into the silence.

Shakira's eyes dart back and forth as she pulls the phone from her ear.

"Is anyone there?" Lucinda calls into the silence again.

Shakira slowly puts the phone back to her ear as she forces her lungs to exhale and inhale deeply.

"I can hear you breathing," Lucinda declares in an accusatory tone. "Who is this?"

A tear falls from Shakira's left eye as she squeezes a word out of her mouth. "Mama..."

Lucinda drops the phone as her heart skips a beat. She draws her hand quickly over her mouth in a gasp as she fumbles to pick the receiver up off the floor. Her wrinkled eyes well up with tears as she responds, "Kira? Baby, is that you?"

"It's... it's me, Mama," Shakira replies.

Both women begin crying as emotions rush over them like a raging river.

"How are you?" Lucinda asks.

"I'm... good, Mama. We are good."

"We?" Lucinda asks. "Are you talking about your son?"

"Yes. He's in college now."

Lucinda can't believe her ears, as a smile fills her expression. "Your father... would be so proud to hear that."

A half smile grows across Shakira's face before she blurts out, "Mama, I want to come home and see you. We both do."

Lucinda closes her eyes at the words she never thought she would hear. The silence is frightening. "Mama?"

"Baby," Lucinda whispers with a resounding tone, "...come home."

A wave of joy overtakes Shakira as she smiles from ear to ear. "How's Mama Rollins, Mama?"

Lucinda's smile diminishes, as the twinkle in her eyes suddenly fades. "Kira," she says in a serious tone, "your grandmother died six years ago."

Shakira's eyes register her horror as these unexpected words cut to her heart. She immediately bursts into tears, sobbing, before being able to pull herself together. "How...?"

Lucinda speaks into the silence, barely able to hold back her own tears. "She had grown sick from diabetes. It was a long battle... but she never once lost her joy. I tried your old number, but it didn't work. You kept moving around so much and no one knew where you were..."

Shakira cries. As does her mother. "Mama, I'm sorry..."

Amidst her tears Lucinda replies, "Just come home, baby. I want to see you both with my own eyes."

"Ok, Mama..."

"When can you come?"

"Treyshawn's next break from school is Christmas."

"Then what a wonderful Christmas it will be."

Chapter Twenty-one

Happy Thanksgiving!

JIM GRABOWSKI'S HOME BUZZES WITH ACTIVITY and excitement as it sits amidst a flowing collage of orange, red and brown foliage. The crisp Westchester air captures the rising smoke from the chimney, while swelling with the scents of food from numerous houses in the neighborhood: oven roasted turkeys, candied yams, hams, corn puddings, cabbage, string beans, stuffing, mashed potatoes, apple cider, sweet potato pies, pumpkin pies, chocolate cookies and many other delicacies.

Mr. Grabowski has a house full as all attendees have arrived: Omar, Curtis and their mother Miranda. Treyshawn and his mother, Shakira. Kelly, her brothers Kevin and Kelvin, and their parents Stacy and Johnny. Jim's daughter Catherine, her husband Cliff and their daughter Cloe.

Festive music trumpets through the home's wireless surround-sound system. Tongues of fire rhythmically lap each other as they flow from slowly burning logs stacked in the fireplace. Lively conversation, sparked with laughter, fills the rooms. Even while being separate families, they react and respond to each other as one single unit that has been united by a common cause. Even Catherine, her husband and child—the newest members to this fellowship—act as if they've known everyone since the beginning.

On this day of thanksgiving, this home—like many—serves as a safe haven from a world filled with pain, turmoil and conflict. As everyone gathers around the dining room table, Mr. Grabowski raises his glass of sparkling apple cider. Everyone quiets down as they hold their own glass.

"A toast." Jim looks around at each person, flashing a heartfelt smile. "We all have a lot to be thankful for. The two most obvious reasons are found in the lives of Curtis and Omar. Both have recently faced the prospect of death. Both have lived to tell the story."

Everyone cheers for Omar and Curtis.

"Everything may not be one hundred percent right in our lives," Miranda adds. "We each have issues that we're dealing with. But we are still here—alive and well."

Jim continues. "And each day we can open our eyes, breathe in fresh air and use our minds to pursue our dreams, is a day to thank God. So God, thank you for life; for good food; and for family and friends!"

"Amen!" everyone proclaims as they drink their sparkling apple cider and make their plates. The evening continues… filled with lively celebration.

Two days later, Treyshawn, Curtis and Kelly stand with their families in the airport terminal. Hugs and kisses are exchanged as the three friends head through the security checkpoint. On the other side, Curtis and Kelly prepare to go in one direction as Treyshawn prepares to go in another.

"It was really good seeing you two," Treyshawn says as they all hug. "It's tough being out in Cali by myself… but I'm makin' it."

"We miss you already," Kelly smiles sympathetically.

Curtis reaches into his bag and pulls out a book. "I wanted to give you this." He hands the book to Treyshawn who immediately sees the heading, 'To My Sons…'

"Is this what I think it is?" Treyshawn asks in awe.

"If my dad were alive I know he'd consider you a son. So, I made you a copy."

Treyshawn looks up at Curtis and Kelly—faintly shaking his head back and forth, in a state of utter disbelief. He lunges at Curtis and gives him the strongest bear hug he can muster. Curtis laughingly cries out due to the intensity of the embrace.

"Thanks Bro," Treyshawn whispers in Curtis' ear. "Thanks…"

An announcement rings over the loud speaker: the flight to Atlanta is boarding at gate 12.

"You guys get outta here." Treyshawn wipes tears from his eyes. "I'll talk to you soon."

"We love you!" Kelly smiles as she and Curtis wave goodbye.

"Love you guys, too," Treyshawn shouts back. He watches as they run to their gate and then he slowly turns and heads for his departure. With every step, he grows more oblivious to his surroundings as his eyes focus on the journal that he holds in his hands.

Chapter Twenty-two

Prodigy

CHASM, CURTIS AND ERICA DESCEND IN one of the many private elevators at the Chasm Group Facilities. The display monitor clearly states the date and time: Thursday, December 6, 2012. 10:00 a.m.

"Curtis, I'm glad you agreed to be one of our student judges," Chasm smiles.

"Are you kidding?" Curtis all-but-shouts, "I'd have to be crazy to turn you down! Thanks to you, I get to judge one of the best college science fairs in the country!"

Chasm chuckles. "Your enthusiasm is appreciated. And your world-wide recognition is helpful as well."

"And your Mach-1 Speedsuit display is fully setup for the public to see," Erica adds as she finishes looking over the information on her digital tablet.

"Conference level 2," a female elevator voice chimes. The double doors slide open as Chasm, Curtis and Erica walk through the second-floor skyway that connects the "A" building to the conference center. Curtis stops for a moment, as a kaleidoscope of light draws his attention to the windows. A water fountain sits below the skyway—glistening in the sunlight. As they approach the special entrance, a wave of voices, mechanical elements and music is heard. A moment later, they find themselves standing on the balcony observatory area, which overlooks a bustling scientific metropolis on the first level of the conference hall floor. Over 1500 students, professors and administrators are in attendance as their display booths line the conference hall floor. Another 300 individuals are present as well, representing the leading government agencies and top science and tech companies in the country. Curtis stands in awe at the sight as Chasm revels in the moment.

The three approach the main podium as Chasm takes the microphone.

He motions to Erica, who presses a button on her digital tablet. Within seconds the music fades, the hall lights dim and two spotlights train on Chasm.

"Attention students, professors, administrators and business leaders!" Chasm bellows.

The crowd comes to attention as everyone faces the balcony. Chasm gazes out over the crowd and smiles.

"Welcome to the 7th annual Montgomery Science & Technology Exhibition!"

The conference hall reverberates as students and professors cheer at the top of their lungs. Chasm allows the cheering to last for a moment before raising his hands to calm the crowd.

"You are here, displaying your scientific exploits because you are the best and brightest that our country's collegiate system has to offer!"

The students cheer again.

"As you know, you will not only present your discoveries to your fellow students, but also to top representatives from every leading technological organization in the country!"

The students cheer again.

"So," Chasm's voice crescendos, "show us your best! Show us your creativity! Show us your scientific methods! Take the risk! And the top three teams that win the coveted prizes, will take their research to the best agencies in the country for an expansion of resources beyond their wildest expectations!"

Once again the crowd erupts into momentous adulation.

"In this room," Chasm continues, "are the individuals who will change the face of this world forever! And it is my aim to discover who—you—are."

A hush falls on the entire crowd, as Chasm's expression grows increasingly serious.

"Over the next two days, in addition to meeting the agency and company reps, I—along with my judges—will review every exhibit. We will scrutinize every detail and will apply the most stringent scientific standards to your work. Wow us! But make sure you know your data."

A light, nervous chuckle circulates among the attendees.

Chasm's mood lightens as he continues. "As you all know, I invite several students, who have great scientific promise, to be guest judges. At the top of this year's list is a young man many of you may know. You have seen him on television. You have watched his world-record videos on the Internet. When he's wearing his Mach-1 Speedsuit he *is* the fastest man alive!"

Students begin to applaud.

"I introduce to you all... Curtis Powers... A.K.A. Jetstream!"

The conference hall attendees burst into cheers as Chasm motions for Curtis to approach the edge of the balcony. Chasm and Curtis stand together—waving to the crowd. The sound of the applause is deafening as Chasm continues, "Let the science exhibition... begin!"

As Chasm, Curtis and Erica make their way down to the main level, several high level representatives greet them.

"Curtis, let me introduce you to several delegates from D.A.R.P.A."

As the day passes, Chasm leads his prodigy through countless impromptu introductions. By evening, an exhausted Curtis takes a break in Chasm's office. While sitting on a plush couch, tired out of his mind, Curtis notices a picture on Chasm's wall. He slowly makes his way over to it and discovers a younger Chasm standing with several extremely well dressed older men. Curtis studies the picture for a moment—his focus never leaving the aged gentleman in the middle of the group.

"Why does he look so familiar to me?" Curtis whispers to himself. As his dazed mind ramps back up to mental clarity, a long forgotten memory rises from his sub-consciousness.

June 19, 2000. New York City. The Architect Group, Inc.

The smell of printer ink fills the air—greeting a smiling 6-year-old Curtis, as he enters the building—holding his father's strong hand firmly. It wasn't everyday that he went to his father's job in the city! And he was very excited to be carrying several tubes strung over his shoulder—containing important blueprints that his father was working on. Malcolm leads his son by the hand through the seemingly endless wood-tiled channels flanked by cubicles on each side.

"Good morning, Mr. Powers," employees say happily as Malcolm acknowledges each person with a wave, smile and hearty 'hello.'

As Curtis walks with his father, many of the employees smile and say to him, "Hey little man." Curtis waves to them while looking up in awestruck wonder at all of the computer displays. Once through the labyrinth, Malcolm and Curtis find themselves standing at a raised platform: affectionately called 'The Island,' which houses the executive assistants. The desks on The Island also serve to guard the way to two grey glass doors—which lead to the executive offices.

Phones ring almost repeatedly as five executive assistants answer in similar tones. "Thank you for calling The Architect Firm of Pierce-Sterling, and Whaley. How may I direct your call?" Beyond this salutation, each conversation varied widely, depending on whom the caller wanted to speak with.

"Marge," Malcolm declares enthusiastically. "How are you on this fine morning?"

"Good morning, Malcolm," Marge replies in her British accent. "I'm well thank you." She hands him a pile of documents, as Curtis pays attention to her somewhat wrinkled skin, her classic silver glasses with a chain on them, and her grey-streaked hair pulled back into a tight bun. She stands and looks over her desk at Malcolm's guest. With a bright smile she asks, "And how are you today, Master Curtis?"

Curtis frowns slightly as he hugs his dad's side. Malcolm looks down at his son, with a smirk. "Hey buddy, it's OK. You remember Ms. Marge, don't you? She's my assistant." Malcolm looks back at her, "I'm sorry Marge. I guess it *has* been a while since he's been here."

Curtis looks up at his dad and smiles before looking at her and saying, "Hello."

Marge stands up straight. "Young man, you may not remember me, but the last time you were here, we had a grand time! You and I went on *several* adventures in the printing room. Last I recalled, you had a lot of ink on your hands and clothes."

Curtis' smile grows, "I remember!"

Marge smiles with a twinkle in her eyes. "And who knows what adventures may be waiting for you and me today! Would you like to go with me to the mail room?"

Curtis nods his head thoroughly and smiles, "Yeah, that would be great!"

"It's yes," Malcolm says, "not yeah. Now, let's get you settled into my office before you go on any early morning adventures."

Curtis frowns slightly. "Bye, Ms. Marge." He and his dad walk pass The Island and through the double glass doors. Once down the plush hall, Curtis crosses the threshold into his father's office. His frown disappears as he enters another world where models of numerous buildings from all over the world surround him. He lets go of his father's hand and runs over to gaze at each of them. Malcolm chuckles at the sight of his son's wonder. Just then, one of the founding partners—an older gentleman—walks into Malcolm's office.

"Malcolm, I need to talk with you in my office."

"Sure thing." Malcolm motions to his son. "John, you remember my son?"

"Why, sure I do!" John exclaims, walking over to the young boy. "Hello Curtis." John smiles while leaning over to shake his hand. "How are you today?"

Curtis looks at his father, who gives him a reassuring nod. Then he shakes John's hand and replies, "I am good," while studying the distinct mole on his chin.

"Great," John says while patting Curtis on his head. "I almost forgot today was 'take your child to work day.' The last time you were here, I was out of town. So it's been about 3 years since we've seen each other. You are growing into a strong, young boy! And your father tells me that you are very inquisitive. That's a great trait to have."

Curtis smiles from ear to ear, "You have a big bump on your chin."

"Curtis!" Malcolm bellows in disbelief.

John laughs. "Not a problem Malcolm. I'm used to it." He turns to Curtis and smiles, "This 'big bump' that you see on my chin is a mole."

"A mole?" Curtis asks curiously.

"Yes, a mole. It's my birthmark."

"I know what a birthmark is," Curtis shouts. "I have one on the back of my leg!"

"That's good to know," John states with a certain amount of amusement.

"Was *your* birthmark that big when you were a baby?" Curtis inquires.

"Curtis!" Malcolm utters with increasing embarrassment, as he slaps his own forehead with his hand.

John lets out a hearty belly laugh. "Oh, he *does* take after you, Malcolm!"

Malcolm shakes his head. "John, I am *so* sorry."

John merely waves his hands. "This is nothing compared to what kids said when I was in elementary and high school." He turns to Curtis with a smile. "No, my mole was not this big when I was a baby."

"Oh, Ok." Curtis responds.

"I need to borrow your father for a few minutes. Is that Ok?"

Curtis nods hesitantly.

"I'll be in the office right next door for a few minutes." Malcolm adds assuredly. "Keep looking at the models. When you're done, you can sit on the couch until I come back, Ok?"

"Ok," Curtis smiles as he begins to study the models again.

The Present.

Curtis' memory dissolves from his mind—leaving only the picture on Chasm's wall. His eyes are once again focused on the man in the center of this group... the one with the noticeable mole on his chin.

The next day is filled with technological demonstrations, judging and autographs. The Science & Technology exhibition ends just after sunset. Curtis is tired; so fatigued that he refuses Chasm's dinner invitation in favor of sleeping the weekend away back in his dorm room.

Curtis opens the door to his room, drops his bags and collapses onto his bed with a deep sigh. "Uhhh, I've never been on my feet for so long," he groans. Just as his eyes close, his cell phone rings. Curtis grumbles as he slowly pulls it out of his coat pocket. It's his mother.

"Hi Mom," he moans dryly.

"What's wrong, baby? Are you alright?"

"Just got home from the science exhibition," Curtis mumbles.

"Aw, my baby is tired," Miranda says sympathetically. "Ok, I'll call you tomorrow."

"Is everything Ok?" Curtis asks.

"Yes. I just wanted to see how your day went and if you saw anything interesting. But we can talk about it later."

"Ok... Talk to you later, Mom."

"Get some rest, baby."

"Mom," Curtis jumps with a start at the memory. "I *did* see something interesting in Mr. Montgomery's office."

"What was it?"

"He had a picture on his wall." Curtis props himself up on his elbows. "He was standing with a bunch of old men."

"Ok..." Miranda states in a nothing-special tone.

"One of them looked like the guy from dad's job."

Miranda's eyebrows wrinkle as she sits up. "What do you mean? Which guy from your father's job?"

"I can't remember his name." Curtis yawns. "John... something. He was a partner."

Miranda stands to her feet. "Do you mean John Whaley?"

"I think so... is he the one with the birthmark on his chin?"

"The mole?"

"Yeah?"

"Son, he's one of the founding partners of the company. Are you sure it was him?"

"Yeah. Small world, right? Isn't it crazy that he would know Mr. Montgomery?"

"Yes, Son. It's a *very* small world. Did you mention this to Mr. Montgomery?"

"No."

"Good. Let's keep this between us for now."

Later that night.

Miranda sits on her bed with the door partially closed—speaking on the phone in hushed tones. Omar rolls his wheelchair to the bottom of the stairs and calls for her, but there's no response. He rolls over to the house phone in the kitchen, slowly picks up the receiver and brings it to his ear.

"I think we should just go and talk with him," Miranda suggests.

"I would advise against that," a female voice replies, "there are too many unknown variables."

"Fine, so what time do you want to meet?" Miranda asks.

Omar's chair creaks as he shifts to find a more comfortable position.

"Is someone else on the phone?" the female voice asks.

"I don't think so," Miranda responds.

"Sorry Ma," Omar states.

"Omar!" Miranda yells.

"I was about to make a call and didn't realize you were using it."

"Let's talk later," the female voice responds before abruptly hanging up.

Omar hangs up the phone as he hears his mother's footsteps coming out of her bedroom, down the hall and down the steps.

"Omar," Miranda almost yells as she switches on the light. "Were you eavesdropping on me?"

"No Ma," Omar feigns ignorance. "I was about to make a call…"

"Omar, your cell phone is on the coffee table!" She points to it. "You don't *need* to use the house phone!"

"Fine Ma," Omar speaks flatly, "I *was* eavesdropping."

Miranda points her finger at him. "You've got no right."

"I know, I know." Omar backs his chair up a little bit. "But I'm worried about you. You've been taking all of these hushed phone calls. And that was *not* Mr. Grabowski on the phone. But that woman's voice did sound familiar. What's going on?"

"What's going on is my business. When I think you need to know, then you'll know."

"Ma—"

"No!" Miranda interjects. "That's it!"

Omar looks silently at his mother... "Since when do we keep secrets, Ma?"

Miranda's expression relaxes as she looks at her son. "Omar..." She takes a deep breath and runs her hands through her hair. "I'm trying to protect you and your brother."

"From who, Ma? Is some guy bothering you? I may be in this wheelchair, but all I have to do is make a call."

"It's not like that." Miranda looks away as she fiddles with her ring.

"So, what is it like then?" His words are met by his mother's silence. "Ma... let me help. With dad gone, you shouldn't have to do everything on your own."

Miranda stares at the family portrait and then sits on the couch.

"Ma," Omar takes a hold of her hands, "what is it?"

Miranda looks at her son with tears in her eyes. "Your father's life insurance cancellation... it wasn't an accident."

"What?" Creases plaster Omar's forehead, as he tries to process his mother's words.

"What do you mean it wasn't an accident? It was a fatal clerical error."

"No." Miranda shakes her head while squeezing her son's hand. "Someone didn't want us to get that money."

"Are you saying that this was deliberate? But who? Why? Why would someone do that? It makes no sense..."

"I know," Miranda groans in a flustered tone while throwing her hands up. "It makes *no* sense at all!"

June 2005. Three Weeks After Malcolm's Death.

Miranda storms into the office of The Architect Group. All eyes are on her as she walks past everyone without uttering a single word. She approaches The Island, sees the unattended desk and addresses one of the other executive assistants.

"Clarice. Where's Marge?" she asks sternly.

"Marjorie is out today," Clarice replies warily. "May I help you with something, Mrs. Powers?"

Miranda visibly winces at the assistant's words.

"I-I am *sorry*," the assistant says awkwardly. "*Miranda*. Is there anything we can do for you?"

"Just tell me where John is," Miranda says.

Clarice hesitates. "He's in a meeting at the moment. Would you like to wait or come back?"

Miranda walks right past The Island towards the double doors.

"Wait," the assistant calls, "you can't go back there!"

Miranda completely disregards those words as she walks through the double doors, pauses momentarily at her husband's vacant office, and then walks down the hall to John's closed door. She opens it without hesitation and barges in with papers in hand. John sits at his desk with the phone to his ear and three people in front of him.

"We need to talk, John," she announces.

"Thank you Clarice," he answers, "she's already here. No, it's fine. No need for security." John hangs up the phone and smiles as he addresses his guests.

"Would you three excuse us for a bit?" The two men and one woman pick up their notebooks and walk out of the room expeditiously, being sure to close the door behind them.

"Miranda," John soothes, "please have a seat."

"I would rather stand."

"Ok," John concedes. "So, what is the matter?"

"What's the matter?" Miranda scoffs. "What's the matter? Let's see. The man I loved—*my husband*—died, leaving me to raise our two sons by myself. And when I contacted the insurance company to see why the life insurance payment is taking so long to kick in, they tell me that the policy had been canceled... by my husband!" She bursts into tears. "Why would he do that?" she asks in desperation before reining in her emotions. "He *wouldn't* do that."

"Miranda," John replies with an air of remorse and sympathy, "this is the first that I've heard of your situation. And the fact that this has happened is completely absurd! Why would Malcolm cancel his life insurance policy mere weeks before he died?" He reaches into his desk drawer, pulls out his checkbook and begins writing. "I will look into this situation—personally. In the meantime, please accept this check from me." He tears the check free from the book and hands it to Miranda, but she doesn't take it.

"I don't want your money, John," Miranda almost yells. "I want what was due to my family!"

John places the check on his desk in front of her. "Please. Take it."

She sits down—her eyes darting back and forth through the room as she processes the situation.

"And this is not a loan," John adds, "Malcolm was more than a partner here; he was my friend. He was a friend to us all. And we will do what we can to help your family during this traumatic time."

Miranda sits for another few moments before slowly picking up the check.

"Thank you," she barely whispers as she stands up and shakes his hand. "I'm sorry for bursting in like this."

"No need to apologize at all," John soothes. "You did what any good wife and mother would do. Take care of your boys and yourself. We will talk soon."

The Present.

Miranda looks off into the distance with her eyes wide and her mouth slightly ajar.

"Ma," Omar waves his hand in front of her face. "Are you Ok?"

"I just," Miranda stammers in a moment of recollection, "I just remembered something."

"What?" Omar sits up in his chair. "What is it?"

"It didn't mean anything when he said it," she continues.

"When *who* said *what* Ma?"

"John Whaley," Miranda recalls. "When he told me he was just hearing the news for the first time, he asked why Malcolm would cancel his own life insurance policy weeks before his death."

"Ok." Omar replies. "What's wrong with that?"

Miranda turns and looks at her son. "I never *told* him the policy was canceled weeks before your father died." They both sit in stunned silence.

"Ma," Omar whispers, "Are you saying that Mr. Whaley lied about this?"

Miranda says nothing.

"But," Omar continues, "they said the cancelation was triggered by an irreversible clerical error. If this isn't true, then you have to go to the police."

"I don't even know who's responsible!" Miranda huffs. "I have no hard evidence. And I don't even know who I can trust."

"So, who was the woman on the phone?"

"That woman is an informant. And she's going to help us get the evidence we need. I can't tell you any more than that. At least, not yet."

Chapter Twenty-three

Adopted Son

BOYS. I HAVE NEVER CONSIDERED MYSELF a poet. But I feel inspired by this thought that has taken up residence in my mind over the last few days. So here is my attempt at being deep:

My son, if you push a man into a corner with no option for retreat

And if he does not faint from fear or crumble under the weight of despair…

That man will come forth swinging harder than he's ever swung

With the sight of life on his lips

And the song of freedom screaming through every clenched fist

And the thought repetitious in his mind: "Purpose is mine to live!"

Push a man into a corner with no option for retreat

And even though forced—he will make his ascent through the melee of resistance

His body, mind and spirit moving in dazzled concert

His eyes wider than they've ever been—his mind clearer than it has ever seen

His heart pounding louder than a thousand suns

For if you push a man to his breaking point—and he survives

Then you have made a man truly rise to a level unheard of—except in distant legends

To a place of possibility turned reality—where nothing is impossible

And faith moves in concert with mental clarity of action

For then… he will be right where God desires him to be—if you push a man.

Love
Your Father, Malcolm.

It's been a long, exhausting day with four classes: 'Psychology 101' at

8:00 a.m. 'English' at 10:00 a.m. 'General Mathematics' at 12:00 noon. 'Art & Design' at 2:00 p.m. Treyshawn lies on his bed in his dorm room. His textbooks are stacked on his desk, next to the mp3 player he uses to listen to them on audio. When he walked into his room three hours ago, he figured he'd read Curtis' journal for a few minutes. Now, it's 8:00 p.m. and he hasn't even touched his homework.

He hasn't eaten or even moved from his spot to go to the bathroom. With each turn of the journal pages, he's laughed and cried. But most of all he's been overwhelmed by the love expressed from a father to his sons.

All of this seems so alien to him. Treyshawn has never experienced love demonstrated like this from anyone—let alone his father. Part of him doesn't want to believe this kind of selfless exhibition of goodwill is even possible. But yet, there it was, on display on every hand-written page. Also, his interaction with Curtis and Omar confirmed that every word, which he read on these pages, was true. Love like this does exist.

"I wonder what his dad's voice sounded like?" Treyshawn muses. "I wish me and my dad had this kind of relationship."

Treyshawn closes the journal and sits up in bed. The more he looks at the cover, the more he smiles as a plan begins to develop within his mind. It's just an inkling, but it's enough to spark a flame of hope in his heart.

"My dad *will* talk to me."

Chapter Twenty-four

Intervention

TYREESE STANDS IN THE QUAD ON Spelman's campus—in shock from the words he just heard. "What you mean you breaking up?"

"Just what I said, Tyreese," Clamille states firmly, "I'm leaving!"

Tyreese looks at her with a sinister grimace. "You ain't leavin' until I say so! And I ain't said so." He quickly pulls his hand back and hauls it swiftly through the air—connecting firmly with Clamille's left cheek. SLAP! Clamille screams out in pain as she stumbles backward.

"Hey!" a voice hollers from behind.

Tyreese turns to see Kelly standing a short distance away.

"Back away from her *right now*!"

Tyreese chuckles while shaking his head. "I knew you had something to do with this." He slowly walks in Kelly's direction. "Didn't I tell you last time that something might happen to you? You need to learn how to mind your business."

"This *is* my business!" Kelly takes a slightly defensive stance. "You think I'm scared of you? I've got two older brothers who are twice your size."

Tyreese stands toe to toe with Kelly. "So, where are they now?" He hauls his arm back and clenches his fist.

SLAM! Before Tyreese knows what hits him, he's body-checked from behind! He lands hard on the ground, clamors to his feet and looks back. A young man stands next to Kelly.

Tyreese rubs the back of his neck. "So, you got help. But he ain't twice my size."

"That's because I'm not her brother," Curtis says sternly, "I'm her boyfriend!"

"The Speedsuit guy," Tyreese mumbles as he takes a step with increasing anger.

Curtis raises his hands in a friendly manner. "There's no need for violence to continue here. Let's talk this through like rational guys."

"Ain't nothin' rational about this," Tyreese counters. "Clamille's *my* woman and you need to mind your business!"

"Dude," Curtis responds, "*Your* woman doesn't mean *your* property. She's not your wife. And even if she were, that still wouldn't give you the right to abuse her."

Tyreese rushes Curtis—throwing two wild punches to his head! Curtis dodges the failed blows, but can't avoid Tyreese's shove—which plants him squarely on the ground. Tyreese raises his leg to stomp Curtis, but others yell his name.

"Tyreese!!!"

He turns to find two sizeable young men approaching.

"You better put your foot down and *back up*!"

A look of panic flashes across Tyreese's face as Kelly smirks. "*Those* two guys are my brothers."

Tyreese slowly backs away—his hands raised as a look of terror smothers his face.

"If you got a problem with our sister, then you *definitely* got a problem with us," Kevin and Kelvin shout in unison.

"And..." another male voice shouts, "If you have a problem with our daughter, then you surely have a problem with us!"

Tyreese turns to find Kelly's parents approaching.

"And if you got a problem with *my* daughter," a woman's voice declares, "then you *most definitely* have a problem with me!"

Tyreese turns around again to find Clamille's mother standing by her side.

"And if you have a problem with one of our students," another voice yells, "then you have a problem with us!"

Tyreese turns yet again and this time finds several campus security guards standing at the ready—with their nightsticks drawn.

Clamille looks at her mother. "Ma! What are you doing here?"

"Making an intervention. Clamille, you should have told me he was beating on you."

Clamille looks down and quietly responds, "But dad..."

"Don't care about what your father did to me," Clamille's mother interjects, "I didn't raise you to be nobody's punching bag."

Tyreese's breathing escalates as he looks around with wild eyes. He is completely surrounded! With a panic-filled yell, he tries to plow through the group with all of his might. Kevin and Kelvin easily catch him by his arms and toss him back to the ground. Clamille's mom motions to her. "Go ahead baby. Finish what you were saying."

Clamille looks around in silence at everyone in the circle—standing ready to protect and support her. Tears fill her eyes as she acknowledges their encouraging expressions of love. Then, with a swelling anger, she glares at a scared Tyreese. Wiping tears from her eyes, she takes a deep breath and speaks.

"Tyreese. When we first met, you made me believe the world revolved around me. And then you made me think that you were my world and I couldn't live without you. And then when I tried to choose my own friends and have a life outside of *us*, you beat me..." Clamille's voice trembles as she continues. "And you *abused* me in ways I can't even say in front of these people. You made me think *I* was the small one. That *I* was the scared one. And you were the *only* one who could set me free."

"But, *you*... are the small one. *You* are the scared one. And now I feel sorry for you."

"Baby," he cries, "don't leave me! Tell them I didn't mean it! I love you with all my heart and I will never hit you again. I promise!"

Everyone in the circle shakes their heads in disbelief.

"Tyreese," Clamille replies, "you said those words before and you've always broken your promise. Today's no different. Like I said before... I'm done. We. Are. Finished."

Tyreese's sad, pitiful expression changes in an instant as he lunges for Clamille! Before he can reach her, the security guards tackle and handcuff him. As they lift him from the ground and take him away, Tyreese repeatedly yells, as saliva trails from his mouth.

"You don't leave me until I say so! And I ain't said so! You hear me Clamille? Do you hear me? I know you hear me! You don't leave until I say so! And I ain't said so!"

As the group rallies around Clamille, Kelly asks, "You *are* pressing charges right?"

"And getting a restraining order," Clamille replies as she hugs Kelly. She then turns to address everyone else. "You all didn't have to do this. But I'm glad you did. Thank you."

Chapter Twenty-five

The Bigger Man

TREYSHAWN'S BAGS ARE PACKED AS HE prepares to leave his dorm room. It's three days before Christmas and he can't wait to get home to his mother. He looks at his watch—fifteen minutes until the cab arrives to take him to the airport. He checks the mirror one last time. Boots, baggy jeans, stylish shirt and fitted hat tilted just to the side—all check. He smiles at his reflection, grabs his bags and rushes out the door.

As soon as Treyshawn exits the dormitory, he sees trouble coming. He turns on an app on his phone and continues walking towards the curb.

"Going somewhere?" Johnny growls, as he and his friends approach.

"I barely made it out my building." Treyshawn huffs, "You stalkin' me now?"

Johnny gets in Treyshawn's face, "I'm sick and tired of your mouth."

"Number one," Treyshawn replies without batting an eye, "You've been messin' with me since the first day I got here and I never did anything to you. Number two. I don't take kindly to people invading my personal space without an invitation."

Johnny pushes Treyshawn! "There you go running your mouth again!"

Treyshawn cracks a restrained smile as he rolls with his adversary's forceful push. "See, now you just pushed me."

"Let's do this right now!" Johnny yells. "You and me!"

Treyshawn notices the growing crowd of students—eagerly looking forward to a fight. BEEP! BEEP! Treyshawn's taxicab arrives at the curb.

"Looks like my ride is here." Treyshawn picks up his bags and takes a step, but Johnny blocks his path. "Excuse me," Treyshawn grins, "that's my ride to the airport."

"You ain't leaving till I say so!" Johnny yells.

"You know what?" Treyshawn drops his bags. "You may be able to beat me, but we'll never know because if you touch me again, I'm gonna report you to security and the dean."

Johnny laughs. "It's your word over mine!"

"Actually," Treyshawn pulls his phone off of its belt holder, "it'll be *your* word against you." He taps the play button and his voice memo app replays the entire conversation.

Nearby students start laughing as, for a moment, Johnny seems hesitant.

"I don't *want* to use this," Treyshawn continues, "but I will if I have to." He picks up his bags again and starts walking towards the taxi.

"You dress like a thug," Johnny retorts, "but when it comes down to it, you're just a punk!"

The students freeze—sure that a fight will start now. Treyshawn turns around, faces his nemesis, and looks at him with a hint of compassion. "You know I used to be you... but you're highly overrated. You can call me what you want. But I know who I am." Treyshawn turns and walks to the taxi amid laughter and applause.

"What's that supposed to mean?" Johnny yells. "What do you mean you used to be me?"

"Merry Christmas," Treyshawn replies as he enters the taxi and closes the door.

Treyshawn doesn't even look back as the vehicle drives away. But if he were to do so, he would see the crowd disperse, leaving a solitary figure standing near the curb.

Chapter Twenty-six

A Boy's Imagination

IT'S A COLD DECEMBER EVENING IN Atlanta, just a few days before Christmas break. Curtis leaves his workshop and walks off campus—down a nearby side street. With his hands snuggled deeply into his winter coat, he passes a small church that seems to be in session. He slows to a stop and looks at the lights shining through the stained-glass windows; smiling slightly as he remembers his mother's words: "If you give God your time, He will give you His time."

Curtis enters the church and sits in the back of the sanctuary while a prayer service takes place. The warmth is soothing as he slowly takes off his coat and hat. He looks around at the twenty or so persons standing and kneeling in various parts of the room. Their prayers and words of worship quietly bathe the atmosphere. Curtis takes a deep breath, sits back in the pew and closes his eyes. "God... it's now or never. Please show me what I'm supposed to do..."

As Curtis prays intently, he can hear children whispering nearby. Suddenly, he senses approaching movement. He opens his left eye. To his surprise, a young Hispanic boy is sitting next to him, grinning from ear to ear.

"You're Curtis Powers," the boy declares excitedly with a slight accent.

"Yes," Curtis smiles slightly, "I am."

"My friends said it wasn't you. And even if you *were* you, they said I didn't have the guts to come over and talk to you." Curtis looks from the boy, over to the far side of the back of the church and sees a group of five kids—all gawking at the sight.

"I've watched you on television. That was scary what you did at that school."

"Listen," Curtis politely interjects, "I've got a lot on my mind and I'm trying to pray here."

"Sorry," the boy sulks, "I just had two questions."

Curtis turns slightly towards the boy and breathes deeply. "Ok. *Two* questions. Then we can talk some more *after* I finish praying."

The boy's eyes light up, as he straightens his posture and fires away. "Do you wear your Speedsuit under your clothes like Superman?"

Curtis laughs out loud and then smothers his mouth with his hands, as the group in front of the church looks back in his direction. "Are you *trying* to get me in trouble?" Curtis whispers as the boy laughs while covering his mouth as well.

"The suit's too bulky to be worn under my clothes." Curtis answers. "By the way… what's your name?"

The boy smiles and extends his hand for a shake. "My name is Javier."

Curtis shakes his hand. "It's nice to meet you Javier. So, what's your second question?"

"Your Speedsuit makes you run faster, but you ever tried making suits that do other things?"

"Actually," Curtis pauses with a slow nod of inspiration, "I… haven't."

"Yeah," Javier continues, "like a suit that controls the wind and one that generates lightning!" Javier's excited voice echoes through the church sanctuary. A woman turns around with a piercing expression and looks in his direction.

"Quick! Duck!" Javier whispers, sliding down into the pew. Curtis looks down at him in amusement, then to the woman and back to him. "Who is she?"

"She's my mother!" Javier whispers forcefully.

Curtis waves to her. Her expression softens as she waves back before turning around to continue her prayers.

"Of course you can make a suit that flies," Javier continues in whisper mode. "Oh! And one that gives you super strength!" He pauses for a moment. "Uh, is it OK to come back up now?"

Curtis chuckles to himself. "Sure. The coast is clear."

Javier scrambles back to his place next to Curtis. "I hope I can be like you when I grow up. I want to inspire people too."

Curtis looks intently at Javier with surprise. "Is that what you think I do? Inspire people?"

"Yep," Javier smiles confidently. "You inspire kids to dream. And then you show us that dreams can come true. But seriously—new suits. You *gotta* do that."

With that, Javier bounces to his feet, waves bye and scrambles back over to where his friends are sitting. Curtis watches as they all break into a hurried, hushed conversation, with Javier at the center of attention.

Curtis thinks to himself as he smiles and looks up at the ceiling: *That kid may be onto something.* Again his mother's words come to mind: "If you give God your time… He will give you His time."

Chapter Twenty-seven

Christmas Heritage

TREYSHAWN SITS ALONE AT A TABLE in the prison visitors center. Surrounding him are many families talking with their inmate relatives and friends about Christmas—which is three days away. A buzz is heard as a thick metal gate opens. A tall, burly guard approaches.

"I'm sorry, but I tried three times. He still won't come out."

"Did he say anything?"

"No. I'm sorry you came here straight from the airport, but, since he won't come out, you will have to leave now."

Treyshawn doesn't move.

"Did you hear me?" The guard asks with a sympathetic but stern tone.

"Yeah. I heard you. Thanks for trying."

The guard watches as Treyshawn gets up and begins to walk away. "Hey."

Treyshawn turns and faces him.

"Fathers can act stupid sometimes. Don't let this ruin your Christmas."

"Thanks," Treyshawn smiles, as he turns and leaves.

The next morning. December 23, 2012.

Shakira is soundly asleep with her head on her son's shoulder. Treyshawn looks out of the window at the passing landscape, as the bus sways back and forth on the highway. The sun barely pierces the horizon, as everything outside seems still and quiet. Treyshawn's hand caresses the cover of the journal that sits on his lap.

The guard's words keep replaying in his mind: *Fathers can act stupid sometimes.* He thinks back over the two last encounters with his dad, his recent encounter with Melvin and the insights he's gained from Curtis' journal. Slowly, as the bus ride stretches into the coming hours, Treyshawn builds a plan upon his initial idea.

The 9:00 p.m. bus pulls out from the depot in a cloud of exhaust, leaving Shakira and Treyshawn standing with their bags. As they begin to look around, Shakira notices a car with its lights on, sitting across the parking lot. A black woman watches them from inside the vehicle. A moment passes before the car door opens and she steps out.

"Mama…" Shakira drops her bags and takes a few steps in the woman's direction. The woman steps away from the car and begins to move towards her, as Shakira starts to run.

"Mama!"

The woman shouts, "Kira!" and hobbles towards her daughter with all the speed she can muster.

Treyshawn watches in amazement as daughter and mother practically tackle each other in their excitement. He then grabs the bags and starts making his way across the parking lot, as Shakira and her mother cry all over each other.

"Mama." Shakira hangs on her mother's neck.

"My baby... My baby!" Lucinda holds her daughter just as tightly.

"Mama," Shakira weeps, "I'm sorry."

"I know," Lucinda beams.

"I'm *really* sorry, Mama," Shakira sobs, "for everything."

"You hush now," her mother soothes. "All that matters is that you're home."

Lucinda pulls away for a moment and wipes her eyes. "Let me look at you!" As she gazes at her daughter's face, her eyes catch movement just behind her. Shakira notices and turns around, both of them wiping away their tears as they face the young man laden with bags.

"Grandma?" Treyshawn inquires with a level of tempered excitement.

"Mama," Shakira affectionately smiles, hesitating slightly, "this is your grandson."

"Treyshawn," Lucinda utters with the awe that only a grandmother can muster. "Drop them bags and come give your grandmother a hug!"

With tears in his eyes, Treyshawn drops his bags, looks at his smiling mother, and hugs the woman he never thought he'd ever meet. As he and Lucinda embrace, he nestles into her strong arms and breathes in the aroma of her perfume. Lucinda holds her grandson and slowly rubs her hand through his hair, while inhaling his musty scent. Her tears flow freely as she whispers softly in his ear, "I'm sorry Treyshawn. I'm sorry for allowing my anger towards your mother to keep me from you."

The floodgates of Treyshawn's heart crumble at her words. And from a place unknown to him—deep in the recesses of his being—buried beneath pain and disappointment—erupts an overwhelming joy which flows through every part of him like a geyser: a joy so great that the only response is to weep. Crying like a newborn baby—he barely stands in place, supported by the strength of his grandmother. Finally. A part of him he never knew… was home.

December 24th. The next morning.

Is this a dream? Treyshawn thinks as he awakens on a king-sized bed, immersed in a plush array of comforters. He lays motionless as the scents of bacon, eggs, fish, grits and pancakes slowly begin to fill the room. He smiles as he rolls over and swims through the comforters to the other side of the king bed. He pulls the thick curtains back from the window and squints hard at the intense sunlight. After a moment's adjustment, he turns back towards the bedroom and yawns. "I don't even remember coming in last night."

He looks down at the bed and pushes against the mattress a few times, before standing up quickly and pulling his feet out from under him. His giggles fill the room as he bounces up and down repeatedly.

Minutes later, he walks out of the bedroom and slowly makes his way down the hall to the stairs. Upon reaching the bottom of the stairs, he leisurely walks towards the sound of cooking coming from the kitchen. He stops in the living room and notices a large Christmas tree adorned with all of the traditional trimmings! Antique couches and bookshelves greet him, as well as numerous family pictures which align the four green-striped walls. He has no idea who he's looking at, but he stares at each person, wondering how he might be connected to them.

As Treyshawn makes his way into the now silent kitchen, he finds his mother and grandmother sitting across from each other at a central wooden table. The light shines through the window casting an angelic glow on both of them as they finish up the food on their plates. Treyshawn immediately notices the way his mother is sitting—so relaxed with one leg crossed under the other as she leans over the table towards her mother. They turn to him in unison and smile.

"So, my grandson is finally up." Lucinda grins.

"What time is it?"

"It's 1:00 o'clock," Shakira smiles. "You were *really* tired. I hope you're hungry."

"Yes." Lucinda adds, "We made *a lot* of food, and somebody has to eat it."

Treyshawn sits down at the table as Shakira gets up and makes his plate. She places the food in front of him and he begins to eat.

"We say grace in this house young man," Lucinda articulates to her grandson.

"Sorry." Treyshawn looks at both of them. "I *do* say grace, but I was so excited I forgot."

"Well, after you finish eating," Lucinda continues, "I need you to get dressed because we have a short trip to take."

"Where are we going?"

"You'll know soon enough."

Two hours later, Lucinda, Shakira and Treyshawn stand in front of the entrance to a cemetery.

"Our family's lot is here," Lucinda states, as they begin to enter the grounds. "Almost every family member for the past five generations is buried here. In fact, this cemetery was established by a newly freed slave who had worked his way to becoming a distinguished businessman... your great, great,

great, grandfather."

"Wow," Treyshawn whispers, as they make their way through a long array of tombstones.

"Treyshawn," his grandmother speaks with a quiet confidence, "you may not know this, but, despite the drama you and your mother have experienced over the years, you come from a great heritage."

A moment later, the three of them are standing in front of a sizeable granite tombstone. The inscription on it reads: Here lies Berneatha Joan McFadden. "Mamma Rollins." Sunrise and Sunset: 1909 - 2006. Daughter. Sister. Niece. Aunt. Wife. Mother. Grandmother. Great-grandmother. Educator. Mentor. Friend. Child of God. "Favor is deceitful, and beauty is vain: but a woman that feareth the LORD, shall be praised. Give her of the fruit of her hands; and let her own works praise her in the gates." – Proverbs 31:30-31.

"Mama Rollins," Shakira utters softly as tears gently roll from her eyes down to her chin—and then drop to the ground.

Treyshawn holds his mother as she leans into his shoulder and begins to cry.

"Never a day went by that she didn't pray for you," Lucinda declares. "She prayed for both of you." She looks at her daughter and grandson. "One of the last things she told me, before she died, was not to worry."

January 27, 2006. Bennitville, South Carolina. Hospital.

Family members surround Mama Rollins. There is not a dry eye in the room as each person has said their goodbyes. Now, Mama Rollins gives her pronouncements over each individual—speaking into their lives. She ends her words of wisdom by looking at her daughter. Amid the sounds of beeping, hissing and weeping, Berneatha smiles brilliantly—even as her aging body continues to shut down.

"I saved you for last," she speaks weakly.

"Mama..." Lucinda cries as she hugs her mother's neck and kisses her cheek. "Please don't leave us."

"Hush child," Berneatha replies. Even in her weakened state, her authority, as family matriarch is not diminished. "We all must go this way at some point. What matters most is how we lived. So listen to what I have to tell you. Now, don't you worry about 'Kira. You hear? Just believe, baby. God showed me something beautiful."

"What Mama?" Lucinda looks at her intently. "What did God show you?"

Berneatha smiles as she whispers, "He showed me the day when she will come home."

"When Mama?" Lucinda asks, trying to hide her desperation.

"It will be some time. But before she comes home—she will call." And with those words, Mama Berneatha Joan McFadden Rollins relaxes into her bed and breathes her last.

The present.

Shakira and Treyshawn look in awe at Lucinda.

"Are you telling the truth?" Shakira exclaims. "Mama Rollins knew that last night was going to happen?"

"Would I have any reason to lie to you?" Lucinda responds.

The three of them stand in a hallowed silence.

Eventually, Lucinda turns to Treyshawn. "Do you want to see your grandfather's grave?"

Later that night.

Shakira and Treyshawn lie in their bed. Their room is illuminated by a nightlight in the corner and the moonlight shining through the window. Treyshawn stares at the ceiling while Shakira faces the wall.

"Ma? Are you awake?"

"Yeah baby. What's on your mind?"

"With this big house that grandma has, why do we have to sleep in the same bed?"

Shakira laughs and turns over to face her son. "With everything you've seen today, I thought you were going to ask something deep."

Treyshawn laughs. "This *is* deep!"

"I'm sure she has her reasons," Shakira laughs. "What's the problem? You don't want to sleep next to your mother?"

"That's *not* even cute, Ma," Treyshawn laughs.

"You got jokes huh? Just keep your cold feet off my legs!"

They laugh.

"Seriously though," Treyshawn continues, "today was an *amazing* day."

"Yes it was," Shakira whispers. "Yes it was."

"I never knew," Treyshawn hesitates, "I never knew that your side of the family... that I came from people who…"

"…People who mattered?"

"That's not what I meant, Ma."

"It's Ok," Shakira smiles. "It *was* good to be reminded about where I came from."

"So what now?" Treyshawn asks.

"Now?" Shakira answers with a slightly raised voice. "We go to sleep."

December 25th. Christmas Morning.

KNOCK. KNOCK. KNOCK. KNOCK. Lucinda opens the bedroom door and leans inside.

"Rise and shine!" she smiles widely. "It's Christmas! Are you two awake yet?"

"What time is it?" Treyshawn mumbles.

"It's time to wake up!"

"Five more minutes, Mama," Shakira mutters.

"You will do no such thing! I need both of you downstairs in the living room in ten minutes! So get up and get dressed... and make sure you use mouthwash!"

Twelve minutes later... Shakira and Treyshawn slowly make their way to the stairs. "MERRY CHRISTMAS!!!!!" The entire house reverberates with the harmonious sounds of forty-plus souls yelling at the top of their lungs. Shakira and Treyshawn are shocked beyond reason as they stand at the top of the stairway. As they look down, their gaze is met by an array of individuals standing on both sides of the staircase.

Applause fills the air as Shakira and Treyshawn slowly descend the steps. Many of the individuals are familiar to Shakira. To Treyshawn, no one is familiar, but they all act as if they've been waiting for him their entire lives.

"Hey Treyshawn," the first middle aged man says, in a southern drawl, "I'm Peter, your third cousin." Before Treyshawn can respond, a woman takes his hand, "Merry Christmas honey. I'm your cousin, Roberta."

Treyshawn and Shakira make their way through the growing entourage of people assembled in the house. As they move forward, a pathway opens up before them as those behind close the path. With each step, they are engulfed by a multitude of hugs and kisses. Soon, they stand in front of Lucinda, next to a large, fully decorated and lit Christmas tree. She hugs them deeply and then turns them around to face the group. The family members immediately hush, as they wait for the first words to be said. Lucinda looks at everyone intently as she speaks:

"Mama Rollins was the matriarch of this entire family. And only those of you who were in the hospital room when she died know that Mama Rollins saw that this day was coming. And I made you swear to never mention her words until they came to pass! Part of me believed what she said, but another part was deftly afraid her words would never come true. Now, here we are."

The family members clap and cheer before Lucinda quiets them down with her raised hands. "In many ways, much of what Mama Rollins was to this family has fallen on me to continue. It is a great responsibility—sometimes a burden—but I am thankful to all of you for making it as light as possible."

Lucinda stops for a moment, takes a deep breath, looks at Shakira and then exclaims:

"My daughter was dead to us... but she is now alive!"

The entire house erupts in a moment of jubilation. After several minutes, Lucinda turns towards Shakira and Treyshawn and points to everyone else in the room. "This..." she utters with quivering lips, "*these people* are *your* family." The family members respond with resounding verbal affirmations. "And you," Lucinda declares with a conviction reminiscent of her mother, "you... are... home!"

Everyone claps and cheers as Shakira cries and hugs her mother.

A moment later, Lucinda finishes her remarks.

"Kira… when you called me and we agreed on you coming here for Christmas, I called up EEH-VER-REE-ONE and told them that they *had* to be here!!!"

Members clap and cheer as one cousin speaks up for them all. "You don't want to know what she said would happen to us if we didn't make it!" They all laugh with knowing expressions.

Lucinda turns the floor over to Shakira. "You got anything you want to say, baby?"

Shakira stands in momentary silence as she looks at all the smiling faces of her family members. "This is all *so* overwhelming. I had been gone for so long… I wasn't sure that I'd ever be accepted again. But it was my son, Treyshawn, who pushed me to make that call. And I'm grateful that he forced me to confront my fears. I think I'll let him speak now. Just know that I love you all."

The group claps for Shakira and then focuses their attention on Treyshawn. He looks at his mother with a slightly fearful expression. But she motions for him to step forward and speak his mind. So, he takes a deep breath and steps forward to address the assembly.

"I thought that God hated me. I mean, why else would I have a mother who couldn't stand me and a father who was locked up and didn't want nothin' to do with me? All I knew was pain and anger… and loneliness. *That's* what I ate for breakfast, lunch and dinner—every day. Twenty-four-seven."

He looks at everyone as he continues. "I had no dreams. And never in my wildest imagination could I have pictured this day. I'm standing in a room full of people—who I don't know—but you are my family and you are cheering for me. Me! The guy who thought his only future was prison or death. The guy who thought about killing himself five years back, just to get things over with."

Treyshawn looks at everyone, including his mother and grandmother, and then slowly cracks a smile as he turns back towards the group. "But your prayers must have worked, cause just after I thought about suicide… things started to change."

Everyone claps and cheers.

"The change wasn't overnight. It wasn't easy. And it sure wasn't painless.

There was drama I had to go through to get to the change... but it happened. And with the help of my friend, Curtis—who back then I was bullying—I began to learn about possibilities and began to see myself and my mother... in a new light."

The group applauds again as Treyshawn clutches his mother's hand.

"Things are still tough for us, but who said life *wouldn't* be tough? We're making it. And with you all, we *will* make it. So, today—on Christmas—I know God doesn't hate me and I thank Him for you all."

And just like that, spontaneous praise and celebration fill the house.

The sanctuary at New Hope Rock Baptist Church is full on this Christmas evening. Several hundred members and guests engage in a dynamic worship of the Creator of the universe. Voices sing harmoniously, while in tune with the vibrant array of musical instruments that are being played by masterful musicians.

The Rollins family sits towards the front of this historic church, filling six pews.

Shakira leans over to her son. "This is the church I grew up in—until I left."

"The Rollins and McFadden families," Lucinda adds as she sits on Treyshawn's other side, "have been here since the church was founded back in 1893."

"That's a long time," Treyshawn answers.

Soon, the pastor—a slightly bent over man in his early seventies—rises from his seat on the pulpit and walks to the podium to begin his message.

"Merry Christmas to us all!" The pastor bellows with a regal tone. "I trust that you have had a wonderful day full of family celebration, gifts and good food!"

The congregation laughs as the pastor continues with increasing enthusiasm.

"We are here tonight to worship God and to share with one another the meaning and reality of Christmas." The pastor pauses a moment and surveys the congregation before continuing. "Did you know that Jesus Christ wasn't born on December 25th? Today is *not* his birthday. However, today *is* the day which Christians the world over, and down through the years, have *chosen* to celebrate his birth. We celebrate this pivotal point in all of human history when God intervened in the affairs of humankind in a way completely unique to any other intervention. 'For God so loved the world that He *gave* His only Son, that whosoever believes in Him should not perish, but have everlasting life!'

"Jesus Christ... Emmanuel... God. With. Us. We celebrate the 'Christ' in Christmas because in Jesus Christ—a humanity that was not worthy of anything good—receives the greatest gift ever to be given. And it is always the prerogative of the giver of the gift whether to give based on merit or on unmerited favor. So, in Jesus Christ, humanity receives what it could not afford to purchase... unmerited favor. In Christ we all get a second chance at life. We can all be forgiven. We all can be reconciled. In Christ, God does for us what we are not able to do for ourselves. Why? Because He chooses to love us. *This* is why we worship and celebrate the birth of Christ. Because He *is* worthy."

The congregation affirms the pastor's words with a round of hearty 'Amens' and 'Hallelujahs.'

"This evening," the pastor continues, "I had the privilege of talking with one of the mothers of this church... our dear sister Lucinda Rollins. And she informed me that her only daughter—who had been away for quite some time—is here worshiping with us tonight. Some of you may remember her daughter's melodious voice which she had since childhood."

Many in the congregation applaud, at their remembrance of her. Shakira looks at her mother, who returns her horrified gaze with a gentle smile.

"Mama," Shakira's eyes widen, "you didn't!"

The pastor continues. "Now Mother Lucinda did not ask me to do this, but *I* am asking Shakira to come up here and bless us with a song!"

The congregation erupts in applause as a frightened Shakira looks at her mother again.

"No," Lucinda smiles, "Actually, I didn't."

"Mama," Shakira blurts out, "I can't—"

"Nonsense." Lucinda raises her hand to her daughter's mouth. "You heard the pastor. Best get up there!"

"Ma," Treyshawn smiles while taking her hand, "you can do this!"

Shakira turns and looks at her son, then back at her mother. She slowly rises from her seat, to growing applause, and makes her way past family members to the aisle and then walks up to the pulpit. The pastor gives her a tender hug as many of the older members in the congregation stand to their feet in celebration.

"It's Ok 'Kira," the pastor whispers, "you were born to do this."

The pastor takes the handheld microphone from the podium and hands it to Shakira. She takes the microphone with a trembling hand and stands almost motionless. The congregation quiets down. A moment passes before she speaks.

"It's... good to be home." Her words are met with shouts of praise from members of the congregation. "Honestly," Shakira continues, "I haven't sang in church since the Sunday before I left South Carolina. And that was a *very* long time ago."

Shakira looks at her son who smiles back at her.

"With everything I've done, I don't feel worthy to stand here and sing. But... as we just heard from pastor, it's not what we do that makes us worthy... but it's what Christ has done and how we respond to Him."

The congregation erupts in praise!

"I've messed up my voice over the years, but as my mother said, I can't say 'no' to the pastor."

The congregation laughs.

"So, Pastor," she looks at him, "I will sing."

The pastor nods in approval.

"Did you have a song you wanted me to sing?" Shakira asks.

The pastor smiles knowingly, as he walks over and borrows the microphone from her.

"You may have been gone a while, but I think you will remember this one. It's the song you sang before you left."

The pastor hands the microphone back to Shakira as she tries to remember what song she sang so many years ago. The pastor looks at the minister of music. She—an elderly woman—nods and raises her hands. The choir stands. She motions to the musicians, gives them a three-count and presses the keys on the organ! At the sound of the first three notes,

Shakira breaks down in tears—almost collapsing to the floor—as a wave of memory-triggered-emotions overtake her. She remembers *this* song... It is "Be Grateful."

The other musicians begin to play as the choir starts to sing the slow opening, "BE-E-E-E-E. Grateful...." Shakira pulls herself together and stands up tall. "BE-E-E-E-E. Grateful...." The organ transitions from the choir's part to Shakira's beginning solo. She starts out softly.

"God... has... not... promised... me... sunshine. That's... not... the way it's going... to be... But... a... little rain..."

"A little rain..." the choir echoes.

"Mixed with God's... sunshine," Shakira continues, "A little... pain."

The choir echoes, "A little pain..."

"Makes me appreciate," Shakira continues, "The good times...."

As the song continues its slow melody, the congregation sways in unison as Shakira's voice becomes stronger and her posture becomes surer. Suddenly, her voice belts out two words as the song immediately picks up in tempo.

"BE GRATEFUL!"

"Be grateful," the choir echoes.

"Because there's someone else, who's worse off than you!" Shakira continues. "BE GRATEFUL!"

The choir echoes, "Grateful."

"Because," Shakira sings, "there's someone else who would love to be in your shoes!"

As the music crescendos, the majority of the congregation rises in bold celebration! Many are clapping! Some are dancing in the aisles. Others are rocking back and forth. Treyshawn stands in awe of his mother and the congregation's response. He claps and rocks as he watches his mother come alive in a way he's never seen before!

There is not a single person in their seat as the song ends as softly as it began. Shakira hands the microphone back to the pastor as they share a warm and powerful embrace. She descends the pulpit steps to thunderous applause—mixed with shouts of joy and praise to God—and makes her way back to her seat.

"Ma," Treyshawn shouts as he gives her a huge hug, "that was awesome!"

Shakira and her son hug for several minutes, embraced as well by Lucinda and many of her family who are standing nearby.

Sleeping relatives adorn every habitable piece of furniture in Lucinda's home as the night gives way to the wee hours of the morning. Only two persons are awake. Shakira sits in her mother's bedroom, surrounded by lit candle fixtures on a desk, a vanity set and several shelves. Lucinda sits right next to her on the bed.

"'Kira," Lucinda says gently. "Today was a good day."

"It was." Shakira's voice is filled with a mixture of happiness and hesitancy. "Mama?"

"What is it baby?"

"I'm sorry that I didn't bring you a gift."

Lucinda gazes at her in surprise. "What are you talking about? You brought me the best two presents I could ever want!"

"What was that Mama?" Shakira stares at her—confused.

Lucinda beams. "Both you and your son *are* the gifts."

Shakira gives her mother a grand hug. "Thank you Mama!"

"You're welcome. Although, I do have a gift for you." Lucinda kneels down, reaches under her bed and retrieves an antique jewelry box. She sits it on her bed next to her daughter.

"This belonged to your grandmother. She gave this to me just before she died. Said it was for you."

Shakira looks from her mother to the box in astonishment. "For me?"

"Yes. For when you returned."

"What's inside?"

"I have no idea. She told me never to open it." Lucinda holds up a silver key. "*This* will open it."

Shakira holds the key in her hands and notices how the candlelight glimmers off of it. She slowly inserts the key into the keyhole and turns it. With a click, the latch pops open. Shakira slowly lifts the lid. Two brown envelopes—one addressed to "Kira" and the other addressed to "Cinda"—sit just inside on the first level of the case.

Both mother and daughter hesitate to touch the envelopes. But after some time, they open them. Inside each is a handwritten letter from Mama Rollins. Shakira and Lucinda sit on the bed across from each other and begin reading their letters.

To 'Kira. My wonderful Granddaughter,

You are headstrong like your mother. Which can be both a blessing and a curse. She never told you, but when she was around the same age as when you left, she and I had a falling out of sorts. She too, took to the wind and wanted to see the world. And who could blame her? For our town was even smaller and more restricted back then. But the difference between her story and yours is two-fold:

1. There was no man involved to further cloud her judgment. 2. She made it as far as the county line before changing her mind and coming back home.

You will never cease to be who you are... no matter how fast or how hard you run. But, if you continue to run away, you will never become who you were meant to be.

With that said, let me also say that never a day has gone by that I have not prayed for you. And when I heard about the birth of your son, I added him to my daily prayers as well.

While I believed that things would work out somehow, I was not sure if you would come back. So many children who leave on regrettable terms, never get a chance to reconcile with their parents and come back home to their family. But, even with my lack of surety, God still compelled me to pray for you every *day, to never speak negatively about you, and to save.*

'What did I save?' you might ask. If you look beneath the second layer in this jewelry box, you will find several envelops with money in them. Every day, I put something aside for you. It didn't matter whether it was a little or a lot. It all added up in the end and the total amount grew to $8,000.00. Use this money to better yourself and your son. Invest it in areas that will yield significant returns.

Remember, 'Kira, with God all things are possible.

I LOVE you more than you know,
Your Mama Rollins

Shakira puts her hand to her mouth and gasps as she finishes the letter. She looks at her mother, who has not stopped crying as she reads her own letter.

My Precious Lucinda,

Out of all ten of my children, you were my favorite. (Actually, I have always said that to each of you.) But you truly have been a joy to raise. Surely we have had our problems and disagreements, but there must be pains when people grow and mature. It is a part of life.

As much as you are your mother's child, 'Kira is your child. And both of you are headstrong—a trait that can be both beneficial and a detriment. In the case of 'Kira wanting to leave home to go with that man, you being headstrong was a benefit. She needed to know that there are rules to live by in life and if she wanted to break those rules, then she had to live with the consequences.

However, you being headstrong became a detriment when your refusal to reach out to your daughter during those early years, most likely served to push her away even further. When you heard she was pregnant, you should have gone to her—at least when it was time for the birth of her son. No woman should give birth without her mother nearby. And even when you didn't want to listen to my counsel, I let you be since she was your daughter and not mine. Yes, there were lessons that she had to learn on her own... and there were lessons you needed to learn as well. And I was wrong for not being more forceful where I felt more force was necessary.

Even so, I watched you over the years... how your anger turned into fear... how you feared that 'Kira might never come back. That is a fear every parent has, whether a child leaves home on good terms or bad. We wonder if our children will forget us... if they will forget every night we stayed awake to make sure they could sleep... if they will forget every meal we cooked for them... every hug... every kiss... every act of love as we strove to raise them to the best of our ability. I understood your fear well, because I experienced it for all of my children.

If you are reading this letter, then you not only have your daughter back, but you also were successful in facing your fear of whether or not she would accept you back. You didn't have to give her the jewelry box, but you did. God not only brought 'Kira back to you, but He has also brought you back to each other. What happens next is up to both of you.

God revealed two things to me: that 'Kira would return and that she would need help getting on her feet. So, I have left your daughter some money to help her. And I know that you will do your best.

With an unending LOVE,
Your Mother

Both mother and daughter quietly sit on the bed: Each one looking at the other—each woman unable to hold back her tears.

"Mama Rollins was *some* woman," Shakira whispers.

"That she was," Lucinda whispers back. "That she was..."

They both rub their hands over the antique jewelry box.

"This was hand-built by your great, great, great, grandfather Hamill and given to your great, great, great, grandmother Estelle in 1866, almost three years after the Emancipation Proclamation was issued by President Lincoln. They couldn't get married under slavery. Their slave master separated and sold them. After they were freed, Hamill searched for eight months and found Estelle. It was a joyous day and they were married several weeks later! Hamill was a man with strong hands and a keen mind. As a sign of his love, he carved this jewelry box from a single block of maple wood and pledged to provide for her in every way possible.

"When Estelle's daughter, Judessa, was to be married, Estelle gave it to her and it has been passed down from mother to eldest daughter ever since." Lucinda turns the lid over. "And here are the names of every woman who owned this box, and the dates when their mothers gave it to them."

Shakira looks at all of the names in awe. "I... never knew."

Lucinda grabs a pen from her dresser door. "We should add our names to this list."

After writing their names, they remove the second inserted shelf, which reveals the envelopes filled with money.

"So," Lucinda asks with a smile, "how much money did Mama Rollins leave you?"

Shakira and Treyshawn exchange hugs with their family at the bus depot.

"We're *so* glad you were able to come down," Lucinda gives them a hug.

"We are too," Treyshawn responds. "I wish we could stay longer."

"Me too," Shakira adds. "But it's the day after Christmas and I have to get back to work."

"We understand," Lucinda replies. "Besides, there's always next year. Just don't wait till Christmas to come back!"

They all laugh as Treyshawn and his mother say in unison, "We won't!"

As they wave goodbye to everyone, one of their cousins yells out, "If you have any problems, all you got to do is call!"

"Thank you!" Shakira yells back as she and Treyshawn get on the bus with the rest of the passengers. After a few moments, the bus roars to life and pulls out of the parking lot. Shakira gives her son a big hug. "Are you ready for another twelve-hour bus ride?"

"Yeah," Treyshawn smirks, "but I miss everybody already."

Shakira reflects on their time together. "It was well worth the trip. Thank you."

"I love you, Ma."

"I love you too, Trey." She kisses him on his forehead. "So, what are you going to do while we ride back to New York?"

Treyshawn pulls out his notebook and pen. "I was planning on writing a letter."

"Really? To who?"

"To someone who can help me understand more of my heritage."

Chapter Twenty-eight

New Year Plans

TREYSHAWN SITS WITH CURTIS AND THE rest of the group at the Powers' residence. It's been two days since he arrived back home. An hour has gone by as Treyshawn has shared his Christmas adventure.

"I'm glad you had a great Christmas Treyshawn," Curtis says.

"Yeah," Kelly adds, "I would love to see what your mother's jewelry box looks like!"

"Thanks guys," Treyshawn replies, "I'm glad you all had a good time here."

Miranda puts some cookies and milk on the table for all to enjoy. Omar's the first to reach in, grab some and takes a couple of quick bites.

"Ma, your cookies are *always* good!"

They all laugh while taking some of the refreshments.

"So what did you guys do?" Treyshawn inquires.

"We all just hung out together," Curtis replies. "Pretty uneventful."

"If you count being around the people you love uneventful," Kelly interjects.

"Hey," Curtis laughs while holding his hands up, "you *know* what I mean. After the past couple of months with guns and police and Omar's injury, I'm *glad* for uneventful." Curtis puts his arm around Kelly. She smiles and puts her head on his shoulder.

"Oh," Curtis adds, "I did receive a letter from Justin and Amanda's parents."

"Those were the bullied kids from the school, right?" Treyshawn asks in between bites.

"Yeah," Curtis smiles. "Their parents thanked me for stepping in and said if I hadn't, they would've been planning funerals instead."

"You really did make a difference that day," Jim responds.

"We both did, Mr. G," Curtis replies. The group sits quietly for a moment.

"So," Jim probes, "the New Year is just a few days away. Anyone have any goals they want to accomplish?"

Omar is the first to respond. "My goal is to walk again—within the next twelve months. Physical therapy is going well. I can stand up for a few minutes at a time now! Just a matter of time before I'm walking again."

"We look forward to that day," Miranda smiles.

"I'm just trying to make it through the rest of the year," Kelly replies next. "I'm glad that things worked out with Clamille. Now we're working to help each other do better in our classes. We'll see what happens with my dancing."

"Kelly," Miranda responds. "I'm glad everything worked out too. I was ready to come down with everyone else to deal with that Tyreese character!" Everyone chuckles.

"Yeah," Curtis adds. "That whole situation could have gone very wrong, very quickly."

"But thank God it didn't," Miranda replies.

"Thank God, is right," Kelly agrees.

"What about you, Treyshawn?" Jim asks.

"I wrote a letter. And I'm going to send it to the warden at the prison where my dad is at."

"Wow," Kelly responds.

"I've got a plan to confront my father, but I'll need the warden's help."

"Whatever we can do," Curtis declares, "just let us know."

"When are you going to mail the letter?" Omar asks.

"Next week," Treyshawn announces confidently.

"We are standing with you," Jim affirms.

"What about you, Curtis?" Treyshawn asks. "Do you got any plans?"

Curtis hesitates. "Actually... I want to create some new suits and design an exhibition summer tour as a way to inspire more people."

"Another project," Jim exclaims.

"Here we go again," Miranda laughs.

"I'm up for some new suit designs," Omar adds.

"What kind of new suits?" Kelly probes.

"Wind and electricity," Curtis declares.

"Now *that's* hot!" Treyshawn hollers.

"How are you going to control the wind?" Kelly asks with a confused look on her face.

"I can't," Curtis answers. "But I can create a suit that incorporates an air compressor."

"Like a hair dryer?" Omar interjects.

"More like a leaf blower," Curtis adds. "That would literally put the wind in the palm of my hands!"

"I can see the tagline now," Treyshawn laughs. "Curtis Powers: the human leaf blower!"

They all laugh!

"And the electricity suit?" Jim asks as the laughing dies down.

"That sounds dangerous," Miranda adds.

"Not if the suit has enough insulation," Curtis replies.

"I meant for everyone else!" Miranda exclaims as they all laugh again.

"Point taken," Curtis laughs. "We'll work on that. But I figure we can modify a Whimshurst machine and strap it onto the back of an insulated suit. Then the wearer can generate strong electrical charges, which can be used to attract and repel light objects and maybe produce short bursts of lightning-like electricity."

"The last time we produced one of your projects, we set a world record," Omar muses. "Why the new suits and the show?"

Curtis looks at everyone for a moment before speaking. "After what happened in Colorado... I figured one way to stop people from bullying others, is to help everyone dream about new possibilities. That's what these suits represent... new possibilities for the bullied, the bully and the bystanders." Everyone looks at each other... knowing what the next step would be.

"I think we're all on the same page," Jim replies as everyone nods their heads. "What do you need us to do?"

Chapter Twenty-nine

From Rags to Riches

IT'S A BRAND NEW YEAR AND Curtis sits in his dorm room with Gavin. They both have spent the last few hours catching up on the events of their Christmas vacation. For the last twenty minutes, Curtis has been explaining his new plan to Gavin.

"So, what do you think?"

"Are you serious?" Gavin yells. "Of course I'm interested! Whatever you need me to do!"

"But you can't say *anything* to anyone," Curtis responds.

"No problem," Gavin assures, "top secret is my middle name!"

"No it's not," Curtis laughs.

"No, it's *not*," Gavin concedes, "but you know what I mean!"

They both laugh.

"So when do we start?"

"My family will take the next few months to plan, research and gather supplies. Then we'll kick it into high gear at the end of the semester. That's where you come in. That'll give us until the end of April, May and the first half of June to get all of the tech ready, as well as figure out how the show will run. My mom has already started reaching out to some venues to secure some dates. The tour will start in July."

Curtis arrives at his on-campus workspace, unlocks the door and walks in. He turns on the lights and gazes at his workbench, couch, file cabinet, desk, vertical corner case, and the many photos and news clippings on the wall.

"Ah, it's good to be back." He smiles broadly and sits in the chair at his desk. But his enjoyment quickly turns into apprehension when he notices something.

"I don't remember leaving this stack of papers over here." Curtis slowly moves a stack of papers from the right side of his desk to the left. He looks over at his file cabinet and notices that one of the drawers is slightly open. He pushes off the desk with his feet and rides his chair to the cabinet. He quickly observes, as he opens the drawer, that his files aren't neatly tucked away.

"Did someone come in here while I was gone?" he says to himself. "The only people who are supposed to have keys are me, the cleaning staff, building administration and campus security." Curtis examines the room some more. "I did leave here in a hurry to make my flight," he says to himself. "So, it was probably me."

Curtis walks over to the large cabinet in the corner. The chains and locks are completely secured. He opens each lock, removes the chains, and opens the double doors. The Mach-1 Speedsuit greets his searching eyes.

"Everything is here," he says with a sigh of relief. Curtis secures the suit and sits at his desk. "Must have been my imagination," he mutters to himself, while unlocking his desk drawer and retrieving his notebook. He opens up to a new page, grabs a pen from his "Team Speedsuit" mug and begins to write.

Journal entry 6,347. January 17, 2013.

"New Project: The team and I are preparing to embark on a new adventure! We will create two new suits to add to the Mach-1 and will take all three on the road in an interactive exhibition designed to inspire kids and adults!

There's a lot to do—like figure out the theme of the show and all of the logistics of how it will work. And, of course, we have to figure out: 1. How the new suits will work. 2. What materials we will need to use to build them. 3. Who we will get to operate them.

There's so much to do, while trying to focus on my classwork and finishing the spring semester strong. One day at a time though... One day at a time."

Several days later: lunch at The Commerce Club...

"So you've never been married?" Curtis asks, as he eats his salad.

"I'm *married* to my work," Chasm responds, "Too busy trying to run a virtual empire, but I've *always* wanted a son: someone to carry on my life's work. Someone who could succeed where I've failed and exceed my greatest accomplishments."

"Wow," Curtis replies, "that's a huge standard to live up to."

Chasm eats his meal, obviously pleased. "You *seem* to be moving in that direction."

Curtis pauses—mid-chew—as he looks at Chasm in surprise.

"Why do you look surprised?" Chasm grins. "You know... your exhibition run at the Olympics really moved me."

"You saw it?"

Chasm cuts a piece of his fig and apple salad and eats it. "Oh yes I did," he says between chews, "with my own eyes."

"You were *in* London?" Curtis blurts out. Others in the restaurant look at him as he bashfully motions an apology and whispers to Chasm, "You were in London?"

"On a business trip," Chasm continues. "In fact, I wasn't far from the entrance you walked through to enter the stadium."

"You *gotta* be kidding!" Curtis chuckles while shaking his head.

"I was sitting close enough to hear the 'click-clack' of your boots as you walked by."

"That is crazy! I can't believe we were so close to each other and I didn't even know it!"

"Seeing your Mach-1 Speedsuit for the first time was amazing. But what moved me was your acknowledgement of your father. I don't think there was a dry eye in the entire stadium. The fact that he served as your motivation for your amazing achievement is admirable."

Curtis looks away from his plate with a slight grimace. "I... I miss him."

"At least you were blessed to have him in your life," Chasm empathizes, "even if it was only for a short while."

"What about *your* dad?" Curtis asks. "What was he like?"

"Well," Chasm wipes his mouth with his napkin, "I never knew my birth father. For that matter, I never knew my birth mother either. Apparently, they left me in a duffle bag in an alley. A garbage man discovered me and took me to the hospital. Eventually, I ended up in the foster care system—shipped around for years from group home to group home until the day when I was finally adopted." He smiles slightly. "That day was just a few months after my 16th birthday."

"Man," Curtis whispers. "How did you survive that?"

"It was my voracious love of learning and my quirky imagination which kept me sane." Chasm motions to the waiter for his usual glass of wine. The waiter brings it immediately. Curtis watches as Chasm admires the color of the red liquid. Chasm swirls the wine in the high stem glass, inhales the aroma and takes a quiet sip. He savors the wine in his mouth—swirling it around for a moment before swallowing and continuing with his story.

"A Caucasian couple adopted me. They were in their sixties and had several failed attempts at having children of their own. They spent their entire adult lives building up wealth and influence, all so they could give it to the right child. After an extensive search—they found me."

"How did you feel?"

"I felt exhilarated!" Chasm's usually reserved body language becomes animated, as he relives the moment in his mind. "Immediately, the world—literally—became my classroom! We traveled extensively and I studied at the best schools. My new parents provided expert tutors who helped me master English, mathematics, the sciences and six languages."

"Six languages!" Curtis exclaims before covering his mouth again, as others in the restaurant look in his direction.

Chasm chuckles, waves at several of the onlookers, and then turns his attention back to his story. "It was a dream come true: to have *nothing* and then to suddenly have *everything*. It was intoxicating, and over time, it fueled my growing arrogance. My initial appreciation slowly transformed into a mindset of entitlement. My 'parents' let my cockiness go unchecked for a while—hoping that I would reign myself in—but when I didn't… they swiftly allowed certain situations to occur to refocus my perspective."

"What kind of situations?" Curtis asks—having not touched his food since the story began.

Chasm sits quietly, contemplating his words. "I'll just say that no amount of money shields you from the fact that there are those who believe the color of your skin makes you less than ideal." The words settle into Curtis' consciousness as they both are bathed in the sounds of the exquisite dining environment.

"Sometimes I still wonder who my birth parents were. Are they still alive? Do they even miss me?"

"You never found them?"

"No. But if my birth parents were in such a state that they chose to leave a defenseless infant in an alley—then maybe I don't need to know who they are."

Curtis looks at Chasm, unsure of what to say. "I'm... sorry."

"Don't be. It is not your burden to carry. What my adoptive parents did was provide an opportunity for the ambition that lived within me. And you remind me *of me* when I was your age; so full of possibilities and dreams. I'm glad we're getting a chance to know each other more."

They continue to eat in silence for several moments.

"So, where do your adopted parents live?" Curtis eagerly inquires.

Chasm hesitates. "They died a number of years ago, after I graduated from college."

Curtis looks away. "I don't know what to say."

"It's Ok. We both know what it's like to lose a loved one. It was a very dark time in my life that, quite honestly, almost destroyed me. If it wasn't for Dr. Winters helping me... I would not be here today."

"It sounds like your mentor is a great guy. Reminds me of Mr. Grabowski."

Chasm smiles at the thought. "I guess we both have been given a wonderful opportunity to know two great men."

"It looks that way," Curtis smiles.

Chasm takes a bite of his Veal Parmesan. "I have to fly to the Midwest in a couple of weeks for an all-day meeting," "Do you want to come along?"

"Really?" Curtis asks with a mouthful of shrimp and pasta in his mouth.

"We'll actually be close to the juvenile detention center," Chasm continues, "where Justin and Amanda are being held."

"Will I be able to visit them?"

"Sure," Chasm responds. "That's why I suggested you come along. It's a great opportunity to see how they are doing. They have a very long road through the judicial process. And the general population grows increasingly polarized over their actions. It might be good for them to see a friendly face."

"That would be good," Curtis replies. "Let me talk to my professors—"

"It's been taken care of," Chasm interjects with a smile. "Everything is already prepared."

"Ok..." Curtis says a bit hesitantly. "What airlines are we taking?"

Chasm smiles. "My boy, it's been a long while since I've taken public transportation *anywhere*."

Chapter Thirty

Alternate Endings

TREYSHAWN ARRIVES BACK AT HIS SCHOOL, returns to his dorm room and settles in. His new class begins the next day. After leaving that class, he marches across campus to the cafeteria.

"You gotta love this California weather!" Treyshawn smiles to himself. "It's January and the temperature is 74 degrees!"

"Hey you!"

Treyshawn turns around, sees Johnny quickly approaching, and throws up his hands in defense. "Dude, I don't have time for this."

Johnny slows his stride—putting his hands up in surrender. "Wait! I don't want to fight. I just wanna talk."

"Uh, huh," Treyshawn answers suspiciously as he looks around for an ambush. "You been wanting to fight me for the whole semester. And now you just wanna talk?"

"Right before Christmas," Johnny replies. "What did you mean by what you said?"

Treyshawn thinks for a moment. "Which part?"

"About you being me," Johnny continues somberly. "What did you mean by that?"

Treyshawn looks at him confused, "Why do you care?"

"If you answer my question, then I'll answer yours."

"You sure you're not gonna try and attack me?"

Johnny stares intently at Treyshawn. "If I did, you couldn't stop me." A few seconds pass before he chuckles and shakes his head. "Nah, man. Serious. I swear. I don't wanna fight."

As they walk, Treyshawn shares his life story—holding nothing back. When he's done, both of them are sitting on a bench. Johnny then begins to share his story.

"I was a star athlete in my town. And my dad worked at the local factory. He was up for a promotion, but lost out to a black man who had just moved into the area. His life spiraled out of control after that and within a few months, he lost his job altogether. That was right before I graduated from high school. My family was torn apart and I took *his* anger as my own. If it wasn't for my scholarship, I wouldn't have been able to come to this school.

"Then I saw you on the first day, and you became the focus of all my rage. So, I bullied you every chance I got! But when you said what you said... I don't know. It did something to me.

"My dad shot himself over Christmas break. His note said he was sorry, but with the bad economy and shortage of jobs, he just couldn't take the pressure anymore. He figured if he couldn't provide for his family, then we'd be better off without him.

"I didn't think I could come back here. But after his funeral, I knew I couldn't stay *there*. I didn't know what to do! I thought I was going to explode! But your words kept playing over and over in my head. Then I knew I had to come see you."

The two young men barely move as they contemplate each others' life experience. Only the wind rustling the leaves on nearby trees is heard.

"*Now*, I get what you meant," Johnny mumbles.

"I'm sorry for your loss," Treyshawn replies. "But if there's anything I've learned in life, it's that, for better *and* for worse, our fathers' actions really do impact us. But I think God gives us the ability to decide how we will respond. We can either play the victim... or do something positive."

January 31, 2013

The Montgomery Group private jet streaks through the sky. Curtis' face is glued to the window as he looks out and sees several airliners flying thousands of feet beneath him.

"Wow," he whispers as he turns in Chasm's direction, "We're flying higher than the airliners?"

Chasm looks up from his business papers, smiles and says matter-of-factly. "That's right. Most commercial airliners fly at a cruise altitude of 30,000 to 35,000 feet. We are currently cruising around 42,000 feet and we're moving *a lot* faster than a commercial plane."

"That is so cool. So, what kind of plane is this?"

"It's a Gulfstream—the latest and most advanced model."

"How much does one of these cost?"

"About $60 million. But that was before I made several modifications."

"What kind of modifications?"

"Perhaps one day I'll show you," Chasm chuckles as he motions to Curtis. "But in the meantime, go ahead and put your seatbelt back on."

Curtis puts his seatbelt on and sits back in his chair as Chasm secures his paperwork and motions to the two flight attendants. They quickly sit down and secure their restraints as Chasm presses a button on his chair. The captain responds, "Yes, Sir?"

Chasm smiles at Curtis as he says, "Captain, please enact maneuver 66."

"Copy sir," the captain replies. "Enacting maneuver 66."

"What's maneuver 66?"

Chasm smiles from ear to ear as three dings are heard throughout the cabin.

The captain's voice rings over the intercom, "Enacting maneuver 66 in 3... 2... 1!" The engines roar as Curtis is pushed back into his chair! The plane climbs steeply through the atmosphere for five seconds before leveling out.

"Wow!" Curtis yells.

"That *wasn't* it," Chasm chuckles, as the plane dives towards the earth— giving everyone on board a sense of weightlessness—before leveling off.

"That was amazing!" Curtis yells.

Chasm laughs, "Wait for it..."

Curtis' eyes open in wonder, "There's more?" Suddenly, the plane engages in 6 rapid spins—causing Curtis to scream the entire time before almost vomiting.

Chasm laughs heartily. "Ok Curtis! *That* was maneuver 66! Do you need a barf bag?"

Curtis takes a moment to settle himself and gain control over the contents of his stomach.

"No," he says a bit weakly. "I think I'm good."

Chasm laughs again. "Now try doing *that* on a commercial airliner!"

"No thanks," Curtis yelps. "It's scary enough on a private jet!"

"And that's the beauty of it!" Chasm says. "The freedom that being influential and wealthy affords a person. While everyone else is below us, crowded like sardines in a flying can, others are soaring in realms that most can't even imagine. There's always more to one's existence, Curtis. The first thing you must decide is if you *want* more or if you're satisfied with what you already have."

Several hours later...

Curtis sits in a sterile, cold room—surrounded by bars, bullet proof glass and fencing. He notices all the tables and benches are bolted to the floor. Several visitors sit at other tables, talking with inmates—some of whom are wearing pink jump suits. Alert guards stand at every doorway.

BUZZ... A large metal door on the left side of the room slides open. Justin walks out in handcuffs, followed by an attentive, male guard. Curtis waves as Justin scans the room. Their eyes meet and they both smile.

BUZZ... A large metal door on the right side of the room opens. Amanda walks out, followed by a female guard. She sees Justin and Curtis and waves to them. Soon, all three sit at the same table.

"You have twenty minutes," the guards say, as they remove the handcuffs and take their positions on the periphery of the room.

Curtis shakes Justin and Amanda's hands.

"It's good to see you two," Curtis smiles.

"It's good to see you, too," Justin replies.

"Yes, it is," Amanda adds, "but I never thought we'd see each other again."

"Thanks to one of my mentors... here I am!"

They sit and smile at each other, when they're not looking around at the room. Curtis notices the many cameras and the eight guards, which stand at the ready—periodically checking their watches. The trio watches as two guards leave their post and approach a table where a group of four is sitting. They are too far across the room to hear what's being said, but their body language speaks volumes.

The youth offender—a boy around 12—grabs his parents' hands as a guard motions for him to stand up. The other guard readies his handcuffs. The boy doesn't move, as his younger sister cries and pushes her way around the table to hug him. The guard—clearly annoyed—motions to the parents, who reluctantly release their son's hands. Still, the boy doesn't move. In a fluid move, the guards hoist the boy to his feet, force his hands together and handcuff him. The boy screams for his parents, as the guards all-but-drag him across the room and through the large metal door.

Curtis looks back at Justin and Amanda. "So, how are you guys holding up?"

Justin looks away. "It's tough in here."

It's really tough, "Amanda adds while wiping away tears, "but we're still alive."

"Killing myself seemed like the way to end all my pain," Justin adds. "But when it looked like I was about to die, I suddenly wanted to live."

"He still won't tell me how he tried to kill himself," Amanda interjects.

"That doesn't matter right now," Justin counters. "After I survived my suicide attempt, I kept seeing these articles where kids just like us killed themselves and the kids who bullied them didn't even care." Justin wipes away tears from his eyes. "That's when I knew they had to pay for what they did. Then one day, I saw Amanda trying to kill herself." Justin reaches over and grabs her hand. "As I pulled her down from that noose, I thought, *'Don't our lives matter?'*"

"He saved me," Amanda whispers, looking at Justin before looking back at Curtis. "Then *you* saved *us*."

"Your lives *do* matter," Curtis smiles. "And now you matter to people around the world."

Justin and Amanda look at each other. "It's crazy watching folks on TV debating about us!"

"Yeah," Curtis replies. "Everyone wants to talk about what could've and should've been done *after* a kid dies. Now, people can ponder that while everyone is *still* alive."

"True," Justin agrees, "and with all of the media coverage, we may be going to trial within a year."

"When you do," confidence marks Curtis' tone, "I'll be there."

Justin and Amanda smile from ear to ear. "Thanks!" they say in unison.

"By the way," Curtis smiles, "tell your parents I received their letters."

"They told us they wrote you," Justin grins.

"They're here every week," Amanda adds.

"So," Justin inquires, "how are *you* doing?"

Curtis sits silently—looking down with a slightly diminished smile.

"Everyone's so focused on us," Amanda adds.

Curtis looks back up. "Honestly, sometimes I have nightmares. But I'm doing better."

"I'm really sorry about that," Justin replies.

"It's a price worth paying," Curtis smiles. "Honestly, my biggest struggle has been to figure out what I'm supposed to do with my life. Since Colorado, I can't help but think about other kids who are being bullied while I'm sitting in my college classes."

"I'm sure you'll figure out something," Justin answers. "After all, you created the Speedsuit."

Two guards leave their post and approach the table with handcuffs at the ready. The time to visit has come to a close.

42,000 feet. Evening.

Curtis stares out of the window of the private jet—still in awe—as it streaks through the clear night sky. He can see the city lights below and the stars and moon above.

"The stars look like you can reach out and touch them."

Chasm takes a quick glance out of the window. "If you think that's beautiful, you should see how the world looks from low earth orbit. The curvature of the planet is awe-inspiring."

Curtis almost gives himself whiplash as he quickly turns towards Chasm. "You've *been* to space?" he exclaims while trying not to choke on his own spit.

Chasm nods with a sly smile.

"How? When?"

"That is a story for another time."

Curtis looks at Chasm in amazement. *Just when I think I know him*, he thinks to himself, *I learn something completely unexpected about him!*

"Curtis," Chasm says rather whimsically, "I want to get your thoughts on an idea."

"Sure thing," Curtis eagerly sits up in his seat.

"The work you've done with your Mach-1 clearly shows ingenuity and promise. You may have wowed the world, but I see your initial attempts as only the beginning. Imagine what we could do to help people like—for instance—our American soldiers. If we took your designs for the suit and Kinetic Redistribution Boots, and gave them a serious upgrade, they could *really* benefit our men and women on the battlefield. And my guess is that you probably have a number of other suit designs as well. If you and I worked together to create the full expression of your ideas, we could truly make a difference. *That* difference would be felt, not only on the battlefield, but across the country in law enforcement, disaster response and other sectors as well."

Curtis thinks for a moment. "That *does* sound great."

Chasm leans forward in his chair. "It's better than great. I can guarantee you high quality, high-level work with top-of-the-line resources and facilities for the next 10-20 years. You would have virtually unlimited resources at your disposal and could 'write your own ticket' creatively and financially. Your family would be set for life, and you could move your mother out of the Bronx to anywhere in the country... or world for that matter."

Chasm leans back and lets the weight of his words sink in.

"That would be a dream come true," Curtis whispers.

"Exactly," Chasm smiles confidently. "I like to think long-term. You may *only* be a freshman, but I can see you twenty years from now. You, Curtis, have the ability to change the world. I want to help you do so. Will you come and work with me?"

"Thank you Mr. Montgomery," Curtis says a bit hesitantly, "but respectfully, I don't like the idea of working on weapons for the military."

"Your brother is in the military."

"Yes. But he's a mechanic."

"A mechanic who repairs fighter jets and weapon platforms. Look. What I'm proposing does include weapons, but it's *so much more* than that.

You don't have to give me an answer right now. Take some time to think about it. But here's the reality: There are bad guys in this world that will use any and every measure to oppress and destroy *good* people. Your ideas and knowledge could help counter that and provide a real sense of security for those in the world who have none."

The rest of the flight is filled with little conversation. Chasm returns to his work and makes several calls while Curtis tries to sleep. But how can he sleep with such an opportunity weighing on him?

The next day...

Curtis leaves his class and begins making his trek across the sprawling campus. As he's walking, another student approaches him.

"Excuse me. You're Curtis Powers, right?"

"That's me," Curtis says cheerfully as he slows to talk.

The other student stops right in front of him and extends his hand. "I'm Trevor Smalley—aeronautical engineer major—Junior."

Curtis shakes his hand. "Nice to meet you. Still not sure what I want to major in yet."

"Well, it's your first year, you've got some time," Trevor laughs. "Nice to *finally* meet you. I just wanted to let you know that what you did out in Colorado was amazing!"

Curtis looks away slightly. "Thanks man."

"I mean," Trevor continues, "to stand before two disgruntled students who were aiming their assault rifles at you... to put your life on the line for total strangers... I don't think I could do that."

"Well," Curtis takes a breath, "you'd be surprised what you can do when given the right motivation."

Trevor chuckles. "You're probably right. Anyway, I saw you walking by and just wanted to let you know how I felt."

"Thanks," Curtis says, as they both shake hands again, "I appreciate you taking the time to tell me."

"Are you heading back to your dorm?" Trevor asks. "We could go get a bite to eat at the food court if you've got the time?"

"Thanks Trevor. But I'm not hungry. Just gonna head over to my workshop."

"You working on the latest upgrades to your Speedsuit?"

"Nope. But I'd love to hear about the kind of work you're doing in your major."

"Cool," Trevor says cheerfully, "Another time then. You have a great day, Curtis!"

"You too," Curtis replies. "Thanks for the encouragement!"

Trevor waves as Curtis continues his trek across campus. While Curtis walks away, Trevor's smile slowly morphs into a devious smirk as he pulls out his phone, dials a number and raises it to his ear. "I just bought you an extra few minutes. Yeah, you better hurry. He's on his way."

As Curtis approaches the door to his on-campus workspace, he immediately notices that the tape he had discreetly placed in several spots on the doorframe had been broken. He enters with caution and slowly looks around. He doesn't like what he finds. He pulls Chasm's card out of his wallet, places it next to his phone and presses the 'call' button. His phone rings twice as Chasm's voice is heard on the other end.

"Curtis, I am in the middle of a meeting at the moment. Is everything alright?"

"No, everything is *not* alright! Someone was in my workspace while we were on your business trip!"

"Calm down," Chasm replies, "It was probably just the cleaning people."

"No, Mr. Montgomery," Curtis counters, "I checked the schedule. They're not due in here until tomorrow!"

"Ok Curtis," Chasm continues, "just calm down. There has to be a logical explanation."

"Yeah, someone went through my files and tried to open up the Mach-1 case. Good thing I put those extra locks and chains on the unit! I'm calling security!"

"You do that," Chasm replies, "I apologize, but this meeting requires my attention. I will notify Erica so she can provide you with any support you may need in my absence."

"Thanks, Mr. Montgomery."

"Don't worry Curtis. We'll get to the bottom of this. Right now, call security and determine what—if anything—was stolen."

Several hours later...

Curtis, Gavin and Erica stand outside the workspace while campus security and the local police department finishes their initial investigation. While Gavin is present for emotional support, he can't help but notice Erica's attractive-but-professional appearance.

"Dude," Gavin whispers to Curtis, "Erica is *hot*! I didn't realize her hair was so long. She usually wears it in a bun."

"Can we focus here?" Curtis says sharply.

"Sorry bro," Gavin concedes quietly. "I'm just saying... And her eyes are amazing! Is she wearing contacts?"

Erica glances in their direction. "I can *hear* you Gavin."

Chasm arrives as the investigation is completed. The primary officer walks over to the group.

"It's good to see you again, Mr. Montgomery."

"You as well, Officer Callahan," Chasm says, "although I wish it were under better circumstances. I do not like theft—especially when it involves one of *my* interns."

"Well," the officer continues, "our initial investigation hasn't turned up much. There was no sign of forced entry. No fingerprints except for Curtis Powers' here. Curtis verified that all of his files are accounted for, but with every smartphone having a built-in camera, no one needs to actually steal paper anymore. So, we're not sure what may have been taken. The only real sign of anything suspicious are the crowbar marks on the large cabinet and the fact that several of the chains had been cut. That cabinet has been reinforced and those chains and locks are heavy duty. What's in there?"

"Why don't you ask Curtis?"

"It's my Mach-1 Speedsuit," Curtis responds. "That's where I keep it."

"Since our investigation is over, you mind opening it up?" the officer asks.

The group enters the workspace and Curtis pulls a keychain from around his neck. With several turns of the key, the four remaining locks disengage and the chains fall to the floor. Curtis opens the reinforced steel doors—revealing the Mach-1 Speedsuit nestled safely inside.

The officer whistles, "What a sight. I can see why someone might want to get his or her hands on *this*. Whether to use it or sell it, this is worth a pretty penny!"

Curtis closes the case.

"What if," Chasm muses, "this incident wasn't about Curtis at all?"

"What are you getting at?" Officer Callahan asks.

"Curtis is one of my interns—and a very *high profile* one at that. Perhaps whoever did this thought they might be able to gain some kind of access to me, through Curtis."

"That's plausible," the officer replies. "You are a very wealthy and influential individual. I'll have my people look into that."

"So will I," Chasm answers.

"Curtis," the officer says, "what do you want to do about your things?"

"Can I move everything out tomorrow?"

"I don't see why not," the officer says. "We'll put a police seal on the door and security will increase their presence overnight. We'll have an officer here tomorrow at 12 noon and you'll be able to pick your things up then."

"Thank you," Curtis replies.

"Yes," Chasm adds, "Thank you Officer Callahan."

"Just doing my job. Y'all have a good night."

Chasm speaks to Curtis as the police officers leave. "Please accept my apologies, since it was my idea to give you a campus workspace. This situation makes me very angry. Let me know what time you want to retrieve your things and I will have movers at the ready. I can get you set up at my facility if you like."

"It's Ok, Mr. Montgomery. I'll take care of it."

"As you wish, Curtis. Call if you need to. You all try and get some rest." With that, Chasm and Erica depart, leaving Curtis and Gavin to head back to their dorm room.

"*That* was crazy!" Gavin declares. "Why did you turn down his offer?"

"I don't know. It just felt right. I don't even know what's going on, how deep this goes or who to trust."

"Yeah, well... How are you going to move everything? Especially that huge storage case?"

Curtis looks at his roommate. "You think your dad will let us borrow his SUV?"

Gavin smiles broadly, "Even better! He's got one of those heavy duty, flat-bed trucks!"

The next day...

Curtis, Gavin and his dad wipe dirt and sweat from their faces as they drive off campus in a rather large pickup truck that's filled to capacity.

"I really appreciate your help, Mr. Pierce."

"No problem, Curtis," Gavin Sr. says. "Any friend of my son is a friend of mine. I'm just glad I was off this week."

"We were too!" Gavin laughs. "Those containers were heavy!"

"Yes, they were," Gavin Sr. agrees. "So, where to?"

"There's a storage place not too far from here. It's reputable and has some great security features. My mom already called ahead and made the arrangements."

Gavin Sr. steps on the gas. "Well then, let's get going!"

Chapter Thirty-one

Prison Plan

TWO GUARDS ESCORT TREYSHAWN PAST SEVERAL armed checkpoints, up a flight of stairs and through consecutive administration and security offices. They stop in front of a red, reinforced door. *Giving up my spring break*, Treyshawn thinks to himself, *sure hope this is worth it.* The guard on the right opens the vertical steel slab and motions for their visitor to enter the warden's office.

Treyshawn expected a tiny, sterile room that was reminiscent of the prison environment levels below; however, what he discovers is quite the opposite. The office is large and colorful, filled with enough paintings and intricate objets d'art that it could be its own museum. Treyshawn is so taken by the interior design that he doesn't even notice the man sitting behind the large mahogany desk.

"Are you surprised, Mr. Jinkins?" the warden says—his sudden speech startling Treyshawn.

"This is definitely... *not* what I expected," Treyshawn gulps.

The warden rises from his chair and extends his hand. As Treyshawn reciprocates, he immediately notices the warden's grip—like a vice. And his skin feels rough like sandpaper.

"Please sit down." The warden motions to one of the two chairs in front of his desk.

Treyshawn sizes up the warden as they sit: he's a short, but stocky man with sandy grey hair and a face with distinguished wrinkles—no doubt from incredible levels of stress. Treyshawn can tell from the size of his neck, and the musculature that's apparent, even through his suit, that the warden is a man who disciplines his body. *He probably has a military background.* Treyshawn thinks to himself.

"With the sterility that is required in a facility such as this," the warden begins, "my office needs to be an oasis of sorts."

"Makes sense to me," Treyshawn responds with a slight, nervous smile. "No use *you* feeling like a prisoner while you're here *watching* the prisoners."

The warden cocks his eyebrow and nods his head in approval. "You are a very determined young man, Mr. Jinkins. It is extremely difficult to get an audience with me. I must admit, the letter you sent was moving. The change your life has undergone is tremendous and your story is quite remarkable. But what you're asking..." The warden lets the sentence trail off while shaking his head slowly.

"I can't move on without knowing why he doesn't want to have a relationship with me," Treyshawn responds. "I *have* to know why. I *need* to know why."

The warden sits quietly in his chair with his hands poised in front of his face. "It *is* true what you said. Children do want to know about their fathers: who they are, what they've done, what has influenced them to act the way they do. It drives us. It defines us." The warden pauses a moment and looks at a picture on his desk—of him, his father and his son. "In this facility even the most hardened criminals—the most brazen of them all—still struggle with their own father issues. But you must move beyond this."

"I know," Treyshawn declares emphatically. "That's why I'm here. I *need* to move beyond this!"

"I'm sorry," replies the warden. "I was not clear. What you are requesting is very... unorthodox. It's *never* been done before. And I'm afraid it can't be done. If something goes wrong, the legal ramifications would be enormous. I'm sorry, but you must move beyond this. Live your life. Don't look back."

"How can I move beyond this when the questions in my mind gnaw at me every day?" Treyshawn asks. "I don't want that kind of torture! It's hard enough trying to do the right thing so I don't end up in a place like this—just like my father. Please... give me this chance."

The warden breathes in deeply and exhales slowly. "I'm sorry," he says curtly.

Treyshawn looks away—wiping a tear from his eye—before looking back at the warden with resolve. "My friend Curtis, who I mentioned in my letter, has questions about his father he may never get answered, because his father's dead. *My* father is alive and he's sitting right in *this* prison, but he won't talk to me!"

"Every prisoner has a *right* not to talk to visitors," the warden replies.

"But keeping his mouth shut doesn't help him or me!" Treyshawn replies. "I thought prison was supposed to be about rehabilitation."

"So," the warden muses, "you think we should just *force* him to talk to you?"

"You force prisoners to do everything else," Treyshawn states matter-of-factly. "Why not this?"

The warden sits quiet and expressionless for a moment before speaking. "You make an interesting argument. Still, I *am* truly sorry. My officers will escort you back to the visitor entrance."

Treyshawn's mouth trembles as he fights back his anger. "Why meet me just to turn me down?" He stands up slowly and extends his hand while taking a calming breath. "It was nice to meet you, sir."

"Thank you," the warden says as he stands and gives a firm handshake. He watches as Treyshawn makes his way to the office door, grasps the nob and begins to turn it.

"Mr. Jinkins."

Treyshawn turns around and faces the warden. "Yes, sir?"

"I will *grant* your request."

"You will?" Treyshawn exclaims. "What... why did you change your mind?"

The warden slowly comes from behind his desk. "My mind was already made up. But I wanted to see if you were—in person—who you claimed to be on paper. That's why I wanted to meet with you. And experience has shown me that a person's character is best measured by how they respond when they *don't* get what they want."

The warden stands directly in front of Treyshawn. "From where I stand, if you *never* get the answers from your father that you seek; and if he *never* does what you feel you need him to do; you have *already* succeeded."

Treyshawn slowly smiles from ear to ear. "Thank you, sir."

"You were right, Mr. Jinkins," the warden says while briskly making his way back to his chair. "We are supposed to be concerned about rehabilitation. And if we never find the courage to face the obstacles in our lives... then whether we are behind bars or in the general populace, we will never truly be free. My assistant will work out the details and get back to you. I'm looking forward to seeing what might come out of this... experiment."

Chapter Thirty-two

Team Speedsuit

AS THE SCHOOL YEAR COMES TO a close, Curtis sits at his desk and contemplates his past and future. He opens his journal and picks up his pen.

Journal Entry 8,229. April 19, 2013.

The school's Spring semester is over. It always amazes me how time flies by when a person has at least one major goal to focus on. Such has been the case with the first four months of the year! Classes were taken and passed. New friendships were established and old friendships were strengthened. Summer plans were solidified and everything is now ready to go!

I am happy to say that Omar is walking now - with the aid of a cane. He gets tired quickly and has to sit down after fifteen minutes or so, but mom says that every week his strength increases.

Phase two of my tour plans kick into full gear next week. We finished designing the two new suits! Now, we'll build and test them over the next two months.

May 1, 2013. 3:23 p.m. A video camera begins recording.

The team stands around Treyshawn who is wearing the first prototype of the wind suit.

"Are you ready?" Curtis asks.

"I'm ready," Treyshawn replies. "Flip the switch."

"3. 2. 1." CLICK. RRROOOOAAAAARRRRRR!!!

Papers blow everywhere, as well as anything not nailed down! The group scrambles for cover as the motor on the back of the wind suit roars at full speed. Massive amounts of compressed air shoot out of several nozzles on the suit at over 200 mph!

"Turn it off!" Treyshawn yells.

"The switch is stuck!" Curtis yells back.

"Unplug the power supply!" Jim shouts.

Treyshawn stumbles in the suit, barely able to keep his balance, as the force of the air pushes him around. Omar runs to the wall socket and pulls the plug. A spark arcs between the socket and the plug as the suit powers down. Papers flip-flop through the air as everyone comes out of their hiding spots.

"You were like a walking hurricane!" Miranda exclaims.

"Yeah," Treyshawn chuckles cautiously. "Maybe this wind suit isn't such a good idea."

"Are you kidding?" Jim counters. "That was amazing! I'm glad we had our safety goggles on, though."

They all laugh.

"Good thing we haven't installed the power cells into the suit yet," Omar adds. "Would have been a whole lot harder to shut you down."

"Yeah," Treyshawn agrees. "Get me outta this thing."

"Wait," Gavin interrupts, "before you take the suit off… how did you feel?"

"Yeah," Kelly adds. "How was it?"

"I could fee the vibration—the power of all that air being forced through the suit and out of my hands. I was scared out of my mind!"

They all laugh again.

"I wonder what will happen when we build the static electricity suit?" Gavin muses out loud. The rest of the group groans at the thought.

"One suit at a time," Miranda cautions. "One. Suit. At. A. Time."

"Well Treyshawn," Curtis jokes, "you always blew hot air back in your bullying days."

"Funny, Curtis," Treyshawn counters with a grin. "Very funny."

May 28, 2013. 4:18 p.m. The video camera begins recording.

A mannequin wears the static electricity suit: housed in a protective, reinforced plexiglass containment unit. The team stands behind an additional protective blast shield—clothed in insulated full-body suits, rubberized gloves, goggles and boots.

"Come on!" Gavin yells. "I can do it!"

"No way," Curtis counters. "This is the first time the suit is being tested. A mannequin is way safer."

"Come on, Curtis! What's the worst that could happen?"

"I've made my decision, Gavin. And it's final."

Curtis nods to Omar. Omar gives the thumbs up to Jim. Jim flips the switch. A low hum is heard from the back of the suit as the modified whimhurst generator begins to spin. An electrical charge builds in the suit's capacitors. A moment later, small electric arcs begin to emanate from the gloves of the suit. Gavin turns to Curtis.

"See! I told you everything would work! I could have been in the suit!"

BOOOOOOOOOOM!

The suit explodes in a blast of electrified bluish-orange fire! The team screams as they huddle together behind the blast shield. No one moves as dark smoke fills the protective containment unit and spews through several large cracks in the plexiglass. Jim and Omar grab their extinguishers and rush to put the fire out!

"I didn't expect that," Curtis shouts.

"What do you think happened?" Omar asks.

"I don't know," Jim replies. "Maybe we put in too many transformers to step up the voltage."

"You think?" Curtis adds with a hint of sarcasm.

Miranda looks at Gavin while shaking her head. "See? You could have been in the suit."

Journal Entry: 8,738. June 15, 2013.

After much trial and error, the wind and electricity suits are operational. Their technical designations are: Compressor Air Suit and the Electrostatic Suit. For security reasons, since they haven't been introduced to the public yet, I won't risk writing their capabilities and their descriptions here in my journal. In a few weeks, people will see them for themselves! And then I can write freely.

Journal Entry: 8,863. July 1, 2013.

Tomorrow we leave for our eight-city tour! Everything is ready to go. Our first venue is local and kicks off on July 3rd! All we need now is a good night's sleep!

July 2, 2013. The tour finally begins.

The sun kisses the horizon just after 5:00 a.m. The entire 11-person team arrives at the meeting area to load the RV with their luggage and to do last minute checks on the performance truck that will be transporting the equipment to each venue. By 6:00 a.m. the team is ready to start the first leg of their four-week, eight-city tour!

"Good morning Team Speedsuit!" Miranda yells excitedly. "This is your first *official* pep talk!"

The 11-person group—dubbed 'Team Speedsuit Powers'—applaud!

"As your tour and show manager," Miranda continues, "I want to say that it's an honor to be here with you! Let me also welcome our new team members: Gavin, Clamille and Johnny. As well as our main team members!"

The team claps again.

"We've got a *big* schedule: eight cities in four weeks. We're starting small with this show, but depending on what kind of response we receive, we could ramp up even more over the coming year. But for now, we're hitting small to medium-sized venues in New York, New Jersey, Connecticut, Massachusetts, Virginia, Washington D.C., Georgia and Illinois.

"Now everyone knows their responsibilities: As tour manager, I will liaison with all venue contacts and manage the overall logistics, including setup/breakdown, media, transportation, hotel costs, food, payments, etc.

"At each venue, there will be a team of ten to twenty or more workers to set up stages, lights, sound, video production—basically everything we need in order to create a great show! Kelly and Clamille will be assisting me. Jim will oversee all technical applications pertaining to the use of the three Powersuits—in their individual and group performances. Omar will assist him with these facets, including the monitoring of suit communications and vitals of each wearer.

"Curtis will wear the Mach-1 Speedsuit. Treyshawn will wear the Compressor Air Suit. Gavin will wear the Electrostatic Suit. Kevin, Kelvin and Johnny will handle the setup and breakdown of all the props. When needed, the drivers from the RV and the truck will assist them. Kevin and Kelvin will also be responsible for hyping up the crowd.

"We've been over this a thousand times... so rest up while we drive and be ready to hit the ground running!"

Venue 1: New York

1000 students and 500 teachers, parents and administrators fill the gymnasium of a high school in the Bronx. Excitement fills the air as they each look through their copies of the Team Speedsuit Powers event program, which is chock-full of pictures, interesting facts, illustrations and stories. Many in the audience are also wearing the two wristbands which came with the program: "Speedsuit Powers: Run Your Dreams" and "Team Speedsuit: No Bullying Allowed."

All in attendance wonder what will take place, as they look at the various large objects stationed on the gymnasium floor. The sound of talking and laughing fills the room, but quickly ceases as the show begins.

Music blasts over the sound system as Kevin and Kelvin burst through the double doors. The students cheer and rise to their feet as the twins take to the stage with extravagant athletic moves! Both are wearing their own custom made Team Speedsuit sports gear: football style for Kevin and basketball style for Kelvin.

"Welcome to the very first Powersuit Performance Show!!!" they both yell in unison as their microphone earpieces amplify the sound.

"Brought to you by Team Speedsuit Powers. I'm Kevin."

"And I'm Kelvin."

"And yes, we are identical twin brothers," both say together. "We have a great show lined up for you!"

"You're gonna see some cool performances built around science," Kevin continues.

"Stuff you've never seen before except in comics or on movie screens," Kelvin adds.

"But the difference," Kevin says, "is that comics and movies are all make-believe and special effects."

"But right here," Kelvin declares, "everything you see today is real!"

"We'll use *real* science to do everything."

"And we'll also share *real* stories about overcoming obstacles and pursuing your dreams."

"So we hope you're ready!" Kevin shouts.

For ten minutes they engage the audience in musical entertainment, provide Speedsuit trivia and invite several teens to assist them in hyping up the crowd!

"Alright!" Kevin yells. "This is the moment you've been waiting for!"

"You've seen him on Youtube!" Kelvin shouts.

"You've seen him on television!" Kevin responds.

"Now," they both say together, "see him live with your own eyes!"

"We present to you... Curtis Powers! A.K.A... JETSTREAM!!!!!!"

The crowd erupts into thunderous applause as a spotlight focuses on the far corner of the gymnasium. An extremely large paper wall printed to resemble a highway road wraps around the entrance. The sound of a turbine powering up is heard as Jetstream bursts through—waving both hands, running towards the crowd! Several obstacles are set up - one of them being an actual wall over six feet high. Using the K.R.B.'s Curtis easily jumps over it with a few feet to spare! The crowd goes wild at the sight.

Seconds later, Curtis stands in front of the crowd.

"How are you all doing?" he yells with a smile while throwing his arms up.

The audience erupts with applause!

"It's great to be here with you!"

"It's great to be here with *you!*" some of the kids yell back from the audience.

"Thank you! We've got a great demonstration prepared for you," Curtis says, as Kevin and Kelvin begin to prepare various setups.

"How many of you have seen the video of me setting the record for the world's fastest man?"

Every hand in the audience shoots up.

"Good. So you all know about my Mach-1 Speedsuit and what it can do." Curtis pulls his helmet-hood back to reveal his face. "I call this my Powersuit. But we also wanted to bring you something you *haven't* seen before! So, let me introduce you to two *new* Powersuits. They are worn by my friends, Treyshawn and Gavin!"

A secondary platform supports a giant box with holes in its walls. The box begins to rumble as flashes of blue light radiate out of the holes, followed by flowing white smoke. The sound of an explosion tears through the gymnasium as the four walls of the box fall to the floor. The light diminishes and the smoke clears, revealing two figures standing in heroic poses.

Curtis bellows, "I present to you... Windstorm and Conduit!"

The crowd cheers as Treyshawn and Gavin jump down from the platform and quickly sprint over to where Curtis is standing. Both of their suits look similar in design to the Mach-1, but with some distinct differences. The most obvious difference is the color scheme. Jetstream's suit is blue and gold. Conduit's suit is black and blue, with silver highlights. Windstorm's color scheme is green and gold, with red highlights.

"Windstorm is wearing what I call a 'Compressor Suit,' " Curtis says. "Windstorm, show everyone what you can do!"

Treyshawn turns towards a wall, three times his size, made out of foam bricks. His suit has a network of hoses built into its design to carry compressed air from the backpack to various nozzles. He raises his hands towards the foam brick wall as the compressor on his back roars to life. A split second later, a large burst of compressed air shoots from his hands and completely demolishes the wall. The audience claps and cheers at the sight.

"Conduit is wearing an 'Electrostatic Suit,'" Curtis continues, "Show these good people what your suit can do, Conduit!"

Gavin walks towards a second platform where Kevin and Kelvin are waiting with two huge cardboard boxes. Conduit's suit also has power cables built into the design to transfer electrons from one part of the suit to the other. As Gavin stands in front of them, both brothers dump several thousand foam peanuts over him—leaving him half covered in the pile.

Kevin and Kelvin step away as Gavin begins to slowly raise his hands until they are stretched out to his sides.

A whirling sound is heard as the modified Wimshurst electrostatic machine on his back revs up. Moments later, the pile of foam peanuts begins to shudder. As seconds pass, a few foam peanuts begin to leap away from Gavin. Within moments, twenty to thirty foam peanuts at a time fly up and away from Gavin. Small sparks begin to extrude from his hands as the foam peanuts completely leap away from him—forming a circle around where he stands. The crowd goes wild with excitement!

Over the next fifteen minutes, Conduit and Windstorm amaze the crowd with their capabilities: Conduit lights bulbs with his hands, attracts a number of objects with a build-up of static electricity and pops balloons with bolts of lightning from his hands. He also holds hands with a line of volunteers who are standing on rubber mats. The static electricity causes their hair to stand on end—which is a funny sight to many—and allows them all to attract and repel a number of light-weight material on several tables in front of them.

Windstorm blows down an array of materials and even juggles two volleyballs without "touching" them—using only the compressed air produced by his suit!

As the volunteers return to their seats, Conduit prepares for his finale! He cranks his Powersuit's settings up to maximum. Electricity crackles and illuminates the air around him. Suddenly, heavy bass-infused music starts playing as he performs a set of martial arts movements in time with the music! Amidst jumps and squats, Gavin throws punch after punch and swings kick after kick—with each strike punctuated by a display of visible electrical arcs!

The music stops as suddenly as it began as Conduit holds his heroic pose. He powers down the suit and bows to the audience. The crowd goes wild with applause as he raises his hands in victory and waves. He runs off to the side of the gym, making room for Windstorm's final act.

"Who wants to help us with a game?" Curtis asks.

A thousand hands fly up as echoes of "Me! Pick Me!" fill the gymnasium! Kevin, Kelvin, Kelly and Clamille run through the audience and pick random volunteers made up of kids and adults. When all is said and done, eight volunteers are culled from the audience, brought down to the floor and given protective goggles. Yellow tape lines the floor, in the shape of a very large rectangle that spans half of the gymnasiums' basketball court. Eight carts, outfitted with various sizes of lightweight balls and blocks, are stationed along the perimeter.

Curtis addresses the crowd.

"Alright! Each volunteer will stand at a cart. Windstorm will stand beneath the basketball hoop at one side of the rectangle. His objective is to move from one end of the rectangle to the other end without getting hit by the objects thrown by our volunteers. Do you think that these eight people can hit Windstorm?"

It's a mixed crowd as many shout 'Yes!' while others shout 'No!'

"There's only *one* way to find out! Windstorm are you ready?" Curtis yells. Windstorm raises his arm, nods his head and gives a hearty 'thumbs up.'

"Volunteers are you ready?" Curtis shouts. Each volunteer yells "Ready!" while grabbing the objects they want to throw. The audience sits on the edge of their seats, barely containing their anticipation.

"Alright," Curtis continues, "Three... two... one... GO!"

Windstorm walks forward and easily dodges the first few balls and bricks that are thrown at him. The crowd cheers as many onlookers yell for the volunteers to hit him!

Windstorm raises his hands at the next round of objects thrown in his direction. His compressor suit roars to life as jets of air shoot from his hands—repelling the objects away from him. As Windstorm makes it to the halfway mark, he is now actively dodging and repelling objects in an effort not to get hit. The volunteers are using every ounce of energy and mental focus to try and hit him—but so far they have all been unsuccessful!

Balls and blocks come from all directions now as Windstorm makes his way through the second half of the rectangle! He's starting to break a sweat as he realizes it's only a matter of time before he's hit. At the very last second when several objects seem to have found their target, Windstorm activates his 'windshield!' Compressed air shoots from every nozzle at once - including the custom nozzles built into his shoulder pads! To the astonishment of the crowd and volunteers, every object thrown is repelled as Windstorm is safely engulfed in a wall of compressed air! Completely unharmed and untouched, he confidently crosses the finish line—without sustaining a single hit! The audience gives a standing ovation as the sound of applause fills the room!

As the volunteers return to their seats and the applause fades, Curtis calls for Team Speedsuit Powers to come to the front. He introduces the team and invites each one to share a key point from their life about overcoming challenges, dealing with bullying and pursuing their dreams.

Kevin and Kelvin: "Because of our size, we don't really get bullied. But because we're athletes, some people underestimate us and think we're not intelligent. Our parents instilled in us a strong desire to do our best with our bodies *and* our minds. So, while we're the most valuable players on the basketball court and football field, we're also honor-roll students in the classroom. Our goal is to go Pro. But if we get injured and can no longer be athletes, we still have the ability to do other productive things. It's always good to have a 'Plan B'."

Kelly: "A good friend once told me that that I didn't have to be perfect... I just had to do my best. That piece of advice really helped to take a lot of pressure off my life. As a ballet dancer, perfection is often held as the end-all-be-all. But, we're all human and we make mistakes. We can't be flawless *all* the time, but we *can* do our best every day. And if we do our best, then the miraculous can happen."

Clamille: "My boyfriend abused me for years. I really loved him and thought that 'love' meant I had to allow him to beat me. It took friends and family to show me that if a person really loves someone, they would never abuse them. Don't let anyone abuse you. A real friend wants to see you thrive and grow. A real friend *won't* manipulate and humiliate you."

Omar: "I'm a big guy like Kevin and Kelvin. And last year, I was injured while serving my country as a Petty Officer Second Class Machinist's Mate in the United States Navy. I was partially paralyzed and in a wheelchair for months. As you can see from my cane, I'm making a lot of progress with my recovery. I wasn't sure how things would work out, but my family and friends cared for me and encouraged me to press forward. This made a big difference during the times when I just wanted to give up."

Johnny: "My dad hated a man who didn't *look* like him. Since he was my dad, I took his hatred as my own. So, when I saw black guys, like Treyshawn here, I saw through the eyes of my dad's hatred. But I also watched his hatred destroy his life, and I realized I needed help so I wouldn't end up the same way. Don't allow someone else's bias to rule your life. Even though we may look different from each other, we all want to be loved, understood and encouraged so we can reach for our dreams."

Treyshawn: "I was a school bully. Because of my bad home life and my learning disability, I was angry at everyone... especially Curtis—who is a genius! I was failing high school *and* life. I had no dreams for myself... I didn't think I had a future. But when I hit my lowest point and felt like I couldn't go on, it was Curtis who helped me. He could have kicked me while I was down, but his act of kindness—at *that* moment—began to change my life *and* my perspective. We slowly became friends, and he helped me to learn and grow. He also connected me to adults who could help me come to terms with my learning disability—Dyslexia. Now, I'm in college and my family life is a *whole* lot better. If we want to stop bullying, we have to start caring about people again... Not just the bullied kids, but the bullies too."

Curtis: "When my dad was alive, he'd always tell me, 'Do your best, so the miraculous can happen.' What he meant was that more opportunities open up for you when you do your best than when you don't. And I never would have thought that my best would have led to where we are today—right *here* and right *now*. Doing your best doesn't mean you won't encounter obstacles. The rest of the team shared stories about overcoming obstacles. And one of the biggest obstacles I've encountered was being bullied. I couldn't see a way out when Treyshawn bullied me, but having the support of my family, friends and teachers gave me hope and the ability to endure. And as Treyshawn said, when he was at his lowest point, I didn't make it worse for him, but tried to help him. And I can't take credit for that. My parents always told me to treat others how I wanted to be treated. If I was down, I wouldn't want someone to make it worse.

"And with all of the bullying going on in our schools and our communities… With all of the kids who see no way out and either take their own lives or the lives of those who bully them… we need to find positive solutions and change the way we act towards each other. Treating others with respect—just how *we* want to be treated—may not work *every* time, but it will work far better than showing hatred and retaliation to those who've hurt us."

Gavin: "Curtis and I are roommates at college. And I have to say *this* is the coolest thing I've ever done! I'm just thankful to be here, on this tour, and with you today. Let me just say that I believe you all are capable of doing anything you put your mind to! When you encounter hard times, don't view them as obstacles, but as opportunities.

"My mother raised me by herself. I didn't meet my father until a year ago. Looking at that reality from the wrong perspective almost destroyed me. I thought I was worthless, but my mother always encouraged and loved me. She helped me turn a hard time, which I saw as an obstacle, into an opportunity to develop my character. Don't let hard times make you bitter—let them make you better!

Mr. Grabowski: "I'm Curtis' former physics teacher. Actually, I'm Kevin and Kelvin's former teacher as well! What you've seen today is all based on science. But, behind the science is imagination, teamwork and discipline. Hard work can pay off when you stay focused on the goal you want to accomplish and keep moving towards it every day!

Miranda: "I'm the manager of this performance and the mother of Curtis and Omar. And while they are special to me, everyone you see here has become a part of my family. They have all spoken well and shared from their heart. And if I can leave you with one message it would be this: in order to be truly successful in life, you can't do it alone. You need a team. You need genuine friends. You need family, teachers and mentors. And most of all—even though it's not popular to say—you need God."

As the performance ends, audience members rush forward to take photos and get autographs. Many of them also buy shirts, posters and other merchandise from the Team Speedsuit Powers sales table. About an hour later, the last guests leave and the team begins breaking down the set. The inaugural tour performance has been a success! Only seven more performances over the next four weeks are left.

Journal Entry: 8,903. July 27, 2013.

Everything that's happened has been beyond my wildest dreams! People love the show! As we went from city to city, crowds grew by the hundreds as favorable media coverage increased. One venue even had to turn people away, and the venue in Atlanta had to be changed in order to accommodate larger crowds! We're now headed to the last city on our tour.

After a whirlwind experience, the last city on the tour finally arrives: Chicago. 20,000 people pack into the United Center arena and none are disappointed. The Chicago performance goes like the previous ones—and the first-ever 'Powersuit Performance Tour' has officially come to an end.

Since this is Gavin's home city, his mother attends the performance, meets the entire team afterwards and celebrates with them at a local restaurant. Being so far away from home, the exhausted team stays an extra night in their hotel to get some much needed rest before making the long drive back home to New York.

Chapter Thirty-three

Stolen

GAVIN AND CURTIS ARE ENGAGED IN a heated conversation inside the equipment trailer in the hotel parking lot. It's been a very long day already and they've been up for hours.

"You're being crazy." Curtis retorts.

"Am I?" Gavin asks.

"Do you even realize what it would take to do that?" Curtis replies.

"Yeah! Everything you have *right here*," Gavin waves his hands at the multiple Powersuits and other technology in the trailer. "You have a cool suit that gives you special abilities—an edge *over* the criminals!"

"Criminals with weapons!" Curtis sits at a console. "You'd need a suit that protects your body from impacts, like being hit with a bat, and bullet proof armor to at least stop small caliber gunfire. The suit would also need some armor plating to stop knives and protect your vital organs. Then the suit needs to be flexible, so your movements aren't restricted and you can be quick on your feet. On top of that, you'd need to conceal your identity."

"With a mask," Gavin shouts.

"A mask won't stop knives to your eyes or a baseball bat to your head," Curtis counters. "You'd need a helmet for that. Then you'd need some defensive and offensive weaponry."

"Yeah," Gavin agrees eagerly. "Some kind of tech to protect you from multiple assaults: like strobes and sonics to disorient your attackers. You can use electricity, too."

"Yeah?" Curtis quips, "And what happens if the suit's power cells run out in the middle of a fight? Your tech is useless!"

"Martial arts!" Gavin yells excitedly. "I've studied for ten years!"

"Gavin, this isn't a videogame or a comic book."

"Says the guy who created three Powersuits," Gavin crosses his arms. "Speed. Wind. Electricity. What else you got brewing in that brain of yours?"

"Gavin," Curtis huffs, "there are too many variables! On top of everything else, you'd need some kind of transportation—something beyond what law enforcement has, or at least comparable. Then you'd need an encrypted communications system, a headquarters and at least one other person to coordinate everything and be an extra pair of eyes and ears while you're on the streets."

"Yeah," Gavin smiles, "like Batman has Alfred."

"This isn't funny!" Curtis yells.

"Who's laughing?" Gavin counters. "I'm serious. We could do this."

Curtis throws his hands up while turning away.

"You say we can't do it," Gavin interjects, "but it seems like you've given this a lot of thought already."

"What comic book geek hasn't?" Curtis fires back. "I'm just saying it's *too* complicated."

"You've built all this," Gavin utters in disbelief, "and all you want to do is go around and put on a show?"

"Gavin," Curtis sits down, "what better way is there to fight crime—to help take the desperation away—than to inspire people to develop goals so they can reach for their dreams? Then they won't have to commit crimes."

"So, a traveling circus inspires people?" Gavin asks sarcastically.

"You know what," Curtis rises from his chair, "if you can't understand why I'm doing what I'm doing, then maybe you don't need to be here."

"Maybe I *should* leave," Gavin counters, "since you *can't* understand why I'm saying what I'm saying."

"I know what you're saying," Curtis says flatly. "You know martial arts. You've worn a suit that puts lightning in the palm of your hands. You want to fight crime. You think it would be cool."

"It's more than that," Gavin yells as he looks at Curtis. "It's more than that..."

Curtis looks at his friend. "Ok... tell me *how* it's more."

"Where I'm from..." Gavin tries to gather his words. "I know you lived in the hood. But you moved there from the suburbs, as a teenager. And where you are now isn't that bad. But I was born in the hood. I grew up in it. Breathed it in every day. I've seen guys shot right in front of me... I've *watched* people die. I've been held up at gunpoint like five times! Cops don't even come around my block unless *they* got backup. People just try to live life—too afraid to pursue their dreams—trapped in their own apartments while gangs and drug dealers run the streets. And if it wasn't for my mom and dad putting me in private school, I don't even know if I would have had any dreams at all—let alone be alive to pursue them."

"But that's why we're here," Curtis declares softly, "to *inspire* people to dream."

"What good is inspiration if you have to deal with being afraid every day of your life? What good is a dream if you have no way to pursue it? If you combined three suits into one or if you got people to use those suits as a team to stop criminals... you could really make a difference."

"Gavin. I understand what you're saying... but it's crazy."

"There are no 'buts'." Gavin counters. "You don't get to back out of this."

"These are *my* suits, Curtis answers sternly. "And this is *my* choice."

"Well, I think you're *choosing* wrong."

"You wanna be a vigilante? Real people can die doing something stupid like that. This isn't a TV show. There's no cheerleader to save, so you can save the world.'"

"Real people die *every* day," Gavin shouts, "while politicians yap their traps and cops barely enforce the laws that are supposed to *protect* people from the criminals! With everything you've done... I thought you'd figure that out by now." Gavin gets up, takes his jacket and leaves Curtis alone in the trailer.

The sound of a beeping alarm awakens Jim Grabowski. He slowly turns over in his bed and looks at the hotel alarm clock. It's 2:30 a.m. He slams his hand on the clock, but the beeping continues. After his grogginess wears off, he realizes that the sound isn't coming from the clock, but from his security communication device sitting *next* to the clock.

"Oh, no," he says while lurching into an upright position on his bed.

Minutes later, he's knocking at another hotel door.

"Curtis! Omar!" Jim yells through the door. "Wake up!"

A sleepy Omar hobbles from the bed with his cane, while Curtis turns over in his bed and covers his head with a pillow. Omar opens the door as Jim pushes past him before he has a moment to complain.

"We have to go, now! Someone's broken into the trailer!"

"What?" Curtis says while leaping to his feet!

Sixty seconds later, the trio makes their way to the elevator—with Omar hobbling as fast as he can and Curtis hopping while trying to get his sneaker on. Once in the hotel parking lot, they approach the trailer cautiously, quickly noticing that the main door is ajar and the alarm is beeping.

Omar reaches into his pocket for his cell phone. "I'm calling the cops."

"Not yet," Jim advises while holding a metal rod. "Not until we know what's going on."

The three of them hesitantly enter the trailer. No one is there.

"Check the suits," Omar commands.

Curtis opens the first sealed container: the Mach-1 is there. He opens the second sealed container: the Compressor Suit is there. He opens the third sealed container:

"The Electrostatic Suit is gone!"

Omar looks around and notices another theft. "The backup KRB's are missing, too!"

"*Who* would have done this?" Jim asks.

"Gavin," Curtis states angrily.

"Gavin?" Jim and Omar respond.

"Long story," Curtis huffs. "Mr. G, we need to track the suit."

"Already on it! " Jim types at a computer console. A moment later, a satellite map of Chicago appears on the screen. Omar and Curtis stand next to Mr. G as the tracking program locates the missing suit.

"There!" Omar points to a pulsing blue dot on the screen. "About eighteen blocks from here! He's moving fast!"

"Let me talk to him." Curtis grabs a headset and puts it on. "I wish we had installed the cameras into the new suits."

With the press of a button, a communications link is established to the missing suit."

Eighteen blocks away, a figure sprints across apartment building rooftops. Gavin yells in excitement, as he leaps from one building to the next!

"So *this* is what it feels like to be him," Gavin says to himself with a smile.

"Gavin!" Curtis' voice blares through the helmet's earpiece.

"Ouch! Curtis?"

"What do you think you're doing!" Curtis yells.

"First—your boots are amazing! Second—I'm going to *prove* my point."

"What you're going to *do* is turn around and get back here!"

"Don't think so, Bro!"

"Gavin," Jim interrupts. "This is not a game. You need to come back here before this gets out of hand. We don't want to have to call the police."

"Go ahead and call 'em. By the time they get to me, I'll have some *real* bad guys waiting to be taken away."

"Gavin," Omar interjects, "what are you trying to prove?"

"Ask Curtis."

"This is ridiculous!" Curtis walks over to the Mach-1 case, opens it and begins suiting up. "I'm going after him."

"I don't know how to stop you guys from talking to me," Gavin says, "but I'm about to hit a hot spot and won't be responding. Sit back and enjoy the show!"

Jim and Omar check the suit's setup protocols: Power levels are at 100%. Internal Climate Control is active. Communications and Visor Display are online.

"Mr. G, I need you to feed Gavin's telemetry to my suit."

"You got it. Omar and I will follow you in the truck."

Curtis looks back once more before exiting the trailer. "Once this is over, we need to install a 'kill switch' in the suits, so this never happens again."

Curtis activates his K.R.B.'s, leaps from the trailer to the ground and runs towards the parking lot's exit with an increasing stride. Once he hits the street, he activates the suit's Vortex Pack. The turbine roars to life as a continuous stream of pressurized air propels him down the block at forty-five miles per hour.

Halfway across town...

"Somebody help me!" A young lady runs for her life as three men chase her down a poorly lit street. She cuts in between two buildings, but discovers the alley is a dead end. She stares at a brick wall with no time to retreat. The three thugs block the only way out of the alley.

"Hey, baby," one guy sneers. "Nowhere for you to go."

"We just wanna talk," another guy taunts.

"Leave me alone!" the girl yells. "Somebody help me!!!"

The three men slowly approach her.

"Yell all you want," one snickers. "Ain't nobody comin' to help you."

One of them brandishes a knife from his back pocket. The woman begins crying profusely as she raises her hands and pleads for her life.

"Please... Please... You don't want to do this."

"Yes we do," one guy replies with a crooked smile. "We *definitely* want to do this."

"I just want to go home!" The woman starts hyperventilating.

"Yeah. You can go home... just take us with you."

Before the young men can take another step, Gavin leaps from the rooftop, cascades down the adjacent brick walls, lands in between the young woman and her assailants and quickly takes a defensive position.

"You heard the woman! Back off!" The voice digitizer in his helmet gives Gavin's words an electrified tone.

The men look at the costume-clad figure in front of them—unsure if they should laugh or fight.

"Don't know who you supposed to be or where you came from," one of the attackers shouts, "but *this* ain't no comic book!"

With almost lightning speed, Gavin leaps towards them, leading his assault with a flying kick that sends the first assailant crashing to the ground. The remaining two thugs pull out their weapons—a machete and a metal tube. They lash out at the costumed figure, but fail to hit him due to his speed and jumping ability.

Gavin leaps over the second guy, turns and parries his machete attack and lands a well placed electrostatically charged palm strike to his chest. A bright blue flash pierces the air at the point of contact, as a mini-thunderclap reverberates loudly. The guy yells as he hurtles almost twenty feet back and crashes into several garbage cans! In the midst of the chaos, the girl makes her escape as Gavin confronts the final assailant.

"What did you do to him?" The third guy shouts nervously.

"Come and find out!" Gavin replies.

The last thug lets out a battle cry and lunges at the vigilante! He swings his metal rod fiercely, but Gavin doges each strike!

"Can you make this difficult for me? Gavin says sarcastically.

"Arghh!" The third guy swings wildly!

The first attacker struggles to his knees—out of Gavin's view—and watches the confrontation. "This dude is fast," he says to himself as he pulls a gun out of his inside jacket pocket.

The third guy swings his rod! FWAP! Gavin catches the rod with his gloved hand while engaging the gauntlet's electrostatic circuits.

"Ahhhhhh!" The guy screams, as electricity passes from Gavin's hand, through the metal rod and into him!

Gavin lets go of the rod as the guy falls to the ground. He stands still— breathing heavily—reveling in his accomplishment, as the two thugs lie semi-conscious on the pavement.

"Wait," Gavin says to himself, "where's the third guy?"

BLAM! BLAM! BLAM! Three shots ring through the night air as Gavin lets out a yelp. His body arches back awkwardly as his arms flail out! He stumbles a few steps and falls to the ground as the first assailant hobbles over to him with his smoking gun.

"Ain't so tough now." He turns to his two cronies. "Come on! We gotta get outta here before someone calls the cops!"

The three of them stumble out of the alley, leaving the costumed would-be vigilante lying motionless on the asphalt.

A minute later, the sound of a roaring turbine echoes through the air, as Curtis arrives. "Gavin!" He kneels down next to him, sees the bullet holes and presses his helmet's communication button. "Guys," he yells in a panic,

"Gavin's been shot! Call an ambulance!"

"We're three blocks away," Omar replies. "By the time the ambulance gets here, we could be at the hospital already."

Curtis turns Gavin over and takes off his helmet. "Gavin! Gavin!! Can you hear me?"

"...Curtis..." Gavin responds while slowly opening his eyes.

"You're alive! "

"I'm... sorry."

Omar and Mr. Grabowski pull up in the truck and rush to Gavin's side to assess his condition before moving him.

The double doors to the ER slide open as Curtis, Omar and Jim enter with Gavin in their arms.

"We need some help here!" yells Omar. Several nurses run over to assist and are immediately hesitant when they see Gavin and Curtis in Powersuits.

"This is way too early for Halloween," a nurse comments.

"Wait," the other nurse answers, "aren't you Curtis Powers?"

"Yes. Please help us! Our friend's been shot!"

"We're part of a performance tour." Jim adds, "We were running some costume tests outside and our cast member was attacked by some guys and shot in the back!"

Several hours later...

Gavin slowly opens his eyes. His body and mind are sluggish, but he can hear the beeping of the monitors next to his bed. As he looks around, he sees Curtis, Omar and Mr. Grabowski sitting in chairs next to his bed. He then feels a hand holding his own and turns to find his mother sitting on the other side of him.

"Mom?" Gavin asks in a weak, dry, bewildered voice.

"Hola hijo," she smiles softly. "How are you feeling?"

Gavin looks at his mother. "Everything hurts. What... happened?"

"You were shot. You're at the hospital. They got all three bullets out."

"How... how did you get here?"

"After you were brought here, Curtis called his mother. She called me." Her expression becomes more serious. "And I called your father."

"What?" Gavin whispers weakly. "Why did you call him?"

"He has a right to know. He wanted to fly out here, but I told him I could handle things."

"How... how is he?" Gavin asks wearily.

His mom pulls out her phone and presses the video chat button. "Ask him yourself."

A moment later, his father's image is on the screen.

"Gavin!" he yells. "How are you? Are you OK?"

"I'm... fine Dad," Gavin smiles slightly.

"Really?" Gavin Sr. asks. "Three bullets to your back and you're fine?"

"Dad, listen. What I did... it was stupid."

"You bet it was stupid!" Gavin Sr. yells back. "I was ready to sue the pants off of Curtis and this entire show until your mother gave me a chance to talk to him, Omar and Jim."

"This was all *my* idea," Gavin confesses.

"I know," his father replies. "Tell me, was getting shot *your* idea too?"

"I got cocky Dad," Gavin admits. "Did they tell you I saved a woman tonight?"

Curtis, Omar and Jim look at each other in surprise. Gavin's mother is astonished.

"No," Gavin Sr. is stunned. "No, they didn't."

"The suits record and relay what the wearer hears," Omar says. "We didn't get a chance to install cameras so we could 'see' what the wearer sees. We only heard the commotion."

"Three guys," Gavin smiles. "I stopped three guys from raping a woman—maybe even killing her. But while I was busy patting myself on the back, I didn't see one of them get up."

"Son," Gavin's father replies, "this is *not* a movie. The doctor said if it wasn't for all of the insulation, padding and plating in the suit, the damage would have been much worse."

"You could have been killed," his mother interjects, "or paralyzed."

"I know," Gavin whispers.

"Son. When your mother and I agreed to let you go on this adventure, we never thought things would end up like this."

"I know, Dad. But I was just trying to prove a point."

"And what point was that?" his father asks.

"That Curtis' inventions could change the world in more ways than he could imagine."

Later that morning...

The entire team is at the hospital saying their goodbyes to Gavin. His mother has prepared to stay and bring him home for the month of August until it's time for him to return to school.

"I can't believe you took on three armed dudes in the hood," Treyshawn laughs. "That was crazy!" He shakes his head. "Still, you could've been killed."

"So could that woman I saved," Gavin grins with a twinkle in his eye.

"True," Treyshawn concedes. "True."

"Either way," Kelly adds, "I'm sure she's grateful to be alive."

"And we're *definitely* grateful that you're alive," Kevin shouts.

"Stupid or not," Kelvin interjects, "You're my hero."

"Yes," Miranda agrees, "but no more suits for you!"

They all laugh.

Miranda continues. "I am *so* glad I didn't skimp on the insurance policy!"

"Gavin," Jim says, "all kidding aside... I know you meant well, but what you did—it was both ill-advised *and* a crime. We're not pressing charges and thank God your parents aren't pressing charges against *us*. But you've put us in a precarious position. Miranda, Omar and I have been filling out paperwork all morning in conjunction with the hospital and the police department."

"You proved your point," Omar adds, "but look at the cost."

"I know..." Gavin replies. "I've got a lot to think about."

"Yes, you do young man," his mother asserts. "But for now, say goodbye and let your friends get on the road."

The group exchanges hugs with their fellow teammate and then vacates the room. Curtis is the last to leave and stands next to Gavin's bed.

"Dude. With everything I've been through, don't *ever* put me in that position again."

"I'm sorry Curtis. I didn't even think about that..."

"I know you didn't," Curtis agrees. "But when I got to that alley and you were lying face down and not moving... I thought you were dead. I felt like my chest was going to explode."

Gavin looks at his friend in silence, as his mother watches from across the room.

"I'll see you in a month?" Gavin asks.

"Count on it."

Gavin's mother smiles as her son and Curtis hug. Curtis walks to the door and stops.

"Hey Gavin. By the way..."

"Yeah?"

"Point taken."

Team Speedsuit returns to New York and disbands for the rest of the summer. For the team, August is a time for relaxation, reflection and family. Local and national media coverage hails their efforts to produce the Powersuit Tour as an inspiring success:

"ELECTRIFYING! BLOWN AWAY! Pass the SPEED LIMIT!" -Time

"From World Record to the Olympics, to a Jaw-Dropping Performance. Curtis Powers and his team have DONE IT AGAIN!" - Newsweek

"The Powersuit Tour is a FEEL GOOD show for the entire family!" - NBC

"ABSOLUTELY RIVETING!" – The Boston Globe

The wonder of it all made me FEEL like a kid again!" –Huffington Post

"SPEED. WIND. LIGHTNING. OH MY! What a treat for people of ANY age!" - ABC

"What a wonderful demonstration of SCIENCE. TECHNOLOGY. ENGINEERING. ARTS and MATHMATICS." – Chicago Sun Times

"Curtis Powers has had a series of AMAZING firsts… I can't even IMAGINE *what he will do next!" – USA Today*

"INSPIRATION. MOTIVATION. EDUCATION. All wrapped up in a POWERSUIT BOW!" – Atlanta Journal-Constitution

Invitations for future events flood in as Miranda, Jim, Curtis and Omar consider the team's next move. Amidst all of the letters from across the country, one arrives from an athletic organizer. But meeting with him will have to wait until the end of the summer.

Dear Curtis Powers and the Powersuit Team,

Congratulations on your completed tour! What you have accomplished is truly amazing. When a colleague of mine showed me a video of your Windstorm suit in action, I knew immediately that we needed to connect.

I would like to meet with you and your decision makers to discuss the possibility of creating an entirely new and unique team sport. As an athletic planning company, my organization plays an integral part in creating and sustaining extreme sports across the globe.

It is my belief that if we can marry your Powersuit invention with my concept, we can create a new form of athletic entertainment that could potentially rival basketball, football and even baseball.

Please contact me at your earliest convenience. Thank you for your time and consideration.

Sincerely,

Roger "Chase" Maxwell
X-Games Athletic Creation Group
Denver, Colorado

Chapter Thirty-four

Taken

SHORTLY AFTER TREYSHAWN'S ARRIVAL BACK IN New York, he and his mother take a trip to Riker's Island.

"Are you sure you don't want me to go with you?" Shakira asks as Treyshawn steps out of the taxicab.

"No thanks, Ma. I'll tell you all about it when I get home."

"Still don't know how I feel about this plan of yours. Your father is not a man to be trifled with."

"Are you trying to make me more nervous than I already am?" he asks.

"No." Shakira looks at him concerned. "I just want you to be fully aware."

"I am," Treyshawn declares confidently. "I can't run from this anymore."

"Good," Shakira replies. "Make sure you keep your arms up and cover your head."

"Ma!"

Shakira chuckles nervously, "Look, I'm just keepin' it real, Ok?"

Treyshawn shakes his head and smiles as he closes the car door. "See you soon, Ma."

"Bye, baby."

As the car drives away, Shakira watches her son through the back window. He stands still for what seems an eternity; and when the car is about to turn out of view, he begins walking toward the prison's entrance.

"My baby," Shakira utters to herself. "He ain't no baby no more."

BZZZZ. The iron gates open as two corrections officers escort a hooded Treyshawn Sr., into the visitors center. They sit him down and leave the room. The buzz is heard again as the gates lock into place. As Treyshawn Sr. removes the black hood and his eyes adjust to the bright lights, he finds himself sitting directly across from his son. He swiftly reaches across the table and grabs his son by the shirt and pulls him towards him.

"What is this?" he shouts. "Where is everyone?"

"It's just us," Treyshawn responds. His father pushes him away, gets up from the table and walks back to the gate.

"I want out of here!" he yells. There's no response. "Hey! C/O! I know you hear me talking to you! Open up!!" The correction officers don't budge and the gate remains shut and locked tightly.

"They're not going to open that gate until the right time," Treyshawn says defiantly.

"And when *is* the right time?" his father asks while turning to face him. "You running things now, Trey?" In a flash, he runs towards his son, grabs him by the neck and lifts him off the ground. "Is the right time when *you* say it is? But what if you can't speak?"

Treyshawn struggles to get free. "Dad…" he sputters.

"I could break your neck before the guards get in here!"

The warden watches the scene unfold from his office monitors. He quickly triggers the intercom to the guard desk. "If he doesn't let go of his son in the next 15 seconds, I want you to go in there and stop him!"

"You prepared to die, Trey?" His father yells. "You ready to die for *this*?"

Treyshawn can barely speak, as he forces out one word: "Y—Yes."

Father and son stare into each other's eyes without wavering. The guards make their way to the gate and prepare to enter, but Treyshawn Sr. lets his son drop to the ground—so they hold their positions. Treyshawn coughs repeatedly while gasping for air. His father turns back towards the gate and watches as the guards move back to their stations.

"Open this gate," Treyshawn Sr. yells as he lunges at the gate and shakes it with his bare hands!

"They're not… opening the gate," Treyhawn tells his father while still trying to regain his voice. "Not… until you tell me… what I want to know."

"I told you to leave me alone!" Treyshawn Sr. says with growing anger.

"All I want to know is why you don't want me!" Treyshawn yells back. He stands to his feet. "Just tell me *why*… and you can go back to your cell!"

Treyshawn Sr. charges at his son again and slams him into the wall. Treyshawn gets the wind knocked out of him, but he doesn't back down.

"Is that… how you always handle things… you don't like?" Treyshawn asks. "You hit stuff?"

Treyshawn Sr. roars as he throws his son across the room. Treyshawn hits the polished floor and slides into the other wall. His father stands in a huff—breathing heavily. Treyshawn forces himself back to his feet. His dad yells again as he rushes him and slams him into the other wall! Treyshawn yells out in pain as his father grabs him by the mouth, with his left hand, and raises his right hand into a fist. His eyes are full of rage! His hand and arm tremble slightly in the air as he prepares to end this conversation once and for all. But before he can strike, his son spurts out a single question.

"So, you're gonna beat me like your father beat you?"

His father's eyes instantly register confusion. His fist loosens as his grip relaxes a bit.

"How… How did you know that?" His confusion gives way to anger as he begins to growl. "Who told you that?"

"Melvin," Treyshawn declares defiantly.

Treyshawn's father releases his grip on his son and stumbles back. "This… this is over *right* now!"

"Not until you tell me *why*," Treyshawn says while slowly moving towards his father.

"Shut up!" His father backs away.

"Not until you tell me!" Treyshawn moves closer to his father.

"Leave me alone!" Treyshawn Sr. stumbles and trips over the bench.

"Not until you tell me!" Treyshawn yells again—gaining strength with each step.

The warden leans forward in his chair as he focuses intently on his video monitor.

"Open that gate!" Treyshawn Sr. yells again as he scrambles to his feet.

"Not until you *tell* me, Dad!!" Treyshawn yells while grabbing his father's jumpsuit. "Tell me… Why you don't want me!!!"

"Because I don't know how to be a father!" Treyshawn Sr., howls at the top of his lungs!

He stands in silence, groping for words that never come. His eyes blink wildly as tears begin to stream down his face. He pushes Treyshawn away from him and starts pacing the floor. Moments pass in silence, as Treyshawn watches his dad struggle to breathe and beat the air as if he was fighting off an invisible assailant. Finally, he calms down enough to repeat the words that revealed what he has always feared.

"I don't know... how to be... a good father." He collapses to the floor in an exhausted heap.

"Dad..." Treyshawn walks over to his father.

He looks up at his son. "All *I* know is that a father beats his kid— constantly. Yells at 'em! Tells 'em they're nothin'. So... I just... don't." He forces himself to his feet and defiantly wipes away his tears. "I'm done."

"Dad, wait," Treyshawn reaches into his bag and pulls out a book. "Wait! I got this for you!"

"You *got* what you wanted," Treyshawn Sr. walks to the gate. He doesn't even turn around to see what Treyshawn is holding. "Now *leave* me alone."

"Dad. Wait!"

Treyshawn Sr. looks over his shoulder at his son, "I'll always hate you for this." He turns back towards the guard station. "Open this gate *now!*" he growls.

BZZZZZ. The guards open the gate. Treyshawn Sr. extends his hands as the guards put the restraints back on him. As the gate closes behind him, Treyshawn yells out.

"Dad, you don't have to be like your father! You can be different! We... can be different!"

Treyshawn stands alone as his father disappears down the corridor. Another corrections officer comes to escort him to the exit.

"If you want," the guard says as they walk, "you can give me the book and I'll make sure he gets it." Treyshawn looks at the guard and then at the book in his hand. He stares at it for a long time before releasing it into the guard's care.

"I'm trusting you with this." Treyshawn looks the guard in his eyes.

"You've got my word," the guard says. "I'll make sure your dad gets it."

As Treyshawn is about to walk through the exit, the guard speaks again.

"I've seen your father almost every day for ten years and I've *never* seen what I just saw. I've never seen him break like that... not even once."

Thirty minutes later...

Treyshawn Sr. lies on his cot, facing the wall, as clanging is heard on the bars to his cell. He slowly turns and sees the guard walking away. Left in his place—just inside the cell on the floor—is a tray with a book on it. He looks at the book for a long time from across his small room. He then turns back over on his cot, facing the wall, and closes his eyes.

In an undisclosed location, a man sits in a dark room, bathed in blue and white light from several computer screens. He sits quietly in the darkness—pensive—watching videos of Curtis' three Powersuits in action. *You have been very busy,* he thinks to himself. At the press of a button, a schematic file displays on the large screens. His cell phone rings.

"Yes? I am reviewing it now. According to your report, this file was relatively easy to acquire. True. It shouldn't surprise me that you figured out his password and unlocked the low-level encryption so easily; after all, you are a prodigy. No. I am not concerned about the other suits. His Mach-1 Speedsuit is the key. Are you sure you can overcome the design flaw issues? No. I don't doubt your ability at all. Yes. The new file is coming in now."

The man smiles slightly as a 3D image of an exosuit—inspired by the Mach-1—renders on the main screen in front of him.

"What do I think? Your upgrades look *very* promising. Move forward with the replication. Initiate the next phase."

Four hours later…

Curtis walks through his neighborhood in shock, as he and Kelly listen to Treyshawn's story over the phone.

"Are you serious?" Curtis asks, as he holds his phone to his ear.

"I know." Treyshawn says as he lies on the living room couch in his house. "I couldn't believe it myself."

"Just like that?" Kelly asks as she stretches on her dance bar in her living room.

"Well not *exactly* just like that." Treyshawn rubs his ribs. "My dad punches *really* hard. Good thing I wore that padding underneath my shirt. Thanks Curtis. Your idea probably saved me from getting a couple of cracked ribs!"

The three of them chuckle.

"Then the guard said he had never seen my dad break down like that—ever."

"Dude, your plan worked!" Curtis exclaims.

"Yeah," Kelly adds.

"How far are you from your house?" Treyshawn asks.

"About a block and a half away," Curtis responds. "The sun's just about to set. I'm gonna take a picture of it and send it to you guys. It's gorgeous."

A car engine roars from behind Curtis as a black sedan screeches to a stop! The doors fly open as three masked men jump out and wrestle Curtis to the ground.

"Hey!" Curtis yells as his phone is knocked under a nearby car. "A black car!" he yells. "Somebody help me!"

"Curtis!" Treyshawn yells while jumping to his feet.

"Curtis!" Kelly cries. "What's happening?"

Curtis yells as one of the kidnappers strikes him on the back of the head with an iron rod! Now unconscious, they gag and tie him up and throw him into the trunk. Treyshawn and Kelly listen intently to the sound of the doors slamming shut, the tires screeching, and the engine roaring into the distance.

"Curtis?" Treyshawn yells.

"Curtis can you hear us?" Kelly bursts into tears.

"Curtis!!!"

But only the wind answers their call... punctuated by the repetitive sound of a nearby car alarm... and then... silence.

Epilogue

Focus

WE ARE SO FOCUSED ON THE minutia of our own lives that we rarely think long and hard enough to see the big picture. We never think when we set out to change the world—or at least the lives of those in our world—that we would encounter so much opposition. We never fathom at the beginning that there would be so many bumps and potholes in the road. If we knew at the start how much resistance we would encounter before the end, many of us would give up on the race before it even began.

There are so many systems of control—layers upon layers. When we break free of one, another is poised, waiting to smother us. There are those who wield the mechanisms, which determine the rise and fall of nations, as well as individuals. They seek to maintain their hold on our reality at all costs. If we can be bought, they will buy us. If we can be coerced, they will intimidate us. If we can be deceived, they will manipulate us. But if we hold to the truth, they will seek to silence us.

Who do these kidnappers work for?

Will Curtis ever see his friends and family again?

Will Miranda's pursuit of the truth behind her husband's canceled policy ever be resolved?

Will Treyshawn be able to build a relationship with his father?

Who is the 'man in the undisclosed location?'

How do all of these pieces fit together?

Discover the answers to these questions and more in BOOK 3 of the SPEEDSUIT POWERS TRILOGY. Coming: Christmas 2015.

Get ready. The phenomenon continues.

Reader's Guide
Selected Themes

Three themes from Book 1 are: The Power of Influence, Purpose & Identity, and The Ability to Choose. Many themes emerge from the pages of this second book. Consider them in terms of the characters' lives and your own. Here are five to get you started....

Theme 1:
Obstacles, Opposition & Temptation

These may seem like separate issues, but they are actually different facets of the same thing: Distractions that can throw you off your game. How do the characters in this book deal with these issues? How do you deal with obstacles, opposition and temptation in your own life?

Theme 2:
The Ability to Choose

This theme is woven throughout each book in the trilogy. The ability to choose is one of the greatest abilities we all posses. The decisions we make affect the trajectory of our lives. Ultimately, this story raises the question, 'You know you can, but should you?' What do you think? Just because a person can do something, should they do something?

Theme 3:
Fatherhood

Curtis, Omar, Treyshawn, Gavin, and even Chasm are dealing with fatherhood issues. How do they handle their issues? How does a father's presence or lack of being present have an affect on their kids? How can a child positively deal with their fatherhood issues?

Theme 4:
Bullying Solutions

Curtis, Treyshawn, Justin, Amanda, Chad, Claire and Johnny have experienced bullying from different perspectives. How do they handle their situations and what can you learn from their experience? Have you encountered bullying in your own life or school? How do you cope? What can you do to deal with bullying? Curtis offers a solution for finding a way for us all to win. How can you find a way for everyone to win?

Theme 5:
Family Heritage

In Book 1, all Treyshawn knows about his life is that his mother and father hate him. As he comes to understand who he is and begins to take ownership of his life, he affects a positive change in his mother. In Book 2, Treyshawn discovers he comes from a rich family heritage he never knew about, which stretches back further than his issues with his mother. How does that discovery further affect his journey? How can discovering more about your distant past help you move forward with your future?

What other themes did you discover in this story?

Visit: **www.APW3.com** to find out more about the themes, story, characters and more!

A Visual Look

Illustrations & Concept Art

Illustrations by Allen Paul Weaver III.
3D Concept Art by Jeff Tyler

3D Chasm Facilities

Chasm Montgomery Facilities Layout

Chasm Montgomery Facilities Main Building

Chasm Montgomery Facilities Entrance

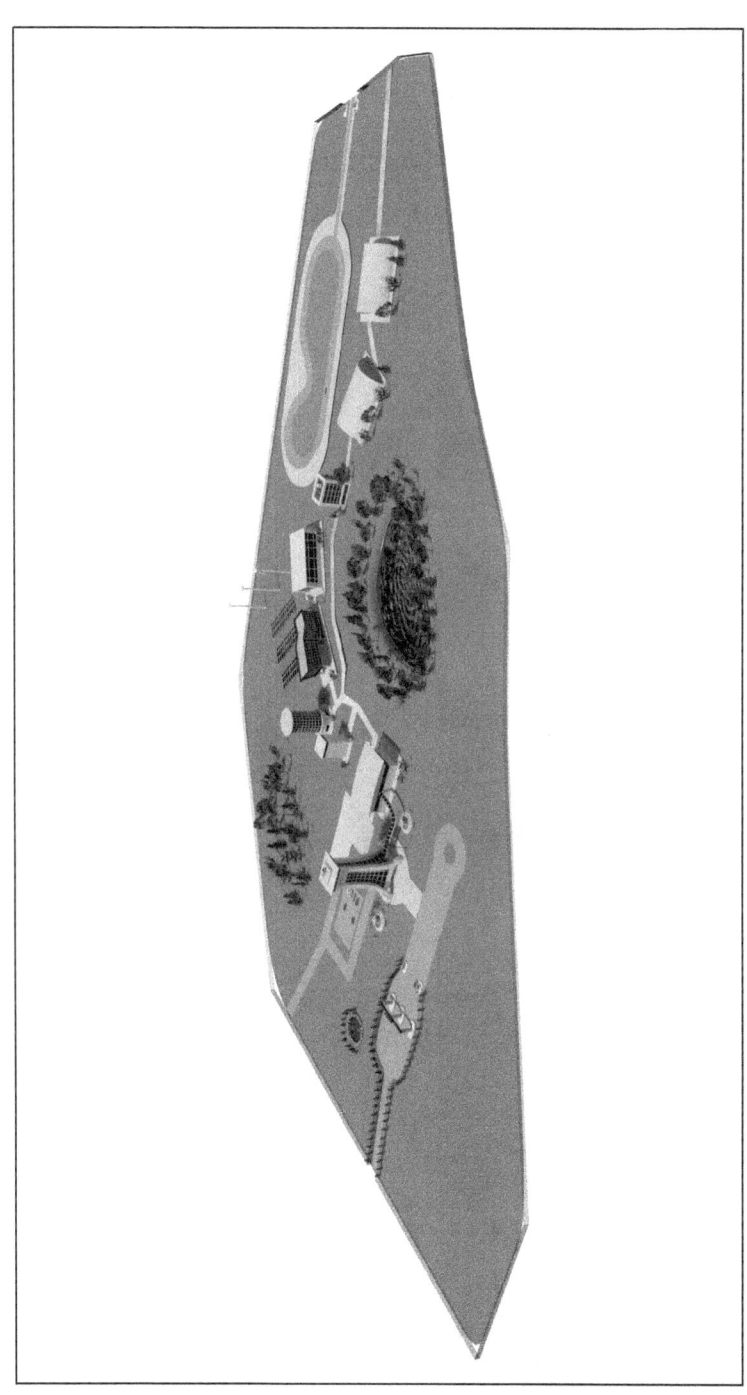

The Montgomery Group Facilities (Aerial Shot)

3D Speedsuit

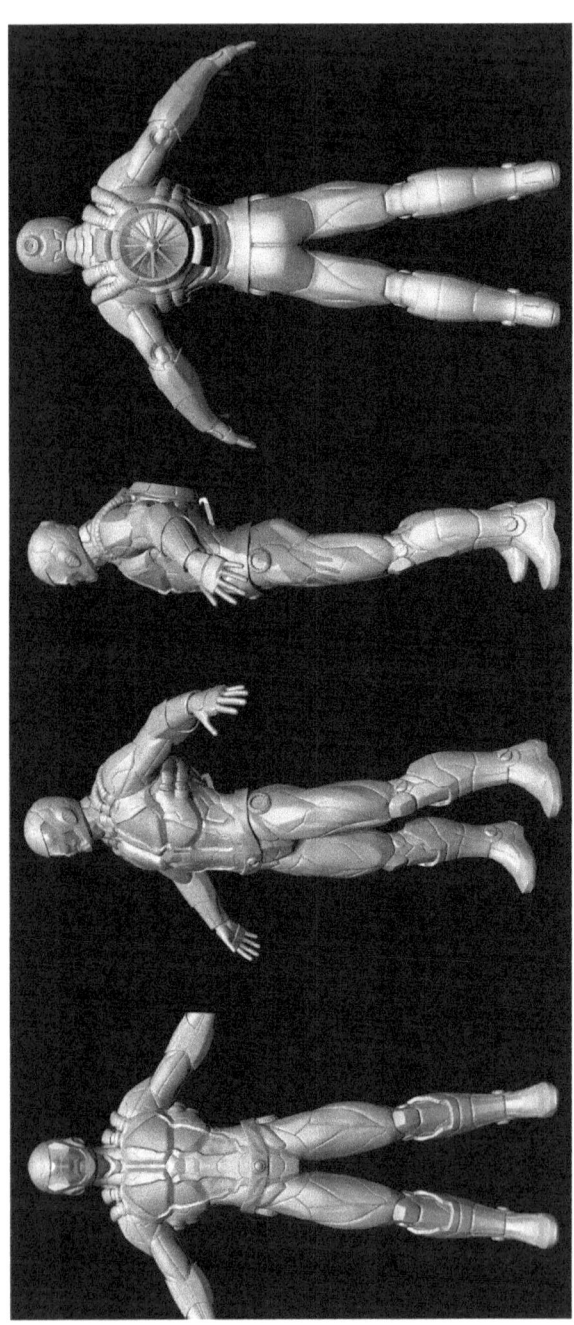

Mach-1 Speedsuit Turnaround

Main Characters

Curtis Powers

Kelly Washington

Treyshawn Jinkins

Malcolm Powers

Miranda Powers

Omar Powers

Jim Grabowski

Secondary Characters

Shakira Rollins

Treyshawn Jinkins Sr.

Gavin Ortiz

Chasm Montgomery

Erica Cosway

Justin and Amanda

Man Undisclosed

Classified Powersuits

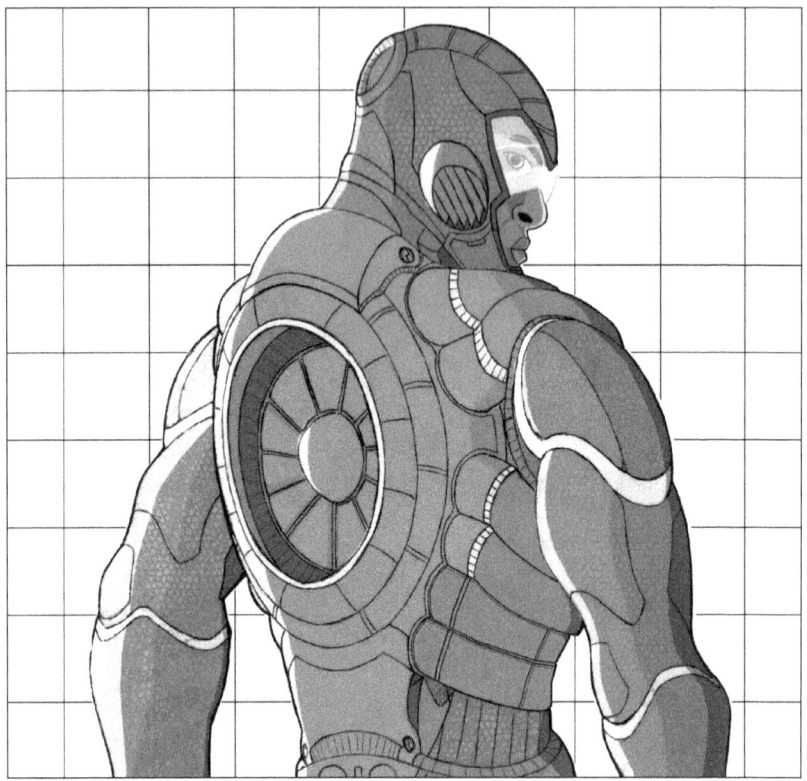

Jetstream Schematic

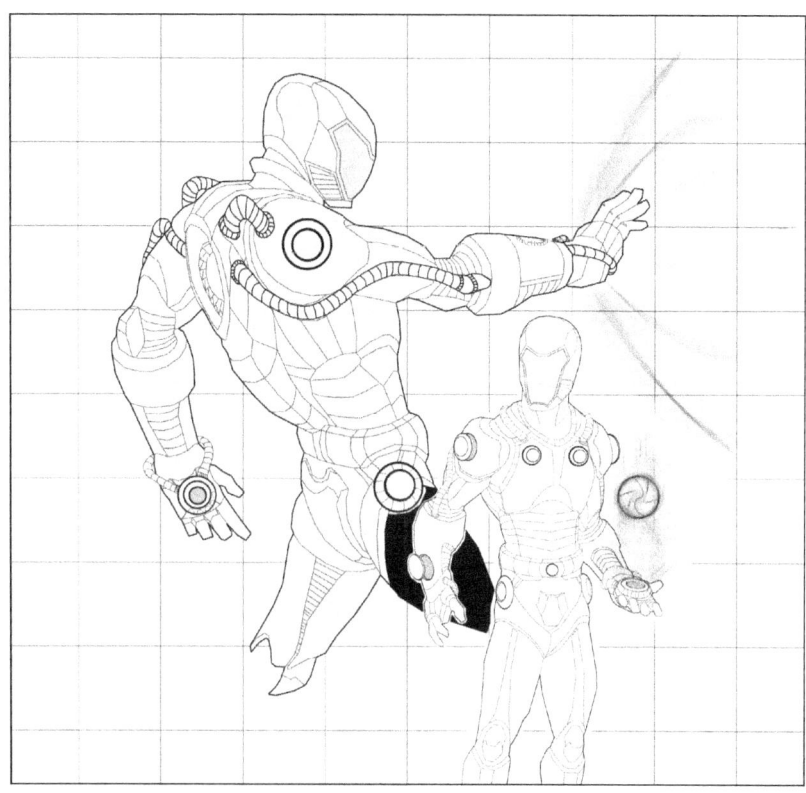

Windstorm Schematic

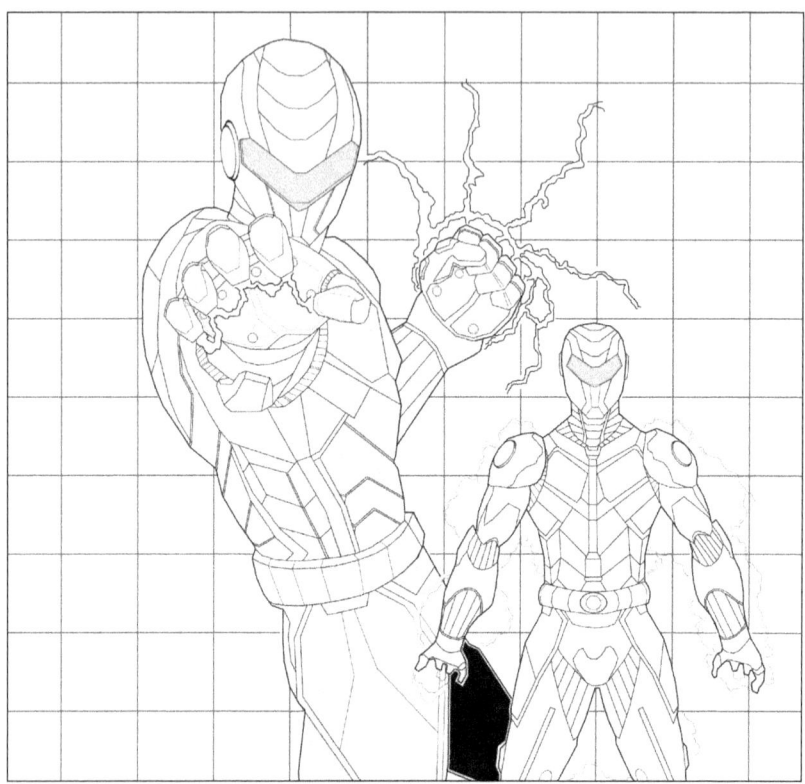

Conduit Schematic

Behind the Speedsuit:

An Interview with Author, Allen Paul Weaver III

Q: So, what's been happening with you since Book One?

A: Book One released in 2009. My wife and I had a son in 2010. My independent film, Speedsuit, was produced in 2011. We screened Speedsuit at 14 venues in 2012. Meanwhile, I also had a change in my employment. I was able to start actively writing Book Two in 2013/2014 and here we are!

Q: Bullying is one of the themes in your book. Were you bullied as a child?

A: I was bullied in elementary, middle and high school. I never really told my parents because I didn't think they could help or that they would make the situation worse. (However, my dad did enroll me in Jujitsu, so I would be able to protect myself if necessary.) I told my friends—especially in high school—where twice they actually stepped in when other students were bullying me. In elementary school, when I did tell an adult (the recess monitor), he took the bully and me out to the middle of the field. Since talking it out was not working, he made us fight it out. (Of course, this tactic is frowned upon today.) But we fought to a tie. The boy never bullied me again.

Q: As a child, did you ever have to protect another child from being bullied?

A: One time in 6th grade, I was on the school bus and had to protect a 4th grader who was being bullied by another 6th grader. The other student and I almost fought, because he wouldn't back down. By the time I got home, the 4th grader's mother had called my parents to thank me because I had stood up for her son.

Q: Why did you choose to escalate the bullying in your story to the point where the two bullied students would bring guns to school to retaliate?

A: Because, this is an unfortunate tragedy that is increasingly happening in our society. Students are bullied and can't get help from parents, teachers, administrators or friends. Then what do they do? They either commit suicide (bullycide) or they retaliate with gun violence. We see it in our schools and our communities. The problem is that often, when the bullied student retaliates (after having undergone tremendous stress at the hands of their bullies) they are looked at as the "monsters" and the bullies are seen as the victims. But this is far from the truth.

If we don't do something, as concerned members of the same society, to help our youth with this issue, more tragic scenarios will happen. No child should commit suicide for any reason—especially bullying. I wanted to address this issue in a way that showed all sides and hopefully, presented a balanced approach to finding solutions to this epidemic.

Q: Fatherhood seems to play a key role in the trilogy. Why is that?

A: I'm not sure what the numbers are for the rest of the world, but in America over 24 million youth are affected by fatherlessness. This is a fatherless generation. Many fathers are absent from their children's lives for many reasons: incarceration, death, divorce, even stress and anxiety from trying to deal with their own demons and issues. Based on the statistics and my own experience, this absenteeism affects kids—plain and simple. And our "fatherhood issues" can affect us for our entire life if not adequately dealt with. We're all susceptible, and much of the angst, at-risk behavior and violence we are seeing in our society can be traced back to the severely strained relationships we have with our fathers. So, I'm trying to do my part to address this issue in a way for everyone to benefit.

Q: Are the Powersuits in your book based on real science? Could they actually be made?

A: Yes. All of the Powersuits in my novels are based on real science. They could actually work—although perhaps not at the levels that I've created in the story. My goal is, at some point in the future, to build a working prototype of each suit for real-world demonstrations. Life imitating art... Art imitating life.

I can remember "well-meaning" adults trying to discourage me from dreaming about fantasy when I was a kid. But, now, government organizations like D.A.R.P.A. and private companies and universities (like M.I.T. Media Labs) are spending billions of dollars to create technology to "do in real life," what is done in comic books and other science fiction genres. Many of these scientists were inspired by science fiction and fantasy in their youth. It is my hope that my Speedsuit Powers Trilogy can serve to inspire our youth towards excellence in a similar way.

Q: How did you determine which Powersuits to include in your books? Can you give us a hint of what new suits might be in Book 3?

A: Curtis will actually create a number of Powersuits. However, I had to devise a way for him to practically approach their creation. The Mach-1 Speedsuit in Book One sets the foundation for all the others. But the process is very organic for him because he never set out to create a bunch of Powersuits. So, each suit has a unique motivation behind them.

His first suit was a result of trying to outrun Treyshawn. (Remember, Curtis initially made the Kinetic Redistribution Boots.) In fact, it was Treyshawn's idea to officially create the Speedsuit after seeing Curtis' progress with the boots and the Slipstream Vest.

Curtis' second and third Powersuit came from the inspiration provided by a young boy who's a really big fan! *"Why not make a suit that controls the wind or generates electricity?"* These two abilities seemed to be the next logical step because the technology already exists. It only requires a bit of tweaking, ingenuity and vision. Also, these two suits will play heavily into Book 3 of the trilogy.

In Book 3, look for Curtis to invent Powersuits that augment human strength, provide added protection against blunt-force trauma and possibly enable pyrotechnic and wall-climbing abilities (among other possibilities).

Q: That brings up another question. Your book is full of S.T.E.A.M. Why is that?

A: S.T.E.A.M. stands for Science. Technology. Engineering. Art. Math. I love science and technology (although Math is not my favorite thing—smile). The world grows increasingly technological and those who understand and apply S.T.E.A.M. principles will be at the forefront of the future. Our kids need to know that these fields are viable options for them, regardless of their race, class or gender. They don't just have to look at being an athlete, entertainer or singer as a way to reach their dreams.

Q: You produced the independent film adaptation of Book 1. Did that have any affect on your writing process for Book 2?

A: Yes, it did. First, when I went back to writing Book 2, after producing the film, the characters were more real to me. The actors from my film were now the characters in my mind. I think that lent a greater sense of gravity and realism to my writing. Second, adapting Book One into a movie script caused me to become more concise and descriptive in my writing. This helped me to move the story forward. Finally, working with the actors inspired me to "write in" several scenes that were not originally part of the Book 2 storyline. For example, "Melvin" was only going to be in Book One, but Steven Strickland, the actor who played "Melvin," did such a great job in the film, that I wanted to find a way to bring his character back.

Q: So, you took a big step by producing most of the illustrations in Book 2 yourself. Why was that?

A: I've been drawing for most of my life. However, my insecurities about my ability have kept me from maximizing this skill that I enjoy so much. Several professional artists have encouraged me to step outside of my comfort zone and do more with my art. I started doing this with the release of the Special Illustrated Edition of Book 1, which has artwork from artist, Shawn Alleyne and myself.

While preparing for Book 2, Shawn wasn't available, due to his own projects. So, I decided to do the artwork myself. I was also able to team up with Jeff Tyler, who is an amazing artist, to take some of my illustrations and translate them into 3D conceptual designs. This was an exciting process! My work has never been produced in 3D before. We are breaking new ground, which is opening up a host of new possibilities!

Q: You've already produced an independent film. Do you see your Trilogy continuing beyond the books?

A: Definitely! We are in the process of pitching the trilogy, in an effort to get it produced by a major studio as a television mini-series, made-for-TV movie or Hollywood blockbuster. We'll see how that goes!

Q: When can we expect Book 3 and what can we expect from that story?

A: Book 3 should be out by Christmas 2015. I'm working hard to finish this trilogy. I don't want to give anything away, but you can expect a continued exploration of each character, while also finding an increase in the action!

Q: What's next after the Speedsuit Powers Trilogy?

A: My hope is to create a 'Radiant City Studios Universe' where new stories and characters will be introduced. Many will somehow be connected to this Speedsuit Powers narrative. Others will not. Also, the Trilogy may be concluding, but the characters will continue in new ways!

As a published author and filmmaker of a story that seriously tackles the issue of school bullying, I seek to provide answers for how our communities can counteract this disturbing trend and help our young people discover and pursue their purpose. Below is an article I wrote to help provide solutions-based-thinking for the school bullying epidemic in our country.

MOVING BEYOND BULLYING:

Laying Groundwork for Discovering School Bullying Solutions that Work for Everyone

By: Allen Paul Weaver III (copyright 2012)

WE HAVE A PROBLEM...

Media reports - including Anderson Cooper 360, Oprah, Dr. Phil - and perhaps our own experiences have made us aware of tragic school bullying stories where deaths are often the result. According to the US Department of Justice bullying report, the situation is so dire, that 160, 000 youth create excuses to skip school every day for fear of torment from bullies. Sadly, many young people are too disillusioned to expect solutions from adult leaders and adults are often too shocked to see beyond the problem.

Is there any way for our communities to move beyond bullying? By saying "beyond" I do not mean we ignore the problem and try to get on with our lives. Rather, we must begin to imagine a reality where the value of each individual is affirmed – thereby nullifying bullying. Then we must implement solutions to move us to that reality.

Let me say, there is no simple solution to this issue. Bullying is a very complex, growing epidemic in our culture; and due to Internet social media, it's mutating – much like a flu virus. No matter how fearful we may feel, we cannot allow the problem to 'frame' the solutions, but rather the solutions must systematically challenge and dismantle this epidemic at every known level. However, if youth and adults unite in meaningful discourse, we can create solutions.

DEFINING THE TERM

Every generation has a tendency to redefine terms used by previous generations. The problem reveals itself when different groups use the same term, but in reality consider the term to mean different things. For genuine discussion and discourse to occur, all parties involved must first agree to the meaning of key terms. The word 'bullying' is one such term.

To some groups of people bullying is seen as teasing and occasional harassment between peers. ("Occasional" because in the past, the harassment usually stopped once the victim came home from school). It is an unfortunate "part of growing up" and a "rite of passage" into adulthood – something you endure and go through. However, to this current technology-driven generation (with access to information and the ability to communicate with one another instantly and constantly), bullying goes beyond teasing and occasional harassment. Bullying, through cell phone and Internet technology, has been elevated to include new forms of mental and emotional torture that happens at school, at home and in almost all locations in between. The result is that many of our youth consider, attempt and succeed at taking their own lives in order to relieve the pain they experience on a daily basis.

Few would deny that the world is an increasingly complex place. Part of that complexity is seen in the following ways: 1) Internet and cell phone technology have enabled youth to make vicious statements with detached anonymity. 2) Youth have an increased lack of anger management, problem solving and coping skills, which leads to an escalation of violence. 3) There is an increasing disregard for the value and sanctity of life among young people and adults. 4) Adults seem unable to stop the bullying - especially in situations where the parents of the bully encourage or support the negative behavior.

CREATING NEW ENVIRONMENTS

We need new environments where bullying is not the norm, but seen by all as a correctable abnormality. One way we create such an environment and move beyond bullying is by striving for authentic relationships. A genuine relationship is one of mutual dealings between two (or more) people; anything else is manipulation. We must learn to establish relationships with identified bullied individuals as well as the bullies themselves. In reality, both the bully and the bullied are victims - just of a different sort. While the bullied is tormented by external factors (the bully); the bully is often tormented by internal issues which may also be a result of their own external factors (home life, self-image, etc…) Both need people they can trust, relationships that promote character development, and visions of a better-alternate reality to the one they are currently experiencing.

Once authentic relationships are established, they can be strengthened through mentor programs focused on the development of the talents of the youth involved - in relation to one another. Within the framework of honest relationships, character building and interpersonal talent development, a new community environment can be fostered where conflict is mediated, differences are celebrated, and common ground is discovered. By implementing positive relationship building through peer-to-peer and adult-to-teen mentoring, this new environment can be created.

Our main obstruction to this new reality is not our youth, but rather the repeated examples of adults (in almost every sphere of life) who no longer value civility as a key ingredient for relating to one another. Our current culture continues to lose sight of what genuine positive relationships look like and how to develop them. As people mistreat one another and don't care to solve conflicts, the result becomes selfishness that causes disparate communities. Society focuses on self-advancement and gratification at the expense of others.

3 KEY CONSIDERATIONS

First, bullying is a symptom of a deeper issue. Every bully has a context for their bullying: family trauma, internal turmoil, inferiority or superiority complex, desire to climb the social ladder of their peers, etc… Context plays a major factor in triggering bullying outbursts. To miss this is to make a grave error.

Beneath context, lies a root issue common to all persons who bully: a lack of value for life. If we are at war with ourselves – we will be at war with others. But if we have a healthy view of ourselves, we will have no reason to cause chaos in the lives of others. We must find a way to help bullies deal with this foundational reality – while taking responsibility for the pain and damage they cause. To understand why they lash out is to open up an entirely new realm of possibilities for positively changing their behavior!

Second, we cannot merely react to bullying. Reacting will always put us behind the problem, because a person cannot react until acted upon by an internal or external force. We need to act – meaning: make decisions based on the facts of the situation; foresee possible outcomes; take preventive measures to structure a bully-free environment; and have appropriate measures in place for when bullying takes place. In short, a proactive approach is necessary.

Rash "knee-jerk" actions often cause more harm than good because they are uninformed actions. The more time we take to examine bullying and walk through practical steps for a variety of scenarios, the more likely we will take appropriate actions when the time comes. The less time we spend seriously considering the reality and outcomes of this bullying epidemic, the more we put ourselves and the lives of our youth at risk. Everyone has his or her own opinion (whether informed or not) about what constitutes "appropriate" action. What standards of determination should we use? The question I propose - regardless of the bully prevention program being used or ignored - is this: "Is this action a "win-win" situation for both the bullied and the bully?" If not, then we must seek additional alternatives.

Third, we must help the bullied AND the bully. If we try to help the bullied, while only removing the bully from the equation, we ultimately participate in a win-lose situation. The bully will be left to his or her own devices, often carrying that negative behavior into adulthood, which puts others at risk, including themselves.

This approach is different from an anti-bullying/zero-tolerance perspective. While anti-bullying/zero-tolerance can be helpful and necessary in many circumstances: removing a bully from the immediate situation – its inherent failure is in its "one size fits all" stance. Zero tolerance says "no bullying will be tolerated under ANY circumstances." The result is a punishment that often doesn't fit the crime. So a first-time bully is given the same punishment as a person who constantly bullies others. And the person who has been a victim of bullying who lashes out because they have no other recourse, is punished just as if they were the bully themselves (often resulting in the actual bully being perceived as the victim!)

In almost every sphere of life, we regard the circumstances of others in an effort to discover context and motivations for actions and best practices for navigating through society. Take parenting as an example: a child's motivation behind an action will greatly influence the type of reaction presented by the parent. If a parent discovers that their car -which they lent to their child the night before - now has major damage, knowing the circumstances behind the damage is crucial! Was their child intoxicated? Or did someone else run a red light and crash into them?

Yet, Zero tolerance disregards circumstances and leaves the bully and/or bullied without a resolution for their present and future. Zero tolerance, as a win-lose approach, may work on some level; but it does not work on all levels. To work on all levels, we need a win-win approach incorporated into this "bullying equation." We need an environment that inspires winning for all instead of winning only for a few.

WHERE IS THE BYSTANDER'S POWER?

Bullying has a negative affect on the bystander community that witnesses such adverse behavior. It creates an atmosphere of fear where well-meaning youth and adults are paralyzed by a sense of powerlessness. A sort of "tunnel vision" takes place, which causes bystanders to feel isolated. Fear often triggers their self-preservation instincts (Fight or Flight) as thoughts play out in their mind, "What if the bully targets me?" The result is that many bystanders will either quietly retreat from conflict or - in an effort to keep themselves from being targeted - will join the negative behavior. What is lost is the fact that bystanders may often outnumber the bullies - providing them a greater advantage for positively changing the situation. "There is strength in numbers."

So, does the bystander have power? Yes. The power comes from the strength of their moral character and their ability to empathize with the person who is being bullied. Bystanders can use their power to influence the outcome of a bullying situation by directly getting involved, indirectly calling for help or providing some type of distraction that helps the bullied child to escape.

The bullied, bully and bystander each have their own power to influence, however, the greatest share of that power is realized by bystanders who unite. If one person musters the courage to intervene, then others will most likely do the same.

When I was a freshman in college, a fellow student had an extremely bad asthma attack in the lobby of my dormitory. When I arrived on the scene, the entire room full of students seemed paralyzed and helpless. To make the situation worse, the student's inhaler was nowhere to be found! We all just watched as the student wallowed on the floor, until one student had the courage to try and help him. As this upperclassman tried to calm our asthmatic classmate down until the ambulance arrived, she yelled out, "Don't just stand there! Somebody help me!" Immediately, I felt compelled to act and jumped to her side. As we tried to calm our fellow classmate, some other students ran outside to try and look for the ambulance.

While this was not a case of "bullying," it does illuminate a point about the nature of group dynamics. Almost all of us were bullied that day - internally coerced by fear and externally restrained by everyone else's lack of action. We felt powerless, but this was a false sense of powerlessness, which was exposed the moment the first student took action and called us to do the same. Bystanders must no longer see themselves as non-participants, as if their inaction has no bearing on the outcome of events.

Sometimes circumstance requires involvement. Instead of "By-standing," those youth and adults who witness bullying must begin to see themselves as being on "Stand-by" - ready to give their assistance when needed. Often bystanders do nothing because they are unsure of the actions they can take. We can help change this reality by clearly presenting ways that they can help.

CAN EVERYBODY WIN?

Our society thrives off of winners and losers. Sports empires and the fans who support them illustrate this fact. Big Business and the consumers who are cheated by them also illustrate this fact. Criminal enterprises are motivated by this fact as well. Somehow, deep down in the back of our psyches it has been ingrained that someone has to lose in order for someone else to be successful. The perception is that there are not enough resources for everyone to be successful. It is "survival of the fittest" and those who are strong enough simply take what they want regardless of the effect it has on others.

But what if we began to ask ourselves, "How can everybody win?" What possibilities would we discover as we looked at the situation from a completely new perspective? What if we were solutions-oriented instead of problem-focused?

Can everybody win? Is there a way for everyone to get what they truly need and not just what they have been coerced into believing was their lot in life? Our young people are dying and if we fail to answer this question correctly and envision a new future that they can see for themselves, then we will all be lost. The task seems insurmountable, but if enough people - youth and adults - can work together– then the dream of a new day will no longer be some future fairytale possibility, but will become a bright new present reality.

Can everybody win? Yes. Everyone CAN win if we are all willing to work together to make the impossible possible.

ACKNOWLEDGEMENTS

I would like to thank my wife, Ijnanya. You constantly push and inspire me to be the best I can be in life and in my writing. Thank you for making time to listen to me read scenes and talk through this process. This trilogy is almost complete. Without you, I wouldn't be this far along on the journey.

I would like to thank my editor, Davina McDonald. You challenged every scene—as a good editor does—so I could make this story as compelling as possible. And you encouraged me to continue this creative literary journey. I value your time, talent and opinion.

Thank you to Tiffany Saunders, Shirley Delph, and Frank Gomez. Your review of this story and your wonderful input has proven to be invaluable!

ABOUT THE AUTHOR

"I never thought I'd make it here," says Allen Paul Weaver III about his life. **"Had my suicide attempt after high school been successful, I wouldn't have. Now I get to tell others, especially youth, that there is life beyond our struggles. We don't have to give in to our fears."**

Allen Paul Weaver III has worked with youth in various capacities since 1997. He is a graduate of Bethune-Cookman University; holding a BA. degree in Speech/Mass Communications. He is also a graduate of Colgate Rochester Crozer Divinity School; holding an MDiv. degree in theology.

Allen has published three other books: *Transition: Breaking Through the Barriers*, an anthology chronicling his journey from adolescence to adulthood; *Speedsuit Powers: Book 1; and MOVE! Your Destiny Is Waiting On You. He has also created two training manuals on book writing and public speaking.*

As a speaker/teacher at retreats, conferences and workshops for youth, men and women, Allen seeks to help mentor others towards their purpose. He believes that "we all have a significant and unique story from which others can learn."

Allen enjoys writing, drawing, producing films, vertical wind tunnel flying, innovating new ideas, and traveling with his wife and son. To date, Allen has traveled to seven African countries, Europe and China. He is currently working on seven other manuscripts for publication.